PRAISE FOR *WHAT WE HIDE*

"Coble and Acker have forged a seamless partnership with a singular voice. I honestly can't tell where one writer starts and the other ends. *What We Hide* is a crisp and hard-charging start to a legal suspense series that tests the boundaries of yesterday's secrets against today's lies, all while trying to escape tomorrow's verdict. From the courtroom to the shadow of a decaying Gothic university, it's a high-stakes ride through love, second chances, and an ending you won't soon forget."

—CHARLES MARTIN, *NEW YORK TIMES* BESTSELLING AUTHOR

"Get ready to be hooked! Brace yourself for a thrill ride as Coble and Acker masterfully weave a web of suspense in *What We Hide*, where secrets simmer and unexpected twists leave you guessing until the shocking finale."

—KATE ANGELO, *PUBLISHERS WEEKLY* BESTSELLING AUTHOR

"This book has it all. Intrigue, suspense, and the mysteries of the heart, woven together masterfully by the great new pairing of Coble and Acker. Fans of their individual books will not be disappointed. New readers will be delighted."

—JAMES SCOTT BELL, INTERNATIONAL THRILLER WRITERS AWARD WINNER

"Much is hidden in Tupelo Grove and Pelican Harbor. In *What We Hide*, expert storytellers Colleen Coble and Rick Acker will take you on a riveting ride through a picturesque Southern town inhabited by characters who will pull you in and make you care. Hidden truths find their way into the light—sometimes quickly, often slowly in the face of great obstacles and danger. Once you start reading, you won't put this book down."

—ROBERT WHITLOW, BESTSELLING AUTHOR

"When you combine two brilliant storytellers such as Coble and Acker, the result is a beautiful, well-crafted legal thriller that keeps the reader utterly riveted. If you're looking for a novel that's edge-of-the-seat compelling, emotionally engaging, and nail-bitingly (I know that's not a word, but it fits) suspenseful, look no further than *What We Hide*. With its compelling narrative, well-rounded characters, and intricate plot, this is a must-read, goes-on-the-keeper-shelf, that will stay with you long after the final page is turned."

—LYNETTE EASON, BESTSELLING, AWARD-WINNING AUTHOR OF THE EXTREME MEASURES SERIES

"*What We Hide* grabbed me with the first chapter and had me reading until two in the morning with its twisty plot and engaging characters."

—PATRICIA BRADLEY, AUTHOR OF THE PEARL RIVER SERIES

WHAT WE HIDE

A TUPELO GROVE NOVEL

COLLEEN COBLE
RICK ACKER

THOMAS NELSON
Since 1798

Published in Nashville, Tennessee, by Thomas Nelson. Thomas Nelson is a registered trademark of HarperCollins Christian Publishing, Inc.

Thomas Nelson titles may be purchased in bulk for educational, business, fundraising, or sales promotional use. For information, please email SpecialMarkets@ ThomasNelson.com.

Scripture quotations are taken from the Holy Bible, New International Version®, NIV®. Copyright © 1973, 1978, 1984, 2011 by Biblica, Inc.® Used by permission of Zondervan. All rights reserved worldwide. www.zondervan.com. The "NIV" and "New International Version" are trademarks registered in the United States Patent and Trademark Office by Biblica, Inc.®

Publisher's Note: This novel is a work of fiction. Names, characters, places, and incidents are either products of the author's imagination or used fictitiously. All characters are fictional, and any similarity to people living or dead is purely coincidental.

Any internet addresses (websites, blogs, etc.) in this book are offered as a resource. They are not intended in any way to be or imply an endorsement by Thomas Nelson, nor does Thomas Nelson vouch for the content of these sites for the life of this book.

Library of Congress Cataloging-in-Publication Data

Names: Coble, Colleen, author. | Acker, Rick, 1966- author.
Title: What we hide / Colleen Coble, Rick Acker.
Description: Nashville, Tennessee: Thomas Nelson, 2024. | Series: Tupelo Grove novel; 1 | Summary: "The only hope they've got is each other, and they're going to have to put their past behind them if they're going to stay alive long enough to uncover all that's hidden"--Provided by publisher.
Identifiers: LCCN 2023059603 (print) | LCCN 2023059604 (ebook) | ISBN 9780840711984 (paperback) | ISBN 9780840712417 (library binding) | ISBN 9780840711991 (e-pub) | ISBN 9780840712042
Subjects: LCGFT: Thrillers (Fiction) | Christian fiction. | Romance fiction. | Novels.
Classification: LCC PS3553.O2285 W47 2024 (print) | LCC PS3553.O2285 (ebook) | DDC 813/.54--dc23/eng/20240108
LC record available at https://lccn.loc.gov/2023059603
LC ebook record available at https://lccn.loc.gov/2023059604

Printed in the United States of America

24 25 26 27 28 LBC 5 4 3 2 1

For our wonderful spouses, Anette Acker and Dave Coble. Words cannot express how grateful we are for your constant help and support!

PROLOGUE

DEATH IS A LONELY BUSINESS.

The Ray Bradbury title pops into my head uninvited. I push it away and try to stay focused. Death is probably coming tonight, either for me or for Luis. Maybe for both of us.

I stare out into the waters off Fort Morgan, waiting for his boat. A waning moon hangs over the Gulf of Mexico, scattering shards of silver light on the uneasy water. Beneath it, a black wall of clouds rises. A storm is coming. It won't arrive for at least half an hour, but the air is already breathless and thick, even by southern Alabama standards. The weather is a complicating factor, but I've accounted for it.

I inhale deeply to calm my nerves, pulling in the mixed scents of sea and land—the wild salt odor of the ocean and the domestic smell of freshly mown grass from the fort's grounds. Perspiration prickles my forehead and I'm tempted to take off my light jacket—though I can't, of course. I shove my hands into my pockets.

I hear Luis's boat before I see it. The veteran smuggler is used to operating without lights. The low cough and chug of his motor comes across the water for several seconds, growing slowly louder before the low silhouette of the boat detaches itself from the shadows around the tip of the peninsula.

I'd expected him to tie up at the little pier a few yards away, which would have put him fully in the moonlight while I stayed partially in the shadows. Instead, he tips his motor up and lets the skiff's momentum carry it up onto the beach. We'll both be fully in the light.

The little boat's bow slides softly onto the sand, and he jumps out. He pulls it up with a sharp tug and turns toward me. He's not a tall man, but he has thick shoulders and gorilla arms. A large pistol is holstered on his right hip.

He starts walking toward me.

"That's close enough," I say when he's about ten feet away.

He frowns but stops. "Where's the money?"

"You've been fully paid. You won't get a bonus by blackmailing me."

He snarls and his hand twitches toward the gun. "I can destroy you!"

"That would be stupid, Luis." I try to keep my voice calm and reasonable. "Think about it. You're making more money now than you ever could smuggling drugs or people. Why ruin it by being greedy?"

"You're greedy!" His hand twitches again, getting a little closer this time. "You give me ten thousand tonight or I tell all those nice rich ladies. I tell the museums. I tell everyone everything! I have the list!"

It's true, unfortunately. He somehow got a partial client list from a delivery driver. The driver has already been dealt with, but Luis is still very much a problem. My problem. "But it won't be just ten thousand tonight, will it? You'll want another ten thousand after you've spent the first one. And your friends will ask where all the money came from, and you'll brag about how you outsmarted the gringos. The other smugglers will hear about it, and they'll figure it's safe to blackmail us too. We can't start down that road. You must see that."

He stares at me for several seconds. He seems uncertain, but it's hard to read his face in the dim gray light. Maybe he's actually considering what I've said.

"Give me ten thousand," he says again, but with less conviction.

"No."

His face hardens. "Give me ten thousand!"

"No."

He puts his hand on the butt of his pistol. "Give me—"

"Take the gun out slowly and drop it. Keep your finger away from the trigger."

His gaze flicks down for a split second. His eyes widen. There's a reason I wore a jacket on this sultry night—and a reason I've had my hands in my pockets during our whole conversation.

He pulls the gun out deliberately, finger off the trigger. But as soon as it's free of the holster, he dodges sideways and points it at me.

He's very fast, and my first shot hits his arm rather than center mass. The impact jerks him as he pulls the trigger, and he shoots into the air.

My second shot hits him in the stomach, and he doubles over. I pull the gun out of my tattered pocket and put a bullet into the top of his head. He collapses onto the beach and lies still.

My heart races and my breath heaves in deep gulps, like I just finished a marathon. I blink away the afterimage of the muzzle flashes and turn in a quick circle, scanning for lights or movement. Nothing. The only sounds I hear over my pounding pulse are the surf and a fitful sea breeze.

I grab Luis by the ankles, drag him back to the boat, and shove him in. I pick up his gun and the bullet casings. The only evidence left on the beach is the dark stain where he had lain, but the coming rain will take care of that.

The storm clouds cover the moon as I push the boat into the water and climb in, and the darkness becomes almost complete. I fumble with the unfamiliar motor, and for a tense moment I'm afraid it won't start. But at last it coughs and comes to life.

The shoreline recedes and I begin to relax. Now I just need to dump the body where the sharks will find it fast. The guns and Luis's wallet will go in the water in separate locations where they're unlikely to be found by divers. Then I'll sink the boat in a different spot and swim back to shore. That's the riskiest part: open-ocean swimming is no joke, especially at night, but I've practiced the swim from the place I picked to scuttle the boat.

I reach an area popular with sharks and put the motor in neutral. I search the stiffening corpse for wallet, watch, phone, and anything else that might identify him and survive the scavengers. His phone lights up at my touch, displaying a snapshot of a young woman holding a little boy. She's wearing a simple white dress that sets off her black hair and caramel skin. The boy has on a Pikachu T-shirt and is reaching toward the camera. They both have beautiful smiles. Their large brown eyes are just like the eyes that have haunted me ever since I saw them watching me from a medieval crucifix in an Italian church years ago.

I click off the phone and put it down, willing myself to forget the picture.

"A lonely business," I say to the darkness.

CHAPTER 1

SAVANNAH WEBSTER SHOULD HAVE KNOWN THE BRIGHT July day would be upsetting the minute she saw old Boo Radley blocking the brick walkway to her classroom. The bull gator roared at her before lumbering off toward the turgid banks of Tupelo Pond where he ruled. She'd forgotten the papers her students had turned in anyway, so while the alligator got out of her way, she retraced her steps to Connor Hall to retrieve her folders.

Most days she loved living in this place of uncommon beauty with its grand old buildings, flowering plants nurtured by the botany majors, and hot, humid days tempered with sweet tea. The gators she could do without.

She reached for the outer door's ornate brass knob, then flinched when a shadow moved to her left near the banks of azaleas and rhododendron into the late afternoon Alabama sunshine. Boo Radley was far less disconcerting than the man who stood regarding her with a half smile.

Her husband, Hezekiah Webster, looked out of place and uncomfortable standing in the garden by the marble angel fountain. He had to be hot in that black suit, and sure enough, he tugged at the buttoned-up collar and red tie at his neck. His dark hair had been freshly trimmed, and his expression seemed pinned in place. She'd always thought him the handsomest man in the room, and he still was with his lean build and strong jawline. His deep voice was as attractive as his striking face with its dark brows and ready smile.

"Hez," she said in an even tone. "I didn't expect to see you here."

She twisted the doorknob and practically fell into the cool recesses of the building. Locking the door against him would do nothing to avoid the coming discussion. Hez was used to taking command of any situation and would smooth-talk his way past her defenses. In this case, capitulation would be the better part of valor. Get him out of here before she fell into his arms again and she'd claim the meeting a victory.

He didn't answer as she hurried to the sanctuary of her classroom, and even if he had spoken, she probably wouldn't have heard him past the clatter of her heels on the marble floor. She set her briefcase on her desk and turned to face Hez with her arms crossed over her chest, waiting for him to speak.

"Thanks for seeing me, Savannah."

His sudden reappearance reached inside and touched something she thought had died when she walked out. She steeled herself. "I don't think I had a choice, Hez. It would have been thoughtful for you to have called first."

He didn't flinch, but then, an experienced DA like Hez never showed his emotions. "Would you have agreed to see me?"

"Probably not."

"I didn't think so, and this was too important." His gaze swept the room and swung to the window frames with the paint peeling. "Tupelo Grove looks a little worse for wear since the last time I was here. Is the university about to fold?"

Did he sound worried, and if so, why would he care? His opinion didn't matter. "Jess has been working hard to revive things here. We've got more students this year than we've seen in ten years. Even the summer class I'm finishing is up in attendance by 20 percent over last year. We'll have nearly four thousand here this year."

"That's great!" His blue eyes lit with what appeared to be relief. "I'm clean now, Savannah. I haven't had a drink or any Vicodin in almost a year." He held out his hand. "Look, no shaking. I want to start a clinic at the law school here. I'll hand-pick the best students, and we'll examine old cases that have merit. I'd like to give innocent prisoners a chance at a new life. The Justice Chamber. Has a nice ring, don't you think?"

"Sounds like a good idea." His DA-turned-defender-of-the-innocent persona was too little too late to impress her. She turned her back on him and threw folders into her briefcase. "I need to go. Good luck, Hez."

He took a step closer. "I won't let you down again. I can do this. I can make a difference in the lives of people unjustly incarcerated and maybe make amends in some small way. There were times when I was a DA, I knew corners had been cut and evidence was presented that shouldn't have been allowed. They weren't my cases, but they happened. I should have confronted it back then, but I was too focused on my career. I was wrong, and I want to make things right."

She looked up at his coaxing voice. For years he'd had juries eating out of his hand, but she'd learned to steel herself against his persuasion. His clear gaze told her he was telling the truth, but that didn't change her gut reaction. Being around him would be too hard, especially since she'd finally made the decision to end this misery.

"I filed for divorce, Hez." She closed her eyes briefly as pain ripped through her chest at the words. How did they even get here? She zipped her briefcase closed, then turned and locked gazes with him. "I struggled with it because of my faith, but I couldn't live in limbo forever. I haven't heard from you in two years. Two years, Hez!"

Didn't she deserve to find another relationship someday and learn to be happy with the remnants of her life? Their tenth wedding anniversary had been two months ago, and she'd slowly realized since then that her life wouldn't change unless she made a conscious effort to repair it.

This time he flinched, and pain filled his eyes. "You blame me for everything, don't you?"

Did she? His career had always been uppermost in his mind. She'd always taken second place. At least it felt that way. She shook her head. "It was your affair with the bottle I couldn't handle."

He shoved his hands in the pockets of his jacket. "Aren't you interested in how I can afford to do this?"

They both knew the DA's office had forced him out when he'd gotten a DUI. They didn't want the scandal. But what did it matter how he'd done it? Their marriage was dead, and she'd signed the death certificate in her attorney's office last week.

She brushed past him toward the cavernous hall. "I've got to go. Find another law school for your clinic."

By the time she hit the front door, she was practically running. The shade from the oak trees festooned with moss cooled her hot face and calmed her agitation. Tupelo trees marched in rows along the brick paths, and the scent of camellias followed her to the administration building. Its steep roof and arching windows had been her sanctuary ever since she arrived at Tupelo Grove University after her world imploded. Her roots went deep into the weedy lawns and old buildings, and the university's fading grandeur welcomed her grief and soothed it with the bright faces of her students and their shared love of history. It had been the perfect haven. Until now.

She'd thought she was healing until she saw Hez's face again.

Savannah's heart still throbbed against her chest wall when she entered the president's office, and she tried to slow her breathing. Ellison Abernathy wasn't her favorite person, and to have to face him after seeing Hez again was more distressing than usual. "Sorry I'm a little late, Ellison."

He raised a brow and pointed his pen at the chair on the other side of his massive desk. Bookcases ran the length of the south wall all the way to the ten-foot ceiling, displaying pictures of Abernathy with politicians and carefully curated mementos of his career. The sun streaming through the mullioned windows would illuminate her distressed face, but she had no choice so she sank into the leather chair.

Abernathy's blond hair was perfectly styled, and his trademark Armani suit was gray today. The white shirt and yellow tie finished the look. He believed clothes made the man, and she'd never seen so much as a piece of fuzz on his jacket.

He steepled his fingers. "You wanted to talk about tenure?"

She nodded. "I have seven years of strong experience already, and I'm working on a book about the Willard Treasure. It's basically finished, but I have to verify a few details." The boast about it going well was a stretch. While the subject was wildly exciting to her, she wasn't certain her passion for the project came across in the manuscript.

"I hope it's accepted before the committee meets. I know when you were hired two years ago, you'd already published a few articles about the Willard Treasure, and with your family connections, you clearly know a lot about the subject. However, Professor Guzman is here now as well. His credentials are stellar with his PhD from Yale and his strong history with pre-Columbian artifacts in general. He's been working on cataloging the Willard Treasure, and once it's done, it will be even more of a draw to pull in archaeology and art students. It will also increase TGU's reputation. So it's a toss-up between which of you would be our best expert on the treasure."

She'd expected this, but it still hurt. The treasure had been part of her family for decades. Some of her earliest memories were of wandering the warehouse and poking through crates of terra-cotta masks and jade statues with her father. The artifacts of an entire city were in those crates, and she had dreams of seeing them set up in the museum. The problem was, much of the art wasn't the shiny objects that drew in visitors, and the museum was still too small to display even a fraction of what the warehouse held. A new wing for the Willard Treasure would be wonderful, but that goal wasn't high on the list for the trustees.

She moistened her lips. "You don't make it sound hopeful. Who is on the tenure committee?"

"I'm not quite certain just yet. Any tenure committee for a history professor will, of course, include the provost and the history chair." His left brow rose. "I've heard you're friends with Beckett Harrison. You might make sure to cultivate that, um, *friendship*. And it wouldn't hurt to be extra *friendly* to Erik Andersen."

Abernathy's practiced smile made her skin crawl. If he meant what she thought he did, it was a disgusting suggestion. "Beckett and I are merely friends. Not *friendly* in any kind of questionable way. I'm not sure what you mean, Ellison." She kept her voice even, but she clenched her fists in the folds of her skirt.

"I didn't mean anything by that, of course. It never hurts to help the process along by being agreeable and on good terms with anyone who holds the reins to your future. Surely you can understand that." His gaze flicked over her legs before rising to linger on her chest. His leering smile left no doubt as to his meaning.

"Thank you, Ellison. This has been very illuminating." Determined not to let him see the tears of rage gathering in her eyes, Savannah rose on wobbly legs. She swung on her heels and stalked out the door. It shut behind her, and she caught a glimpse of his secretary's surprised face as Savannah stormed past. She shoved open the exterior door and stepped outside to draw in air untainted by the odious president's presence.

That tenure position belonged to her. Ellison had practically promised it to her when she accepted the professorship. She couldn't leave here. Too much of her past anchored her to this place, and she couldn't leave the little grave in the family cemetery. Not yet. Maybe not ever. And now Hez had shown up. Could the day get any worse?

CHAPTER 2

———

DIVORCE. THE UGLY WORD HUNG IN THE CLASSROOM'S stale air after the sound of Savannah's steps faded into silence.

Hez wanted to go after her, but it would be futile. No one ran away from problems as fast as Savannah Webster. He'd just hoped she might not think of him as a problem anymore.

He had spent the last two years getting clean, rebuilding his life, and laying the plans for the Justice Chamber. It had been grindingly hard work, but he hadn't given up. Always in the back of his mind, he imagined how Savannah would react when she saw the finished product, how thrilled she would be by the new Hez. She would immediately see that he was a much better man than he had ever been during their marriage. Then, after a few suitably gushing words, she would melt into his arms.

He'd played that stupid scene in his head a hundred times, most recently on the drive down from his court hearing in Mobile today. Reality had actually matched his fantasy, at least for a few seconds. He spotted her a moment before she saw him, and she'd been just as breathtaking as the first time he'd seen her. The late afternoon sun caught the red-gold highlights in her shoulder-length auburn hair, and her sleeveless top showed off her toned arms.

She noticed him walking up and turned, giving him a quick glimpse of her profile—still perfect at thirty-five. Then he was looking into those big green eyes again, so close he could see the tiny flecks of gold. He'd always liked that she was tall so he could study those amazing colors in her eyes. He had been about to launch into his big planned speech . . . and the moment was over before it began. She hadn't listened to a word he said. New Hez, old Hez—it was all the same to her.

It didn't matter if he had changed—the past hadn't. And Savannah still blamed him. Of course she did.

His vision blurred and he wanted a drink. Just one to take the edge off the pain. He took a deep breath and shook his head. No. He knew where that path led.

He had kidded himself that the door back into Savannah's heart was still open a crack because she hadn't filed for divorce. But she probably just hadn't gotten around to it because thinking about their marriage—about him—had been too painful. She had stuffed their failed marriage into that enormous mental closet full of things she didn't want to deal with. Until now.

A new idea hit him like a kidney punch: Did she have a boyfriend? Was that why she'd finally filed for divorce? That would also explain why she pushed him away so hard just now.

If she was seeing someone, he couldn't blame her. The last time she had set eyes on him, he was "all messed up with no place to go," as he admitted at the time. He was a workaholic alcoholic who had destroyed his family and his future. Why would someone like her wait around for two years on the slim chance that he might turn himself around? It would make perfect sense for her to move on.

He took a deep breath and blew it out slowly. Maybe it was time for him to move on too.

"Can I help you?" a reedy voice said.

Hez turned and saw an ancient security guard standing in the door. The guy's uniform was probably as old as he was. His name tag read Oscar Pickwick.

"I was just visiting someone, but I'm done now." He walked out past the guard, who trailed him until he left the building.

It was after five o'clock, but the sun still turned his jacket into a personal sauna the minute he stepped outside. He took it off, then pulled off his tie and unbuttoned his collar for good measure.

He looked for a shaded spot away from students where he could sit for a few minutes. A rickety bronze bench, green with age, stood under a nearby tupelo tree. He tested it and it wobbled, but it seemed sturdy enough to hold him. A plaque announced that it was the *Gift of the Class of 1956*. Cheap class.

He sat down and surveyed his surroundings. Despite Savannah's assurances, Tupelo Grove University looked more threadbare than he remembered. The dead limbs on the towering oaks in the quad needed trimming. Weeds and grass sprouted from the brick paths. Legare Hall, the grandiose marble administration building Savannah's father started twenty years ago when he was university president, still wasn't finished. Even from Hez's vantage point over a hundred yards away, it was clear that construction stopped a long time ago and the half-built hall was slowly decaying into the perfect setting for a Stephen King story. Tupelo Grove certainly wasn't "Harvard on the Bayou" anymore. Much of its five hundred acres was still swampland and planted fields for the agricultural department.

If anyone could turn this place around, it was Savannah's sister, Jessica Legare. Jess was a financial wizard who had spent eight years at a cutthroat Wall Street investment bank before taking the CFO job at Tupelo Grove three years ago. She had the brains and intestinal fortitude to fix the university—if it was fixable. He hoped it was, for Savannah's sake if not his own.

Hez's phone buzzed in his pants pocket, and he pulled it out. It was Jimmy Little, Hez's friend and head of his current law firm. He took the call, happy to think about work for a few minutes. "Hey, Jimmy."

"How'd the hearing go?"

Hez smiled at his boss's impatience. "We won."

"Yes!" Hez could almost see Jimmy punching the air. "Tell me all about it."

Hez gave a blow-by-blow description, which took twice as long thanks to Jimmy's frequent interjections and questions.

"Are you on the road back to Birmingham?" Jimmy asked when Hez finished his story. "I'll buy you dinner at Highlands."

"Thanks, but I figured I'd spend the night down in Pelican Harbor. I'm having dinner at Billy's and staying at a little B and B on the water."

"Oh." Jimmy paused. "That's pretty close to Tupelo Grove, right?"

"Yeah. I'm actually at TGU right now."

"Are you there about the Justice Chamber?" Jimmy's voice was wary now. He knew the Justice Chamber was Hez's dream. After a couple of long conversations, Jimmy had reluctantly agreed that Hez could have six months of paid leave to start the clinic someday—but he also clearly hoped someday never came.

Hez sighed and ran his fingers through his hair. "Yeah, but it doesn't look like it'll work out."

"I'm sorry, man." Jimmy's tone conveyed the exact opposite of his words.

"It's fine. It was a mistake for me to come down here."

I wait until Savannah goes home, which seems to take forever. At least I have a tracker on her phone, so I don't need to spend hours watching for her to leave.

Finally, the blue dot labeled *S* begins to move on my screen. I move too. Ten minutes after she walks out of the building, I walk in.

This old pile of ivy-covered brick and stone has a unique stink to it, like all of TGU. It's more of a feeling than an actual smell: the stench of generations of dirty laundry that has never been washed or aired. The pile just grows higher as the years roll by.

My first stop is the classroom where that idiot left the provenance letters he was supposed to pick up. Those letters were basically certificates of authenticity for every artifact in the last shipment. Without them, we won't be able to sell a single one. Where are they? Did Savannah grab all of them? Peter thought he saw her take the whole stack as he was going back to get them, but he's not a particularly reliable source, especially when he's agitated. Maybe she left some of the letters behind.

I do a quick search of the desk and trash. Nothing. I walk up and down the rows of student seats, glancing down each. I see only dust and the occasional snack wrapper or soda can.

Next I go to her office. A little ripple of adrenaline runs through me as I open the door. I have a cover story for being in the building, but not here.

I close the door and look around. The early evening sunlight slants through her windows, making the room warm and stuffy. I step behind her well-organized desk and flip through the papers on it. Student essays to be graded, university paperwork, scholarly magazines and newsletters. No provenance letters. I check the desk drawers and credenza. Nothing there either.

A bead of sweat runs down my temple. I've been here too long already, but I can't leave until my search is done.

I scan the room, looking for any other place she might have left the letters. The bookshelves hold only books. The top of the credenza has the standard TGU computer and some family pictures.

One of the pictures catches my eye. A wedding photo showing a radiant Savannah and a self-satisfied Hez wearing a smirking smile. My fists clench and I resist the urge to tear the picture from the frame and rip it to shreds. Why is that still here? He's supposed to be out of her life!

I take a deep breath and blow it out through my nose. Maybe I need to take the Hez situation into my own hands.

I check the tracker on my phone. Savannah has left her house and is walking back toward campus. She's probably walking her dog, but she might stop by her office. She's brought him here before.

Time to go. I skim my gaze over the office one last time,

skipping the wedding picture. Then I slip out, close the door behind me, and hurry down the back stairwell. A quick check of my phone shows Savannah walking around the pond. Good.

I exit the building and head for my car, keeping to the lengthening shadows. She might have taken the provenance letters home. Maybe I can get in and search before she returns.

I make the short drive to her neighborhood and park a block from her cottage. But the blue dot is heading back now. She'll be home in just a few minutes. I'll need to wait until she's asleep.

Another jolt of adrenaline hits my bloodstream, and it's much stronger this time. What exactly will I do if she wakes while I'm in her home?

CHAPTER 3

SAVANNAH'S EYES POPPED OPEN IN HER BEDROOM. THE
room was quiet except for Marley's low growl, and the only
light was from her bedside clock shining out the time of almost
three in the morning. Her Aussie always let her know if anyone
stepped foot in the yard. Her frozen muscles finally released,
and she sat up to reach for Marley's soft fur. He stood on the
floor beside the bed, his attention focused on the window.

She licked dry lips. "What is it, boy?" she whispered.

He uttered another growl. Her room was at the back of the
small shotgun-style home and looked out on a small pond.
Marley and Boo Radley had a mutual hatred for each other,
and she stepped to the window to see if the gator had wandered
into the yard. She peeked through the blinds and saw nothing
but the moonlight glimmering on the koi pond and nearby
bench. Nothing moved.

The floor creaked down the hall toward the kitchen, and her
pulse rocketed again. Marley's attention never wavered from
the window, so she tried to tell herself she was alone in the
house, but that didn't comfort her.

She flipped on the lights, and the glow pushed back the
shadows. Her neat bedroom looked exactly the same. The

small desk area where she worked was the only spot of disarray with its stacks of homework folders. Was the picture of her and Hez with Ella out of place?

"Come," she told Marley. With the dog beside her, Savannah explored the house.

The kitchen still carried the faint aroma of the roast chicken she'd had for dinner. The living room and bathroom were clean and empty. In spite of the noise she'd heard, she found nothing out of place. Marley might have caught a whiff of Boo Radley's scent outside.

When she returned to the bedroom, she knew she'd never be able to sleep. She might as well grade papers for an hour or so. Seeing Hez again had so discombobulated her that she hadn't graded a single essay. She picked up the first folder and began to read through the paper. The shock and pain in his face when he'd heard she'd filed for divorce kept intruding on the job in front of her.

Working steadily, she was down to the final folder in an hour.

She took the last folder and frowned. It was much heavier than the rest. And the feel of the folder was different too—it wasn't the standard school-grade folder but a heavier stock. She flipped it open and scanned the top page. It appeared to be some kind of document on school letterhead.

The substance of the letter caught her attention. It was a letter of provenance for some pre-Columbian artifacts. The letter didn't interest Savannah until she realized the provenance was listed as proof of sale for the listed statues. As far as she knew, the university wasn't planning to sell any of their pieces. The value of the artifacts was enormous in so many ways, and she almost felt they were part of her personal history.

She flipped through the rest of the folder and found multiple letters like the top one. Was someone selling off museum assets without permission? Savannah had suspected something was amiss at the museum when she tried to find a box of historical documents to show her students last year and found them missing. Selling items with fake documentation would increase their value substantially.

Was the university in more trouble than she knew? If this was as bad as it looked, it could be the end of the school her family had dedicated their lives to for over a century. She owed it to the school and to her family to ferret out the truth. But she was a lowly history professor, not an investigator.

She could go to Ellison Abernathy, but everything in her rebelled at the idea. He was the slimy sort, just like her father. Ellison reminded her of an old-time snake-oil salesman with his too-perfect hair and toothy grin. All flash and no substance.

Savannah couldn't tell Jess yet either. Her sister had her hands full trying to keep the university in the black, and this kind of news would be too distracting. Better to wait until Savannah got to the bottom of it.

Hez could help me.

It was the worst possible idea. But no one was better at figuring out cases than Hez. The thought of working with him made acid churn in her stomach—and how could she ask him for help just hours after dropping the divorce bomb? No, there had to be a better option. But who?

"Beckett." She answered her own question with a relieved

sigh. As provost, Beckett Harrison was in charge of Tupelo Grove's bureaucracy, so hopefully he would know if these were legitimate sales. And if they weren't, he'd be able to put a stop to them.

She glanced at the clock. It wasn't quite four o'clock, but she could kill time for two hours by working on lesson plans. She picked up her laptop and got to work. She worked steadily until light crept into the room. Just after six, so she could call now.

She grabbed her phone from its charger and called Beckett.

He answered on the first ring. "Morning, Savannah. You're up early. Something wrong?"

"I'm not really sure. I found some strange documents mixed in with a stack of essays."

"What kind of documents?"

"Provenance letters. Whenever an ancient artifact is sold, there should be some sort of proof that it's not fake and wasn't looted. These are letters attesting to the provenance of Aztec artifacts from the university's collection." She took a deep breath. "Beckett, are we selling the Willard Treasure? Are we in that much financial trouble?"

"Wow . . . I—I . . ." Shock rattled his usually smooth and confident baritone. He cleared his throat and started again. "This is stunning. No, we're not selling anything from our collection, especially the Willard Treasure. That's the history department's pride and joy. Are you sure these letters mean someone is selling our artifacts?"

"Yes," she said without hesitation. "The letters specifically talk about sales."

"I see." He paused. "How did they wind up mixed in with a stack of your essays?"

The memory of her surprise meeting with Hez popped into her head, flustering her more than it should have. "I . . . was a little distracted when I left yesterday, and I must have accidentally grabbed them with my students' papers." She hurried on before he could ask what had distracted her. "Someone must've left them there by mistake, but who? We can't let someone pilfer those artifacts—they're worth so much, in both monetary and cultural value."

He was silent for a moment. "Do you have any idea who it might be?"

As soon as he asked the question, she knew the answer. "Someone who has access to the Willard Treasure, the university seal, and our letterhead. And who likes to live larger than his university salary allows."

"I think I know who you have in mind."

"Ellison."

He sighed. "It's possible you're right, Savannah—but you'll need more evidence. A lot more. Bringing down a university president isn't easy, and trying is dangerous."

"I know." She bit her lip. "I'll need help from someone high up in the administration, someone who really knows the system."

"Someone like the provost." He took her unsubtle hint, a note of resignation in his voice. "Okay. I'll need to see those provenance documents. Give me the weekend to see what I can find out."

Hez had planned to take a mini vacation on the Gulf shore. He'd have dinner at Billy's—hopefully with Savannah—and spend the night at the Bayfront Inn, a cozy little B and B he and Savannah had stayed at a few times. The morning would be devoted to old Pelican Harbor favorites: a run in the park before it got too hot, takeout beignets from Petit Charms, a walk along the beach (hopefully also with Savannah), and coffee at one of the little shops that dotted downtown.

It was, of course, a terrible plan from beginning to end. He knew it the moment he walked into Billy's. The smell of grilling oysters should have made his mouth water, but instead it made his stomach churn. Savannah loved them almost as much as he did, and they'd often shared an order when they came here for dinner. He left after barely being able to choke down a cup of crab-and-corn chowder.

The Bayfront Inn was even worse. It had been a rambling old mansion before being converted to a bed-and-breakfast twenty years ago, and rumors abounded that it was haunted. And for Hez, at least, it was: the ghost of his dead marriage followed his every step. There was their favorite nook in the dining area. And the stairs leading up to the suite on the top floor where they'd stayed on their anniversary, the one with the skylights and the panoramic view of the bay.

He lay awake until after two, then finally fell asleep.

Hez moved through the house, but his legs dragged like lumps of concrete. Where was Ella? He wanted his little girl's arms around his neck. Door after door opened in his hand, but each space stood empty. He had to find her.

He tried to call her name, but his vocal cords made no sound. The last door loomed before him, and he reached for it with trembling fingers. It didn't budge when he yanked on it, but it released on the second try.

He stared into the abyss, then backed away. He needed to scream, but he couldn't open his mouth.

Hez bolted upright in bed, shaking and covered in sweat, iron bands of grief and guilt still coiled tight around his heart. He'd never get back to sleep, so he went for a run at four. He was back by five o'clock and on the road back to Birmingham by six.

It was a relief to see Pelican Harbor in the rearview mirror. The first rays of dawn gilded the tops of the highest buildings as he pulled out of the inn's parking lot, and he could hear the gulls crying as they flapped out to follow the shrimpers. He loved the little town, but it was crowded with memories and had no room for him anymore.

He spent the four-hour trip listening to continuing-education podcasts, pausing occasionally to dictate notes when he came across something useful for one of his cases. It was mostly dull stuff, but it forced him to get his mind out of the past. It worked—by the time he reached the parking lot for his apartment building in Birmingham, he had new ideas for a couple of cases and a tentative list of schools to call about the Justice Chamber.

As he walked to the building, a man got out of a car and intercepted him. The guy was a twentysomething in khakis with a neat beard and shoulder-length black hair. He was carrying a thick envelope and looked vaguely like an upscale messenger.

"Hezekiah Webster?"

"Yes."

The guy thrust the envelope into Hez's hands, then stepped back and snapped a picture with his phone. "You've been served."

The guy got back into his car and drove off as Hez opened the envelope. It contained a stack of legal documents. The top one was titled "Divorce Complaint" and was captioned "Savannah Webster v. Hezekiah Webster."

CHAPTER 4

SPANISH MOSS HANGING FROM THE TUPELO TREES THAT
lined the pond blocked the breeze as well as the morning
sunshine. Savannah sat on a bench and fanned herself with
the folder in her hand. Beckett should be here any minute. The
trees around this garden area shielded their meeting from
students walking along the path to class.

She spotted the gator sunning himself on the other side of
the water. The back of her neck prickled as if someone was
peering at her from the foliage around the pond, but she saw no
one. Nerves, most likely. She wanted concrete evidence so she
could confront President Abernathy. He was so good at lying,
and they'd have to have something he couldn't explain away.

She spotted a flash of red and saw Beckett striding toward
her. For a heart-stopping moment, she thought it was Hez. How
had she missed Beckett's resemblance to Hez until now? Same
erect carriage, same dark hair. His eyes were brown instead of
blue like her husband's, but the resemblance was startling from
a distance. She didn't want to examine why she might have
been drawn to him in the first place. So far she'd managed to
turn aside his dinner invitations, and realizing he resembled
Hez made her doubly glad she'd turned him down.

She stood and smoothed her navy skirt. "Thanks for coming so quickly."

He took her hand and squeezed it. "Of course, Savannah. This is too important to put off."

She handed him the folder. "This is what I found."

He perused it silently, then handed it back. "He also ordered a ream of history department letterhead."

"He's a law guy. What reason did Ellison give for the order?"

Beckett shrugged. "I doubt anyone questioned him. Most people know better."

She held up the folder. "Should we call the police?"

"I think we should confront him first. We'd look pretty stupid if he has a perfectly good explanation for all of it."

"What explanation could there be?"

"I have no idea, but you know Ellison. He's quick on his feet. I'm ready to go now if you are."

The president's office was across the green belt and down Oak Lane. They could walk there in five minutes. Savannah would barely have time to compose herself before confronting Ellison Abernathy, but she didn't want Beckett to see her reluctance. They gave Boo Radley a wide berth on the way to the sidewalk, and the trip went far too quickly for Savannah. Her heart rate increased with every step closer to the ivy-covered brick building until they stood in front of the green door.

Beckett swiped his pass at the door and opened it.

She took a deep breath and stepped through the doorway into the foyer. It smelled of the fresh disinfectant the cleaner had used. This early, Abernathy would probably be the only one in his office, and she let Beckett lead the way.

The door to the presidential office suite wasn't quite shut. Beckett frowned. "It's usually closed until his secretary arrives." He pushed it open and walked in. The small secretarial office in front of the president's office was empty. Beyond it, the door to the president's office stood ajar. "Ellison?"

Savannah grabbed Beckett's arm. "Something's wrong, Beckett. I can feel it. We should call campus security."

"If he's hurt, we need to do more than call security. I'm going in." Beckett walked past the secretary's neat desk and pushed open the door to the president's office.

Savannah had no choice but to follow him into the cavernous space. Abernathy's giant desk occupied its usual space by the mullioned windows looking out onto the campus, but he wasn't seated behind it.

"He's not here." A peculiar odor she couldn't identify hung in the air, but it raised the hair on the back of her neck. "Something's wrong."

She didn't wait for an answer but pulled out her phone and called the campus police to request assistance. Before someone picked up on the other end, she spotted a black shoe. A Salvatore Ferragamo like Abernathy always wore. She dropped her phone and rushed around the edge of the desk to kneel at Abernathy's side.

A pool of blood spread out from the president's head and from around his torso. His color was odd. Savannah vainly tried to find a pulse in his wrist before she moved to his neck with the same results. Nothing. Finding him like this brought back the horror of the day her little girl died.

She scrambled back on her haunches, not aware of the keening sound erupting from her throat until Beckett called her name.

Breathe. In and out.

Beckett helped her up, but she was barely aware of him. Abernathy took all her focus. He was dressed in a crisp white shirt and red tie under a navy Armani suit, but his hair was in disarray. Could he have fallen and hit his head on the edge of the desk as he went down? Head wounds tended to bleed heavily.

Then her gaze fell on the note pinned to his lapel. She leaned down to take a better look.

Something Wicked This Way Comes.

The familiar title by Ray Bradbury was in her own library. It took a moment for reality to sink in—this was murder. Someone had killed the university president.

Savannah's office was usually her refuge on campus where her favorite books surrounded her, but not today. Her hands shook as she made fresh coffee for her and the detective who stood peering at her bookcases.

Savannah turned and went to her desk. "I already told the officers everything I knew yesterday at the scene." Yesterday was a blur in her mind. The police had peppered her with questions, and the news had rocketed through the small student body finishing up summer classes.

She'd met Detective Augusta Richards several times at the hardware store her husband owned. She wore her short brown hair in a no-nonsense cap around her face and was tall and lanky with kind brown eyes. Her quiet, unruffled demeanor should have soothed Savannah's agitation, but the fact she was here at all had raised her hackles.

Pelican Harbor provided police services to the university under a century-old agreement. Savannah wished she could call her best friend, Nora Craft, for moral support, but Nora was a forensics tech in the Pelican Harbor Police Department, and Savannah didn't want to place her friend in the middle of this mess. Besides, Nora was out of town for the next couple of weeks.

The detective stepped closer. "I'm sure you did, but I need to go over it again with you in case there's something you remember this morning." Her gaze softened. "You're exhausted. Did you get any sleep last night?"

Savannah dropped into her chair and fiddled with her bracelet. "Not much. I kept seeing his face." Her voice wobbled, and she shuddered.

Richards moved to the other chair and settled in it with her notebook and pen out. "That had to have been upsetting. Were you and President Abernathy close friends?"

"No, not at all. Business acquaintances only. I don't have much use for people who take advantage of their positions. He loved making sure everyone knew he was the university president."

She told the detective about the provenance letters she'd found. "I told the provost about it, and he checked who had access to the warehouses where the artifacts were stored. Abernathy had logged in there at midnight two weeks ago. He easily could have been the one selling off the Willard Treasure pieces. He also ordered history department letterhead, which is what was used to create the provenance letters."

"Did you call the police and report it? Or campus security?"

"No, the provost, Beckett Harrison, suggested we should

confront Abernathy ourselves first and see if there was a good explanation."

"It sounds like you don't really like him."

Savannah gave a tiny shrug. "It's not a requirement to be buddies with the university president. And honestly, he has asked me out several times, which offended me since he's married. So no, he's not someone I liked being around." Technically, she was married too, but she left out that detail.

Richards wrote in her notebook. "Did he have any good friends among the professors?"

Savannah remembered the last Christmas party Abernathy had thrown. Most of the professors had shown up, but no one milled around Abernathy talking. "Not that I know of. Most of the professors have mentioned they detested him. That probably widens your suspect pool quite a lot."

"Your family has deep ties to the university, is that correct? Did your family start it?"

"Well, not exactly. It was originally named Universitates Nova Cambridge Willardius when it was founded after the Civil War."

"That's a mouthful."

Savannah nodded in agreement. "Joseph Willard bought a defunct plantation for a song and wanted to start a school that would rival Harvard. There were some, um, incidents with several burlesque dancers from New Orleans, some unpaid tax bills, and then a large fire. The board of trustees renamed it after all the tupelo trees on its premises. One of my ancestors was on the board back then, and he appointed his son as president, much to the dismay of Willard's son. My father eventually took over."

"And this Joseph Willard is the one who amassed the pre-Columbian artifacts that seem to be disappearing?"

"Exactly."

Detective Richards pointed her pencil toward the bookshelves. "Interesting that you have a book titled *Something Wicked This Way Comes*. That's what was written on the note pinned to Mr. Abernathy's jacket."

"It's by Ray Bradbury and is very famous. But his title is taken from a famous line in Shakespeare's *Macbeth* that goes: 'By the pricking of my thumbs, something wicked this way comes.' It's difficult to say what the killer was referencing."

"I see. Thank you for that clarification. Would you mind coming to the station for a little longer chat?"

"I'd be happy to come down." Though happy wasn't really what she felt, she didn't have any choice but to agree.

Richards left, and Savannah sank into her chair. Was it her imagination that the detective had looked at her with suspicion?

All the stories Hez had told her throughout their marriage came flooding back. The person who discovered the body was often a suspect. She held her hand to her mouth as the realization coalesced that she might be a suspect. Would the police arrest her?

CHAPTER 5

HEZ LEANED AGAINST A TREE AND SMILED. HE LOVED TAKING his rescue, Cody, to the dog park during his lunch break. Cody got his exercise and Hez got a free live comedy show.

Just looking at Cody was entertaining. He seemed to be made out of leftover parts from random breeds: Chihuahua legs, Great Dane ears, greyhound body, and an elegant—but crooked—Chesapeake Bay tail. He had wispy brown-gray fur with several severe cowlicks, so he always looked like a hurricane-force wind was blowing from his right. The final flourish to Cody's unique look was what Hez called the "crazy tooth"—an incisor on Cody's lower jaw that stuck out when his mouth was closed and gave him a vaguely rabid look, even when he was sleeping.

Fortunately, none of the other dogs cared what Cody looked like. He liked to play and didn't get mad at puppies or yappy little dogs, so he was popular at the dog park. Right now, he was trying to get a reserved, aristocratic-looking dog to play. The other dog was much taller than Cody, so he was jumping to make eye contact—leaping so high on his tiny legs that he almost appeared to be levitating.

After watching Cody bounce for half a minute, the aristocratic dog finally smiled, did an elegant little jump, and trotted toward Cody, who put his ears back and tore off like a furry missile with the other dog loping in pursuit.

"It looks like my dog made a new friend. Yours?"

Hez turned and saw a pretty redhead walking toward him. "Cody is mine or I'm his, depending on how you look at it." He nodded toward the dogs. "Yours is beautiful—is she a greyhound?"

"Saluki. And Cody is . . . ?"

"Mostly dog, I think."

She let out a sunny laugh. "He's adorable. I'm Dani, by the way."

"I'm Hez. Nice to meet—" He was interrupted by his phone ringing. Fortunately, Cody was playing with the saluki and didn't notice. He hated the way cell phones suddenly and randomly came to life, which he felt was deeply inappropriate behavior for an inanimate object.

Hez was about to send the call to voice mail, but he stopped when he saw who was calling. A hard knot formed in his gut. "I'm sorry. I need to take this." He turned and walked to an empty grassy area as he answered the call. "Savannah?"

"I-I'm sorry to bother you, Hez." Her voice trembled. "I didn't know who else to call."

The knot in his gut wound even tighter. What could be so bad that she felt she needed to call him two days after serving him divorce papers? "What is it?"

"There's been a murder. I think the police suspect me."

"What? Why? Who was killed?"

She told him about Abernathy's death and Richards's interrogation and request to come to the station. "Do you think I'm a suspect?"

"There's no doubt they'll be looking hard at you, Savannah. The police play good cop for a reason—they can get a suspect to relax and share things they shouldn't. You just told her you didn't like Abernathy and that you might have a motive because of the missing artifacts. You have a vested interest in the school and the artifacts because of your family connection." He paused as a new thought hit him. "Hold on, where are you now?"

"On my way to the police station."

"Are you under arrest?"

"I—I don't think so."

"You'd know if you were. Okay, the first thing you need to do is turn around. Don't go to the station and don't talk to the police anymore."

"But won't that make them think I'm guilty?"

"Tell them your lawyer told you to do it."

"You'll be my lawyer?" The hopeful note in her voice made him wince. He'd said that reflexively without thinking it through.

"I . . . Well, I guess I can represent you for right now," he said lamely. "That will make our conversation privileged, so the police can't ask you about it. Beyond that, I'll need to think about it."

"Oh, okay." She was silent for a heartbeat. "I think there's more going on than just Abernathy's murder. A lot more. I . . . I need your help."

The vulnerability in her voice struck a chord in his heart—and sent up a big red flag. The midday heat beat down on him, and a bead of sweat trickled down his neck into the collar of his oxford shirt. "Sure, give me a call tonight."

"Could we discuss it in person? I'm sorry, I know I'm asking a lot."

Three days ago, she couldn't get away from him fast enough. What was going on? Conflicting emotions roiled in his chest. The ink was barely dry on her divorce complaint, and his Spidey-sense warned him to stay outside the blast radius of whatever this was—but he couldn't bring himself to say no to her. And then he realized he had to.

"Actually, I can't represent you. I have a conflict of interest because we're, um, adverse parties in another matter."

"I trust you, Hez. I don't know what to do or who else to ask. And honestly, I'm sorry I even filed without talking to you first. I feel bad."

Hez stood rooted to the ground, her words echoing in his mind. *"I'm sorry I even filed."* Part of him had been aching to hear those words, but another part warned him not to get his hopes up. She needed him now and the divorce was getting in the way, so now she was "sorry."

What would happen when she didn't need him anymore? She hadn't said that she felt bad for filing divorce papers, only that she hadn't talked to him first. So when he was done helping her, would she refile but talk to him first? That seemed to be what she was implying.

A burst of motion caught his eye. He turned in time to see one of Birmingham's resident peregrine falcons catch an unsuspecting pigeon, killing it instantly in a burst of feathers. Would Savannah be like that pigeon, caught by brutal forces she didn't really understand? He knew the world of criminal justice and deadly conspiracies, but she didn't. She'd somehow wandered into that world, and she could easily wind up in prison or even dead. Could he let that happen to her?

"Hez, are you there?"

"Yeah, I was just thinking. Um, I'll come down tomorrow morning. I'm not sure what I can do to help, but we can talk about it over coffee."

"Thank you!" The relief in her voice was palpable. "We can meet at University Grounds in Nova Cambridge at ten thirty. My treat."

He ended the call as Cody came trotting up, panting and grinning. Hez scratched his ears. "Hey, buddy. I think your dad just did something dumb."

Hez looked every bit the polished attorney who would rescue Savannah from the legal morass where she floundered. Seemingly unfazed by the noise of steam wands frothing milk and the din of student chatter, he sat erect and alert in a corner table at University Grounds. Two cups and her favorite beignets were already on the table.

Hez spotted her and stood to pull out her chair. His appreciative glance made her glad she'd picked out the red A-line dress that skimmed her hips. Did she hug him, shake his hand, or what? A brief memory of meeting him at their favorite coffee shop in Birmingham hit her. It was the day she'd come in to tell him she was pregnant. He'd picked her up and swung her around the room while other patrons laughed and clapped. No one was laughing now.

She settled in the chair. "I hope you weren't waiting long."

"I just got here." He scooted in her chair before resuming his seat. "I hope you still drink peppermint mochas."

"And you've got black coffee in your cup, right? No froufrou drinks for you."

His wide grin emerged. "It's really great coffee. How long has this place been here? It looks new."

She inhaled the aroma of espresso before she took a quick sip of the bold flavor of peppermint and chocolate. "It is. The old Hotel Tupelo was going to be torn down, but an investor rescued it and turned it into office and retail space last year. The students love the modern vibe, and we professors love the excellent coffee." She reached for the beignet. "And they make the best beignets around." She took a bite of the powdered sugar treat to force herself to quit babbling.

He arched an eyebrow. "You always make small talk when you're nervous. Is it that bad?"

"It's not good. I feel like the police are circling like sharks around a bleeding dolphin, and I don't know what to do."

"You're the easy target, Savannah. The detective finding that book title made for easy pickings. Do you have any idea who might have killed Abernathy? Anyone have a grudge against him?"

"I don't think many of us liked him. He was the sleazy sort." She set down her mocha and leaned forward. "Hez, I told you that someone has been raiding the Willard Treasure and selling the artifacts after authenticating the pieces. Maybe Abernathy was involved in it too. Or maybe he discovered what was going on and was killed to keep it quiet."

Hez's brow furrowed, and he took a sip of his coffee. She watched his mouth touch the edge of the cup and a sudden memory of the feel of his lips on hers hit her out of nowhere. How could she still feel such a draw to him after all that had happened? His sudden reappearance showed her how little progress she'd made to forge a life without him. Would she ever be free of him? Did she even want to be?

He tapped his fingers on the tabletop. "Someone in your department has to be involved, which will occur to the police too. The mastermind would need someone who had access to the artifacts as well as the ability to know how to write an authentic-sounding provenance letter. And they'd need the university seal, which Abernathy had in his possession."

"Why would he need someone in the history department when he had access to history department letterhead on his own?"

He lifted a brow. "How do you know he had access to letterhead?"

"Beckett told me."

"Beckett? Who's Beckett?"

Heat rose in her cheeks, and she lowered her gaze to her coffee cup. "Beckett Harrison. He's the provost, and he discovered an order Abernathy placed for history department letterhead."

"He just blurted this out to you?"

"Ah, w-we're good friends, and I called him when I found the fake provenance letters. He promised to poke around and talked me out of calling the police until we had a chance to ask Abernathy about it. He'd hoped Abernathy had a good reason for the order."

"So he was with you when the body was discovered?"

She gave a quick bob of her head. "Yes."

Her cheeks had to be bright red. Hez was the smartest man she'd ever known. He would see right through her "good friends" comment and realize at least a potential relationship might exist there.

She lifted her gaze to Hez's face and saw the realization dawn in those blue eyes that missed nothing. "He's asked me out, but I've always said no. I-I'm not ready to date. Besides, we're still married."

"I see."

The hurt in his voice squeezed her chest. "I'll pull back the divorce papers. I never should have filed without talking to you."

"Why would you do that, Savannah? Just so I'll represent you, or because you're willing to give us a second chance?"

She opened and closed the clasp on her bracelet. Her emotions were in such a jumble she didn't know how to answer. There was so much pain and complexity in what went wrong in their marriage. Could any relationship be saved after going through what she had with Hez? She'd always been a hopeful person, but losing Ella had stripped Savannah of her optimism. Sometimes things went horribly wrong, and like Humpty Dumpty, they could never be put back together again.

"Savannah?"

His patient tone cut her worse than a harsh retort. They'd both changed, but while he seemed to have become kinder, she'd morphed into a person who dashed in for a quick slash of the verbal blade without warning. Being served with divorce papers couldn't have been easy on him when he'd come, hat in hand, to ask for a second chance. And she hadn't even considered his plea. Not once.

She lifted her gaze to meet his again. "I don't know, Hez. Reconciliation is a long, painful process. I'm under so much stress right now, I can't think." She swiped her palm across her forehead. "Can we postpone talking about starting over until I'm not under suspicion for murder? You'll represent me if I pull back the divorce, won't you?"

His steady gaze lingered on her face before he rose and picked up his coffee. "I don't know, Savannah. I'll have to think about it. If I decide I can't do it, I'll find another attorney for you."

She watched him walk out the door. Was he really leaving her to face the police alone? She didn't want some other attorney—she wanted Hez. And what did that say about how she felt about him? It took every bit of strength she had not to run after him.

CHAPTER 6

THIS WOULD NOT GO WELL. HER SISTER BLAMED HEZ FOR ELLA'S death and for Savannah's pain. Savannah smoothed her skirt with damp fingers, pulled in a deep breath of the lingering scent of wax on the tile floors, then pushed open the door marked *Jessica Legare*. Jess didn't notice her at first, and Savannah watched her a moment.

She was thirty-three, two years younger than Savannah, but she looked twenty-five. Her chin-length blonde hair was tucked behind her ears, and she wore a slim blue sheath that enhanced her creamy complexion. She was small with quick movements, and Savannah's five-ten height towered over her. Savannah had always wondered why she'd never married, but Jess claimed to never want to be in the horrid position their mother had endured. Savannah thought it had more to do with her broken engagement a decade ago.

Savannah pinned a neutral expression in place and held up an iced caramel latte from University Grounds. "Good morning."

Her sister looked up from behind her big desk. "What are you doing here so early? I suppose it's about Abernathy's death? I should have called when I heard you'd found the body, but I was out of town until last night." She ran her hand through her hair. "And I'm nowhere near ready for the fall semester to start, so I have a ton of work to wrap up."

"I'm sorry to bother you, but I have something important to discuss with you."

Jess glanced at a paper on her desk. "And I have an invitation for you to speak to the Mobile Historical Society next month. It will look good on your vitae for tenure."

The thought of tenure was a constantly looming weight, and Savannah hated this kind of request, but she gave a curt nod. "Text me the details. I need just a few minutes this morning."

"Can't it wait?" Jess's slim hand gestured at the piles of paper-work on her desk. "I have exactly two hours to get this report done for the trustee meeting."

As CFO of the university, Jess was always busy, and a warm flush worked its way up Savannah's neck at the obvious brush-off. "I'm afraid not. I'll try to only take a minute." If only this could wait.

Jess held out her hand for the coffee. "Have a seat and read the numbers in the first column off to me. I'll work while you talk."

Savannah took the page in Jess's hand and read the first line. "$10,213. I want you to give Hez a teaching position. He wants to start a law clinic here."

Jess set the coffee on the desk with a careful motion. "Out of the question."

"I need him, Jess," Savannah said in a low voice. Admitting it made her chest ache. "The police think I had something to do with Abernathy's death."

Jess's hazel eyes went wide, and she leaned back in her chair. "Start at the beginning."

Though she hadn't wanted to tell Jess about the provenance letters, the police knew, so it was time to tell her sister. She spilled out the events of the last few days. The color slipped from her sister's cheeks when Savannah got to the part about the Ray Bradbury book the police saw on her bookcase.

"You know Hez is the best attorney I could get. And he won't charge me." Savannah omitted the part about Hez wanting a second chance. "Birmingham isn't close enough, and he'll need a job if he takes a leave of absence to help me."

"Savannah, you are barely holding your head above water. The anniversary of Ella's death is approaching. The last thing you need is to have that anchor back around your neck. He hurt you badly, and I don't want to see it happen again. Think this through."

Savannah barely managed to hold back a flinch. "I already did. Do you have another attorney as good as Hez? One who won't charge me an arm and a leg?"

Jess sighed and rubbed her forehead. "You know I don't."

Savannah should have been elated at the note of resignation in her sister's voice, but even now she wasn't sure how she would handle being around Hez every day. She'd managed to steel herself before scheduled meetings, but running into him would be a constant occurrence. And the idea of a reconciliation would be dangled in front of her every second. It was a temptation she had to resist for her sanity.

She leaned forward with the paper still clutched in her hand. "Then you'll arrange it?"

"I don't have a choice. I hope you know what you're doing."

More for her own sake than for her sister's, Savannah gave a vigorous nod. "I'm sure it's the right thing. I have to go in to the police station for an interview, and it will help so much to have Hez there. I already said more than I should have. That whole good cop / bad cop thing."

Jess held out her hand. "Give me my paper and get out of here. Though I have no idea how I can concentrate on work when you dropped a bombshell in my lap."

Guilt, a familiar companion, compressed Savannah's heart. She handed Jess the paper and stood. "I'm sorry."

Her sister pointed at the door. "We can talk more when this meeting is over. I need to get back to work."

"Of course. Thanks so much. I'll let Hez know he can start on Monday."

Jess made a nondescript noise in reply and waved her hand again. Savannah retreated into the hallway and pulled the door shut behind her. At least it was over. Her sister had never liked Hez, not from the first moment they'd met. Savannah had always thought Jess was jealous.

When Dad had yelled at Jess, it was always Savannah who comforted her. Their mother was too afraid of Dad to buck him when it came to much of anything. Once Mom had been forced to come crawling back after one of his affairs, her life spiraled down even more until its sad, sorry end.

Dad always knew Jess wasn't his—and made sure she knew as well. When Jess started standing up to their father, she'd been thrown out of the house, and Savannah had gone with her instead of living at home during college. They'd moved into an off-campus house, and it had been the two of them against the world.

Hez's entrance into their lives had changed everything. It was no longer just her and Jess, and Savannah had been unable to prevent Jess's resentment of Hez's intrusion. Her recovery might be jeopardized by dealing with Hez in her life again, but there was no choice.

Hez didn't see the hippo until it was too late. He cast his fly and let the breeze carry it to the edge of the reedy area near the shore of the pond where his cousin and good friend, Blake Lawson, had taken him fishing. Blake had just returned to town after a stint in the Marines. It was a perfect cast—or would have been if there hadn't been a hippo lounging in the mud. Its massive head rose at the sudden motion from Hez, and it fixed its eyes on him.

"Careful." Blake spoke in a low voice from the back of the bass boat, which suddenly felt small and fragile. He didn't increase their slow speed, but he did angle them farther from the reeds. "Don't bother Bertha."

"Sorry." Hez sat motionless, letting his line drift. Blake had cautioned him multiple times to keep an eye out for hippos. They were a lot more dangerous than most people realized, and even females without calves—the only kind at the animal sanctuary owned by Blake and his mother—could be deadly if provoked.

"It's okay. Bertha has never acted aggressively, and I wouldn't have taken us here if I thought there might be a problem. But better safe than sorry."

Bertha watched the retreating boat for a few seconds, then settled back down into the muck. Hez relaxed and retrieved his line. His fly hung over the warm green water, a brilliant gem of wet red and yellow feather, almost completely hiding the sharp steel hook. "I should've seen her. I was distracted. I've got a lot on my mind."

His cousin was thirty and unmarried. His single state had never kept him from voicing an opinion though, and the odd thing was, he usually put his finger on Hez's problem.

Blake glanced at Hez, keen intelligence in his blue eyes. "When we talked on Friday, you said you would be meeting Savannah for coffee. Might that have something to do with why you're distracted?"

"It might." He recounted their meeting at University Grounds, ending with Savannah's admission that Beckett had asked her out. "She said she turned him down, but I got the impression she was interested. I'm thinking of just letting the divorce go through and referring her to someone else. I know plenty of good criminal defense attorneys, and a clean break might be best for both of us."

A sympathetic grimace creased Blake's tan face. "I'm sorry, man. Did she change her mind about withdrawing the divorce case?"

"No, but she's only doing it so I'll represent her."

"Did she say that?"

"Basically. I asked her whether she was just doing it so I'd be her lawyer, or whether she was willing to give us a second chance. She gave me a nonanswer about how stressed she is and said maybe she'd think about reconciliation after this is all over. She couldn't even look me in the eyes while she said it."

"Do you blame her?"

Hez frowned at his cousin. "What's that supposed to mean?"

Blake shrugged his broad shoulders. "Do you blame her for divorcing the guy you were two years ago?"

"But I'm not that guy anymore."

"Does she know that?"

Hez chewed his lip for a moment. They'd met twice and spent less than thirty minutes together. Could she really tell he'd changed from just that? "Maybe not. But I'm not sure it matters. She still blames me for Ella's death. She'll never forgive me for that."

"Did she say that?"

"I could tell."

Blake looked him in the eyes. "Have you forgiven yourself?"

Hez sighed. "There's only one person who can really forgive me, and she's buried in a little grave on top of a hill a few miles from here."

"God can forgive you."

Hez looked away from his cousin's steady gaze and fixed his eyes on the water. A breeze wrinkled the surface, scattering gleams of sunlight. It was a good day, and he didn't want to ruin it.

Blake meant well, of course. So did all the people who had tried to console him with heartfelt Christianese at Ella's funeral. But it was all white noise to him, empty phrases he'd heard a thousand times growing up. How exactly was he supposed to "accept God's forgiveness," "experience healing grace," and so on? None of those platitudes would let him go back and undo that terrible day. None of them had saved Ella, and none would bring her back.

Hez could feel Blake watching him, but his cousin accepted his silence. Hez appreciated that. Blake knew him well enough to realize that pressing the subject would only result in an argument.

The pond surface swirled and Hez's fly vanished. His line snapped taut, and the rod tip dipped toward the water. He spent the next thirty seconds battling a huge bluegill. The animal sanctuary's ponds weren't open to the public and had some of the best fishing in Alabama as a result. If Hez were actually fishing seriously, he'd probably be getting a bite on every cast.

Blake netted the fish and dropped it in the boat's live well. "Here's the thing. A week ago, all you wanted was a chance to show Savannah the new Hez. Well, now you've got your shot. The circumstances might not be quite what you had in mind, but she's practically begging you to spend time with her."

"The circumstances aren't at all what I had in mind. And this guy she's interested in—he's a key witness. I'd need him to testify persuasively and hold up under cross-examination. I'd have to spend hours with him and build a good rapport, and all the while I'll want to punch him in the face." He took a deep breath and blew it out. "I don't know if I can do it."

"So you're ready to let her walk because you're too much of a wimp to face down a rival? Show her how you've changed? You'd be a fool to walk now when you've got a second chance waiting for you to take it. Where's your fight, man?"

Blake had been the one who'd found Hez's support group, and he'd talked him off a ledge once or twice after Savannah had left. Hez had learned the hard way to listen to his cousin's advice.

"Fine. But you'd better be ready to bail me out of jail."

CHAPTER 7

SAVANNAH EYED THE RUN-DOWN BUNGALOW ON THE OUT-
skirts of Nova Cambridge. Peeling green paint hung in strips
from the decaying shutters, and the siding held hardly any
color at all. One porch post hung at an angle, and as she
approached the front door, she spotted the way the bottom of
the post wasn't secured to the floorboards. The whole thing
could come down in a puff of wind.

She didn't want to be here. This ramshackle little home
scared her more than any haunted house ever had. But the
path to tenure went through that crooked door, and she was
determined to follow it. She took a deep breath and walked up
the weedy path. Once she verified a handful of facts, her book
would be ready to submit.

The wood door swung open before she could knock, and
a tiny woman barely five feet tall appeared. Her white hair
curled around her face and highlighted her faded brown eyes
that nearly disappeared into wrinkles when she smiled. She
wore a pink blouse tucked into gray slacks.

"You must be Savannah Webster. I'm Helen Willard. Come
in." She scooped up an orange cat that was about to bolt
through the door.

She didn't remember Savannah. That was a big relief. Their paths hadn't crossed since she'd left for college, but she still vividly recalled "Miz Willard's" dislike of all things Legare. The miniature woman in front of her was a sharp contrast to the female powerhouse she'd feared all her life.

She followed Helen through a warren of pathways constructed through boxes stacked nearly to the ceiling. Savannah sneezed at the smell of must and old paper. When they reached the living room, she glanced around for a place to sit, and Helen moved a pile of photo albums out of the way.

Antiques stuffed the small room, and Savannah instantly coveted the barrister bookshelves with their glass fronts. She couldn't identify any of the titles inside, but she edged toward that end of the old sofa in hopes of making out some of them. They might be helpful for her book.

"It's so kind of you to agree to see me." Savannah pulled her notebook and pen from her purse. "Nothing has been published of the early history of TGU and the Willard Treasure, and I plan to change that. You know more about it than anyone else."

Helen gestured at the stacks of boxes. "I'm sure you think I'm just a hoarder, but someone had to save the history. These boxes contain memorabilia and newspaper articles about my family's past. I hoped this day would come and there would be a resurgence of interest in my great-grandfather. I remember him as a dashingly handsome gray-haired man with a booming voice and a kind manner. He deserves to be remembered for the visionary he was."

Savannah had always thought Joseph Willard was a lot like her dad—bigger than life and a hero to those who didn't know him well. Scratch beneath those likable surfaces and the rot underneath became all too clear.

She nodded. "I'd love to hear the story of how and why he founded TGU. He was quite wealthy?"

"Nouveau riche, not inherited. Like so many after the Civil War, he was a carpetbagger, which made the woman he wanted to marry turn up her nose. She was one of the Cabots, and they only married Harvard men. He wanted to push her face in his success, so he came south with a plan. He managed to buy some abandoned plantations, and he immediately loved the one here in southern Alabama. He had a scheme to create a southern university that could rival Harvard and Yale. Grand architecture with equally excellent instruction."

Savannah had never heard about Willard's broken heart and motivation, and she jotted it in her notebook. "That had to have cost a lot of money."

Helen shrugged frail shoulders. "He sank most of his fortune into the venture. Top architects clamored to design the buildings, and when they were completed, he hired the best minds to be professors. He never wanted the Harvard-educated Boston Brahmins to snub him again. And so Universitates Nova Cambridge Willardius was born."

Savannah turned a warm, encouraging smile on Helen. "And we still have Nova Cambridge as part of the area's heritage."

Helen preened at the comment. "You're a nice young lady and well versed in the events, it seems. I wasn't going to let you see the letters about the Willard Treasure, but I've changed my mind." She rose and dug through a box before she handed over a stack of envelopes.

Savannah could hardly wait to read them. She opened the letters and snapped pictures of them with her phone. "These are wonderful, Miz Willard."

The woman handed her the albums, and Savannah snapped pictures of the old photos too. Savannah could see her book morphing with this previously unpublished information.

She stopped at a faded image of three burlesque dancers. "What can you tell me about this photo? They were from New Orleans, correct?"

Savannah knew the story, of course. A fire started during a burlesque show, and its aftermath turned up unpaid taxes. Willard vanished before he could be arrested. The school's trustees knew the tarnished university wouldn't survive without major intervention, so they changed the name to Tupelo Grove University and tried to erase its unsavory beginnings.

Helen bristled, but before she answered, the sound of a door opening managed to push its way past all the boxes, and a man's voice called out, "Gram!"

A thirtyish man with sandy-brown hair and his grandmother's brown eyes burst out of the narrow path through the boxes. He pointed a finger at Savannah. "Gram, this woman isn't who you think. She's a Legare!"

Helen gasped and put her hand to her neck. "B-but her name is Webster. Are you sure, Deke?"

"Her married name. Her father is Pierre Legare." He pointed in the vicinity of the front door. "Get out and leave our family alone. You should have known better than to come here after you evicted Gram."

"She was evicted from her house?"

He sneered. "Your innocent act doesn't fool me, Savannah Legare. You knew exactly what you were doing. The Legares have taken advantage of our family for years. You won't get away with it forever, you know. Your sins will find you out eventually. All of you, especially your father."

The bad blood between the Legares and the Willards was long-standing, so Savannah didn't bother trying to defend herself or her father. At least she had her notes and pictures of the letters and old photographs.

Savannah's phone rang when she reached her vehicle, and she tensed when she saw the detective's name on her screen. Her hands shook as she slid into her Honda Civic, and she set her head against the steering wheel. *Don't answer.* She swallowed and waited until the ringing stopped.

A few moments later, her phone chirped with a message, and she read it in her text app. Augusta wanted to know when they could finish their conversation. Never, if Savannah had her way. Why couldn't Augusta realize she had nothing to do with Abernathy's death? Savannah felt penned in and hopeless. Was this how every defendant felt before they were arrested? How did she clear her name?

Everything in her longed to call Hez. He'd know what to do. But she'd sent him an email about working at the university, and he hadn't answered yet, and it had been five days. Maybe he was going to turn her down, and she would have to figure this out herself.

The dash lights glowed when she switched on the engine. It was only nine, and a plan sprang to life. She could search the warehouse. Maybe she could examine the Willard Treasure room and find a clue as to who had done this. Abernathy's murder had to be tied to the sale of artifacts.

She drove back to Tupelo Grove and got to the warehouse just before ten. A few students lingered on the park benches and near the pond, but the streets and sidewalks were mostly empty. Fall classes would start on Monday. She parked behind the warehouse and dug out her key card. One quick swipe and she was inside and out of sight of curious eyes.

The place smelled of age and dirt. She felt along the wall for a switch and found it. The dim fluorescents overhead flickered as they turned on, and the hum was a welcome distraction from the too-quiet space. She'd been inside the Willard Treasure room a hundred times over her lifetime. Her father had often taken her here to wander through the treasures his predecessor had accumulated. She had loved wandering through the stacks of boxes.

Her feet unerringly led her to the room in the back of the warehouse, and she unlocked it and stepped inside. She locked the door behind her, then switched on the light. The rows of boxes and statues seemed much the same as the last time she'd been in here. Or did they?

She studied the enormous stone carvings and frescoes torn from the walls of Aztec tombs. Where was that huge one that had been her favorite for so long? He was so ugly she'd felt sympathy and a real connection to him. Oh, there he was, hidden behind boxes. Had someone moved him? She snapped pictures as she walked along the rows past boxes labeled "Assorted Pottery from Building 3" and another row of boxes with the itemized contents labeled.

By the time she was done, she was sure items were missing. She couldn't be sure how much had been stolen because boxes and artifacts had been moved around, probably to hide the thefts. But who was the thief? The log of who had accessed the room should be in the front office by the door. She flipped off the light and crossed under the humming lights to the office. She unlocked it and went to the computer.

It required a password, so she typed hers in, and the screen accepted it. Someone else would be able to tell she'd been in here, but that was all right. She taught classes on the ancient peoples of the Americas, so she had every right to examine anything in this warehouse. She navigated to the visitors' list of the Willard Treasure room. There were more than she'd expected. Who would have such interest in the old artifacts?

She pulled out her phone and took a snapshot of eight names. Several of them had legitimate interest, including some of the professors in her department, but three of them gave her pause. Why would they be in here?

She went to the next page, but there was nothing else of interest, so she closed the page and left the computer idle like she'd found it. A soft, sliding noise came from her right as she exited the office, and she froze. Her blood pounded in her ears, and she barely breathed. She waited for what seemed an eternity, but there was no other sound.

Maybe it had been her imagination. Or a raccoon. The thought of an animal being in here with her wasn't much of a comfort, and she retraced her steps to the back of the building.

Her breath came fast as she strained to hear any movement behind her. Maybe coming here alone hadn't been a good idea.

She reached the door and exhaled in relief. She started to unlock the warehouse's outer door and it opened when she touched it. It hadn't even been latched. She'd locked it after she entered, hadn't she? Her pulse rocketed again, and she hurried outside and pulled the door shut without bothering to turn off the lights.

With the door shut, darkness pressed in on every side and her anxiety increased. She had to get home where she could breathe again. Her hands shook as she locked the door and turned to run to her car.

Something rustled to her right, and somebody struck her on the head. Darkness rushed down to claim her in its folds.

Something jolted Hez awake. It took him a few seconds to recognize his phone's ring. He opened his eyes and blinked from the light of the iPhone screen a foot from his face. Jessica Legare was calling. Cody barked at the phone.

He groaned. A conversation with Jess was never fun, especially not at—he glanced at the clock on his bedside table—1:23 a.m. What could she be calling about at this hour?

The answer popped into his sleep-fogged mind: Savannah.

He grabbed the phone from its charger and took the call. "Hello?"

"Savannah is in the hospital," Jess said without preamble. "She asked me to call you while they take her in for an MRI."

He bolted upright. "What? What happened?"

"Someone attacked her as she was leaving the history department warehouse. They hit her on the head, and she woke up around midnight." Jess paused as though expecting a response, but he was too shocked and groggy to say anything. "She went in there by herself at night because the police called her again and she felt she needed to try to clear her name. You hadn't responded to her email, so she decided she had to do something on her own."

"Oh. I—I . . ." His voice trailed off as he fumbled for words. "Is she okay?"

"I hope so. The doctor just walked in. Get down here." She ended the call.

He stared stupidly at the now-dark phone for several seconds, stunned. How serious was Savannah's injury? He should have asked more questions.

Savannah had to be all right.

He shook himself and switched on the bedside light, illuminating the entirety of his tiny studio apartment. He pulled on some clothes, grabbed a couple cans of cold coffee from the fridge, and stumbled out the door. Savannah needed him, and he should have been there. Someone had actually attacked her—this was real. She was in danger, and he would be too.

He took a moment and decided to grab his Glock 22 and bullets from the safe. He had a concealed-carry permit, and he wanted to be prepared.

Ten minutes later, he was headed south on I-65 with Cody in the back seat. He collected his scattered thoughts as he drove. Savannah's email had offered him a teaching job and a home for the Justice Chamber if he'd represent her. He hadn't responded because he didn't know what to say. He could easily represent her from Birmingham—Little & Associates had clients all over Alabama. A local PI could do the legwork, and Hez could drive down for court hearings and key witness interviews, and he could invite Savannah out for dinner whenever he was in town. Simple—and very different from what Savannah had in mind.

She wanted him to take a leave of absence from his job, move to Nova Cambridge or Pelican Harbor, and take a position as a professor and legal aid clinic director. He'd proposed basically the same thing when he visited her at TGU, of course, but a lot had happened since then. She'd turned him down, filed for divorce, implied she was interested in someone else, and said she wouldn't even consider getting back together until this was all over.

Did he really want to try to start a new life at Tupelo Grove when there was a good chance he'd wind up living it on his own? Could he bear seeing her on campus every day with another man's ring on her finger?

He'd started to write a response email thanking her for the offer and gently declining. He'd represent her, but he'd do it from Birmingham. But his conversation with Blake yesterday made him rethink that. It dawned on him that Savannah was implicitly saying she wanted him back in her life, even though his presence made her deeply uncomfortable. Was it because part of her still loved him despite the pain? Or was it because she was more afraid than he realized and she trusted him to protect her? Which he'd utterly failed to do.

A cold wave of guilt washed over him, settling in an icy lump in his stomach.

Hez pulled into Pelican Harbor just after dawn. He'd called ahead and found a pet boarding place that agreed to take his dog for a few hours, and it only took moments to drop Cody off. Hez turned into the hospital parking lot. Long shadows stretched across the mostly empty asphalt. He parked as close to the entrance as possible and hurried in. Once the front desk verified he was Savannah's husband, a nurse guided him to her room. Fluorescent lights buzzed overhead, and the scent of disinfectant lingered in the tiled hallways.

Savannah was eating breakfast in bed when Hez walked in. To his relief, she seemed more or less okay. Her auburn hair was pulled back in a ponytail that revealed a lump near the back of her head. The early morning light showed smudges of yesterday's makeup on her smooth tan skin and caught the gold flecks in her tired green eyes. She looked beautiful.

She noticed him in the doorway and put down her fork. "Oh! Thanks for coming so quickly—I wasn't expecting you for another half hour or so. I must be a mess."

He smiled. "I was just thinking how good you look. You've got first-thing-in-the-morning beauty. How are you doing?"

Color crept up her cheeks, but she held his gaze. "You're sweet. I'm doing fine, except for a headache, some brain fog, and a nasty bump. The neurologist says that should all resolve soon. I've had a concussion, but there's no bleeding on the brain. They're going to release me this morning."

"That's great! Have you talked to the police?"

"Yes." A shadow crossed her face. "I should have waited for you, shouldn't I? I'm sorry."

"Don't worry about it. You're a crime victim this time, not a potential suspect. I'm sure it was fine. What did they say?"

"There weren't any witnesses, and whoever attacked me seemed to know the locations of all the cameras. All the police have is a partial image of the back of someone wearing a gray hoodie. The crime techs are out checking for fingerprints, but they didn't seem optimistic." She hesitated. "Do you think you can help?"

He shrugged. "I know a couple of good investigators down here, but I'm not sure how much they can add to what the police are doing."

She bit her lip. "What about you? You worked the biggest investigations yourself when you were at the DA's office, didn't you?"

He had, which was a big factor behind his 98 percent conviction rate in murder cases. "Yes."

"Did—did you get my email?"

He took a deep breath. "I did. I'm sorry I didn't respond. I'll talk to Jimmy and see if I can find a place down here. My lease is up next month anyway."

"Oh, good! You'll love Tupelo Grove. It's the perfect place for your clinic."

He cleared his throat. "I, uh, won't be starting the clinic, though I might take on a pro bono case or two. I'm going to take a one-semester teaching contract at the university and see if I can still do some remote part-time work for Jimmy."

Her lips flattened. "Oh."

"I'll be here for you until this is over, Savannah. Don't worry about that. But I just . . . well, making long-term plans didn't seem like a good idea in light of how things are between us."

She smiled, but it seemed forced. "You're right. It's for the best this way."

CHAPTER 8

SAVANNAH'S LIVING ROOM WAS ENTIRELY TOO SMALL TO
hold the animosity radiating between Hez and Beckett sitting
at opposite ends.

"Here you go." She handed mugs of strong coffee to both
men, but even the happy sunflower design on the cups wouldn't
quell the tension.

Beckett wore a gray suit while Hez had opted for khaki
slacks and a polo shirt. Had he deliberately chosen to dress
down to show he didn't need a suit to appear competent and in
charge? Because in spite of the more casual attire, he was the
one who drew her gaze.

She studied him for a quick moment. Was he feeling the
weight of the impending anniversary of Ella's death too? Every
morning she awakened to a sense of dread that only grew as
each day passed. Their baby girl had been everything to her.
To Hez too. September first would be the third anniversary of
that terrible day, and every year she'd thought it wouldn't hurt
so much when the calendar flipped to that date. Judging by the
heaviness in her spirit, it wouldn't be that way this year either.

Hez's blue eyes looked shadowed, and she suspected he
wasn't sleeping any better than she was. In the old days she

would have caught his hand and dragged him off for a nap that turned into much more. Her cheeks flared with heat.

He caught her gaze and sipped his coffee. "Good stuff." He glanced around the room. "Cute place you have here too. It feels like you. Comfortable furniture, and you've painted it your favorite green-gray."

"I was lucky to get it."

At least he hadn't been able to read her mind. When her dog stared at Hez's pooch, Cody, with a challenge in his dark eyes, she moved her stockinged feet to Marley's back and gave him a foot massage, which usually calmed him.

Cody yipped and showed his snaggle tooth before he lunged at her moving feet. "Hez, your dog is a maniac." She snatched her feet back toward the sofa. "Where did you get him? He's, uh—interesting."

"He's great, isn't he? You never know what you're going to get with a rescue. They're like a box of chocolates—except chocolates usually don't freak out if you walk past a statue or eat your five-hundred-dollar arguing-in-the-Supreme-Court shoes."

"So you're telling me to keep my new Jimmy Choo pumps in the closet?"

"And your jogging shoes and your sandals. I appreciate you keeping him until I find a place. The hotel manager hates dogs."

Savannah eyed Cody again. "Maybe it's just your dog."

He grinned at her comment. "Hey, I've got a lead on a rental. It's a condo in downtown Pelican Harbor. Jane Dixon owns it."

"I know Jane," Savannah said. "I could talk to her, put in a good word for you."

"I'm meeting her at the condo at three on Saturday. You could meet us there."

Beckett frowned and shifted in his chair. "You're moving here?"

"I need to be near enough to help find who's behind this."

"I'm perfectly capable of helping."

Hez didn't speak, but his slightly contemptuous gaze flicked over Beckett. He focused his attention back on Savannah. "And get this, babe—the police chief owns it. I thought I might cozy into her good graces and find out who her detective actually suspects in Abernathy's murder."

That "babe" was entirely for Beckett's benefit, so Savannah pressed her lips together and decided to ignore how the endearment caused butterflies to take up residence in her tummy. "You think I'm in the clear?"

"I wish I could say that, but no. I'm sure you're their top suspect. It's my job to point their attention in a different direction."

She sipped her coffee and hoped it would help the headache that had been her constant companion since she'd awakened yesterday. "So where do we go next? I hope it's somewhere without the crowbar someone used on my head."

Beckett straightened in the brown armchair. "The guy hit you with a crowbar?"

She wanted to laugh, but with his earnest expression, she knew he'd take it wrong. "I was joking. I didn't see what he hit me with, but my head still hurts. He took my phone, which was almost as bad." She held up her new phone. "Got another one this morning after the hospital sprang me."

Beckett's brow smoothed. "It's always smart to follow the money. As provost I have access to TGU's financial data. If

Abernathy and his coconspirators were selling artifacts from the university's collection, some traces should exist in the financial records. They would have wanted to run the funds through the school's bank."

"Not necessarily." Hez flipped open the red file folder on his lap. "You said you spotted a couple of names that seemed out of place. We could start by interviewing them. I want to know what they were looking for in the warehouse. Savannah, I wish we had the pictures you took with your phone. They might give us more information."

She rubbed the lump on the back of her head. "Whoever it was, he was serious about making sure I didn't find anything of value."

Her gaze fell on her MacBook Air. "Hey, wait a minute. The concussion must be clouding my brain. I didn't even think about the cloud. Any pictures I took should have been uploaded."

She grabbed the laptop off the coffee table and navigated to the library of pictures. There they were—the last photos from her phone. Six snapshots of the room containing the Willard Treasure and one of the computer screen containing the names of the professors who'd accessed the warehouse.

"I'd forgotten some of the names, but here they are. I'll print them out. I know all of them, so I'll go with you to interview them. They might be more relaxed with me there."

Hez shot a triumphant grin toward Beckett, who looked away. Maybe it had been a mistake to invite both of them here at the same time, but she hadn't expected Beckett to act like they were a thing. She didn't want Hez to believe they were a thing. Her gaze strayed back to him. The only man who had ever stirred her heart that way had been Hez.

Why on earth had she agreed to talk to Jane? Savannah parked in front of the beignet shop in Pelican Harbor and shut off the engine. It had seemed a good idea at the time to make sure Hez found a place and was nearby to help her, but now that she was faced with walking through a condo with him, it felt much too intimate. Plus, she was still a potential murder suspect, so she might find herself sitting on the other side of a courtroom from Jane someday.

The police chief's condo was in the cutest block of Pelican Harbor's French Quarter. The town sat along the blue water of Bon Secour Bay between Oyster Bay and Barnwell, and visitors said its charm reminded them of New Orleans's French Quarter. Pelican Harbor had been a favorite place to visit when she and Hez were married, and Savannah had mostly avoided it since she'd taken a job at TGU.

She found it hard not to let her gaze stray to the Bayfront Inn down the way and across the street. There were too many reminders of a life that could never be regained.

She forced herself to get out and walk to the black iron staircase on the side of the Petit Charms brick building. The door at the top of the stairs stood open, and she walked up and stepped into a kitchen with gray cabinets and marble counters. It was part of an open space with a vaulted ceiling. The sweet aromas from the beignet shop under the condo wafted in the open door.

She walked across the wood floors into the living room, beautifully furnished in gray and white. Through the big window overlooking the street, she spotted an iron balcony with two chairs and a table. No sign of Hez or Jane. "Hello?" she called.

"We're in the bedroom," Hez called.

She followed the sound of his voice through a doorway that opened into a spacious bedroom with an attached bath. The gray and white furnishings in here were as tasteful as the rest of the space.

Jane Hardy Dixon turned to face her with a smile. The police chief was in her early thirties with chin-length light brown hair and hazel eyes. She wore white shorts and a blue tee instead of a uniform. Her tiny stature and face shape had always reminded Savannah of Reese Witherspoon. The two of them had met at a charity event when Savannah first moved to TGU.

Jane inclined her head toward Hez. "Hello, Savannah. I understand you're his local reference."

So Hez had already worked his charm with Jane. Savannah had been a fool to think her recommendation was needed. "I think it's safe to lease your beautiful condo to him."

"I usually like a year's lease, but he says he'll only be here through December."

"That's the plan for now. It might be extended." When Savannah saw Hez's eyes widen, she regretted her choice of words. She'd made him no promises for anything more than a semester, and she didn't want him to think she was already planning to repair their marriage.

Though being in this coastal town where they'd spent so many romantic weekends had her emotions in a jumble.

"I'd appreciate it if you could make an exception for me," Hez said. "If circumstances change and I'm able to stay longer,

I'll sign an extension immediately. And I'll take good care of your beautiful place."

"Mama!"

Savannah turned toward the childish voice and spotted a little girl who looked enough like Ella to take her breath away. Blue eyes peeked from under a mop of blonde curls, and chubby legs churned under her lilac sundress as she ran toward Jane, who scooped her up. The little girl wrapped her arms around her mother's neck, and Savannah could almost feel the tight squeeze and smell the sweet scent of the child's skin.

A fierce longing for Ella enveloped Savannah and nearly buckled her knees. Her gaze instinctively sought Hez's. Deep pain roiled in his blue eyes. It took all her strength not to go to him and comfort him.

Jane bounced the little girl in her arms. "This is Dolly. She's two. Say hello, sweetheart."

"Hello." The word was muffled as Dolly buried her face in Jane's neck.

Savannah couldn't help staring. "She's beautiful, Jane. And her name is perfect."

"It means 'gift of God,' and she certainly is that." Jane kissed the curly mop of her daughter's hair. "We're all smitten with her. She has her daddy wrapped around her little finger, and her big brother, Will, hated the thought of leaving her so much, he took TGU's football scholarship offer instead of heading to Ole Miss like he'd planned. He decided against living in the dorm so he could see her every day. She's a charmer."

Savannah tore her gaze from the little girl before she begged to hold her. She made a show of glancing at her watch. "I need to get back to TGU. I hope you'll consider Hez for your condo."

Jane smiled and set her daughter down. "It's a done deal. I have the lease agreement with me if you're ready to sign, Hez." Her smile faltered when she looked at Savannah.

"Thank you so much." Savannah swallowed past the constriction in her throat. "I—I need to go now."

Hez's gaze swung to her, concern creasing his face. He opened his mouth, but she was out the door before he could say anything. She shook her head, ashamed that she couldn't hold herself together. But she didn't slow down until she was at the bottom of the staircase and heading for the sound of the waves and the scent of water.

God had given Jane a beautiful daughter but had taken Savannah's. The harsh reality settled in her heart that she didn't just blame Hez. She blamed God. She had sensed him with her, but he could have prevented all of this from happening. Why hadn't he?

CHAPTER 9

HEZ LEFT HIS NEW "OFFICE"—ACTUALLY LABELED A STORAGE room on the floor plan—and made the ten-minute trek across campus to the history department offices in Connor Hall. Gaggles of students hurried along the weedy brick paths linking the old limestone-and-brick buildings. Hez weaved his way among them, marveling at how young they looked. Three weeks ago, he'd felt like he hadn't really changed since he left college fifteen years ago. Now he felt like an island of almost middle age surrounded by a sea of youth.

He reached Savannah's office, took a deep breath, and knocked on the door.

"Come in," she called.

He opened the door and walked in. Built-in bookshelves along two walls held neat rows of scholarly treatises on pre-Columbian North America, Savannah's main area of specialty. A smaller bookcase by her desk was stuffed with the classic fantasy and horror stories she loved. There was her old boxed set of *The Lord of the Rings*, the bindings cracked and worn from a dozen readings. A familiar-looking book lay open on the top of the bookshelf, and he smiled: Seamus Heaney's translation of *Beowulf* that Hez had given her for her birthday while they were engaged. They'd read it aloud to each other one stormy weekend, savoring the poetic rhythms in the ancient tale of monsters and mead halls.

Savannah sat behind her desk, smiling back at him. She wore a cream blouse and khaki slacks that gave her a crisp, professional appearance but didn't hide her curves. A picture of Ella faced him from the credenza, stabbing his heart. The anniversary of her death was in two days, and he'd been trying not to think about it.

"Did you see Beckett's email to the history faculty?" she asked. "That should make these interviews easier."

He focused on Savannah, glad to be distracted from the picture behind her. "No, my university email isn't working yet. What does it say?"

She turned to her computer and read, "Dear colleagues, the provost's office is investigating whether certain items may have been improperly removed from the collections commonly known as the Willard Treasure. Please cooperate with the investigation and make yourselves available for interviews upon request. The provost's office will be assisted by Professor Savannah Webster and recently hired law instructor Hezekiah Webster."

Hez grimaced at the power play. He and Savannah weren't "assisting" Beckett's investigation, and the interviews had been Hez's idea. Plus, it hadn't really been necessary to point out that he was a lowly "instructor," which put him at the bottom of TGU's academic pecking order. Still, Savannah was right that this would make their job easier—none of the professors on her list could refuse to talk to them now.

"Great," he said without enthusiasm. "Who do you want to talk to first?"

"Let's start with old Charlie Hinkle. His office is just down the hall."

They left her office and walked a few paces down the corridor and entered a room that was more fire hazard than office. Stacks of paper and books covered every available surface, including most of the floor. A narrow clutter-free corridor led back to a battered old desk, behind which sat what appeared to be a living garden gnome, minus the pointy hat.

"Good morning, Charlie!" Savannah said, brightening the dusty room with her smile. "Do you have a few minutes?"

The gnome looked up from an enormous book festooned with yellow sticky notes. Rheumy brown eyes peered from under bristling white brows. "Ah, Savannah. Of course I have a few minutes for you." He gestured at two chairs, each of which held a foot-high stack of papers, books, and magazines. "Sorry for the mess. Feel free to clear those off and have a seat."

"That's all right," Savannah said. "Hez and I only need a few minutes of your time. We're here about some missing items from the Willard Treasure. Did you see Beckett's email?"

"Yes, yes, yes." Hinkle shifted in his seat. "I, um, I'm sorry about that."

Hez's ears perked up. "Sorry about what exactly?"

Hinkle pointed at the tome he'd been reading when they came in. "I'm updating my book on late Aztec pottery, and I may have borrowed one or two pieces from the warehouse without, um, formally checking them out."

"Which pieces?" Savannah asked.

"Oh, they're over here." Hinkle pointed to a spot behind his desk. He lifted a small orange vase with a jaguar-shaped handle. "The others are a little too big to pick up."

They picked their way around the desk, with Savannah in the lead. Half a dozen pots, dishes, and other items lay haphazardly on piles of paper. She snapped pictures of the items with her phone.

A stone sculpture of a flat-nosed man's head wearing a helmet sat on a small table. Hez pointed to it. "Can I see that?"

Hinkle glanced at it in surprise. "Oh, that's not from our collection. It's not even Aztec. That's a loan from the University of Alabama."

Hez nodded. "I'd still like to see it. Could you hand it to me?"

Hinkle hesitated for a moment, but then he grasped the head with spidery-veined, age-spotted hands and strained. It scraped across the table and tilted up, but he couldn't lift it. "I'm sorry. Could you come around here?"

Hez squeezed past Hinkle and picked up the head. He guesstimated its weight at twenty-five pounds. No more than thirty. He turned it over and saw a University of Alabama museum catalog sticker. He put the head back on the table. "Thank you for your time, Professor Hinkle. I have no further questions."

Hez retraced his steps through the obstacle course covering the floor while Savannah said goodbye and got Hinkle to promise to check out the artifacts in his office.

Once they were back in the hall, Hez turned to Savannah. "Well, it wasn't him. He's not strong enough to pick up that head. There's no way he could have knocked you out and dragged you off the path."

She nodded while staring at the pictures on her phone. "True, though he does have three of the pieces I noticed were missing." She stopped and frowned.

Hez stopped too. "What is it?"

She shook her head. "I don't know. There's something off about these pictures of the warehouse. I feel like I'm missing something, but I don't know what. This stupid postconcussion brain fog makes it hard to focus."

Hez looked over her shoulder, catching a faint whiff of the tropical scent of her shampoo. With an effort he focused on the pictures rather than her. They showed a dimly lit room lined with metal shelves, which were mostly full of boxes and crates of different sizes. One shelf held a row of old ledger books. A utilitarian table and a few chairs stood in the middle of the room, presumably for use in examining artifacts from the boxes on the shelves. "For what it's worth, nothing looks strange to me."

She sighed and pocketed her phone. "Maybe it's nothing. Okay, let's talk to Tony Guzman next."

CHAPTER 10

GUZMAN'S OFFICE WAS AS SPARTAN AS HINKLE'S WAS CLUT-tered. Three large windows and spotless white walls gave the room a bright, airy feel. A small bookcase held an American flag in a case flanked by two small Mexican flags. There were also several pictures of Hispanic men in uniform, including a photo of Guzman in uniform shaking hands with a gray-haired officer. The credenza held only a computer, two large monitors, and a phone. Hez suspected he could do the white-glove test on any surface and not find a speck of dust.

Guzman sat behind a neat and almost empty desk. A muscular, fit man about Hez's age of thirty-seven, he clearly had the strength to knock out Savannah and carry her several yards. And based on his pictures, he had at least some combat training. Savannah had also mentioned that she and Guzman were competing for the same tenure spot—could that be related to recent events somehow?

As soon as they finished introductions, Guzman said, "I'm glad you stopped by."

Savannah arched an eyebrow. "Why is that, Tony?"

"Because the so-called Willard Treasure has bothered me for years. It contains thousands of priceless artifacts—the looted heritage of an entire city of my ancestors—and no one has ever even done a proper catalog of them. You could steal half of what's there and no one would ever notice. So I'm glad someone is at least investigating missing items."

Guzman's choice of words caught Hez's attention. "You said 'looted.' Do those artifacts rightfully belong to the university, in your view?"

Guzman didn't hesitate. "No, they rightfully belong to the people of Mexico, especially the native inhabitants of Veracruz. Do you know the story of how all those artifacts wound up here?"

Hez shook his head. Out of the corner of his eye, he could see Savannah fidgeting with her bracelet, which she often did when something bothered her.

"A gambling debt." Guzman's dark brown eyes flashed, but he kept his voice even. "Our esteemed founder, Joe Willard, liked to gamble in New Orleans. He won a lot, and a number of powerful men owed large debts to him. One of those was an exiled Mexican general. Willard let it ride. When the political winds shifted in Mexico, the general went home to become governor of Veracruz province."

"I think I've heard you mention him," Savannah said.

Guzman ignored her. "By that time Willard had founded his university and was trying to raise its prestige. One way to do that was to give it a museum stuffed with spectacular artifacts, so Willard wrote to his old gambling buddy and said that they'd be even if Willard's school could have exclusive rights to a top-notch Mexican site. The governor happily agreed and found Willard a pristine Aztec site deep in the jungle. Willard sent down a huge team with pickaxes and shovels."

Guzman shook his head. "The place looked like a war zone when they left. They shipped back a literal boatload of artifacts—intricate gold work, enormous stone carvings, and frescoes torn from the walls of tombs. The flashier items went into the museum, but a lot of the 'boring' artifacts went into boxes labeled 'Assorted pottery from northeast building' and stuff like that. They went straight into storage, where they've stayed ever since."

"I see," Hez said. "So in your view, it all really belongs to the people of Veracruz, especially the descendants of the Aztecs."

Guzman nodded. "Exactly."

"Like you."

Guzman gave Hez a pointed stare. "What do you mean?"

Hez shrugged. "Well, if it belongs to you, then you'd be entirely within your rights to take a few pieces, wouldn't you?"

Guzman's face darkened. "So that's where this is going. Look, if I took any of those artifacts for myself, I'd be just as bad as Willard. Worse actually—I'd be stealing from my own people. They belong in a museum where they can be studied and people can see them, but that museum should be in Veracruz."

Savannah leaned forward. "I understand how you feel, Tony. We're just trying to figure out where the missing artifacts might have gone. We have evidence that you recently visited the warehouse where they were kept. Would you mind telling us what you were doing there?"

"Not at all." Guzman's color started to fade back to normal. "I was making a catalog. It's been over a century—it's time someone finally did it. You're welcome to a copy of what I have so far. Maybe it will help with your investigation."

Savannah smiled. "Thanks, Tony. That would be great."

"Yes, thanks." Hez thought for a moment. "I don't have any further questions, at least for now."

Once they were back in the hall, Hez turned to Savannah. "I'm less positive about him, but my gut says no."

She nodded. "I'm pretty sure he meant everything he said. I've heard his gambling-debt speech at least half a dozen times, usually followed by a proposal to fund a museum in Veracruz. And he does have a point about how we got the Willard Treasure. It wasn't illegal—especially back then—but it's also not a story we're very proud of. Tony can be a little bit of a zealot, but I don't think he's a thief."

"Or a murderer."

She nodded again, then glanced at the screenshotted list on her phone—and grimaced. "Okay, we've saved the best for last: Erik Andersen."

"It doesn't sound like he's a favorite of yours." He frowned. "Wait, is this the guy Jess dated?"

"Yes. I was surprised to find him still working here. He's the department chair and is pretty full of himself."

Hez wanted to ask more questions about Andersen's personal history, but he restrained himself. The details of his relationship with Jess were a little murky. All Hez really remembered was that the ending had been ugly. Maybe that was why Jess was still single—and still on guard around the male species. "He's a European history professor, isn't he?"

"Yep, which makes it odd that he was in a warehouse that doesn't contain any European artifacts." She stopped outside Andersen's office and knocked on the half-open door.

"Come in," a deep male voice called.

They walked into an office that seemed more suited to a politician than a professor. The polished walnut bookcases and matching table were mostly decorated with awards and honorary degrees Andersen had received and pictures of him with famous people. The man himself sat behind an ornate walnut desk, smiling at them with too-perfect teeth. He was a big man, and Hez guessed that he'd probably been handsome in a rugged-Viking way about ten years ago. He still had the thick blond hair, broad shoulders, and square jaw, but he'd gotten squishy in the middle and florid in the face.

Andersen steepled his fingers. "What can I do for you?"

Hez cleared his throat. "We're investigating the removal of artifacts from the Willard Treasure warehouse."

"Oh yes. Beckett sent an email about that, didn't he?" Andersen glanced at an expensive-looking watch. "I don't know anything about it. Is there anything else? I've got a meeting I need to get ready for."

"Just one thing: Why were you in the warehouse?"

His face went blank for an instant, but he recovered quickly. He furrowed his brows. "Hmm. I'm not sure what you're talking about. I can't recall the last time I was in there."

Hez nodded to Savannah, who took out her phone and held up the screenshot of the log. "It was just over a week ago," he said. "We know you were there."

Another hint of terror flashed across his face as Andersen stared at her phone, followed by another fast recovery. "Oh . . . oh yes. Thanks for reminding me. I was just looking around. As head of the department it behooves me to look in on our collections from time to time, of course. Now, I'm sorry, but you really must excuse me. If you have more questions, please contact my secretary to schedule an appointment."

"I think we have all we need," Hez said. "For now."

Back outside, Hez stared up the hill toward the cemetery. Savannah turned to stare that way too. "It's the day after tomorrow."

"I know," was all he could say. Part of him wanted to suggest they go together, but he didn't think he could bear the condemnation he was sure would be in Savannah's eyes when they stood at their daughter's grave.

Savannah hadn't been able to sleep, and she rose with the sun and headed to the cemetery. The shade of the tupelo trees along the path up the hill cooled her heated cheeks, but the freezing sensation moving over her skin came from dread.

Three years.

Jess struggled to keep up in her heels. "I should have changed to my running shoes," she muttered. "Wait up, Savannah."

Savannah always stopped at this spot anyway. Marley flopped down in a shady spot, and she settled onto a chipped marble bench. It was the oldest place in the cemetery, and if such places could be beautiful, this one fit the bill. Most of the old graveyard had been neglected since many of the family members had moved away or gone on to eternity themselves, but this family plot at the top of the hill was a lovely gothic garden. Overgrown wildflowers and sprawling trees were sprinkled among pillared crypts and ornate headstones of stained and decaying marble.

Jess reached her, and her expression softened. "You doing okay, Savannah? I don't know that it's healthy to come here every year. Being confronted with it first thing in the morning sets you up for a terrible day. I worry about you."

Savannah had her gaze fixed on her goal ahead. "Three years ago today, I lost everything that mattered to me, Jess. My daughter, my marriage, my happiness. This day will never bring anything but pain and loss. If it hadn't been for a deep sense of God's presence with me, I don't know how I would have survived it all."

She knew Jess would flinch, and she did. She hated it when Savannah brought up her faith. Savannah reached over to squeeze her hand. "You didn't have to come, Jess. I know it's not easy—not for any of us."

Jess tucked a stray blonde lock back into place. Her hazel eyes filled with tears as she gripped Savannah's hand. "You've been happier lately. Well, at least until Hez had to come back into your life. Now you're sad again. I can't stand it."

"I'd probably be in jail if he hadn't."

Savannah began walking along a weedy oyster-shell path toward Ella's grave. Aware of where they were going, Marley ran on ahead to sit atop Ella's grave. She'd tried to keep up the headstones and crypts of the immediate family—their grandparents, their mother, and of course her precious baby girl.

As she drew near to the spot, her pulse raced and her mouth went dry. She fell to her knees in front of the black oval stone with Ella's picture etched onto its surface and reached out to trace her daughter's smiling face. The sweet scent of wildflowers filled her head.

She and Hez had chosen a verse from Luke to be inscribed below Ella's image: *"For where your treasure is, there your heart will be also."* Though she knew with every fiber of her being that she'd see Ella again someday, it was the *now* that was so painful. She struggled to hold back the tears so she didn't upset her sister.

She preferred to come here alone, but Jess had insisted on being with her. Savannah had been afraid Hez's return would make this year's anniversary all the more painful. And maybe it had. Seeing him brought back memories of that horrible day.

She stretched out over the grave and let the fresh scent of grass push out the memory of the wail of the ambulance and the screams that had erupted from her own throat when she heard the news.

Her friend Nora always reminded her to remember the good times, and Savannah would try to focus on those today.

She sat up and wiped the moisture from her cheeks, then leaned over to pluck weeds from around the gravesite. The last statue she'd brought, one of an Aussie, still seemed in good condition. She traced the lines of the dog's fur, and an unexpected smile lifted her lips. At least the artist hadn't had to try to carve that wild tooth of Hez's dog. Cody would have been a hard dog to create.

She became aware of Jess's hovering presence. "Ella loved dogs. Any dog, but especially Marley. I think there have to be dogs in heaven."

Marley woofed at the sound of his name.

Jess stirred and settled on the bench. "It's such a peaceful place up here. Do you come up often?"

"When Ella first died, I came every day, sometimes more than once. Now I come often, but it's not a compulsion." She glanced at her sister's somber face. "Remember how Ella would squeal when you came to see us? She'd run with her arms outstretched the minute she spotted your car."

Jess bit her lip and tucked her chin down. "She was a special little girl, Savannah. I didn't mean to imply earlier that any of us would ever forget her. I miss her too. Why does there have to be so much pain in life?"

"Pain and loss are part of life. We all know that. You and I more than most." Her gaze wandered to the headstone over their mother's grave. "It was hard to lose Mom." There was a plot for her father someday when he died, but it wasn't a spot her sister would care about.

Jess looked up and followed Savannah's gaze. "I might come up here and dance on his grave when the old man finally has the good sense to die."

Savannah sighed. "You need to forgive him, Jess. Your hatred only hurts you."

"Oh, I know he doesn't care how I feel. He's always made it abundantly clear. I wish I'd realized sooner I wasn't his own child. It might have made the abuse easier to tolerate."

Jess didn't often talk about this, but Savannah wasn't ready to delve into that pain on an already agonizing day.

Jess glanced at her. "You're a lot like Mom, you know. Beauty, brains, and a fatal problem with trusting the wrong man. Look where it got her—bruises and tongue-lashings? I'm so afraid Hez is going to hurt you. It would kill me to see you in so much pain again."

Savannah's cheeks went hot. Discussing how she felt about Hez wasn't something she wanted to do. Not today. "Hez is nothing like Dad."

"You're defending him like Mom defended your dad."

Savannah struggled to keep from raising her voice. Her sister was speaking out of love. "How can you talk to me like this on today of all days?" Her voice broke, and she reached out to touch Ella's picture again. Her baby. Sobs built in her chest again, and she had to let them out. But the hot tears rolling down her cheeks brought no relief—they only amplified how much she missed the sweet scent of Ella's skin and hair and the feel of her small arms wrapped around Savannah's neck.

She rocked back and forth, and her cries echoed back at her from the canopy of trees overhead. "Ella, my Ella," she sobbed.

"I'm sorry, so sorry!" Jess put her arm around Savannah's waist and lifted her to her feet. "Come on, honey. I'll cancel my meeting and your classes, and we'll get you a peppermint mocha."

Jess only wanted to help, so Savannah let her lead her away. No solace was here anyway—only the insistent knowledge that her life would never be the same. Not ever.

Jess paused near the top of the hillside and frowned at one of the trees. Savannah didn't care enough to ask why Jess seemed distracted. It was an opportunity for her to pull out of her sister's grip and choke back her sobs. She took several deep breaths and tried to gather her composure.

People had remarked on how strong she'd been through the tragedy, but today the grief had taken her down to the depths. The only way to fight it was to run, just for a little while. Until tomorrow came, and she didn't have to remember every detail of when the light went out of her life.

How was Hez handling the anniversary? She prayed he wasn't falling apart like her.

CHAPTER 11

JIMMY'S CALL CAME JUST AFTER DAWN, WHILE HEZ WAS
still on his first cup of coffee. He didn't need to ask the purpose
of the call. "Hey, Jimmy. Thanks for calling." Cody growled at
the demon phone, gave Hez a disapproving glare, and trotted
out of the room.

"Hey, Hez." Jimmy's deep voice rumbled through the phone.
"I'm your sponsor and your friend. Of course I'm going to check
on you today. Probably more than once. How are you doing?"

"I'm fine." Hez took a sip of the rich black brew. "As fine as
I can be, anyway."

"Uh-huh. What are your plans for the day? You're going to
keep yourself busy, right?" Jimmy firmly believed that activity
was a great substitute for alcohol, especially on a hard day. A
year ago—the first anniversary of Ella's death that Hez had
spent sober—Jimmy had insisted on taking Hez for a long
hike, followed by a huge dinner at a noisy barbecue place and
then an outdoor jazz concert. It had worked. By the time Hez
finally got back to his apartment, he'd been too exhausted to
even think about having a drink. It was all he could do to take
Cody out for a ten-minute walk, which the dog had considered
utterly inadequate.

"Yep." Hez drew in a deep breath, and the scent of fresh beignets from the restaurant below reminded him that he hadn't eaten. "I'm going to grab a little breakfast and then go for a long run, with a stop at Ella's grave. Then errands and paperwork for the rest of the day. I've got a to-do list a foot long."

"Sounds like a plan." Jimmy paused. "Are you going to be on your own?"

"Yeah. Blake is tied up today."

Jimmy was silent for a moment. "Wish I could be there. I'll give you a call later. And I'll be praying for you."

"Thanks, man." Hez ended the call and discovered a voice mail from Blake, who was also checking on him before heading out to a remote part of the animal sanctuary that had no cell coverage. Hez appreciated the concern, but he really felt fine. He was more worried about Savannah—he knew how deep her grief ran.

He pulled on his running clothes, eating a banana and some granola as he dressed. The fragrant smell of beignets still tempted him, and he promised himself one when he returned from his run. He picked up the little stuffed puppy he planned to leave at the grave and shoved it in his pocket. Then he headed out.

Hez jogged slowly through town, then picked up the pace when he reached the path at the edge of the village park. It was a scenic trail with a six-mile loop that ran over the bridge connecting the points at Weeks Bay before curving into sun-dappled forest. The beautiful spot was rife with memories of watching the sunset with Savannah in happier days. He'd run it several times, but he hadn't had the courage to visit Ella's grave yet.

As he ran, Ella filled his thoughts. He shied away from memories of her death, making himself focus on her all-too-short life. She'd been a carbon copy of Savannah, except that she had his blue eyes—which had been gorgeous on her. They sparkled when she laughed, which she did often, especially after they brought home Marley as a puppy. The two of them had been best friends. If only Hez had paid attention when Marley started barking that day, maybe . . .

No. He wouldn't go there. That painful path had led him to the bottom of many a bottle. Today he was going to focus on the good memories—like how much she loved his shrimp bisque, which he made with real North Sea shrimp and considered much superior to the bigger but less flavorful Gulf prawns. He'd taught her to call those "tofu of the sea." Savannah hadn't found it quite as funny as he did. He decided to make shrimp bisque tonight in memory of those good times.

And then he was there. A crushed oyster-shell path led off the main trail and up a gentle wooded hill. He stopped, took a deep breath, pulled the little puppy out of his shorts pocket, and walked toward his daughter's grave. The air was still under the leafy roof, and the crunching of his footsteps on the path sounded unnaturally loud.

A dilapidated iron fence marked the border of the cemetery. The rusted gate stood open, but he hesitated before going in. He felt like an intruder here, in the burial ground of Savannah's ancestors. But it was Ella's burial ground too. He gripped the puppy in both hands like a protective talisman and went in.

A distant sound stopped him as he neared the top of the hill. It took him a second to recognize it: sobbing. A woman sobbing. Savannah.

He ran to the hilltop and the scene came into view. Savannah and Jess, standing in bright sunlight at Ella's grave. Savannah's back was to him, her shoulders heaving with grief. Jess had her arm around her sister, comforting her. He took a step forward into the light, instinctively wanting to comfort his wife.

Something alerted Jess to his presence, and she spotted him. The tenderness vanished from her face. She shot him a glare filled with so much accusation and anger that it hit him like a blow.

He stepped back and tripped over a tree root. He landed on his back. The breath whooshed out of him and he lay gasping for a moment. He turned and saw the stuffed puppy gazing at him with blank, glassy eyes.

Ella's eyes had the exact same empty stare when he pulled her body from that pool.

All at once he was on his feet and running again. He raced pell-mell down the hill, away from the suffocating fog of guilt and death that shrouded the ground around his daughter's grave. He passed the gate and the edge of the grove, and he didn't slow down until he was almost back to Pelican Harbor.

His breath sawed in and out in ragged gulps, and sweat streamed down his face. He felt like an idiot and a coward. One nasty look from Jess and he ran like a little kid who thought he saw a ghost? But no, that wasn't it. He could face Jessica Legare. What he couldn't face was the memory of that day.

So he wouldn't face it. Not now anyway. He'd run some errands, make some shrimp bisque, and remember his daughter's infectious laugh.

He needed cayenne pepper and a few other items for the bisque. His wallet was back in the condo, but Publix had Apple

Pay, so he could just use his watch. He spotted a store off the path and headed for it. Hopefully, he wouldn't see anyone he knew.

He grabbed a cart and hunted for the items he needed. His gaze landed on a display of Justin's peanut butter cups, and the memories he'd been avoiding ambushed him.

Savannah had stood in the doorway to his home office at nine on a Saturday morning. "I have some errands to run, Hez. Can you watch Ella for an hour?"

He hesitated. "I have work to do, babe. This brief is due on Monday."

She pressed her lips together. "You always have work to do. It's the weekend, and she needs some time with her daddy."

"I was going to take her to the park when this is done."

"Take her now. I won't be gone long."

He pushed back from the desk. "You're right. The time crunch will be better when this trial is over." She didn't have to tell him he always said that, and his workload got heavier, not lighter. He kissed her goodbye and went to get Ella.

He plopped her in front of a TV and turned on *Moana*, her favorite movie. Marley jumped on the sofa with her. Hez shot a glance back as he left the room. Ella was already entranced by the opening scenes, leaning back into the sofa cushions with her chubby little legs splayed out in front of her. He smiled at how cute she was and glanced at his watch. She loved this part, and he could do fifteen minutes on the brief.

Hez went back to his home office and left the door ajar—enough so he'd hear what was going on, but the movie wouldn't distract him. He soon lost himself in the brief, honing his argument that the other side had misinterpreted a key statute.

If he could just convince the judge on this point, everything else would fall into place. It was a nuanced issue, so he needed to word this section exactly right.

Marley's barking broke into his thoughts, but Hez ignored it. The puppy barked whenever he saw a squirrel, FedEx dropped off a package, or someone turned on a leaf blower anywhere in a three-block radius. He even barked when the wind blew.

Wait, the barking was coming from *outside*. Hadn't he left Marley on the sofa beside Ella? He sighed. He'd better investigate.

He walked past the room where he'd left his daughter and dog and glanced in. The movie was still playing, but the sofa was empty.

"Ella?"

No answer.

"Ella?" he called in a louder voice as he walked down the hall.

Still no answer.

The first little wave of fear rippled through him. "Ella!"

He heard a sound and jogged toward it. He found Marley in the family room, standing just inside the sliding door. It was open. Ella had just learned how to open it.

Hez ran outside. What he saw would be seared into his memory for the rest of his life: the flagstone path leading out to the pool, the white Adirondack chairs Savannah loved, and the little table between them holding her mug and a package of Justin's peanut butter cups—Ella's favorite candy.

And in the pool itself, Ella floated face down. Her golden hair spread out around her little head like a halo.

Hez jumped in and frantically started CPR, but he knew it was too late as soon as he saw her face. Her blue eyes stared at him, glassy and empty.

The rest of the day had been a blur. Scattered memories cut through him like glass shards—the sirens, the EMTs, Savannah's screams when she came home, the grocery bags she dropped on the kitchen floor. The only thing he clearly remembered was fighting over the candy. He yelled at Savannah for leaving it where Ella could see it from inside, and she yelled back that he must have done it. It was the first skirmish in his losing war against guilt.

"Mr. Webster," a vaguely familiar voice said, breaking him out of his thoughts.

Hez looked around and saw a wizened little man looking up at him. It took a second to place him. Hinkle, that was it. Charlie Hinkle. "Oh, hi, Professor Hinkle."

"I just wanted to let you know I checked them out."

Hez blinked. "Checked out . . . what?"

"The pieces for my book. The ones you and Savannah came to see me about."

"Oh, uh, yes. Thank you."

Hinkle's gaze went to Hez's cart. "Oh, the Mondavi cabernet. Is it good with beef? We're having a couple of old friends over for dinner and . . ."

But Hez wasn't listening. He was staring down into his shopping cart. Two bottles of wine were in it. He had no memory of putting them in, but he'd been on autopilot ever since he walked into the store. And apparently this was what he still did on autopilot.

"I'm sorry," he said, interrupting Hinkle. "I have to go." And Hez walked out of the store, leaving his cart and the startled professor behind.

He went straight to his condo, where he grabbed his phone from its charger and called Jimmy.

Jimmy picked up on the first ring. "Hi, Hez. You okay?"

"No. No, I'm not." Hez recounted everything that had happened since he walked into the cemetery.

Jimmy whistled. "Man, that's rough. Wow. When was the last time you prayed the Serenity Prayer?"

"The last time we were at a meeting together."

"So it's been a little while. Let's pray it together now. 'God, grant me the serenity to accept the things I cannot change, courage to change the things I can, and wisdom to know the difference.'"

Hez mumbled the familiar words along with him, but they didn't help. "The thing is, it's my fault that she's dead, and I can't change it. How can I accept that?" He pictured her lifeless face staring up at him as he held her in his arms in the pool. His throat swelled and his vision blurred. "How can I ever . . . ?"

Jimmy was silent for a long moment. "Yeah, serenity can be hard, especially when you're trying to do it on your own. Could be there's some serenity down at that Pelican Harbor beach you've been bragging on. What do you say we go down there and throw a football around and do some barbecuing or something? Maybe we'll find a little serenity while we're at it."

"It's a long drive."

"Yeah, perfect for listening to a book I just downloaded."

"I don't know, Jimmy. I—"

"Don't you argue with me, Hez. I'm still your boss. Don't you forget that. And I'll pick up some burgers and charcoal on the way. No more grocery stores for you today."

Hez managed a chuckle. "Thanks, Jimmy. I really appreciate it."

He ended the call and went out on the balcony. Pelican Harbor's bustling little French Quarter spread out below him. His shaky breathing became even, and a light breeze cooled his face, bringing the scent of beignets and the faint strains of jazz.

He felt calmer, steadier. The dark weight of guilt and grief had lifted a little—but it still hung over him, waiting to crash down again with crushing force.

CHAPTER 12

THE EARLY SEPTEMBER BREEZE, DAMP AND CHILL, BLOWS
in off the water. I zip my jacket and shove my hands deep into
the pockets. It's not really cold—my car dashboard showed
seventy-three degrees when I parked—but even that gets
uncomfortable when you've been standing in the wind on a
beach for an hour in the middle of the night. I'd like to wait in
my car, but that's out of the question, of course.

I'm not on this dark, deserted strip of sand at Pelican State
Park by choice. We had to tighten operational security after the
blackmail incident with Luis. He knew what he was smuggling,
and he managed to get a driver to tell him where it was going,
which gave him enough information to threaten us. Now the
packages are sealed at the source in Mexico or Guatemala, and
the shippers are under strict instructions not to tell anyone
what they contain. And drivers no longer pick up shipments at
the water's edge. I do.

The new system seems to be working, but I don't like it. I'm
too involved. Much more involved than I ever wanted or planned
to be. This was supposed to be safe and easy—something I could
handle from behind my desk while drinking my morning coffee.
I also wasn't supposed to have to kill anyone.

Luis's right foot washed ashore last week. The police think it belonged to a drowned fisherman or migrant, but they found it near where I dumped the body. Also, the foot was in a black cowboy boot, and I can still feel the leather of his boots as I dragged the body across the beach to his boat.

I shiver, but not from the cold.

Finally, a boat approaches. Its lights are off, so it's little more than a black shape in the water a couple hundred yards offshore.

A helicopter roars overhead, flying low. Its spotlight snaps on as it zooms over the water. A cone of light picks out the boat almost immediately. A man sits in the stern. He's already gunning the powerful motor and turning away from shore. Another boat appears out of the darkness, speeding toward the first. It will be a race, but I have no doubt who will win.

Coast Guard or cops. Maybe both. They knew he was coming, so they knew he was meeting someone onshore. I turn and run for my car.

I'm too late. A police car is already parked in the entrance to the parking lot, engine running and lights on. My car is the only vehicle in the lot, and it's lit up like an opera star singing a solo.

Panic rises in my chest, but I fight it back. I need to think, fast and hard. They'll be searching the shore, so running probably won't work. I might be able to escape by swimming, but they've seen my car, so they'll know I was here. My only advantage is that I almost certainly don't fit the profile of the smuggler they think they're hunting.

I make my decision, take a deep breath, and walk into the beams from the police car's lights. I hear a car door open, but I can't see anything in the glare. I shade my eyes. "Is everything all right, Officer?"

A male silhouette appears in the light, hand on his gun. "Let me see your license." I can't see his face, but the voice sounds young.

I take it out and hand it to him. "What's going on? That helicopter scared me half to death." Which is absolutely true. The best way to hide lies is to bury them in a pile of truths, which is my plan.

"What are you doing out here?"

"Walking on the beach."

"At one in the morning?"

"I couldn't sleep. My job can be pretty stressful."

"Did you see anyone on the beach?"

"No, but I noticed a pickup parked on the side of the road about a half mile back."

He nodded. "We saw it. Mind if I search your car?"

"Not at all." I'm glad my gun is in my pocket rather than my glove compartment. I click the key fob. The car chirps and the lights flash as it unlocks.

The cop walks over and opens the door. I get my first look at his face. He is very young. He checks the interior, then opens the glove compartment and the trunk. When he finishes, he turns to me. "Okay, you can wait in the car while I check your license."

I get in the car and take deep breaths to relieve the tension in my body. Something went terribly wrong tonight, but what? Did someone talk? And then it hits me: the organization will think it was me, especially if anyone saw me with the police tonight.

My pulse starts to race again. I need to find out where the leak is and plug it fast. If I don't—

A tap at my window makes me jump. The young officer is smiling. "Sorry to startle you," he says as I roll down the window. He hands me my license. "You can go now. You shouldn't come down here during the night. It's not safe."

I nod. "Yes. Yes, I realize that now."

Savannah could have done without the hostile glances between the two men on opposite sides of the table in her office. The tantalizing scents of coffee and beignets should have had them all relaxed and smiling, but instead they were ready to engage fencing blades.

She slid a coffee from University Grounds toward Hez. "Since I asked you both to be here so early, the least I could do was bring coffee. Looks like you brought beignets." She handed Beckett a water. "Here you go, weirdo. I thought about getting you an herbal tea, but I knew it would be a waste of my money."

He grinned. "Sleep, good food, exercise, and sunshine. That's all a body needs." His nose wrinkled when he glanced at the open box of beignets. "Those don't qualify as healthy."

"You can look away when we eat them then. I'll be glad to have yours."

A corner of Beckett's lips lifted. "You with powdered sugar on your face would be way more tempting than the beignet."

They'd never even gone on a date, and it was a very unfair parry in the verbal fencing skirmish. He'd only said something so provocative to annoy Hez, so she didn't answer as she sat in a chair between them and opened her laptop. Besides, his vote on her tenure was important.

Hez's posture went rigid at their friendly exchange, and her gaze swung back to him. Except for the tired lines around his eyes, she never would have guessed yesterday had been as tough for him as it had been for her. And maybe it hadn't. He'd always been a master at compartmentalizing his life. Once he got over the shock of Ella's death, the stacks of folders and his distraction with work had only grown.

And so had the mound of empty liquor bottles.

For all she knew, a pile was in his trash can right now. He claimed to have changed, but she wasn't so sure. The mint she'd caught on his breath this morning might have been meant to cover a much more distasteful scent. If she'd had any choice at all, he wouldn't be sitting across from her in his khaki slacks and blue shirt. He wouldn't be looking at her with eyes that reminded her so painfully of her daughter's. And even worse, that gaze brought a flood of memories of the first time she'd seen him. She'd fallen in love with that direct, open gaze at first sight.

She'd been at his office for him to take her statement before she testified at the first murder trial he prosecuted. It had been a small piece of evidence—just placing a car she'd seen outside the coffee shop at a specific time—but she'd sensed a definite spark between them. She'd been disappointed when he didn't call her and thought she'd misjudged his interest. Two months later when the jury came back, her phone had rung and she heard that deep, compelling voice asking her to dinner and a football game. Their relationship had traveled at warp speed. And they'd been happy, so happy. Until the unthinkable happened.

She blinked and refocused her attention on the problem facing them. "Sorry, what did you say?"

Hez pulled out his phone and glanced at it. "Andersen is a definite possibility. His reason for being there is flimsy. In my view a lie immediately takes a suspect to the top of the list."

Savannah's tension ebbed at his calm voice. "There could have been no possible reason for him to look at the artifacts there. None of them have any bearing on his area of expertise. And he was in a hurry to get us out of his office. I'm not saying he killed Abernathy, but his stated purpose for being in that warehouse was a lie."

Hez took a sip of his coffee. "I'd like to contact Augusta and tell her what we've discovered. If we can find another direction for her to aim her focus, maybe she won't harass you for another interview." He leaned back with a confident expression. "I'm skilled at coaxing information from the police, and she might reveal a line of inquiry we haven't investigated ourselves."

This time Beckett stiffened. "We don't have to lean on the police to learn more. I've studied the financials I have access to, and there are troubling and unexplained deposits. They appear in TGU's records and almost immediately disappear."

"Well done," Savannah said. "Any hint of where the money is coming from?"

Beckett's smile spread to his brown eyes. "I have no proof, but I suspect the deposits are from sales of the artifacts and they are transferred out by the thief."

"Shouldn't the report show where the money came from and where it went?" Hez said.

"The reports I can access are general without the detail we need. We need more information."

Hez glanced at Savannah. "Who would have complete access? Jess?"

She saw where this was heading and nodded. "Jess is the CFO and can see everything."

"I asked for access, and she denied it," Beckett said. "And with Abernathy dead, no one can override her. But I'm sure she would let you have the password, Savannah. She'll want to help you."

Was he really that clueless? Savannah's gut clenched at the thought of asking her sister to let her into the school's financial records. Jess's job was sacrosanct to her, and she wouldn't likely agree to let anyone have access. Not even her sister.

Hez huffed. "You don't know my sister-in-law well, do you, Harrison? Money is power to her, and she isn't easily cajoled into anything. We'd have better luck getting the police to ask for a search warrant. And right now the investigation centers on Abernathy's murder. A judge won't grant that kind of access without probable cause that it's related."

Beckett bristled at Hez's tone, and Savannah suppressed a sigh. Did Hez have to remind Beckett of their former relationship every other minute? "I'll talk to her about it and explain how important it is to figure out who is behind this. But we have to remember the embezzler has likely hidden his or her tracks."

Hez took another sip of coffee. "True enough. We'll likely have to take some rabbit trails to discover their identity, but I've handled many convoluted cases in my career."

Enough of this kind of verbal sparring. She closed her laptop and rose with it tucked under her arm. "Let me know what you find out from Augusta, Hez. I'll tackle Jess and see how far I get. If you hear a thud, it's because she's kicked me to the curb."

Beckett chuckled, but Hez's eyes narrowed. He'd likely charge to her defense if he deemed it necessary. The thought of having him as a protector brought more comfort than it should.

She exited the office and stepped into the sunshine. Maybe before she talked to Jess, she'd see if Hez had taken anything to Ella's grave. It shouldn't matter how he processed his grief, but she wanted to make sure he felt something. Right now she wasn't so sure.

And an hour later she was even less sure. There was no sign he'd been to Ella's grave at all.

CHAPTER 13

HEZ'S VISIT WITH DETECTIVE RICHARDS BROUGHT BACK fond memories. He hadn't been in the Pelican Harbor police station since he was a brand-new lawyer working his first case for the DA's office. He'd been sent down to collect some physical evidence needed for a murder case. It was a menial task, but his supervisor insisted that new hires personally learn every step of building a case—an education that proved invaluable later in his career.

The quaint redbrick building hadn't changed, but the police chief had. The old chief, Charles Hardy, had been replaced by his daughter, Jane—who was also Hez's landlord. Hez made a quick stop by her office to drop off his rent check and thank her for clueing him in to a local dog park where Cody had made several new friends. He said nothing about the Abernathy murder case, of course, but it never hurt to be on friendly terms with the police chief.

Chief Dixon directed him to Detective Richards's office. She looked up from a stack of papers on her desk. "Good morning, Mr. Webster. Have a seat. Sorry for the delay. I was just showing a new hire around. You said you had some information for me?"

Hez settled into the chair in front of her desk. "Thanks for meeting with me. Yes, the university is investigating the theft of artifacts. We think there might be a connection to the Abernathy murder, particularly in light of the attack at the warehouse."

Richards nodded. "That occurred to me too. Do you have any hard evidence?"

"Not yet, but we have started interviewing potential suspects." He recounted Savannah's and his conversations with the three professors. Richards took notes as he spoke, which was encouraging.

"Have you pulled surveillance videos from the professors' visits to the warehouse?"

He nodded. "TGU only saves security video for sixty days, so we don't have everything. I've asked them to load the backup tapes to see if they can find more."

"Good thinking. Can you send me a copy of anything you find?"

"Of course. We're also checking the university's finances. If the murder is tied to the artifact theft, I wouldn't be surprised to find a money trail linking Abernathy to his killer."

She looked up from her notes, a hint of concern in her brown eyes. "Are you preserving the metadata?"

"We are—I thought of that too. We want to make sure any evidence we find is admissible."

She relaxed. "Thanks. I'm glad TGU has a former prosecutor handling this. We're pretty busy, and I don't have time to get out there as often as I'd like. I appreciate your doing some of the preliminary legwork for me."

Another encouraging sign. He decided to push his luck a little and see if she'd tell him anything about her investigation.

"Of course. We're happy to help. Is there anything you can share that might make our investigation more efficient? For example, are there any indications that this might have been a burglary that went wrong?"

She shook her head. "No signs of forced entry or a struggle, and nothing appears to have been stolen. Also, Abernathy died from a single deep stab wound in the back. So it seems he trusted his killer enough to let that person get behind him."

"Time of death?"

"He carded into the building at five thirty that morning and the body was found shortly after seven, so presumably somewhere in that window."

"Unless the murderer killed him somewhere else and used his card to get in and dump the body."

She glanced at her watch. "That's pretty unlikely given the amount of blood around the body."

"Good point. Did anyone else card in after him?"

She shook her head again. "Not until Savannah and Beckett, so presumably Abernathy's killer either broke in or Abernathy opened the door for his murderer."

"Got it. Well, I won't take up any more of your time. I'll let you know what we find."

He did his best to keep from grinning like an idiot until he left the station. The meeting could not have gone any better. Richards had given him more information about the case than she really had to, though he would have been entitled to it eventually if Savannah were charged. But more importantly— much more importantly—Richards didn't act like Savannah was likely to ever be charged. This had been a collaborative meeting between two investigators, not a cop meeting with a suspect's attorney. Hez had been in both types of meetings, and he knew the difference.

Thinking of Savannah brought a flash flood of memories about Ella. Hez's smile vanished and his stomach muscles tightened. He paused with his hand on the door of his car.

He struggled with his pain briefly before he was able to force his mind back to the just-finished meeting. He visualized telling the good news to Savannah. She'd thank him and reward him with one of those smiles where her whole face lit up. She might even hug him. And maybe Beckett would be there to see it. Hez chuckled at the idea—and at himself for thinking like a teenager competing for a girl.

His equilibrium restored, he got in his car and headed back to campus. Someday he'd have to confront his responsibility for his daughter's death, but not today. It was still too fresh—his meltdown the other day made that clear. He didn't want to think about what would have happened if he hadn't run into Professor Hinkle at Publix.

He needed to be more careful when he approached the dark places in his memory where the demons lurked. And he should stay away from them whenever possible, especially when he was alone. Maybe next year he'd be ready to wrestle with them. Or the year after that.

Jess's mansion on the outskirts of Pelican Harbor oozed privilege and power. The sunset painted the Greek Revival house in oranges and gold, giving it a warm and inviting look that Savannah knew was entirely external. Jess lived alone and only used the larger rooms when she was throwing upscale parties for donors or financiers. The only parts of the house that got regular use were the home office and pool, where Jess put in miles each day. The rest of it felt lifeless and dusty, even though Jess's maid service kept it spotless.

Savannah had stayed in the house briefly when she returned to Tupelo Grove after the collapse of her marriage, but she moved out as soon as she found her cottage. She'd felt guilty for leaving her sister all by herself, but she just couldn't live somewhere that felt like a cross between a luxury furniture showroom and a mausoleum.

She rang the bell, and Jess opened the door in a bathing cover-up. "I was just about to go for a swim." Her gaze fell on the Mac's Irish Pub box in Savannah's hands. "You brought shepherd's pie? I suppose I could cancel my swim for now, but you should have called."

Savannah followed her inside. Why was it always this way with her sister? Savannah had no trouble standing up for herself, but informing her sister of unpleasant news was always a chore she would rather avoid. Nevertheless, this had to be done.

The sooner the better. She wouldn't be able to eat a bite with the argument looming over her head. "I have something important to discuss with you."

Jess eyed her warily. "What?"

"Whoever killed Abernathy might have left clues in the university's fiscal records, but they're behind a firewall in the computer system." Savannah set the box of food on the dining table and drew in a breath. "You need to give Beckett access to the full school financials."

Jess pulled the box of shepherd's pie toward her and lifted the lid. She inhaled and smiled. "No one makes shepherd's pie like Mac's."

Savannah crossed her arms over her chest. "Did you hear me?"

Jess sighed. "Look, Savannah, I don't want to fight with you. The school is my responsibility, and no one has full access but me. Not Beckett. Just me." She stared at Savannah. "Hez is behind this, isn't he?"

Savannah's cheeks warmed. "We all thought it was a good idea. The police suspect me. I could feel it, and Hez confirmed it. We're trying to throw the investigation in another direction—hopefully the right one. Whoever is selling off the artifacts has to be running the money through the school's books."

"You think I'm stupid? That I wouldn't notice it? I know my job, even if you don't think so. There's nothing in the records to be seen."

"You're the smartest person I know, Jess, and maybe I'm wrong. I can concede I might be." Aware she was babbling, Savannah silently counted to ten and tried to calm her racing pulse. She had to convince Jess somehow. Hez and Beckett were depending on her. "What could it hurt to let Beckett poke around? He knows the inner workings of the history department, and he might spot some small detail that will lead us in the right direction."

"I never should have hired Hez. He's the best lawyer I've ever met, but . . ." Jess shook her head. "I don't want him to hurt you again, and I'm afraid you'll let him. You have blinders on when it comes to him."

"I see more than you know." Savannah wet her lips. "You've always been there for me, and I need your help. I don't know where to search next if you say no. I might as well turn myself in and let them put me in jail."

"You're so melodramatic." Jess pulled out a chair and sank onto it. "If you didn't need something from me, I'd still be in the dark about the investigation. That has to stop. If I let Beckett look at the financials, you have to keep me apprised on what's happening. And Beckett examines nothing without my being there. Is that clear?"

"Of course." Savannah felt faint with relief. Though it was nothing short of a miracle, she'd convinced Jess. "Thank you so much. I love you, Jess."

She made a move toward her sister, but Jess held up her hand. "If I do this, I want you to promise me you'll keep Hez at arm's length. He's here for one reason only, and you know it. He wants you to come back to him, and that can't happen, Savannah Elaine Webster. Do you understand?"

"He's only here for one semester—and remember, that was his idea. Would he have suggested that if he was really trying to win me back?" It surprised her how much it stung to admit that.

"True. You're saying all the right things, but I can see he still touches a place in your heart. He nearly destroyed you once, and I won't stand by and let that happen again."

"I feel like I don't really know him anymore. There's such a disconnect between our lives now. I mean, there always was really. And after Ella's death, it all became crystal clear." Her eyes misted and she fought to keep her voice even. "I—I don't even think he went to Ella's grave yesterday. There were no flowers or anything that suggested he'd been to visit her."

Jess put a hand on Savannah's arm. "I'm sorry. Fortunately, he's only here for a few months. Once Christmas comes, he'll be out of your hair."

Jess opened the box of shepherd's pie, releasing the rich aroma of beef, garlic, and potatoes. But Savannah's appetite vanished at the thought of Hez leaving the college. She was afraid to examine why.

CHAPTER 14

HEZ COULDN'T WAIT TO TELL SAVANNAH THE GOOD NEWS— but he had to. She wasn't in her office when he got back to campus, which was a little surprising since she usually stayed until at least five o'clock. He could wait until he was sure she was back home.

Besides, he had something else he'd been meaning to do. He picked up his desk phone and dialed.

A familiar female voice answered. "Paige Alexander, Federal Public Defender's Office."

"Hey, Paige. It's Hez Webster."

"Hez? I haven't heard from you in years! Are you still with the DA's office? Or did you finally decide to join the Light Side?"

He laughed. He and Paige had been razzing each other ever since they were in law school together at Tulane. "I went into private practice, so I guess you could say I joined the Green Side. If I'm going to defend criminals, I might as well get paid good money for it. You have no excuse."

"Hey, everybody is entitled to a defense. Except maybe you. I'd probably plead your butt straight into a nice, long sentence. Prison would be good for you."

He laughed again. "That's actually what I'm calling about—everyone deserving a defense, that is. Not you committing malpractice to get me behind bars. I'm taking a leave of absence from my firm and teaching at Tupelo Grove. I'd like to do some pro bono work while I'm here and maybe involve a couple of my students. Does the PD ever refer out cases?"

"That's awesome! You'd make a great professor. As for the referrals, yeah, we make them—usually misdemeanors. But that seems like a waste when we've got you available. Hold on a sec." He caught bits and pieces of a muffled conversation, including "excellent lawyer" and "drunk." Then Paige was back. "You sober, Hez?"

He was used to—and usually appreciated—Paige's bluntness. "Yep. I haven't had a drink for almost two years and I'm in AA."

"Cool. One more minute." More muffled conversation ensued. "Okay, we've got a felony drug case down there that we don't have the bandwidth to handle. A guy named Hernando Morales got picked up by the Coast Guard off Fort Morgan at 1:00 a.m. about a week ago. He said he was fishing, but the Coasties say he didn't have lights on his boat and he tried to evade them. They also claim he threw something overboard, but they couldn't find anything."

"They couldn't find anything?" Hez echoed. "No drugs?"

"None. They even brought out a dog after they towed his boat to shore. Nada. The only thing in the boat was a fishing pole."

That didn't add up. "So why is this a drug case, let alone a felony case?"

"Excellent question. Morales is from Biloxi, so he drove a long way to do some night fishing. And he had a drug-trafficking arrest in Mexico ten years ago. That's it."

"Seems thin."

"Very thin, but the U.S. Attorney's Office is threatening to throw the book at him. If he won't cooperate, they say they'll charge it as 1-A intent to distribute, plus a Travel Act violation."

Hez whistled. "So they're asking for ten years to life. Wow." He drummed his fingers on the desk for a moment. He loved a challenge, and the case sounded like it had some intriguing issues. "This doesn't make sense. There must be more going on."

"I'm sure there is, but the USAO won't tell us, and we don't have the time or resources to figure out what it is. You want the case? It could be a lot of work."

Hez didn't hesitate. "Yes."

Savannah drove home along Willard Street. There was a group grief session tonight, and she should go, but she couldn't face talking about her loss. Not with her life and heart in so much turmoil. She needed to talk to Nora. She had gotten in last night, and Savannah desperately wanted her best friend's moral support. Plus, Nora worked for the police department. She would never disclose anything confidential, but her body language might give Savannah a hint as to how worried she should be.

When she stopped at a light, she texted Nora and asked if she'd mind meeting at the coffee shop instead. The lights and hubbub of University Grounds would distract from the memories that kept trying to surface. Someday maybe she'd be able to take them out and examine them, but not now.

A message from Nora pinged back almost immediately. *Got you covered, girlfriend. Already at a back table with their first batch of spiced cider in hand.*

Savannah exhaled and turned down Magnolia Street. Nora almost always stopped to get them a treat on the way to group. Savannah parked behind her friend's white Nissan and hurried past students sipping their drinks on the expansive porch of the renovated hotel. The scent of spiced cider overlaid the usual aroma of espresso, and the sound of the steamer hissing was like a relaxing hug to her soul.

She dawdled at the memorabilia wall when she spotted an old photo of Jess and her at a TGU game when the school had won their one and only national football title. She and her sister wore identical joyous expressions. When had she last seen Jess wearing a smile like that? A pang lodged in the region of Savannah's heart. Jess had lost whatever happiness she'd once had.

She glanced around and saw Nora at a back table. She must have come straight from work because she wore her forensic tech blue uniform. The two of them had met at a group meeting for parents who'd lost a child. Nora's six-month-old son had died of an asthma attack, and her husband had died in an accident on a military chopper a year later. The two had been friends from the moment they met.

Nora tucked a curl of dark hair behind her ear and stood. "You just missed meeting my niece Tammy. She's starting work with me at the police station." Nora took Savannah's hand and squeezed it. "I can count on one hand the meetings you've missed. What's gotten you in such a tizzy?"

Savannah collapsed onto the chair and reached for the comfort of the hot drink. "My life is a mess."

"Is it about Abernathy's murder? Augusta is a good and fair detective, so try not to worry."

Savannah relaxed a little. "That's part of it, but not all. Hez showed up out of the blue and asked for another chance."

Nora's brown eyes went wide behind her glasses. "I—I don't know what to say. How do you feel about it?"

"I blew him off at first, but once it was clear I was under suspicion for Abernathy's death, I knew I needed his help. I agreed to drop the divorce for now so there's no conflict of interest."

"There are other attorneys."

Savannah appreciated her friend's cautious tone. "I know, but Hez is the best."

Nora's pert nose wrinkled. "You sure that's the only reason? Something has prevented you from filing for divorce before now. I know your faith kept you hanging on, just like it did me. We've talked about everything over the past two years except for your husband. You freeze whenever his name is brought up. Even when you told me you were filing for divorce, you didn't want to talk about it. You just did it without any discussion."

Savannah took a sip of her cider so she didn't have to answer right away. She finally set her cup back on the table. "It's normal to avoid talking about painful subjects."

"Oh please, this is me you're talking to. You've heard me blather on about Nathan's death ad nauseam over the past three years. I talk about how much I loved him and how much I miss him. I've told you about the affair he had when he was deployed to Japan and how God reminded me of my own sin when he came crawling back. We've discussed how hard it was to rebuild our marriage and how excited he was when

Preston was born. But you're as silent as a fence post about your relationship with Hez. You've kept back every detail except that he drank too much and took Vicodin after Ella's death."

"It's hard to talk about it."

"Do you still blame him for Ella's death?"

Savannah shook her head. "I never did blame him. At least I didn't think I did. It could have happened to anyone. Ella had just learned to open that door, and I had found her outside the day before she drowned. She'd slipped out on me too."

"But you found her. You paid attention. Wasn't he supposed to be watching her?"

"Yes." The old horrifying memories tried to surface, and Savannah swallowed them back down. "He always cared more about his job than he did us. Or at least it felt that way. No matter how carefully we planned a vacation or an event, work always intruded."

"Isn't that kind of normal for an attorney?"

Savannah bobbed her head. "I knew before I married him how it would be. I thought I could handle it, but we'd started fighting about his preoccupation with his work. We'd go to parties with his associates and I saw how distant some of the couples seemed to be. I didn't want that to be us."

"Did you talk to him about Ella? It might have been helpful to go to the cemetery together."

"I never heard from him. The day came and went like any other day. I even stopped by the grave later in the evening to see if he'd left anything. There was no sign he'd even been there." She shredded a paper napkin into strips. "I've hardly slept because it upset me so much."

"Did you call him? Text him?"

"Well, no."

"Maybe he was hurt he didn't hear from you."

"I never thought about calling him."

Maybe she should have reached out, but things felt so awkward between them ever since he'd walked back into her life. She didn't know how to repair a marriage that had splintered into a thousand pieces. But maybe she could try. Wouldn't God want her to at least see if anything was left?

"Do you want to try again with Hez?"

Savannah slumped in her chair. "I don't know." She palmed her forehead. "I'm such an idiot. I keep thinking about how it was with Hez. He's always been bigger than life, and his smile could light up my whole life. He'd come home after a big case was settled and carry me off to a romantic weekend at the beach. It's hard to forget all that."

"The heart wants what the heart wants. Has Hez changed?"

"He's trying. It's too early to know if it will hold. He's been going to AA. But he still works too much, and I don't think he's come to terms with Ella's death. Before we decided to attempt to reconcile, we'd have to really talk. I'd have to be sure he's changed."

"So talk. You are so good at your job and can take charge of any situation except this one."

"I can't stand the thought of ripping that wound wide open again when it's finally scabbed over a bit." She toyed with a napkin. "And to be honest, the second I saw him I wanted to be in his arms again. Crazy, isn't it?"

"I get it, but you can't heal yourself without talking to him. It's time, Savannah. Past time."

Savannah bit her lip and held Nora's gaze. "I realized the other day that I blame God more than Hez. He could have prevented Ella's death, but he didn't. I don't know how to get past that."

"I've had to deal with that, too, Savannah. I think every parent who has lost a child feels that."

"How did you get past it?"

"I didn't really 'get past it'—I don't think anyone does. Honestly, I don't understand why God took my precious boy and I probably never will—at least not in this life. Why couldn't God let Preston grow up into a wonderful man, do great things in the world, get married, have children of his own? Why—?" Nora's voice faltered and she wiped her eyes. She took a deep breath. "God doesn't always call us to understand, though, does he? But he always calls us to trust him. I remind myself that God loves Preston even more than I do. I remind myself of that every day. I have to. My son will never have to suffer in this life. He's in a perfect place. It's hard for us to see eternity. Our children are experiencing it right now, though."

Savannah let the words seep into her heart and wished she could trust the way Nora did. She believed what Nora said was true, but her heart still questioned. It would take time.

Nora got a text and read it. "I have to go in to work. I'm sorry. Will you be okay?"

Savannah forced confidence into her voice. "I'll be fine. You go ahead and go. I'll just hang out here for a while." She could fill some of the hours with work, but the thought held no appeal.

Nora slung her bag over her shoulder. "I'll call you later."

Savannah's phone rang, and she glanced at the screen. Maybe he had new information. "Hey, Beckett."

"You doing okay, Savannah? I wanted to see how your visit to Ella's grave went. I hope you weren't alone."

How sweet that he'd remembered it was the anniversary of Ella's death. "I survived."

The contrast between Hez and Beckett squeezed her chest. Why had she waited so long to see if Hez had changed? No matter what excuses Nora made for him, the fact remained he hadn't been concerned enough about her to text or call. "University Grounds has their autumn cider tonight. Want to join me?"

"I can be there in thirty minutes."

The lilt to his voice touched her, and she smiled. "I'll meet you on the porch."

The thought of a pleasant few hours to fill her evening lifted her spirits. Beckett was easy to talk to, and she wouldn't have to think about ripping open that wound with Hez again. It wasn't a date—just some cider with a friend. She'd have to be careful not to give Beckett the wrong idea.

CHAPTER 15

HEZ LEANED BACK FROM HIS DESK AND STRETCHED. HIS SPINE crackled, which always occurred when he'd been sitting still for too long. His stomach rumbled and he glanced at his watch: 7:32. Paige had sent him the initial documents in the Morales case, and Hez had gotten more sucked in than he intended. He'd read through the entire thing and done some preliminary legal research—both tasks he'd planned to accomplish tomorrow. Litigation could be almost as addictive as Vicodin.

Time to give Savannah the good news about his discussion with Detective Richards. He took out his phone to call her, but he hesitated before dialing. Was her grief support group done meeting? He wasn't sure how long it ran, but he couldn't hang around campus all night.

His stomach rumbled again. Maybe he could tell her over dinner. What was the name of that little Italian place on the Pelican Harbor boardwalk by the old hotel? Maria's—that was it. They used to go there when they were dating. They'd spend hours talking and laughing over an enormous family-style bowl of pasta. The boardwalk was right on the beach, so when they finished their meal, they'd take off their shoes and walk in the sand under the stars.

He pictured her sitting across a little table from him now, her beautiful face lit by candlelight as she listened appreciatively to his description of his meeting with Augusta. His pulse quickened at the thought, and he smiled.

He decided to text her. *Hi! I've got some news about your case. When would be a good time to talk? Happy to buy you dinner if you haven't eaten.*

A few seconds later, the pulsing ellipsis appeared. Then, *Now is fine. I'm at University Grounds.* The ellipsis appeared again before he could respond. *With Beckett.*

He frowned. There went his dinner idea. He'd get to score some points in front of his rival, but he really didn't like the idea of Beckett and Savannah being out together.

On my way, he texted back.

He switched off his computer and headed out. University Grounds was about a block from the edge of campus, where the oldest part of TGU bordered the oldest part of Nova Cambridge. He weaved his way among groups of students as he walked down narrow cobbled streets that had been designed for horse-drawn carriages rather than cars. Neoclassical statues presided over several corners, including a heroic marble figure of Joseph Willard looking much taller and more muscular than the old pictures Hez had seen. There was also a bronze bust of Louis Legare, Savannah's great-great-grandfather. He had been TGU's second president and the first in a long line of Legares who taught at the school.

Hez reached University Grounds after a five-minute walk. Strings of patio lights cast a warm yellow glow on the wrought-iron tables and chairs on the broad porch of the old hotel that housed the coffee shop. The tables were mostly full of students and faculty, and it took Hez a few seconds to spot Beckett and Savannah. They sat close together in a dimly lit corner along the porch rail, chatting and laughing. Beckett had his arm on the rail behind her—not touching her but familiar and possessive. Savannah noticed Hez and waved him over.

Rather than weave his way through the patrons, Hez walked over outside the rail. The scent of cinnamon and nutmeg hung in the cool evening air. He sniffed appreciatively. "Mmm. University Grounds makes the best cider."

"They really do." Savannah took a long sip as if to illustrate the point. "You said you had news. What's up?"

So she wasn't going to invite him to join them. Maybe that was because the porch was crowded. Maybe.

"I talked to Augusta this afternoon." He recounted his conversation with the detective, doing his best to navigate safely between bragging and false modesty. It seemed to work— Savannah seemed impressed, and a small frown creased Beckett's forehead and the corners of his mouth.

"That's awesome, Hez," Savannah said when he finished. "I definitely picked the right lawyer! Do you think I'll be in the clear by the end of the semester?"

"I think you're in the clear now, but we should have more certainty in a couple of months." Hez couldn't help a note of lawyerly caution. "You never can be sure, of course."

She gave a relieved smile. "Excellent—for both of us. You must be looking forward to getting back to Birmingham."

"I, uh, haven't made a decision about that." Hez cleared his throat. "You know, Tupelo Grove has been growing on me."

She looked down into her cup and swirled it. "Hmm. You'll need to talk to Jess about that. I don't know if she has a position budgeted for you after December."

He blinked and swallowed. Savannah had trouble being direct about anything negative concerning their relationship, but her message came through loud and clear. She hadn't asked him to stay or even hinted that she'd like it if he did. Instead, she punted to Jess, who had always resented him as an intruder. "Ah, okay. Good to know," he forced out.

"Thanks for stopping by," Beckett said, his frown now transformed into a smug grin.

"No problem. I just finished work and was on my way to grab some dinner." Hez patted his midsection, though he didn't feel hungry anymore.

A hint of concern showed in Savannah's eyes. "You just finished work?"

He mentally kicked himself. Why had he forgotten that she hated his workaholism almost as much as his alcoholism? "I was just killing time until you were done with your grief support group. I know how hard this time of year is for both of us." The memory of her sobbing at Ella's grave sent a sudden jag of pain and guilt through his heart.

Savannah stared down into her cup again and said nothing.

Hez decided to leave before things got even more awkward. "Have a good evening." He turned and walked away.

Before he'd gone a hundred yards, Hez realized he was heading in the wrong direction. He was walking toward downtown Nova Cambridge, which had a collection of restaurants catering to faculty and students. But that was the last place he wanted to go now. His gut felt like it was full of cold gravel, and he couldn't think of anything more depressing than sitting alone in a restaurant while Savannah was out with Beckett. Besides, he needed to get back home to Cody, who hadn't been out since noon.

He cut across a parking lot and walked back on a parallel street so he wouldn't have to go past his wife and rival again. Stately old homes lined the mostly deserted sidewalks. Antique streetlamps cast pools of light but did little to relieve the darkness. Hez didn't mind. It fit his mood.

A movement in the shadows half a block away caught Hez's eye. Someone was standing beside a huge Spanish moss–draped oak tree. Hez froze, peering into the night. The figure moved again. The man was looking down a side street, watching something. Hez realized he was near University Grounds, and the man would have a good view of the porch—especially the corner where Savannah and Beckett were sitting.

Something about the guy seemed familiar, but Hez couldn't place it. He stepped closer. Staying away from the streetlamps, he crossed the street and snuck up behind the guy. As he approached, his view came in line with the man's—and it was clear that he was watching Savannah and Beckett or someone sitting right next to them.

The guy ran his fingers through shaggy hair—and Hez knew why he looked familiar. His hand shook and his movements were jerky and fidgety. Hez had seen it at least a hundred times in the past two years: The guy was an addict going through the first symptoms of withdrawal. He was hours past due for his next fix or drink, and it was starting to affect him. So why was he out here rather than feeding his craving?

He whirled and caught sight of Hez. His eyes widened and he dashed off without a word, almost instantly vanishing into the night.

Hez stood on the sidewalk, trying to commit the man's face to memory. Wavy brown hair, glasses, dark brown eyes, thin nose and lips, early thirties, about five-foot-two. It was dark and Hez had only gotten a split-second look, but he was sure he'd recognize the man if he saw him again.

Part of the reason he could picture the man's face so clearly was that he'd seen it before in better light. But where?

Savannah took a sip of her cider. The cooling temperatures had plummeted her mood, not the desolate expression she'd glimpsed on Hez's face as he walked away from University Grounds.

The number of students on the porch had thinned out, and she was ready to call it a night herself. Hez's appearance had upended the evening.

Beckett's arm dropped from the back of her chair enough for his hand to settle on her shoulder. "You okay?"

Maybe he'd gotten the wrong idea from her invitation. "I'm fine. It's getting chilly."

His arm didn't return to its former position. "Supposed to go down to forty-eight or so tonight."

The warmth radiated off his skin, and she leaned forward to curl her cold fingers around her mug of hot cider. When she leaned back, he'd pulled his arm to his side. She breathed a sigh of relief.

"I'd love to spend more evenings like this with you. Sans an impromptu appearance by Hez, of course." Beckett's eyes went cold. "Has he always liked making an entrance to try to upset you?"

"He wasn't trying to upset me—he wanted to make sure I was okay." She rolled the taste of cinnamon and nutmeg around on her tongue before continuing. "He's an attorney. They're used to attention."

But was that fair to say about Hez? He had always cared about the law and justice. It was one thing that had attracted her early in their relationship. He worked too many hours, and while that pattern obviously hadn't changed, his motives were good.

Beckett took her hand in his warm grip. "I care about you, Savannah. More than you know, more than I should since you're still married. I have to guard my feelings right now. It wouldn't be right to move in a more serious direction yet. Do you have a time frame of when you hope to finalize things with Hez?"

She shifted in the chair and pulled her hand away. "Let's stick with being friends for now, okay, Beckett? I have too much to worry about to think about anything else."

Her phone dinged with a message. She snatched it out of her purse with relief she struggled to hide. It was from Hez.

You okay? I spotted an addict watching you. I've seen him before, but I can't think where. Wavy brown hair, glasses, dark brown eyes, thin nose and lips, early thirties, about 5'2". Want me to check out your house?

No thanks, I'm still with Beckett, and he will make sure I'm safe.

The way her pulse blipped when she hit Send told her she wanted to upset him. Sometimes she didn't understand her own behavior.

She exhaled and told Beckett about the man Hez had spotted. "It's probably nothing."

"I'll walk you home," he said. "Let's get out of here before he comes back."

Ten minutes later, they were outside her cottage. Things seemed normal from the sidewalk. The porch light pushed back the shadows, and the lamp she'd left on sent out a welcoming glow from the window.

Beckett held out his hand for the keys, and she dropped them into his palm. "I'll unlock the house and check it out. You wait here."

She hugged herself against the chill while he opened the door. Marley darted past Beckett's legs and raced to her side. He stared up at Savannah with an outraged expression as if to ask what she'd been thinking when she brought this man home.

When Beckett disappeared inside her house, she put her hand on Marley's head. "He's just making sure I'm safe. I know you would have warned me if there was an intruder." What was she doing explaining her behavior to her dog? Marley crouched on his haunches and tipped his head to one side. "You should like Beckett more than Hez, you know. He doesn't have a dog, so you don't have to share his attention."

Marley sneered in the way only a dog can, and she sighed. "Yeah, I know that's a crazy thing to say. You adore Hez and always have. I'm sure he loves you more than Cody. A guy never forgets his first dog."

Marley laid his head on his paws as if he was finally content with something she said. Boo Radley roared from the pond across the road, and the dog jumped to his feet with his ears pricked forward.

"Stay," she said.

The door opened, and Beckett gestured for her to join him. She loosened fists she hadn't realized she'd clenched. "All clear?"

"I didn't see anything out of order after checking the bathrooms, closets, and under the beds. The back door and windows are all locked down."

She exhaled at the realization she wasn't in danger here. Her neighbors on one side were professors who gardened every free moment, and the ones on the other side were joggers. One of them would have noticed an intruder, so she'd been stressing for no reason. Her quiet street was safe, no matter what Hez claimed to have seen.

Her self-talk bolstered her confidence, and she smiled up at Beckett. "I'm sure it's fine. And I have Marley too." The dog lifted his head at the mention of his name and gave an assertive woof. "Thank you, Beckett."

"Anytime."

He hesitated and his gaze searched hers. It was easy to guess his intention, but she hadn't kissed anyone but Hez in years, and now wasn't the time to start. She took a step back. "I'd better get inside."

His strained smile didn't reach his eyes. "I sure wish you were single, Savannah," he said in a husky voice. He went down the two steps on the porch and walked away without looking back.

She rubbed her forehead and went inside. The investigation had enough drama on its own without adding more.

CHAPTER 16

WORK WAS MORE FUN FOR HEZ THAN DAYS OF A PAINFUL
postmortem on yet another failed attempt to score points with
Savannah—though it was tough not to do one. How did those
attempts always go wrong? Had he caused her so much pain
that she could never let him close again? Was her heart so
seared that she could feel nothing toward him except regret?

He shook his head and forced his thoughts back to the task
in front of him. He'd been given the law faculty's collective
least favorite course: legal writing. The other professors hated
it because there were no interesting cases or legal theories to
discuss, just piles of bad writing to fix. Most of the writing
really was terrible, but Hez got satisfaction from the work. He
knew that good—or even just competent—writing would be a
lot more important to his students' careers than understanding the development of international human rights law or one
of the other ivory-tower topics his new colleagues loved.

Hez's students seemed to be learning—and one in particular
caught Hez's attention: Eduardo Hernandez. Ed was a varsity
swimmer who was only in law school because he had an extra
year of athletic eligibility. Hez originally wrote him off as a
jock just using up his scholarship, but Ed had turned out to be

a surprisingly good student with a strong interest in criminal law. He was smart, paid attention, turned assignments in on time, and was never late to class. He also spoke Spanish fluently, which made him perfect for what Hez had in mind. And when Hez had asked for volunteers to help with the Morales case, Ed had been the first to sign up.

Hez pulled up Ed's number on his class chart and sent a short text, asking him to call.

Hez's phone rang just as he finished grading papers. He could hear locker room noise in the background. "Hi, Professor. I just saw your text. What can I do for you?"

"Hi, Ed. You said you're interested in helping with that pro bono case I mentioned in class. You would help with the interviews and investigation. We can even get you some courtroom experience, too, though you wouldn't have a speaking role. What do you think?"

"That would be awesome! Swimming season is in full swing, but I'll make the time. What's the case about? And when can I start?"

Hez smiled at the young man's enthusiasm. "Let's talk tomorrow after class. This is the oddest drug-smuggling case I've seen in a long time, but I'll save the details for our meeting. I'll have a few projects for you too. The probable cause hearing is next Tuesday at eleven o'clock, and we'll need to be ready."

Hez chuckled as he ended the call. This guy was as excited as a caffeinated puppy. The thought reminded him that he needed to walk Cody when he got home—but first he had one final project to finish.

The video clips from the warehouse security camera had finally arrived—over two weeks after he'd requested them—while he was in class yesterday, but he hadn't opened them until he was sure he had the building to himself. The last thing he wanted was for a colleague or a student to pop in for a chat and see someone they knew on his monitor. He went to the door and took a quick peek down the hall—no one in sight and all the other offices were dark.

He started downloading the clips. While his computer worked, he poured himself a cup of stale coffee and grabbed a couple of protein bars from the stash he kept in his desk for when he worked through a meal. Then he sat back to watch.

The first dozen or so clips were all Tony Guzman. He followed the same pattern each time—open a box of artifacts, carefully take one out, photograph it with his phone, carefully put it back, take out the next one, and so on. In other words, he appeared to be doing exactly what he'd said: creating a detailed photographic catalog of the Willard Treasure. Hez was sorely tempted to hit fast-forward, but he decided against it because he might miss some crucial detail. An hour later, he regretted that decision.

The Charlie Hinkle clips were a little more entertaining—like a dull reality show with no sound but occasional funny moments. The little old professor would spend ten minutes rummaging through a box, talking to himself the whole time. Then he'd leave with an artifact, usually forgetting a notepad or something, which he'd retrieve in a clip time-stamped an hour or so later. He spent one entire clip searching for his glasses, then realizing they were sitting on his forehead. By the time he finished watching the Hinkle Show, Hez was convinced that he was innocent too. Which left Erik Andersen.

Hez poured himself a fresh—or new anyway—cup of coffee and started the Andersen clips. In the first one Andersen walked in carrying a duffel bag. Hez expected him to start shoving artifacts into it. But instead he took out a wine bottle, corkscrew, glasses, and candles. He arranged these on a little table in the corner next to a couch Hez hadn't noticed before. He returned a few minutes later with a young woman wearing a sorority sweatshirt.

"Well, now I know what you were hiding." Hez shook his head. It was hard to believe Jess had fallen for such a dirtbag, but she had been a lot younger then.

Hez was left with the same questions he had started with. Who was stealing artifacts? And who had attacked Savannah?

Savannah gave the warehouse door a dubious look. It was her first time back since she was attacked, and a little tendril of unease stroked her spine.

"Here you go, Miz Savannah. Yer safe—nobody in here but the rats." The old guard, Oscar Pickwick, stood out of the way for Savannah to enter.

The drooping skin around his rheumy brown eyes wrinkled in a smile. "Just funnin' you. My old tomcat, Meowth, keeps the rodent population under control. I'll be outside if you need me."

As he turned to leave her to begin her task, he lifted his phone and touched the screen. The opening music to his *Pokémon Go* app began to play. Savannah had been in his path when he was playing his game once, and he'd nearly knocked her into the pond. She was probably safer with the remaining rats.

She stepped into the cavernous room, and the odor of must and old wood hit her. A fluorescent light flickering on and off made the place seem even more like a nightmarish scene from *Raiders of the Lost Ark*. She eyed the mountains of old crates stacked nearly to the twenty-foot ceiling in the old warehouse. How did she even begin?

Crowbar in hand, she forced herself to move down the line to the bigger crates. She'd always been intrigued by pre-Columbian art. It wasn't just about Mayan and Incan art, but there were smaller groups who had their own distinctive pieces. Anything created by indigenous people from five hundred years before Christ up through the time of Columbus was of interest to collectors.

She clambered up on a smaller crate she'd already examined and slid the tip of the metal bar under the lid. The old pine was in remarkably good condition and resisted her amateur efforts until the tight nails gave a final squeal and the lid began to move. She managed to get it open and peered inside. A large stone "temple" was inside. It looked to be from the Mezcala culture with its colonnades. It had probably been used in an ancient funeral.

She pulled a copy of Professor Guzman's updated inventory from the back pocket of her jeans and found the item listed. Could any pieces have been removed before the inventory was done? She had no way of knowing. After checking it off, she replaced the top and moved to the one on the other side to repeat the process. The next crate held an assortment of jade that had been highly prized all across Mesoamerica, especially by the Mayans.

She repeated the process down the long line of crates and, hours later, found nothing missing now that Professor Hinkle had checked out the items he'd taken. Even the gold pieces were still present. There were still crates to go through, but Savannah had the sinking feeling she would find no information for the long hours she'd spent. Maybe she should take a break and run out for coffee.

She spread the printout atop one of the crates and studied it. Frustration gathered in her chest, and she exhaled. She had to be overlooking something.

Soft footfalls from outside the door caught her attention, and she glanced that way to see Beckett enter the warehouse with cups from University Grounds in his hands. He was dressed in biker shorts and a tee, and his skin glistened from a recent workout.

"You read my mind!" She crossed the distance between them and wiped a filthy hand down the side of her jeans before she took the cup he held out. "Thank you, thank you."

"I thought you'd need a break by now." With one hand now free, he reached out and rubbed at her cheek with his thumb. "Dirt. In fact, you might need two showers." His gaze swept down over her red tee and worn jeans. "You might need to wash your clothes twice too."

"I don't think I even want to look in the mirror." She took a sip of her mocha and sighed. "Heavenly." Her stomach rumbled and she realized she'd missed lunch, but the milk in her drink would dull the hunger pangs.

He glanced around the huge room. "Find anything?"

"Nothing. It's so frustrating. I wouldn't have been attacked unless someone wanted to keep me from discovering something criminal."

"You look stressed. A workout would fix that. I've got an extra bike, and we could pedal down to the beach."

A mere nine miles for him, but a hard trek for her when she hadn't been on a bike in years. She and Hez used to have bikes they'd take out for leisurely rides with Ella in her little helmet perched in a seat behind one of them. The sudden memory pushed out the frustration of her lack of progress on the case.

"You okay?"

She nodded and rubbed the back of her neck. "Fine."

He didn't take her word for it and came around to lay his warm hand on her shoulders. "Tight. Have a seat and I'll see if I can get rid of those knots in your shoulder." He moved her to a crate.

Now that he'd mentioned it, she realized the tightness in her shoulders had brought the beginning twinges of a bad head-ache. Though she should finish her task, she didn't protest as his strong fingers probed the sore spots in her shoulders and neck. In moments the muscles began to release the pain pulsing at her temples.

"Better?" he asked.

"So much better."

But for an instant she wished Hez were here with her and not Beckett. She was still skittish and reluctant to have another man touch her, even in such a platonic way. What did that say about feelings she wasn't ready to admit even to herself?

CHAPTER 17

HEZ GLANCED AT HIS PHONE AS SOON AS CLASS WAS OVER. He'd texted Savannah two hours ago. She still hadn't responded, and the texts showed as delivered but not read. A ripple of unease rolled over him. Maybe she was just busy, but what if the explanation was more sinister?

He'd go find her. Ed would be stopping by in half an hour to go through the latest dump of Spanish-language evidence from the U.S. Attorney's Office, but Hez wouldn't be able to focus if he was worried about Savannah.

His first stop was the history department. Savannah's secretary said she'd left hours ago and taken the old security guard with her. That didn't reassure Hez—it meant she'd gone somewhere unsafe enough that she wanted protection, but she hadn't brought it. The guard was more likely to be napping or staring at his phone than protecting Savannah.

So where did she go? The guard's jurisdiction was limited to TGU, so Savannah presumably was somewhere on campus. The warehouse. That must be it. She was at the warehouse—and she wasn't responding to texts. Had she been attacked again?

He hurried to the warehouse, dodging students on the way. He passed the guard—sure enough, the man was staring at his phone and tapping on the screen. He didn't even glance up as Hez half jogged by him. The warehouse door was open, and the inner door leading to the climate-controlled room holding the Willard Treasure was also ajar. Concern tightened his chest.

He pushed open the inner door—and froze. She sat on a box with Beckett leaning over her with his hands on her shoulders. Her eyes were closed and her perfect lips curved in a half smile.

Her eyes opened wide. "Hez! What are you doing here?"

His concern congealed into a lump of ice that sank into his gut. "You weren't responding to texts, and I was worried."

"Oh, sorry. The reception is terrible in here." She stood and pulled her phone out of her jeans pocket. "I've been going through boxes for the past few hours." She looked down, apparently remembering that wasn't what she'd been doing when Hez walked in. "Um, Beckett just stopped by to bring me some coffee."

Beckett smiled broadly but said nothing.

Hez kept his eyes on Savannah. "I see."

She stared down at her phone. "Your messages still haven't shown up. Did you have news?"

"Yes. I got the security camera video." He described what he'd seen. Both Beckett and Savannah grew visibly concerned when he told them about Erik Andersen's covert trysts.

Beckett responded first. "Thanks for bringing this to my attention. My office will have to investigate, of course." He glanced at the table and sofa in the corner and grimaced. "If he's having an affair with a student, that would be highly inappropriate. We have very strict rules about faculty-student relationships."

Savannah bit her lip and seemed lost in thought. Was she wondering how to break the news to her sister?

"That reminds me—I have some news of my own," Beckett continued. "Now that I have access to the full CFO database, I've been able to track down a series of suspicious transactions. The amounts coming in vary from around fifty thousand to over a million, but the amounts going out are all just under ten thousand. All anonymized, of course."

Hez wasn't surprised. "Someone is smurfing."

Beckett nodded. "I thought the same thing, Hez."

"Smurfing?" Savannah frowned. "Sorry, you lost me."

"Banks have to report any cash transaction of ten thousand or over," Hez replied. "Criminals don't want their money tracked, of course, so when they're moving a lot of cash, they often break it up into a series of transactions that are just under the reporting limit. That's called smurfing. Don't ask me why."

Savannah got to her feet and walked over to a crate that had papers spread across the top. "How many inbound transactions?"

Beckett cocked his head. "Inbound transactions?"

Savannah's head moved from side to side as she scanned the papers. "Transactions where money is coming into the university. We're assuming those are payments for stolen artifacts, right? So the number of inbound transactions gives us at least a clue as to the number of artifacts that should be missing from the warehouse."

Beckett stared into the middle distance for a few seconds. "About thirty inbound transactions, I believe."

"And how much money are we talking about in total?" she asked.

"About twelve million."

Hez whistled. His mind went back to financial fraud cases he'd prosecuted. "Did the money always get smurfed out on the same day?"

Beckett nodded again. "Yes, same hour usually. Sometimes even the same minute. The money stayed on the university's books for as little time as possible. And all the transactions went through an obscure account that seems to have been set up specifically for money laundering. If you're not in the right database and specifically looking for suspicious transactions, you'd never find it."

Hez thought for a moment. Whoever had done this was pretty sophisticated, but some parts of the scheme would be hard to fake. But which ones? He searched his memory for a moment, then snapped his fingers. "The bank will have verified the identity of whoever opened the account. Who was it?"

"It was . . ." Beckett took a deep breath and looked at Savannah, who was still poring over her papers. "The account was opened by someone claiming to be Jessica Legare."

Savannah placed small pumpkins among the deep red chrysanthemums on Ella's grave. The flowers and pumpkins added a bright splash of color. The earthy, pungent scent of the mums mingled with the odor of decaying vegetation in the wooded area around the cemetery. The leaves wouldn't start falling for another month, and she'd need to do cleanup from then until February.

She moved around to the back of the headstone and stopped at the sight of a waterlogged stuffed puppy lying upside down as if it had fallen off. She picked it up and saw a tag that read "Daddy loves you." Her throat tightened at the realization Hez had to have placed it on the headstone. She battled the sting in her eyes at the thought of him coming here alone like she did. If only they could have faced this battle together these past years.

She turned at the sound of crunching oyster shells echoing up the hillside. Jess's blonde hair came into view. Savannah dusted the dirt from her fingers on her jeans and went to await her sister on the bench overlooking the peaceful scene. It might not have been the best idea to meet here, but she'd wanted to make sure no one overheard them. Jess was apt to raise her voice at the news Savannah meant to share.

Jess wore jeans and a bright blue cotton sweater. She dropped onto the bench beside Savannah. "Are you all right? I was worried when you wanted to meet up here."

"I'm fine. I wanted to decorate Ella's grave for fall."

Jess glanced over at the mounds of flowers and pumpkins. "It's so pretty. I remember how Ella's eyes widened when she helped pull the goo out of the pumpkin's innards when she was a year old. It was so funny. I still have a picture of her."

Her daughter had died too early that second autumn to decorate a pumpkin. "I remember." Savannah couldn't let anything swamp her and keep her from launching into the reason she'd asked to see her sister. "I have some news on the investigation to share with you."

Jess's brows winged up. "What's happened?"

"Hez got the security camera video. Tony Guzman is clean. He was doing exactly what he'd said. Professor Hinkle was also legit." She licked her lips. "I can't say the same for Erik Andersen. He went in with a duffel bag."

"He carried out artifacts?"

Savannah shook her head. "He took things out—a wine bottle, corkscrew, glasses, and candles."

Jess stilled. "That sounds like he was expecting a—a woman."

"Exactly. A young woman showed up for a romantic tryst. He appears to be using the warehouse to hide an affair with a student."

"That's strictly against university policy."

"I know." Savannah examined her sister's expression. The hooded eyes and tight mouth spoke of suppressed pain. "Do you still see him at all?"

Jess lowered her head to stare at her hands. "Not in ages." She lifted her head again and caught Savannah's gaze. "Don't go all sympathetic on me. I got over Erik a long time ago."

Jess could say that all she wanted, but Savannah had her doubts. They'd been engaged eleven years ago, and she'd never seen her sister so happy. When their relationship collapsed, Jess had retreated into her own world, and she'd never let Savannah back inside. Or anyone else, for that matter. Jess had vanished into the all-consuming world of New York finance for almost a decade. When she moved back to TGU two years ago, she'd brought back some of that Wall Street intensity. She had thrown herself into her work and rarely had time for outside activities. She still went to New York for business regularly, but Savannah hadn't seen her go out with a man since Erik. Had she discovered him cheating?

Jess stood and paced in front of the park bench. "I'll need to do something about this. It can't continue." She stopped and thrust her hands in the pockets of her cotton sweater. "What about Beckett's investigation into the financials? I want him to quit poking around as soon as possible, and he's had ample time to evaluate them."

Savannah hadn't been prepared for that question. "You'll have to talk to him about that." She rose and went to pluck a weed from her daughter's grave.

Jess followed her. "What's going on, Savannah? You're hiding something."

Savannah was terrible at keeping secrets. She tossed the weed away and turned to face her sister. "He found evidence of something called 'smurfing.' Twelve million dollars have gone through the account and back out again in a matter of minutes. It's an obscure account that seems to have been set up to launder money."

"Money laundering." Jess shook her head. "Listen to yourself. This isn't a movie. No one is laundering money through any of our accounts. Beckett is hardly an expert on finances. I don't believe it—not for a second."

Savannah didn't believe it either, and she didn't want to try to explain something she didn't understand. "You'll need to talk to him for more details."

"Oh, I will! Does he have an opinion on who's done it? *If* it's been done, which I highly doubt."

"Um, he says you created the account, Jess. I don't believe that, of course. But someone seems to have gone to great trouble to implicate you. Beckett can tell you more."

Her eyes widened. "Did he actually believe I'd do something like that?"

"He said he checked with the bank, and the person had presented documents claiming to be you."

"I'll get to the bottom of this! They surely have a copy of the ID and any other proof the thief used in my name. I guess I should be grateful Beckett saw something so I can put an end to it and figure out what's going on here." Jess's expression turned thoughtful. "Could Abernathy have been involved? Maybe there's a connection with his murder. Will Hez tell the police what your little investigative group has uncovered?"

"I—I assume so, but we haven't talked about it."

Wasn't Jess worried the police might turn their attention to her? Savannah couldn't let that happen. While she wanted the police to realize she was innocent, she didn't want her sister to come under scrutiny in her place. She'd have to check with Hez and see what he thought.

CHAPTER 18

HEZ WALKED INTO HIS OFFICE AFTER CLASS AND FOUND A voice mail and three missed calls on his phone. He tossed his notes on the well-used plywood desk he'd been given and hit the Play button. A deep male voice boomed from a staticky speaker. "Hez! It's Don Hale from the U.S. Attorney's Office. Glad to see you filed an appearance in the Morales case—it's been too long since we worked together. Give me a call when you get this. There's a little scheduling hiccup we need to discuss ASAP."

All three missed calls came from the same number, presumably Hale's. And all three had come while Hez was in class. Hale must really want to talk.

Hez sighed. Don Hale—often called "the Whale" behind his back—was a large man with an even larger ego. He won a string of high-profile mafia and drug cartel cases in the early 2000s, which convinced him he was the best lawyer in any courtroom he walked into. When Hez worked with him on a couple of joint state-federal cases, he'd treated Hez like a junior associate. When Hez put together a very good plea deal resolving one of the cases, Hale had called a press conference to announce "his" victory—and he hadn't mentioned Hez, of course.

The phone rang again. Same number. Hez plopped into his office chair and picked up the receiver. "Hi, Don. What can I do for you?"

"Hez! Good to hear your voice. Hey, on this Morales case, could you do me a favor and waive the preliminary hearing? It's set for next Tuesday, and I've had a conflict come up."

It was a routine request, but something felt a little off. In fact, something felt off about the whole case. Hez decided to push for more information. "I can work with you on scheduling, but I'd like to see what you have on Morales. When are you going to actually indict him?"

"We're working on it."

"Great, but when will I see the indictment?"

"When we're done and the grand jury issues it. Hez, don't give me a hard time about this." His voice had the tone of a teacher warning a mouthy student.

Hez wasn't about to back down. "You can't just hold Morales in jail until you get around to indicting him. If you can't show probable cause, you have to let him go. A prelim sets a deadline for you to do that. I'm not just going to waive it without more."

"I know what a prelim does," Hale snapped. "You've got the complaint. That tells you all you need to know."

"No, it doesn't. It's a bare-bones copy-and-paste job with a boilerplate affidavit that doesn't even identify the drugs. I want to see the evidence backing it up. If Tuesday doesn't work for you, how about Wednesday? And if that doesn't work, why not have someone cover the hearing for you—or better yet, just get the indictment?"

"Look, Hez, read the complaint again. I've got confidential witnesses saying there's a smuggling operation and that there was supposed to be a delivery coming in by boat at 1:00 a.m. on the night of September third. Your guy showed up at 1:00 a.m. on the night of September third in a boat, and he was acting exactly like a cartel smuggler—no lights, he ran when the Coast Guard showed up, and he threw something overboard. Sounds like Sinaloa, don't you think? That's enough to show probable cause. Forcing us all to go through a prelim will just tick off me and the judge."

Hale might be right, but there were weird gaps in the complaint, like the failure to identify the drugs Morales was supposedly smuggling. And if Hale was so sure he could show probable cause, why not just put his evidence in front of a grand jury and get an indictment? That would be easier for him and would automatically cancel the prelim. Something was off, and Hez's Spidey-sense was tingling. "Sorry, Don. I guess I'll be seeing you in court on Tuesday."

"You're gonna regret this," Hale growled. He hung up without waiting for Hez's response.

Hez stared at the phone, wondering if Hale was right.

Grading papers had turned into a chore, especially on a Friday when Savannah would rather be at the pregame rally like everyone else. She usually enjoyed seeing her students' fresh perspectives on discovering history, but she kept tensing with every new sheet she pulled from the stack in case she ran across more provenance papers. Abernathy's death had rattled her even more, and it felt like the entire university held its breath while waiting for the next shoe to drop.

She rubbed her aching neck and stared out the window toward the lights of the football field. Her first date with Hez had been to a football game, and he'd kissed her that night with the taste of butter and popcorn still on his lips. She touched her lips and smiled. For the first time a seed of hope unfurled and pushed its way to the surface. Was there any chance of a reconciliation?

The sun had begun to fall past the tops of the tupelo trees on the horizon. The campus felt deserted with most students at the game. One more paper and she'd head for coffee and some food. Hunger twisted in her stomach.

"Knock knock," a male voice announced.

She turned and saw Erik Andersen standing in the doorway. "Professor Andersen, what can I do for you?"

Dressed in pressed slacks and a tight shirt that showed his biceps, he shut the door behind him and advanced into her office. "Aren't you ever going to call me Erik again? Your sister and I broke up years ago. Don't you think it's about time you got over that? I'm a pretty nice guy, actually." His mouth widened in a leer.

While Jess had gone on with her life after his betrayal, her inner light had gone out and had never returned. Savannah blamed Erik for snuffing it out.

When she didn't answer, he sighed and came closer. "Any more ideas on who stole the artifacts? I hear Hez got hold of some video footage, and I thought maybe he had solved the case by now."

His tone made her study his expression. Was that tension? Fear? Did he have something to do with it? "Oh, did he? If he found any evidence, I'm sure he turned it over to the police."

"That's good. I mean, whatever Abernathy was involved with, it was clearly dangerous. I wouldn't want you getting in the way of danger too. Jess would never survive something happening to you."

Savannah tensed. Was he warning her off? "Luckily, she'll never have to face that."

"I sure hope not." He perched on the edge of her desk and picked up the snow globe on the desktop. "Pretty. Almost as mesmerizing as you."

She resisted the urge to snatch it from his hand, and her fingers curled into her palms. Ella had loved it, and it was a reminder of the winter weekend they'd spent as a family in Michigan.

She rose and began stuffing papers into her briefcase. "Well, I don't know anything about the videos. You could ask Hez directly."

"Maybe I'll do that. What do you say we go get some food and some drinks? You haven't been out of the office all day, and you have to be starved. Maybe we could bury the hatchet. I've always liked you, Savannah." His gaze fell on a picture of her and Hez with Ella, and he frowned. "Looks like you're still carrying a torch for that loser. I'd like to show you I'm not such a bad guy."

She straightened and stared him down. "Professor, I have no interest in a personal relationship with you, and your comments are offensive." She snapped the latch on her briefcase and headed for the door. "I'll lock the door behind you."

He brushed past her a little too closely, as if intentionally invading her personal space. "It's dark out there tonight, Savannah. Be careful walking home."

Another veiled threat? She shuddered and locked the door once his footsteps faded down the hall.

***

Hez wasn't wrestling with a question of life or death—but it was a question of life, so he needed to focus. Specifically, the question was how to defend Hernando Morales from a ridiculously overcharged complaint that could put him in federal prison for the rest of his life. Hez needed to be 100 percent mentally present while he and Ed prepared for the probable cause hearing—even though he was tired and there was somewhere else his mind very much wanted to go.

Hez suspected Don Hale was trying to scare Hernando into cooperating. Hez thought he could get the charges dropped down a long way—possibly even dismissed entirely—if Hernando was willing to play ball with the FBI. There were just two problems with that approach. First, Hez didn't like giving in to bullies, and Hale was a bully. But Hez could have swallowed his pride and gone along with it if not for the second problem: Hernando was a lot more scared of the consequences of cooperating than not cooperating. But scared of whom?

Hez turned to Ed, who sat across a cluttered table in the empty office they were using as a war room. "Who do you think he's working for?"

Ed gave him a blank stare. "Excuse me?"

"Hernando. Who do you think he's working for? He was pretty tight-lipped about that when we interviewed him at the jail."

Ed shrugged muscular shoulders. "He was pretty tight-lipped about everything." He paused for a moment. "Maybe one of the big drug cartels?"

"Hale hinted that it was the Sinaloa cartel, but that didn't seem quite right for some reason." Hez snapped his fingers. "The file we got from the jail—where is it?"

Ed grabbed a neatly organized accordion folder from the top of a gun metal–gray credenza and handed it to Hez, who quickly found what he was searching for. "He's in B block. There's no way he'd be there if he had anything to do with Sinaloa."

Ed stared at him in confusion.

Hez was too exhausted to explain. It was after seven o'clock, and he'd hardly slept the night before after seeing that addict watching Savannah. "It'll make sense when we're at the hearing. Trust me." He yawned and handed the file back to Ed. "This goes on our exhibit list."

Ed nodded. "I'll make five copies and pre-mark them with exhibit stickers."

Hez kicked himself for not having checked the jail records earlier. He'd gotten them shortly after he walked in on Savannah and Beckett at the warehouse, and he'd been too distracted to give them a close read. He needed to take Cody for a long walk to clear his head. And then he needed a good night's sleep. "I'm going home. And you should too. You've been spending a lot of time on this case, and I don't want your classwork to suffer."

"Yes, Dad." Ed grinned. "I'll make the copies and then head over to the library."

Two minutes later, Hez walked out the law school door and into the gathering night. The air wasn't quite cool, but it no longer held the day's heat as tightly as summer evenings did. The leaves hadn't started to change colors yet, but that would come soon. He smelled woodsmoke—probably from one of the firepits so popular at the fraternity and sorority houses. A few students strolled in the twilight. A faint babble of conversation and laughter came from a party somewhere. A few early stars twinkled in the deep blue sky overhead.

Savannah used to love going for walks on evenings like this. So did Ella. They'd just started teaching her to count, and she'd ride on his shoulders and count the stars as they emerged, squealing with excitement every time she spotted a new one.

Hez wished with all his heart that he could go back to that time—somehow hit Reset on his life and avoid all the failures that had led to him walking through this perfect evening alone. But the past was carved in immutable granite. Maybe he needed to accept that.

Everything he'd done over the past few months had been an attempt to undo the past. He had forced Savannah to withdraw the divorce petition and tried to cajole her into coming back to him. Then they could have another baby and start over from where he messed everything up. But it hadn't worked—and even if it had, the past wouldn't be undone and Ella would still be dead.

Maybe it was time to move on—and to let Savannah move on. She'd made it very clear that's what she wanted. She had shown no interest in getting back together despite seeing the "new Hez" at close range for over a month. And he vividly remembered the contented smile on her face when Beckett was massaging her. How many moments like that had the two of them shared when he wasn't around to interrupt?

Hez's unhappy train of thought was derailed when he glimpsed a familiar male figure in the dusk ahead of him, hurrying along one of the brick paths that crisscrossed the campus. Hez couldn't tell for sure if it was him in the dim light, so he followed at a distance, staying in the shadows.

The man went to the administration building. He avoided the well-lit main entrance and circled around to the side. He pulled open a door and ducked inside, but not before Hez got a glimpse of his face in the brief splash of light from inside the building. A moment later, a light came on in the CFO's office. It was the same guy he'd caught watching Savannah and Beckett at University Grounds. And he just went into Jess's office.

CHAPTER 19

SAVANNAH SPOTTED JESS AT THE END OF THE GULF STATE
Park Fishing Pier. She sat dangling her feet off the edge. She
wore khaki shorts and a blue top, and she swung her legs like
she used to when they were kids. It was such an uncharacter-
istic pose for her sister that Savannah stopped and watched
for a moment with Marley dancing impatiently beside her.
Jess stared out over the water in the fading light as if she was
searching for the meaning of life. Savannah hadn't seen her so
pensive in a long time.

Jess was such a contradiction at times—caring and supportive
yet so closemouthed about her own dreams and desires. Her
job seemed to be enough, but was it really? Savannah had often
wished to see her sister happily married with a couple of kids.
She'd been an attentive and loving aunt to Ella and had been
devastated at her death.

Marley barked, and Jess turned her head and spotted
Savannah. The pathos on her face morphed into a smile, and
she waved. "There you are."

Savannah walked out to meet her and dropped down onto
the rough boards beside her. She licked the salt from her lips.
"Been here long?"

"Just a few minutes." Jess inhaled a breath and blew it out. "I love the smell of the sea. It beats the stale air of my office any day. It's been ages since we came out here. I was glad you suggested it. I was just watching a pod of dolphins."

There were no dolphins that Savannah could see. Her memories of this place were full of fishing trips with Dad and Jess, but more often than not, he and Jess were bickering by the time they'd left. "I wanted to talk where we wouldn't be overheard." The pier held a few fishermen, but they were far enough away that no one would hear what she wanted to talk to Jess about.

"You said you needed to talk. What's up?"

"Hez spotted someone watching me." Savannah gave her sister the brief description Hez had given her. "And last night he saw him going into your office. Does the description ring a bell?"

Jess pursed her lips, and a frown creased her forehead. "It sounds like Peter Cardin, my accounting assistant. I'm sure it's nothing. He probably forgot something."

"Hez says he's an addict. He spotted some telltale signs."

Jess stared out over the water before she shrugged. "I find that hard to believe."

"Hez is genuinely concerned. He'd like to take a look at the guy's background and turn it over to Augusta. We have to consider the possibility this Peter is the one hiding the money. Maybe it's to support his habit. It would make sense."

Jess pleated her shorts with her fingers and still didn't look at Savannah. "Fine. I'll pull his file when I'm in the office and send it to Hez. I want this all over. I don't like him poking into the school's records and implicating my staff."

Why was she acting so defensive about this? Was it because she felt responsible for hiring Peter? "If Hez finds out who is behind all this, it will be over. The more help you can give him, the faster that will happen."

"I suppose you're right." Jess's phone sounded with a message, and she glanced at it before she rose. "I need to make a private call. Let's head back to the parking lot."

Business or pleasure? Savannah had caught a hint of softness around her sister's mouth when she read the text. Was she seeing someone? If only she would open up and talk to her like when they were younger.

Hez had been right to have Savannah tackle this conversation. As prickly as Jess had been about it, she would have turned down Hez's request immediately.

They walked back to the parking lot in silence. Marley nosed along the gravel along the way. A pelican scooped up water and a fish before taking off overhead again, and Savannah watched the big brown bird soar into the darkening sky. Sometimes she felt like that hapless fish. No matter how she tried to escape into a new life, she felt caught. Not that Hez was a predatory pelican. She knew he still loved her, but that love felt like a trap some days. Or maybe it was her own feelings confining her in the same place.

Did she even want to wriggle out? Whenever she was around Hez, she felt the same old pull, even though she fought against it. The inexorable tide dragging her into the old patterns was nearly impossible to resist. When she'd married Hez, neither of them had any idea of the challenges and heartache they would face, but wasn't that the way it was with any marriage? Even losing Ella hadn't killed her love for Hez. It was only when he chose booze over her that Savannah had begun to consider what life without him would look like.

And now that he was back, she wasn't so sure she wanted to let go. The realization had been growing ever since he walked back into her life. Her heartbeat rocketed at the thought of seeing the hope ignite in his eyes when she told him that. Maybe it was time.

Lost in thought, she missed her sister's comment when she stopped at her car. "I'm sorry?"

Jess wore a troubled frown. "I was just saying goodbye." She glanced at her phone. "Listen, I have to fly to London and need to book a flight to leave tomorrow morning. Can that file wait until I get back? I'll just be gone five days. I'll be back on Tuesday."

"Not really. Can't you swing by the office and email it to Hez before you leave? And why such a last-minute trip?"

"I was already planning to go, but I made a mistake on the date and I need to go tomorrow." When Savannah didn't answer, Jess sighed. "Fine. I'll run by the office. Can you reschedule my flight while I pack and finish up a few things? I'll text you the confirmation code. I need to go out first thing in the morning."

"Out of Pensacola or Mobile?"

"Either will work."

"I'll be glad to do it."

As her sister drove off, Savannah's phone dinged with a message with the code. She got in her car and ran the window down to enjoy the breeze while she pulled up the airline website. The existing flight was out of Mobile into London for next Thursday, so it was off by a week. It wasn't like Jess to make a mistake. Savannah was able to reschedule it for six tomorrow morning.

She hoped whoever Jess was meeting in London made it worth the change fee. Was it a man? Maybe Jess wasn't all about business like Savannah thought.

Tuesday afternoon Hez walked into a courtroom in the Mobile federal courthouse and surveyed the scene. He could identify everyone in the room—with one exception. The familiar clerk and bailiff sat on either side of the bench, flanking the judge's currently empty chair. Hez's witnesses were sitting with Ed in one of the front benches of the gallery. Hernando Morales was in the first bench with a guard beside him. Hale sat at the prosecution table, one of two that faced the judge's bench across the open space known as the well of the courtroom. He was built like an oversize mailbox—a wide head atop a bull neck and thickset body from his shoulders to his shoes.

A short, muscular man of about forty in an off-the-rack blue suit was immediately behind Hale. The guy wasn't wearing a sign that said "FBI agent," but he might as well have been. And then there was a broad-shouldered young man in the back row who didn't have an obvious role. He was watching Hez, but he dropped his gaze to his phone when Hez looked his way.

Hez didn't have time to wonder who the stranger was. The bailiff rose as Hez walked in, signaling that the judge was about to appear. Hez hurried to take his place at the defense table.

"All rise," the bailiff intoned. "The United States District Court for the Southern District of Alabama is now in session, the Honorable Daphne Montpelier presiding."

Metal clinked as Hernando and his guard rose from the bench behind Hez. A creak came from the prosecution table as Hale stood.

Judge Montpelier bustled in through a door behind the bench. She was a tall, rail-thin woman of eighty-two, and she'd been on the bench for almost half her life. She was still mentally sharp and had plenty of energy, though, and she had a reputation for being a stickler who insisted on exact compliance with rules and statutes. That trait usually annoyed lawyers, but Hez hoped it would be on full display today. It was his only hope of victory.

The judge lowered herself into the tall black leather chair behind the bench. "Good afternoon. Please be seated. Mr. Hardwick, please call the case."

The clerk, seated below and to the right of the judge, nodded. "*United States v. Hernando Antonio Morales.* Appearances, please."

Hale pushed himself to his feet again. "Donald Hale for the United States."

Hez stood. "Hezekiah Webster for Mr. Morales."

The judge looked at Hernando. "Mr. Morales, we're here for a preliminary hearing that will answer two questions. First, is there probable cause to believe a crime was committed? Second, is there probable cause to believe you committed it?" She spoke in a quick, smooth monotone, repeating words she must have said thousands of times over the decades. She turned to Hale. "Counsel, call your first witness."

Hale looked back into the gallery. "The government calls Special Agent Harold Jenkins."

The man in the blue suit rose and walked down the aisle. He passed through the well of the courtroom and took the witness stand. The clerk swore him in and he settled into the witness chair, looking comfortable and a little bored.

Hale picked up a manila folder and notepad, then strode to the lectern. "Agent Jenkins, how long have you been with the FBI?"

"Ten years, the last eight in the Mobile office."

"Please tell the court how you came to be involved in the investigation that led to the arrest of Mr. Morales."

"For the past five years, I've been assigned to a multiagency drug interdiction task force. We received a tip that a delivery would be made by boat at approximately 1:00 a.m. on September third to the east end of the beach in Pelican State Park."

Hale pulled a document out of the folder. "May I approach the witness?"

The judge nodded. "You may."

Hale handed the document to Agent Jenkins, then returned to the lectern. "Is this the tip you mentioned?"

Jenkins glanced at the document, which Hez recognized. A heavily redacted transcript of a Spanish-language phone call with an English translation stapled to it. "Yes."

"Did the task force in fact intercept a boat headed for that location at approximately 1:00 a.m. on September third?"

Jenkins nodded. "Yes. We intercepted Mr. Morales's boat."

"Other than the fact that the time and place matched the tip, was there anything that indicated Mr. Morales was smuggling drugs?"

"He was operating his boat without lights, which is illegal at night. He also tried to evade the Coast Guard vessel that performed the intercept. Finally, he resides in Biloxi, which is over forty miles away by water and longer if you're driving."

"Were drugs found in his boat when he was apprehended?"

"No, but personnel on the Coast Guard vessel saw him throw something overboard while they were pursuing him."

Hale closed the manila folder and put his notes on top of it. "Based on your years of law enforcement experience, do you believe there is probable cause to support each and every element of each of the offenses alleged in this complaint?"

Hez rose. "Objection, lack of foundation."

The judge and Hale both looked at Hez in surprise. The rules of evidence didn't apply at preliminary hearings, so objections were very rare. That actually was the main reason Hez objected—he wanted to disrupt Hale's rhythm and signal that he didn't consider this hearing just a routine formality.

When no one spoke immediately, Hez pushed a little more. "All we know is that Mr. Jenkins has been assigned to a task force for five years. We don't know how many drug-smuggling cases he has handled, let alone maritime cases such as this one. Therefore, no foundation has been laid for him to render what amounts to an expert opinion on the probability that Mr. Morales was engaged in drug smuggling."

The judge leaned forward. "Overruled, but I'll take that into account in determining the weight I give the witness's testimony on this point." She turned to Jenkins. "You may answer."

"Yes, I think there's a fair probability that he committed the charged crimes."

Hale shot an annoyed look at Hez. "I won't waste the court's time by cataloging every drug case Agent Jenkins has handled. Pass the witness." He picked up his papers and returned to his seat.

Hez stepped up to the lectern. "Agent Jenkins, I'll cut right to the chase. Mr. Morales is accused of drug smuggling. Where are the drugs?"

Jenkins shrugged. "Probably somewhere on the bottom of the Gulf of Mexico."

"You've had divers looking for them, correct?"

"Yes."

"And in two weeks of looking, you haven't found the drugs Mr. Morales allegedly threw overboard, correct?"

"Well, yes—but we're still looking."

"That's a shallow area with good visibility and well-known currents, correct?"

"I don't know. I'm not a diver."

Hez decided to take a gamble and ask a question he didn't know the answer to. "And what did you find in your search?"

The agent shrugged again. "A couple of key chains, a Coke bottle, a bracelet, an old knife, a little statue, and a cooler with no lid."

"No drugs?"

"No."

"Why hasn't the task force been able to find the drugs in two weeks of searching?"

Jenkins opened and closed his mouth twice before answering. "I don't know."

"I'd like you to look at exhibit one, the tip received by the task force. It simply refers to a 'delivery'—or *entrega* in

Spanish. It doesn't contain any actual reference to drugs, correct?"

"Not an explicit reference, no."

"And no drugs were found when Mr. Morales and his boat were searched—not even trace amounts, correct?"

"Correct."

"The only thing in his boat was fishing gear, correct?"

"Yes, but there were no fish and he didn't have a license."

Hez smiled. "Thanks, you anticipated my next two questions. If he was fishing without a license, might that explain why he didn't have his lights on and why he tried to evade law enforcement?"

Jenkins's eyes widened. "I . . . I can't speculate on that. He would've come a long way just to fish."

"And if he threw his illegal catch overboard while being chased, that would explain both what the Coast Guard saw and why your divers haven't been able to find any drugs, correct?"

Tiny beads of perspiration dotted Jenkins's hairline. "Again, I can't speculate on that. It wouldn't explain why he was 'fishing' at the time and place indicated by our source."

"Is illegal night fishing unusual in that area?"

"I have no idea."

"Switching gears, drug smuggling in the Gulf of Mexico is controlled by the Mexican cartels, correct?"

"In general, yes."

"And when individuals associated with different cartels are incarcerated, they're separated to prevent violence, correct?"

Jenkins eyed Hez warily. "I can't comment on Bureau of Prisons policies."

Hez turned to the judge. "Your Honor, I have a witness who can testify to this policy, but I believe it is well known to both the court and the prosecution, so hopefully a stipulation will be possible."

Judge Montpelier nodded. "Hopefully. And if not, I've handled enough of these cases that I can take judicial notice of it."

Hale stood. "The government so stipulates."

"Will the government also stipulate that cell block B, where Mr. Morales is currently housed, is not used to house cartel prisoners?"

Hale sighed and shuffled through the papers in front of him. He picked up the jail records Hez recognized from his prep session with Ed. "This is getting very far afield, but yes, the government will stipulate to that."

"Thank you." Hez turned back to the judge. "Pass the witness."

Judge Montpelier looked at Hale. "Any redirect?"

"Just one question. Agent Jenkins, do you continue to believe there is probable cause to support each and every element of each of the offenses alleged in this complaint?"

"Yes."

"No further questions. The government rests."

"You may step down, Agent Jenkins," the judge said. "Mr. Webster, please call your first witness."

Hez reached back to the table to get his binder of witness notes. "Thank you, Your Honor. The defense calls Alfred Smith."

A weathered old man with rheumy blue eyes ambled up to the witness stand just vacated by the FBI agent. He wore a wide-lapel powder-blue three-piece polyester suit that had doubtless been the height of fashion in 1979. He situated himself in the witness chair and the clerk swore him in.

"Mr. Smith, what is your occupation?"

"I'm a shrimper."

"Do you know the waters off Pelican State Park?"

The old man bobbed his head. "Know 'em better than my own bathtub."

"Is the fishing good?"

"Some of the best fishing in the South," the old man said with a touch of pride.

"Good enough to make someone drive from Biloxi?"

Smith nodded. "Absolutely. Fact is, I've seen boats all the way from Miami."

"Do they always have licenses?"

"No." He cast a disapproving glance toward Morales. "'Specially the ones out at night. And you can't hardly see 'em if they have their lights off and there's no moon. Almost ran into 'em a couple of times."

"Is it fair to say that unlicensed night fishing is a problem?"

"Yep. Parasites. Worse than ticks on a hound dog."

"How deep is the water there?"

Smith shrugged one shoulder. "Varies depending on the tides and where you are, but not more than thirty feet."

"Are the currents strong or unpredictable?"

"Not particularly."

"Have you ever gone diving there?"

"Sure, 'specially when I was younger. There's shipwrecks going all the way back to the Civil War. Sometimes we'd go spearfishing too."

"How's the visibility?"

"Good enough for spearfishing. Lot better than Mobile Bay."

"Is it easy to see objects on the bottom?"

Smith nodded. "Sandy bottom, not a lot of weeds."

"Would it be hard to find an object dropped from a boat in that area?"

"Nope. Fact is, a lady tourist once lost her sunglasses in there and paid me twenty dollars to find 'em. Said they were 'designer glasses' and was all frantic." He chuckled. "She sure had her knickers in a knot."

"Did it take you two weeks?"

"More like twenty minutes. It was easy money."

"Impressive. Would you consider working for the U.S. government?"

Smith laughed and the judge smiled. Hale sat stone-faced.

"Pass the witness."

Hale replaced Hez at the lectern. "Mr. Smith, do you have any experience with drug smuggling?"

"No, sir."

"Pass the witness."

Hez stood. "No redirect, Your Honor. The defense rests."

"All right," the judge said. "I'll hear closing arguments now. Mr. Hale?"

Hale drew himself up to his full height, looming over the courtroom. "Thank you, Your Honor. As the court is well aware, the government need only show that there is a substantial chance that Mr. Morales committed criminal acts. That is enough to establish probable cause for his arrest and detention. The evidence presented today clearly meets that standard." He held up a thick forefinger. "First, the drug interdiction task force got a tip indicating that a smuggler would make a delivery at a particular time and place." Another finger. "Second, Mr. Morales's appearance at the time and place from the tip." And another finger. "Third, Mr. Morales's behavior was entirely consistent with smuggling. He had no lights on his boat, he fled when he saw the Coast Guard, and he threw something overboard. That is more than enough. Further, we don't need to rule out other possibilities. The defense's evidence establishes, at most, that it's also possible that the defendant might have been fishing. But that's irrelevant. The question before the court is whether there's a substantial chance that the defendant was smuggling drugs. It does not matter that there may also be a substantial chance he was doing something else."

Judge Montpelier nodded. "Thank you, Mr. Hale. Mr. Webster?"

"Thank you, Your Honor." Hez stepped to the lectern. "This is a drug case with a fatal flaw: no drugs. No drugs in the government's tip—that just mentioned a 'delivery.' No drugs on Mr. Morales or in his boat. No drugs on the bottom of the ocean. The Bureau of Prisons isn't even treating Mr. Morales like a drug smuggler. They're housing him with the general noncartel population— presumably because both he and the cartels said he's not one of their members. In fact, I'd wager that the lack of drugs is why we're all here today. If the government had evidence that Mr. Morales was smuggling drugs, they would have presented it to a grand jury and gotten an indictment. They didn't. They've been looking for that evidence, trying to find it before the clock ran out on them, but they failed. All they can prove is that Mr. Morales may have violated Alabama's fishing and boating rules. The law does not allow them to lock him in a federal cell for that. They do not have probable cause to hold him for any of the crimes alleged in the complaint, and he must be released."

"Thank you." The judge turned to Hale. "Any rebuttal?"

He shook his head. "No, Your Honor. The evidence speaks for itself."

"Indeed it does." The judge picked up the complaint and flipped through it. "And it says the defendant was certainly acting suspicious. But acting suspicious is not a federal offense. Every crime charged in this case requires proof that the defendant possessed, trafficked, or sold illegal drugs. The complete absence of *any* evidence of illegal drugs is problematic. Very problematic." She fell silent again, staring into the middle distance. She steepled her fingers and tapped the tips together rhythmically. After a long moment, she shook her head. "I don't see a way around it. No drugs, no probable cause." She turned to Morales. "You're free to go."

CHAPTER 20

I'M WAITING FOR NEWS, WHICH I HATE. I WISH I COULD have been at the preliminary hearing. That was impossible, of course, so I'll have to rely on a secondhand report. In the meantime I'm sitting here jiggling my leg, unable to focus.

The report will at least come from a credible source: Lamont Dawkins, a veteran criminal defense lawyer from Mobile. He had assured me that neither Hez Webster nor Don Hale would recognize him. I hired him to monitor the Morales case, and he sat in the back of the courtroom throughout the hearing.

A text pops up on the burner phone I use to communicate with him: *Hearing over. Opening Zoom.*

His text includes a Zoom link, which I open. I keep my camera off. He doesn't know my name or face, which is safest for both of us. I use a voice-altering app for the same reason. "How did the hearing go? What did we find out about the government's case?"

"Well, we found out they don't have one, at least not yet." He shakes his head in disbelief. "That's the first time I've seen the prosecution lose one of these."

"What?" I can hardly believe my ears. Dawkins had told me this should be an easy win for the prosecution. The most we could hope for was a preview of their evidence against Morales. Actual victory wasn't a real possibility. "I thought all they had to do was show there was a substantial chance Morales committed a crime. How did they lose?"

"They came in ready to tell their story, and they did a decent job. They still don't have the drugs or whatever Morales threw overboard, but they did build a circumstantial case against him. Hez Webster was ready for them at each point, though—and they weren't ready for him. It was like . . ." Dawkins pauses and shrugs burly shoulders. "I used to box, and the best analogy I can think of is a fighter who throws a good punch, but he doesn't see the counterpunch coming. Webster counter-punched really well and scored a knockout."

"So what happens now? Is the case over?"

Dawkins hesitates and frowns. "Yes, for the moment. Morales walked out of the courtroom a free man, but they can rearrest him the minute they have more evidence—and you can bet they're looking for it very, very hard. Hale got embarrassed today, and he'll want to erase that embarrassment ASAP by putting Morales back behind bars and keeping him there."

So that was the fly in the ointment. I knew there must be one. "I see. Let me know if there are any further developments."

I end the call and immediately make arrangements to get Morales out of the country. Once he's beyond the government's reach, we'll be safe again—or as safe as possible, anyway. We've already dealt with the source of the leak that got Morales arrested.

Ten minutes later, a driver picks up Morales and whisks him to a waiting private plane. The knots in my stomach loosen and I take a sip of my tea, which is now lukewarm but still good.

I lean back in my chair, stare out at the rain-shrouded land-scape, and smile. This day has turned out much better than I expected, and I have Hez Webster to thank.

I chuckle at the thought of being grateful to him of all people. He's been a dangerous wild card ever since he arrived—who would have guessed he'd also turn out to be my ace in the hole? Still, he has to go, and the sooner the better. Today's performance is further proof. If he has the brains and intuition to find the chinks in the prosecution's case and win an ordinarily unwinnable hearing, then he also has the brains and intuition to piece together what's going on at TGU. And if he does that, things will get very messy very fast.

Hez gasped for breath as he reached the top of the last hill. It was a beautiful Sunday afternoon, perfect for a run. He'd skimped on his workouts in the weeks leading up to the prelim, and he was paying the price now. Maybe he should have stuck with running in his neighborhood instead of driving out to the sanctuary for a jog with Blake.

He paused to admire the view, which he did even when he wasn't searching for an excuse to stop running. He could see most of the animal refuge, and it was remarkable. Covered, open-air safari trucks lumbered along the roads on the African bush excursion. A lion sunbathed on a rock outcropping half a mile away. Birdlike hoots from a forest grove in the other direction told him that the sanctuary's family of bonobos was nearby, probably laughing at the silly humans running for no reason. A giraffe's head appeared from behind an acacia tree beside the road. Its long-lashed brown eyes watched him for a moment as it chewed lazily. Apparently satisfied that he was harmless, it turned back to its meal.

"Sightseeing or just out of shape?" Blake called from fifty yards ahead.

"A little of both." Hez started running again and caught up with his cousin by the time they reached the sanctuary's office.

Hez followed Blake into the tiny kitchen, which barely held the two of them. Blake took carafes of cold-brew coffee and fresh cream out of the fridge and got two glasses from the cupboard. He filled both with coffee and a splash of cream, then handed one to Hez.

Hez took a long sip and the icy drink hit his tongue in a satisfying wallop of caffeine. He let out an appreciative sigh. "Perfect, especially after a good run. I could live out here and do this every day."

Blake chuckled. "No, you couldn't. You'd be bored in less than a week."

Hez looked at his glass, watching the tendrils of cream and coffee slowly mix. "Yeah, I guess I do like to keep busy."

"That you do. I'm glad you're taking a little downtime. What's up next for you? More action on that Morales case you told me about?"

Hez shook his head. "Probably not. The feds could rearrest him, but they'd have to find him first. I called him this morning to check in, but his phone was disconnected. So I drove over to his house. He was gone. It looked like he'd left in a hurry."

"Think he's okay?"

"I hope so. He mentioned that he had family back in Mexico. Maybe he's headed back to them." That was all part of a defense attorney's job—he couldn't judge a defendant's guilt or innocence. All he could do was put the government to its proof and ensure his client's rights were respected.

"That would make sense, especially if he's afraid of getting picked up again if he stays around here." Blake set his glass on the Formica counter and crossed his muscular arms. "So if it's not the Morales case, what is next? I know you've got something in the hopper, and I'm sure it's interesting."

Hez laughed. "You know me too well. After the hearing yesterday, I got two calls offering me work. One came from my old buddy Paige in the public defender's office. They've got a murder case they'd like to refer. The other call came from Jimmy Little. He wants me to help with a crypto case. I probably only have time for one of them."

"Which one?"

"I'm leaning toward Jimmy's case. The crypto stuff is really interesting, and I could use the money. It's venued in Birmingham, so I'd need to move back up there."

Blake arched an eyebrow. "What about Savannah?"

Hez swallowed the rest of his coffee. "Things don't seem to be working out."

Blake grimaced in sympathy. "Sorry to hear it."

Hez stared down into his glass. "I gave it my best shot. She knows about the changes I've made, and we've spent a lot of time together—but my presence mostly seems to upset her. It's hard to admit, but the only moments I've seen her relaxed and happy have been a couple of glimpses of her and another guy when she didn't know I was there. Maybe coming down here was a mistake."

Blake shook his head. "A mistake to show your wife who you are now and let her know how you feel? No. You did the right thing. But you can't force her to love you back."

And that was exactly what he'd been trying to do. Savannah needed help, and he leveraged that into making her dismiss the divorce case and not complain when he shoved his way into the new life she'd built for herself. It was like she asked him to put out a fire in her house, and he decided to move into her spare bedroom.

He knew what he needed to do. He used his law degree to get into her life again, and he could use it to get back out. Aside from burying Ella, it would be the most painful thing he'd ever done, though.

CHAPTER 21

THIS IS IT.

Savannah jumped to her feet and took a deep breath when she heard the car door outside. Marley's excited bark told her it was Hez.

Her pulse jumped at the thought of the coming conversation. Hez had called an hour ago saying he needed to talk to her, and she began to plan what she might say. The thought that there might be a "them" in their future had her struggling to breathe. Nora had told her they needed to talk it out, but what if there was no resolution? Savannah would still be stuck in the same situation where she wanted either never to hear his voice again or to rush straight into his arms.

She was a crazy person.

She slicked on peach lip gloss in the mirror in the entry, then opened the door. The late afternoon sun outlined his broad shoulders, and she caught her breath as a wave of longing hit her. He wore slacks and a blue shirt that amplified the color of his eyes. His pulse throbbed in the open collar of his shirt, betraying his nervousness.

Marley, tail wagging, went to push his head against Hez's hand. As his long fingers ruffed up the dog's ears, she had a stab of longing that he would cup her face in those hands.

In that moment she knew she was going to say yes when he asked to start over. She missed him. Every cell in her body vibrated to his deep voice when he spoke. They'd always said they were soul mates. Maybe that was why it had been so impossible to forget him.

He held up a white box. "I brought a peace offering of beignets." A manila envelope was tucked under his arm.

"And I made coffee." Savannah clamped her lips against the nervous words that wanted to spill out. "Come on in."

He followed her into the living room, where he settled on the sofa and didn't speak. She rushed to the kitchen and poured two cups of coffee with trembling hands.

Could she do this—put the past behind her and demolish the walls she'd put up? Carrying the coffee, she rejoined him in the living room and handed him a cup.

"Thanks." He inhaled the coffee's aroma and took a sip. "You've always made the best coffee."

He spoke faster than normal. Did he think she was going to shoot him down again? Yesterday she might have. But not today. Something had changed her. Maybe it was the tentative way he'd called or the pain and fear in those blue eyes. She didn't want either of them to hurt like this any longer.

She settled on the sofa beside him with one leg tucked under her. The scent of his spicy cologne made her want to move closer. She opened the Petit Charms box and took a beignet. It was a perfect snack to celebrate what was about to happen.

Her defensive walls had tumbled the minute she opened the door.

Hez set down his mug beside the envelope he'd brought. "I have so much to apologize for."

Her smile faltered. "You've apologized, Hez. It's not necessary."

"It is." He pressed his lips in a determined line. "Just let me get through this. I'm so sorry, Savannah. I lost our daughter, the most precious person in our lives. I became a man I didn't recognize, let alone respect. I didn't listen when you pleaded with me not to work so much. After Ella's death, it got worse. My job was as much of a drug as the Vicodin and alcohol. I went from bad to worse, yet you still hung in there for so long. But I didn't stop there with taking you for granted. I got clean and assumed you would forgive all of it. How presumptuous of me. I'm so sorry. So very sorry." His voice choked, and he swallowed.

"I—I didn't think it was presumptuous. I'm glad you're clean, Hez. Really."

He went on as if she hadn't spoken. "I didn't take your feelings into account at all when I showed up here asking for a second chance. I forced my way back into your life without listening to a word you said. I used my law degree like a club to get you to do what I wanted." He leaned forward and took her hand. "There was only one thing I could think of that might help you forgive me."

She clung to his hand. "I already forgave you, Hez." This wasn't going the way she'd anticipated. Misgivings stirred to life at his grave expression.

"I have the power to give you want you want. So I'm going to do just that, Savannah." He picked up the envelope he'd placed on the table and handed it to her. "I'm giving you your freedom with these divorce papers. You can move on with Beckett, and I'll stay out of the way. I'll work on the investigation and keep it strictly business. All I want is for you to be happy, and I've realized that's out of my power now. I blew my chance. Once the semester ends, I'll be out of your hair. The pro bono case has been wrapped up, and there won't be a reason for me to stay. In the meantime I'll try my best not to run into you."

"B-but . . ." She barely got the word out before he stood and strode to the door.

The door closing behind him felt so final. She stared at the envelope in her hands before she threw it to the floor. The hateful word *divorce* wasn't something she could read right now. Marley whined and bumped her hand with his nose. She leaned down and buried her face in his comforting thick coat before letting the tears fall.

Savannah parked behind Nora's white Nissan on the outskirts of Pelican Harbor. The security light pushed back the night's shadows but did nothing to cast out the ones in Savannah's heart. Her pulse jumped every time she looked at the manila envelope on the seat beside her. She still hadn't opened it.

She got out of the car and approached Nora's cute shotgun home. The door swung open before she could press the bell, and Nora, dressed in pink pajamas, stood in the doorway. "Savannah, get in here and tell me what's happened. You can't text me a 'Help, I talked to Hez' without more explanation. I've been dying waiting for you to get here."

Savannah practically fell into her friend's arms, where she sobbed while Nora made soothing noises and patted her back. "He's divorcing me," she managed to choke out before she got her tears in check.

"Come inside." Nora led her into the living room where a diffuser wafted lavender oil into the room.

Savannah plopped onto the sofa and hugged herself until she stopped shaking. So many emotions swirled in her heart—fear that she'd lost Hez forever, relief it was over, and the pain of fresh rejection.

"Here." Nora thrust a mug of tea into her hand. "It's passionflower. It will calm you down."

Savannah nodded and took a sip but tasted nothing. There was too much turmoil for her senses to work. Why hadn't she had this reaction when she filed for divorce? Was this how Hez felt when he'd been served? Maybe it had been even worse for him. She hadn't given him the courtesy of delivering the papers to him herself. At least he'd shown up to do the deed himself.

Nora sat beside her on the sofa. "Tell me."

Savannah started at the beginning and went through every nuance of how her feelings had changed when he showed up. "I was floored when he handed me the papers."

"What did you say?"

"Nothing. I was too shocked to say anything, and he was out the door before I could stop him."

Nora took a sip of her tea. "Hmm," was all she said.

"What's that mean?"

"Just that your attitude took a major shift. Last time we talked you didn't want to still love him."

"I know, right?" Tea sloshed in the mug when Savannah set it down on the table. "I'm such an idiot. Everything I thought I wanted was a smoke screen to cover my feelings. I should have paid attention when he showed up that first day. I've always had such a visceral reaction to him. Even the day we met, I just knew. It's probably why it took me so long to file for divorce. I thought it was what I should do, but I didn't really want to."

"So what comes next?"

"I don't know. Maybe he's right. There's so much pain in our past. Can we ever get beyond it? He was so sincere, Nora. I saw the old Hez standing at the door tonight, and it all came rushing back in a big jumble of emotion. He was so sincere in his apology. The divorce papers were proof he wanted me to be happy." Tears burned her eyes. "Why am I such a mess?" She stared at Nora. "You were shocked I filed. Was it because you knew I still loved Hez?"

Nora stared at her over the rim of her cup before she lowered it and set it carefully on the coffee table. "I was shocked because I had no idea you were even considering divorce. And only you know if you still love Hez, even if it's taking you a little while to figure that out. I won't tell you what I think you should do because I can't make that decision for you. What do *you* want?"

A boulder formed in Savannah's throat, and she swallowed it down. "I thought I knew before he gave me those papers. Now I'm so confused. Maybe it was a second chance to think it through." She shivered and hugged herself again. "If I'd told him we could try again, I might have regretted it in the morning."

She was already second-guessing her reaction to seeing him standing in the door to her house. The attraction between them had always been so powerful, and that much hadn't changed.

But was it enough to overcome Ella's death? Him blindsiding her like this left the bad taste of distrust. He'd said she should have talked to him before she filed, so shouldn't he have done the same thing? She'd had no idea he was thinking about this. Every time they'd been together, hope shone through his eyes.

The adrenaline coursing through her since Hez had shown up began to drain away, and she was so tired she could have lain on the sofa and gone to sleep.

Nora eyed her. "I think I'd better fix coffee while you figure out what you want before it's too late."

Too late.

The words shot straight to her heart like an arrow. Maybe it had been too late when she came home to flashing police car lights. How did they find the power to overcome it all? She'd clung to her faith and her hope of seeing Ella in heaven, but she hadn't been able to muster the same faith about her marriage.

She rose and turned toward the door. "I think I'll just go home, Nora. Thanks for letting me cry on your shoulder." She eyed the damp spot on her friend's pajamas. "Literally."

Nora walked her to the door. "Remember, nothing is impossible with God. Don't count him out when you're trying to make your decision."

Savannah nodded and hurried toward her car. She couldn't think about it tonight. Hez had been so final. And maybe he was right.

CHAPTER 22

WHO WAS PETER CARDIN, AND WHAT WAS HE UP TO?

Hez stared at his office wall, mind whirring. He'd spent every free minute trying to answer that question. He'd told Savannah he would wrap up the investigation by the end of the semester, and he intended to keep that promise. Also, staying focused on the investigation kept him from thinking about her. He was lucky he'd managed to deliver his rehearsed speech, hand her the papers, and get out the door without falling apart.

Work helped him hold it together this past week. It kept his mind off the memory of her hand in his, the tropical scent of her auburn hair as she sat close to him on the sofa, the surprise in her green eyes when he handed her the papers. What else had he seen in her face? Not the relief he'd expected. Had he glimpsed something more tender? Or was he just projecting?

He shook his head and muttered, "Focus!"

He needed to keep his mind on the investigation. Thinking about Savannah was a black hole that kept trying to suck him in. He couldn't let it.

Cardin was the key. Hez was sure of it, and his certainty grew as he worked. The personnel file Jess sent over contained a very interesting résumé. Cardin had an accounting degree from Northwestern and three years' experience in PwC's education group—one of the best accounting practices focused on colleges and universities—but his employment there ended two years before he started at TGU. Where had he spent that time? Prison, as Hez soon discovered. Searches of a couple of legal databases revealed that Cardin pled guilty to embezzling from clients and spent a year and a half behind bars.

Hez had asked for access to Cardin's email account, but Jess refused. She said his emails probably contained confidential financial information about TGU students and employees, which Hez wasn't authorized to see. She agreed to run some searches herself, but Hez almost didn't care what the results showed. Cardin probably wasn't dumb enough to leave anything incriminating in his work email. The important fact was that he had access to confidential financial data, which meant he could be responsible for the suspicious transactions Beckett found.

Next, Hez turned to TGU's security cameras. He couldn't just ask for clips for particular times from a particular camera, like he had with the Willard Treasure warehouse. He wanted to track Cardin's movements around campus, a massive job of reviewing thousands of hours of video from over a dozen cameras scattered around Tupelo Grove. He couldn't do that on his own, of course. He needed help, and he knew exactly who to call: Bruno Rubinelli.

Bruno was a semiretired San Francisco software genius who had founded and sold two companies before he was thirty. He spent most of his time skateboarding now, but he sometimes took on criminal cases that interested him. Hez managed to hook Bruno with the words "Willard Treasure" and reel him in with tales of Willard's exploits and Abernathy's murder. By the end of a thirty-minute call, Bruno had agreed to run his custom facial-recognition software on the TGU security camera video, culling it down to only clips that showed Cardin.

Two hours later, Hez had ninety-three minutes of video to watch. It mostly showed Cardin entering and leaving Jess's office suite, but he also made a lot of trips to the history building after hours, which seemed odd. Hez jotted down a note to ask Jess about that.

His stomach rumbled, and he checked his watch: after three and he'd worked through lunch. Again. And he'd gone through all the protein bars in his desk while skipping earlier meals. Maybe Savannah had a point about him working too much.

Another rumble. "Okay, okay," he told his abdomen.

He stretched and reached for his mouse to pause the video. Time to stretch his legs and get something to eat. The student-run café had good shrimp gumbo, and they only charged $3.99 per bowl.

He froze with his hand on the mouse. The video showed Cardin arguing with a man in the parking lot behind the history building. The time stamp was July 27, 7:34 p.m. The same day Hez arrived on campus—and the day Savannah unwittingly picked up the forged provenance documents. He didn't recall the exact time, but he remembered the hot late afternoon sun on his back as he walked out of the building alone, and he'd had dinner reservations at Billy's at 7:00. Had Cardin accidentally left the documents, realized his mistake a few hours later, and come back looking for them? The biggest piece of info in Hez's view was that Cardin was wearing a gray hoodie. A strange thing to wear on a humid summer evening. Was he the man who'd attacked Savannah in the warehouse?

And who was Cardin arguing with? The man's back was to the camera, but he looked vaguely familiar. He had light hair and broad shoulders and was tall—probably a few inches over six feet.

Cardin talked almost nonstop, and he seemed twitchy and nervous. The video quality was too poor for lip reading. He pointed at the building a couple of times, then shrugged and held his hands palms up. The other man took a step forward and Cardin cringed back.

Hez was sure he'd recognize the man if he could only get a glimpse of his face. "Turn around. Come on, turn around."

Almost as if he'd heard Hez, the man turned abruptly and stalked off, with Cardin trailing after him, mouth still going. It was Erik Andersen.

There he was. Savannah caught her breath at the sight of Hez waiting for her in the hall outside Jess's office. He stood studying the trophies in the display case and hadn't seen her yet, so she let her gaze linger on his features and strong jaw. The divorce papers still sat unsigned on top of her desk, and she looked away every time she spotted them.

She should have been glad he'd taken the decision out of her hands, but she wished she'd been able to tell him how she felt.

He turned from the display case and spotted her. The skin around his blue eyes crinkled in a warm smile that curled her toes. "Good morning." Heat flooded her cheeks, and she checked the impulse to press the iced caramel latte to her face.

He took a step toward her. "Do you have some papers for me?"

She shook her head. "I don't want all our savings, Hez. You'll need a down payment on a house at some point. It's not a fair division of the money left from the sale of the house."

He shrugged. "I don't plan on buying a home anytime soon. I don't know what the future holds yet, now that . . ." His gaze shuttered, and he looked away.

She heard the rest of his unspoken sentence in her heart. *Now that we aren't ever going to be together.* The end of their marriage was something she thought she wanted, but now that she faced the finality of a divorce decree, she couldn't bear it. Her eyes burned with the effort to hold back tears.

"We can talk about it later. Jess is expecting us, and I don't want her to get started on some other project and shortchange our discussion."

"Want me to take the lead, or do you want to do that?"

"She's always prickly with you, but you're the one who knows more about Cardin. I'll jump in if she pushes back."

He nodded and rapped his knuckles on the office door. When Jess answered, "Come in," he opened the door and gestured for Savannah to go first. She went ahead of him and spotted Jess behind her desk. Sunlight streamed through the big window and touched her sister's face. Jess looked older this morning, tired and anxious. Was it the situation with Cardin or a late night?

Savannah crossed the office to hand her sister the iced latte. "Early morning?"

"I was here at five." Her gaze went past Savannah to Hez. "I don't have much time."

Hez appeared in calm command as he strolled over to face Jess. "I have some concerns about Peter Cardin. After looking over the personnel file you gave me, I wanted to find out about the employment gaps. Did you know he'd been in prison for embezzling money from clients?"

Jess's face reddened. "You are invading Peter's privacy! Yes, he got into trouble. He had a cocaine habit that he kicked. You, of all people, ought to understand giving someone a second chance. You asked Savannah to intercede for you and give you a chance here. Should I do less for Peter? He's been a good and reliable employee."

"I watched ninety-three minutes of video. He went in and out of the history building on sixteen occasions. Don't you find that a little excessive? What would he be doing there? I believe we have to consider the possibility Cardin might be the one selling artifacts and running the funds through the school's accounts. Especially in light of his embezzlement history. And another thing—he was wearing a gray hoodie in the video. He might be the man who attacked Savannah at the warehouse."

Jess waved her hand in a dismissive gesture. "He delivers messages to the professors all the time. Some of our history faculty hate email and prefer to receive important or sensitive documents by hand. You're trying to pin something on him that's completely innocent."

Savannah heard the way her sister's voice vibrated and knew she should step in, but Hez shot her a warning glance, so she kept silent. Why was Jess defending Peter so strenuously?

"I understand," Hez said in a calm voice. "One more thing and we'll let you get on with your day. Can you think of any reason why Cardin and Andersen might get into an argument?"

Jess took a quick breath. She glanced at Savannah with an appeal in her eyes, but Savannah let the silence stretch out. Jess knew something and didn't want to answer.

"Any ideas?" Hez asked again.

Jess took a sip of her latte, then set it on her desk. "No idea. Now if you'll excuse me, I need to get back to work."

"Fair warning—Augusta will need to hear what I've discovered," Hez said.

Jess stood and leaned forward with her hands on her desk. "You discovered nothing, Hez, but just like you always do, you're trying to turn a nothing-burger into something it's not. You're going to look foolish."

"Augusta might agree with you, but we'll let her decide."

He turned toward the door, and a muscle twitched in his jaw. Savannah wanted to say something to defuse the tension in the air, but she turned and followed Hez out the door. Once the door shut on her sister's angry face, she put her hand on Hez's arm. "I think Jess knows exactly why Peter was arguing with Erik."

He nodded. "I wondered if she didn't want me investigating Cardin because she knew it would lead to Erik. Do you think she still cares about him?"

"She says she doesn't, but Jess has always been so private that it's hard to know for sure. She couldn't wait for us to get out of there. I wouldn't be surprised if she called Erik and Peter right away. What do you think Augusta will do?"

"I'll soon find out. I'll go see her right away and turn over the video. Something's there, Savannah. I'm sure of it." He held her gaze for a long moment. "Be careful. Things may heat up if Augusta pokes in deeper."

She wasn't aware for a few seconds that she'd taken his hand, but he didn't pull away. His firm grip was a reminder of everything in their past, but it broke her heart to think that her contact with him would soon end.

CHAPTER 23

SLOW-BUILDING TENSION HAD PLAGUED HEZ FOR THE PAST
two days, but it began to evaporate as he ran with Cody trailing
behind. The distant rhythm of breakers on the beach paced
him for the first couple of miles. As his path moved farther
from Bon Secour Bay, the music of the waves gave way to
woodland sounds. Early morning breezes rustled the branches
overhead and sent ripples through the long grass in the occasional meadows. The forest wore the tired, faded greens of late
September, signaling that fall was just around the corner.

Nervous energy had built up in him like a static charge
after his talk with Augusta. When she'd heard about Cardin,
she immediately asked Hez, Savannah, and Beckett to put
their investigation on hold while the Pelican Harbor Police
Department worked the case. As a former prosecutor, Hez
understood perfectly. Having private citizens and the police actively investigating simultaneously created legal and
logistical risks that could easily destroy a case. So Augusta's
request held logic—but Hez still hated being stuck on the
sidelines.

He reached the side path leading to the cemetery where
Ella was buried. He hesitated for a moment. Might he run into

Savannah at the grave? No, she had class now. He turned off the main trail, and the crushed oyster shells crunched under his feet as he jogged up the gentle slope to the graveyard. The rusty gate still stood open. He slowed to a walk and went in. His panting dog followed him, tongue lolling out of the side of his mouth.

The air felt cooler and fresher than the last time he'd come here, and a clean light wind greeted him. Spanish moss hung from the arching limbs of ancient trees, waving gently like the remnants of old flags. Green bronze angels watched over monuments of stained marble and lichen-crusted granite. Weeds crowded the path, grabbing at his ankles and shins as he passed.

The genteel decay vanished when Hez reached the two newest graves in the Legare section of the cemetery. Bright sunlight fell on the weedless grass covering the graves of Ella and her maternal grandmother, and no moss or lichen grew on their headstones. Fresh flowers adorned each.

Ella would have liked this place. He could almost picture her playing in the grass and asking him the names of the flowers on her grave.

A lump formed in his throat and he felt familiar pangs of guilt—and also a new undercurrent of peace. Looking at his daughter's grave hurt, but he could also see the beauty and love Savannah had brought to this place. Coming here would never be a happy experience, but it didn't have to bring searing pain.

He had been gripping the past like shards of a broken crystal sculpture, trying to force the shattered pieces back together with bloody fingers. He needed to let go and accept what had happened. The sculpture could never be made whole again, but the pieces held a broken beauty of their own, especially when touched with healing light. Like this place. There was wisdom here.

Would memories of his failed marriage feel the same way in a few years? Could days like their anniversary become times of happy memory and gentle regret? Maybe, if he could learn to let go with grace.

His eyes fell on the inscription on Ella's stone: *"For where your treasure is, there your heart will be also."* The verse had been Savannah's choice, but he had never liked it. It seemed beautiful but depressing—a reminder that one of his greatest treasures lay buried in the ground and a big piece of his heart had gone in the grave with her.

He couldn't leave his heart buried forever. Maybe that was the point of the quote. Hez had never paid much attention in Sunday school, so he wasn't sure what the context was for that verse. Perhaps it was actually a warning not to treasure something that had slipped forever beyond your reach. He should look it up someday.

And he needed to visit Ella's grave more often. A lesson for him resided here.

He walked back toward the path, patting the top of Ella's headstone as he passed. The black granite was warm and smooth. "Love you, honey. I'll be back."

Savannah couldn't seem to shake the dark cloud riding on her shoulder ever since Hez served the divorce papers, and it was already October sixth. Her class this morning didn't start until eight, and she'd hoped an early walk around the pond with Marley would clear her head and help her focus on a different future than she'd envisioned. After notating an even split of their assets, she'd finally signed the papers, made a copy, and brought everything back to Hez yesterday evening. She had also included her engagement ring and wedding band, with a note asking him to sell them and donate the proceeds to the Justice Chamber. She'd had to pray for the strength to do it, and she finally managed to pull the trigger. To her relief, he'd been out, so she had shoved everything through the old-fashioned mail slot in the front door of his condo.

She zipped her hoodie sweatshirt up to guard against the sixty-degree breeze whipping up waves in the pond, then tugged on Marley's leash to direct him toward the oyster-shell path around the pond. Boo Radley roared in the distance, but he was far enough away she didn't have to worry about the gator lunging out of the darkness.

The pond path was deserted this early, and the warm glow of streetlamps gave the familiar landscape an otherworldly ambience. Even though Hez had asked her not to wander around on her own, she had Marley with her. Legare Hall loomed in the distance. The unfinished building had fallen into decay, but Jess had mentioned plans to convert it into student apartments. It would take more money than Savannah could imagine to renovate the building her father had started twenty years ago. Its imposing exterior masked the massive work needed inside. Another of her father's failed grandiose ideas.

Savannah squinted through the darkness toward the gothic-style building. Was that a light? She shook her head. She'd never seen anyone poking around the old building. Numerous signs warned students to stay out. The place wasn't safe and had been roped off for the past two years after a student crashed through a floor and broke a leg. She'd had to resist the urge to explore herself more than once.

She pulled out her phone to call security when Marley barked and pulled his leash from her hand. He darted toward Legare Hall and didn't turn when she called for him. He howled in a way she'd never heard, and the hair rose on the back of her neck. She stepped from the path and ducked under Spanish moss hanging from the trees around the hall.

Everything about this felt wrong. An impulse erupted to call Hez, but she pushed it away. He'd made it clear she was supposed to start a new life without him. The smart thing to do would be to call security, but she had to retrieve her dog.

She started up the slope toward the building. "Marley, come!"

Her dog whined from the deeper darkness closer to the hall. Was he hurt? Marley howled again, a mournful sound that made her gasp. She turned on her phone's flashlight and moved toward where she'd heard the dog. The light made her feel a little better, and its wavering beams touched Marley's black coat.

"There you are, boy." She squatted beside him and ran her hands over his coat. No blood. "You okay?"

He whined before launching into a full-throated howl again. "What's wrong, boy?" She rose and shone the light around the area.

They were near the entrance to Legare Hall, and shattered glass sparkled in the flashlight's beam. Savannah grasped Marley's leash, then tugged him toward the pond. "Let's get out of here. I want to see you in the light."

Marley barked and jerked away again. Even though she'd been prepared for a lunge, he managed to escape again, and he darted through the entry door into the old building. Why was it even open? Probably students again.

The flashlight on her phone pushed back the shadows and illuminated the way into the dark maw of the derelict hall. She pushed the door open wider. "Marley?" He made no noise, and she lifted the phone higher to shine the light around the space.

The grand foyer rose twenty feet into a rounded dome that had partially collapsed sometime in the past few years. Support beams lay askew on the banister of the curving staircase up to the next story. They'd also gouged some of the mahogany floors, and she winced to see them in such condition. Grotesque shadows danced in the light of her flashlight, and all Savannah wanted was to find her dog and get out of here. It was a treacherous space, and if she wasn't careful, she'd end up with some broken bones or a bashed-in skull.

She spun in a circle with the light, and her sneakers kicked up dirt. She sneezed at the stale scent of mold and filth. "Marley, come."

The dog whined from a doorway to her right, and she went that way. It opened to a spacious office, at least judging from the wall of bookshelves. Maybe her father had planned it for himself. Something moved in the shadows just out of range of her light. "Marley?"

The dog whined, and she went toward him. She stumbled over something on the floor and dropped her phone. With the light snuffed out, the room plunged into suffocating darkness. Her phone must have fallen upside down. She knelt and touched the wooden floor, then ran her fingers through the debris. Where was her phone? Her fingers touched something warm and pliable, and she instinctively shuddered and jerked her hand back.

The rising sun's rays filtering through a big window to the east illuminated a small section of floor, and she spotted her phone. As soon as she lifted it off its face, its light landed on a figure on the floor.

Peter Cardin. His eyes stared up toward the ceiling, but she didn't think he was conscious.

She squatted beside him and touched her cold fingers to his neck. No matter where she moved her hand, she couldn't detect a pulse. She laid her hand on his motionless chest. No movement. She tried to find a pulse in his wrist. When she took her hand away, her fingers brushed a piece of paper.

She picked it up and put it under the light of her flashlight. The words on the paper made no sense at first. *Death Is a Lonely Business*. It was the title of another Ray Bradbury novel.

Someone had murdered Peter Cardin.

CHAPTER 24

HEZ DIDN'T LIKE IT. IN THE TEN DAYS SINCE CARDIN'S murder, Detective Richards had gone radio silent. He'd called three times, and she hadn't picked up. So he left a voice mail volunteering to help and asking if there was anything he should tell campus security about the threat posed by a killer on the loose. No response—but he did learn from TGU's security chief that the PHPD had reached out to him directly to say they believed this was a targeted killing and there was no increased risk to campus residents. Augusta Richards was clearly avoiding him—the question was why.

When Hez was in the DA's office, he routinely told cops not to talk to lawyers who were close to potential targets, especially if the cop had a preexisting relationship with the lawyer. Was that what was going on here? Did the police suspect Savannah?

Hez squirmed on the worn cushion of his office chair. Savannah had discovered the body. Again. She had an unfortunate habit of finding the corpses of men she disliked.

That didn't mean she was the killer, of course, but it did make her a natural suspect—especially since, by her own admission, Cardin's body was still warm when she'd found him. It would be reasonable for the police to think Savannah might have spotted him stalking her and decided to take matters into her own hands. Was that what Detective Richards was thinking?

The air in Hez's shoebox "office" suddenly felt stuffy. He needed to go for a walk—and Cody probably did too. He shoved his to-be-graded stack of papers into his briefcase and headed out.

Twenty minutes later, he was walking down the stairs outside his condo. Cody scrambled after him, his nails making a sound like someone was pouring gravel down the steps. The smell of beignets from Petit Charms greeted him, but Hez was too tense to be hungry. Maybe a walk along the water would help him relax.

They turned away from Pelican Harbor's quaint French Quarter and headed toward Bon Secour Bay. A brisk breeze blew in his face and he inhaled deeply, savoring the cool salt smell. They reached the waterside park, and Cody immediately did his business and set about putting squirrels in their place, which drew an annoyed squawk from Pete the Pelican, the semi-tame bird that was Pelican Harbor's unofficial mascot. Alfie Smith sat on a bench, eating his lunch. He looked up at Cody's yapping and gave Hez a friendly wave. Hez waved back.

When they were in town, he and Savannah used to get beignets at Petit Charms and eat them here. Early in their relationship, a summer rain squall caught them by surprise while they were at the park. The rain was warm and they were drenched in seconds, so there was no point in running for shelter. Hez did a terrible impression of Gene Kelly from *Singin' in the Rain*, which got Savannah laughing so hard she couldn't speak. He could still see her in his mind's eye, utterly soaked and full of carefree joy.

He caught himself wishing he could stay. There were good memories here, and he'd settled into the rhythms of university and small-town life faster than he'd expected. It would be hard to go back to Birmingham. Hard, but necessary. She'd returned the signed divorce papers, eliminating any doubt about her intentions. Her insistence on an even split of the assets had been touching, unnecessary, and very Savannah. And then there were the rings, of course. Even at the end, she had insisted on being more generous than he deserved.

It took everything in him to file the divorce papers for the judge's signature, but he did it. For her. And he would move back to Birmingham for the same reason. A clean break would be best for both of them.

But would a clean break be possible if she was accused of murder? She would probably ask him to represent her, and he would say yes. He already knew the evidence, and he would be the obvious best choice to represent her. But that would mean regular contact with her for the duration of the case, which could be a year or more.

His phone buzzed and he pulled it out of his pocket. Savannah. His pulse quickened as he accepted the call. "Hey, what's up?"

"The police just showed up with a search warrant!" Her voice shook. "Can you come over here? Please?"

So the other shoe had finally dropped. "Where are you?"

"Jess's house."

He blinked. "Jess's house?"

"Yes. We were having coffee when someone knocked on the door. She answered, and the next thing I knew, police were swarming everywhere. Please come."

"Yeah, of course. On my way."

Hez ended the call and headed for his car. The legal wheels whirred in his head during the ten-minute drive as he tried to figure out what the police were up to. Jess didn't have any apparent motive to kill Cardin—or Abernathy, for that matter—but it would be natural for her to help Savannah. Jess was highly competent, fiercely protective of her sister, and cold and hard as Arctic ice. If Savannah killed someone, Jess wouldn't hesitate to get rid of the body and destroy evidence. Was that why the police were searching her home?

A familiar scene came into view as Hez reached Jess's place. Two police vans were parked in front of the ornate Greek Revival portico, and a team of officers in acronym-emblazoned blue windbreakers moved in and out of the house. Hez also glimpsed what looked like evidence techs in the grove of trees in the backyard.

Savannah and Jess stood close together between the marble columns. Savannah hugged herself and shifted her weight from foot to foot, while Jess was a steel statue. Detective Richards stood a few feet away, keeping an eye on both them and the officers.

Hez pulled up behind the rear van and got out. A wave of relief swept over Savannah's face as she saw him approaching, but Jess's face remained an expressionless mask.

"Thank you!" Savannah put her hand on his arm as he walked up. Her touch sent a thrill through him, despite the circumstances.

He patted her hand. "Of course. Happy to help." He turned to Detective Richards. "Can I see the search warrant?"

The detective glanced over her shoulder. "You'll have to ask her."

Hez's gaze traveled past the detective to a severe-looking young woman in a suit standing behind the vans. She caught his eye and walked over. "Deputy District Attorney Virginia Samson. Can I help you?"

So they had a prosecutor overseeing the search. Interesting. They must think they were likely to find critical evidence, so they wanted to ensure everything was done exactly right. "Yes. My name is Hezekiah Webster and I represent Savannah Webster. I'd like to see a copy of the search warrant."

"That won't be possible at this time."

Hez arched an eyebrow. That was an unusual response. "It'll be possible pretty soon. If you use any evidence from this search against my client, I'll be entitled to the warrant, the supporting affidavit, and the application. Even if you don't charge her, the property owner can sue if you guys go beyond the scope of the warrant, and you'll have to produce the warrant during that lawsuit. So why not give it to me now?"

Samson frowned, accentuating the sharp planes of her face. "Do you represent the property owner too?"

So that was why she wouldn't give Hez the warrant—it wasn't targeted at his client, Savannah, but at Jess. He gave Jess an inquiring look. Her face remained stony, but uncertainty flickered in her eyes for a moment. And was that fear he saw too? It was gone before he could be sure.

Jess turned to Samson. "Yes, he represents me."

Before Samson could respond, an officer and a tech approached and motioned for her and Detective Richards. They walked a little distance away and talked in tense, low tones for a few minutes. Then they came back, and Detective Richards appeared as grim as Samson. She walked up to Jess. "Jessica Legare, you are under arrest for the murders of Ellison Abernathy and Peter Cardin."

———

Savannah ducked under the low-hanging moss on the huge live oak tree and ran after the detective as she loaded Jess into the police van. "Please, there must be some kind of mistake." Detective Richards didn't answer, and Savannah swung around to search out Hez. She found him jogging close behind her. "Do something!"

He took her hand and pulled her against him. "Breathe, babe. There's nothing we can do right now. They're going to take Jess downtown and book her. We can't interfere."

She allowed herself to slump into the circle of his arms and nestle against his chest. His familiar cologne with its earthy sandalwood notes slowed the frantic beat of her heart, and she closed her eyes. When she lifted her head, the van carrying her sister was disappearing down the road.

She took a shuddering breath. "I hate injustice." She didn't even like to watch shows about false arrests and other mistreatment. Maybe it brought back too many memories of how her dad would accuse Jess of things that weren't her fault.

His expression went somber. "I remember."

The understanding in his gaze wrapped around her like a warm blanket. The history of their love for each other couldn't be wiped away by a piece of paper. Not even Ella's death had destroyed the pull she'd always felt toward him. Yet here they were with that document proclaiming they were done as a couple.

She took a step back. "Why did they arrest her, Hez? She couldn't have anything to do with this. It's insane. They didn't even tell her why so she could explain."

He shoved his hands into his pockets. "From the firepower they brought, it's clear they expected to find something incriminating. Whatever that was, it had to have been very bad for them to arrest her on the spot without a warrant."

"Didn't they need a warrant to search her house?"

"Yes, but a search warrant wouldn't let them arrest her. They'd need an arrest warrant for that—and if they had one, they would have cuffed her as soon as they arrived."

"Can we get her out today?"

He shook his head. "This will have to play out for now. They'll arraign her as quickly as they can arrange it—probably tomorrow morning. The court will set bail at the same time."

She felt a surge of hope. "So maybe I can get her home tomorrow?"

He grimaced. "She's been arrested for murder, and the formal charge will probably be capital murder. The prosecution will argue against bail, and even if bail is granted, it's likely to be very expensive. Let's deal with that problem when we get there. In the next few days the DA will lay out what evidence they have against her in a preliminary hearing, and her lawyer will get to look at it."

"Why did you say 'her lawyer' like that? You're her lawyer."

"Maybe you weren't looking when she told Richards I was representing her. I'm not sure that's what Jess wants. She was only asking me to represent her so we could see the search warrant. She hasn't asked me to represent her in a murder case."

The distance in his gaze and manner alarmed her. She took hold of his forearm. "But you will represent her, won't you, Hez? Please, you have to. There's no one I trust more than you."

He hesitated before his shoulders relaxed and he nodded. "If she asks me, I'll do what I can to help. Things spiraled quickly here, and I'm curious what evidence they have. I've been trying to get in touch with Detective Richards for days, and she's been dodging me. When you called to tell me they were executing a search warrant, I was afraid you were the target. You found both bodies, and the police targeting you made more sense than them looking at Jess. Did any of the officers mention what they hoped to find?"

She thought back to the morning before shaking her head. "There was no explanation. They barged in and said they had a search warrant, but we never saw it." She turned to stare at her sister's house. "Can I clean up in there? They trashed the place. All her beautiful things are lying around on the floor. It's outrageous the police don't put things back the way they found them."

"They aren't done yet. Once they release the house, you can go in and set it to rights. I'll help you."

She was beginning to see this new Hez wasn't the same man she'd walked away from two years ago. This new Hez was ready to help even if it meant cleaning up the house of a woman who hated him. He was trying so hard. Maybe it really would stick.

She reached out without thinking before pulling back her hand. He might not welcome her need to touch him for reassurance, and she didn't want to give him false hope when she didn't know herself how to start over. "I can do it. You've already done so much.

Is there any way you can find out what evidence they have before the preliminary hearing?"

He shook his head. "Sorry, our hands are tied for now."

"Can we see her before she's arraigned?"

"I can. I'll go see her right away."

"What about me?"

"She can request a visit with you, and they'll probably grant it." He took her hand again. "Try not to stress about this, Savannah. I know it's hard, but we're stuck until we know more."

Her fingers curled around his, and she took comfort in his strong grip. "You will get her acquitted, won't you, Hez?" Even as the words came out of her mouth, she knew it was an unfair question. He couldn't possibly know what the state had against her, but she wanted some kind of reassurance to help her deal with this.

He squeezed her fingers. "All I can do is promise my best. She's your sister, and I'll do everything I can."

That reassurance meant more than he knew. Hez had always been a man who took pride in his knowledge of the law, and his power in the courtroom was something Jess was going to need.

CHAPTER 25

"WHY CAN'T I EVER SAY NO TO HER?" HEZ ASKED THE WIND-
shield as he drove to the Baldwin County jail in Bay Minette.
He had been torn at the thought of representing Savannah if
she had been arrested, but he had no conflicting feelings about
representing her sister in a murder case. He didn't want to do
it. At all. They had never gotten along, and there was no reason to think that would change now. Also, representing Jess
would force him either to stay in Pelican Harbor or to make
regular four-hour trips from Birmingham. Besides, Jess didn't
need him—she had the money and connections to hire the best
criminal defense attorneys in the state. And yet here he was
driving to a jailhouse interview with her.

None of the excellent reasons to say no had mattered. Not
when Savannah was in his arms with the sun catching the
hints of gold in her auburn hair and green eyes, looking up at
him with pleading terror.

Oh well. Maybe Jess wouldn't even want him to represent
her. It was entirely possible he would walk into the meeting
room and she would tell him that he'd wasted his time because
she had already hired some heavyweight lawyer from Mobile.
Which wouldn't bother him in the least.

The jail loomed into view. It was an enormous redbrick cube with a low, flat-roofed building in front. Well-trimmed bushes and palm trees lined the parking lot and gave the compound the appearance of a government office building, at least until a visitor spotted the razor wire–topped fences.

Hez noticed the unique smell of prison as soon as he walked in. A combination of unwashed bodies, cheap disinfectant, and something else—the indefinable odor of despair.

A guard walked him back to the attorney interview room reserved for his meeting with Jess. She was already there, sitting behind a utilitarian table and watching him as he entered. She looked small and young in her prison uniform, but her posture was erect and her hazel eyes full of icy defiance.

"I thought you were only representing me regarding that search warrant," Jess said as soon as the guard closed the door.

"So did I." He chuckled as he sat in a chair across the table from her. "But here I am offering to defend you against two murder charges and all the various and sundry related charges the prosecution will throw at you."

Her eyes narrowed slightly. "I didn't ask you to."

"No, but Savannah did."

"Did she ask—or did you suggest it?"

He arched an eyebrow. "Why would I do that?"

"Because you're still trying to win her back."

"You may not have heard, but I filed for divorce."

"But the papers aren't final yet, are they? And I see how you look at her."

The mention of the divorce brought a sharp stab of pain. "We're here to discuss your criminal case, not my marriage." He tried to keep the anger out of his voice, but he wasn't entirely successful. "Do you want me to represent you or not? And it's totally fine if the answer is not. I'd actually prefer it. I want to be back in Birmingham permanently by Christmas."

She folded her arms across her chest. "Promise me you won't use this to try to worm your way back into her heart."

"That's it." He pushed his chair back and stood. "You should have a lawyer you trust, and that clearly isn't me. Let me know if you want a referral." He turned toward the door and put his hand on the knob.

"Wait."

He sighed and turned back. "What?"

A calculating expression creased her face. Had she been testing him? "I want you to represent me."

"Are you sure? I know some very good local defense attorneys, and I'd be happy to—"

"I'll pay you the same rate as my New York lawyers—fifteen hundred dollars an hour. Will that be satisfactory?"

He blinked. That kind of money would be a big help when he was finally able to start the Justice Chamber. "Sure."

"Good. How soon can you get me out on bail?"

He returned to his seat. "The earliest opportunity would be when you're arraigned tomorrow morning. I'll ask for bail, but don't get your hopes up."

She leaned forward, and there was new urgency in her voice. "I need you to get me out in the next week. What will that take?"

"Persuading the judge that you're not a flight risk or a danger to the community. And if there's a specific reason you need to be out, it's good to mention that too."

She hesitated. "I have a very important meeting. It's confidential school business."

"Okay, well, I'll see what I can do."

She laid a hand on his arm. Her fine-boned fingers were surprisingly strong. "Hez, you have to win this."

Savannah sat in a waiting room at the Baldwin County Corrections Facility. She'd been relegated to this room for over an hour already. Was Hez still with Jess? It would explain the long wait, but it might be that Jess didn't want to see her. She had to approve the visit before Savannah could go back.

The door opened, and Nora stepped into the room with a University Grounds coffee in her hand. "I came as soon as I heard."

Savannah jumped up and embraced her friend. Her eyes burned, but if she let out the tears, she'd be unable to marshal her strength for a while—and she needed every bit of control she possessed to get through this. She released Nora and pulled her over to sit with her. "It's insane, Nora. Why would they accuse Jess of something like this? She didn't kill anyone."

Nora handed her the coffee cup. "You know I can't talk about the case, but let me just say they do have some evidence."

Savannah's knees went weak, and she sank onto the chair. "Someone must be framing her, and the police are buying it. I thought the police were the good guys. Aren't they supposed to dig until they actually find the truth?"

Nora sat on the chair beside her. "I know you're hurting, Savannah, but you have to let this play out. Who's her attorney?"

"Hez. He might be in there right now. They haven't let me back yet."

"He's a great attorney."

Savannah took the lid off her coffee and inhaled the aroma that pushed aside the stench of despair permeating the building. "He's not confident he can get her off. He even warned me he might not get her out on bail. The trial will take a long time— and he's moving away in a couple of months. I think his attention will be split, and he won't be here to find out the truth."

The thought of being on her own with such a huge task felt overwhelming. Could she do it? Her thoughts whirled. Jess's future—her whole life—depended on her being exonerated. If the police wouldn't do it, and Hez wasn't here and fully committed, that left only Savannah to get to the bottom of what was going on at the campus. She had to step up and do this. Jess could spend the rest of her life in prison. Even worse, she could be executed. There had been two murders, and she was being accused of committing both.

"I see the wheels turning," Nora said.

Savannah fingered her bracelet. "I just realized I have to figure this out myself. I can't depend on the police or Hez. He filed for divorce for a reason."

"He filed to make you happy."

"I'd like to believe that, but maybe he's tired of the chaos too. Maybe he needs to move on to heal, and that won't happen as long as he's living here. At the first sign of a problem, I rush into his arms."

Nora lifted a brow. "Oh? And how did he react?"

"He held me while I fell apart. I asked him to go see Jess and represent her. I don't think he really wanted to do that." She knew her husband's every expression, and he'd only agreed because she asked. How was that fair to him?

"Maybe Beckett would help. He might have the power to get into files and places you can't."

Savannah tensed. "I don't think so. To tell you the truth, Beckett is a little too possessive even though we aren't dating. It's like he expects me to run into his arms the minute my divorce is final. I'm trying to keep some distance between us, at least until I'm completely sure about Hez."

"I can understand that, and I think that's wise. What about your dad? He's got the money to hire a private investigator."

"Maybe. He and Jess don't get along." Had she explained the family dynamics to Nora? Probably not. It wasn't a pleasant topic of conversation.

A female officer opened the door and peered in. Her glance bounced from Nora to Savannah. "Come with me, Ms. Webster. Your sister has agreed to see you."

Savannah sprang to her feet. "Thanks for coming, Nora. I'll talk to you later." She followed the officer down a tiled hallway to a room where she spotted her sister behind plexiglass. When Jess saw her, she grabbed a phone. Savannah slid into a chair and picked up the handset.

Seeing her sister in a prison uniform choked off Savannah's initial greeting. Jess saw her shock and smiled. "The highest fashion they could offer me. It's fine, Savannah. It's only clothes."

"We've got to get you out of here. You saw Hez?"

Jess nodded. "He agreed to represent me."

Savannah leaned forward and put her hand on the plexiglass. If only she could touch Jess, comfort her. "Have you heard the evidence against you yet?"

"Not yet. Hez says that will come at a hearing."

"I know you didn't hurt anyone. I'm going to find out who's behind this."

Jess shook her head. "Someone killed two people and broke into my house to plant evidence. Whoever is behind this is determined and dangerous. If they find out you're poking your nose into this, you'll be in their crosshairs. I want you to stay out of it. Let Hez figure it out. That's what I'm paying him for."

Savannah lifted her chin. "I'm not staying out of this, Jess. You're my sister and I love you. I promise you I'll figure it out. I'll do whatever it takes to exonerate you."

Jess's eyes filled with tears, and Savannah's throat closed at the unfamiliar sight. Jess needed her, and she *would* find a way to free her.

CHAPTER 26

HEZ GOT HIS FIRST GLIMPSE OF HOPE—QUITE LITERALLY—
when he walked into the courtroom. Deputy District Attorney
Hope Norcross sat at the prosecution table, chatting with the
bailiff. Hez knew her well from a gang case they'd prosecuted
together five years ago. She had been fresh out of law school,
and he had rescued her from several rookie mistakes. They
stayed in touch, and he informally mentored her until his
booze-fueled collapse. He hadn't talked to her since, but if
anyone in the DA's office would show some flexibility on his
bail motion, she would.

As he walked up the center aisle, the side door opened. A
deputy emerged, followed by Jess and a second officer. Jess
caught his eye and motioned him over. The deputies depos-
ited Jess at the defense table and sat behind her. Hez took the
seat next to her.

Jess leaned over and whispered, "Give me an update. I hate
that I can't have a phone."

"I just got the complaint this morning," he whispered back.
"They're charging you with two counts of capital murder and a
bunch of included offenses. The only real surprise was a charge
for embezzlement. I—"

"What about bail?"

"That will be decided today. The judge will also schedule the prelim, which is where we'll get our first real look at the prosecution's case."

"All rise," the bailiff intoned. "The District Court for Baldwin County is now in session, the Honorable Judge Achilles Hopkins presiding."

Judge Hopkins limped to his seat and settled in while everyone in the courtroom stood silently. He was a burly, middle-aged former cop who went to law school after a teen-aged carjacker ended Hopkins's law enforcement career by ramming his police cruiser while trying to get through a road-block, crushing Hopkins's right hip. Unsurprisingly, he was a tough-on-crime judge who tended to give the prosecution what it asked for—so Hez's real job today wasn't to persuade the judge to grant bail. He needed to persuade Hope.

After a couple of minutes of formal appearances and other "legal liturgy," as Hez's first boss called it, the judge got down to business. "Okay, is your client waiving the reading of the complaint, Mr. Webster?"

Hez stood. "Yes, Your Honor. We received a copy this morning. No need for a formal reading."

"Good. And how does your client plead?"

"Not guilty, Your Honor."

The judge nodded and jotted down a note on a yellow pad. "Next on the agenda is setting a preliminary hearing." He turned to a large paper calendar hanging on the courtroom wall. "I've got a trial starting tomorrow that will last the rest of the week. Ms. Norcross, does October twenty-three at nine work for the DA's office?"

Hope pulled out her phone and scrolled for a moment. "Could we make it the twenty-fifth at nine, Your Honor?"

The judge nodded. "That works for me. Mr. Webster?"

"We would prefer an earlier date, Your Honor, but I have no problem accommodating Ms. Norcross." He glanced at her, and she smiled and mouthed, *Thank you.*

The judge made another note. "All right, the final item on our agenda is pretrial detention. Mr. Webster, is your client requesting bail?"

"Yes, Your Honor. We recognize that Ms. Legare is charged with very serious crimes, but every other factor argues in favor of pretrial release with an appropriate bond. First, she has no criminal history. None. Second, she has strong ties to the community. All her family is here. Her job is here. Her home is here. Third, she is the chief financial officer at Tupelo Grove University. That's a critically important role, and depriving the university of her services will harm its employees, students, and hundreds—if not thousands—of others who rely on the university."

Judge Hopkins shifted in his seat. He was up for reelection in less than a year, and he hopefully didn't want to needlessly antagonize a large chunk of the electorate.

"Finally, based on the foregoing, it's clear that Ms. Legare is not a flight risk. This is her home, and she will stay here to clear her name. We think a bond of one hundred fifty thousand dollars is more than sufficient. That's double the maximum bond for regular murder. But if Ms. Norcross disagrees, we'll work with her to find a mutually acceptable amount."

Hez sat down and turned to watch Hope. Bail was a long shot in any capital murder case because of the aggravating factors that separated that crime from regular murder. Still, if any capital murder defendant deserved bail, it was Jess. And if any prosecutor would agree to bail, it was Hope.

The judge turned to Hope. "Ms. Norcross?"

Hope gave Hez a look that he couldn't quite read. Sympathy? Doubt? At least she seemed uncertain, which he took as a good sign.

She slowly got to her feet. "Your Honor, there appears to be, um, some sort of misunderstanding or mistake here. Ms. Legare not only is a flight risk; she actually has a flight booked for the day after tomorrow. She has chartered a private plane from Birmingham to London, England. We discovered the charter documents on her computer this morning and confirmed with the airport just before this hearing. We cannot agree to bail under these circumstances, of course." She sat down, avoiding Hez's stunned gaze.

The bottom dropped out of Hez's stomach. This couldn't be true, could it? Hope must be the one making a mistake. He turned to Jess, whose face was set in grim lines.

"Mr. Webster, is this true?" the judge demanded.

Hez stood, his mind reeling. "I . . . Could we have a five-minute recess, Your Honor?"

The judge glowered at him. "Two minutes." He turned to the court reporter. "Off the record."

Hez sat and swiveled to Jess. "What's going on?" he hissed in her ear.

She gave him an icy look. "I said I had an important meeting. You didn't ask where."

"What?!" Several heads turned toward him. He took a deep breath and lowered his voice. "Why do you have to go to London?"

"I can't tell you that."

Hez barely resisted quitting on the spot and walking out of the courtroom. "If you can't be straight with me, Jess, I can't represent you."

She folded her arms and pressed her lips into a thin line.

"Okay, recess is over," Judge Hopkins announced. "Back on the record. Mr. Webster, is the defense still requesting bail?"

Hez didn't bother consulting Jess before he rose. "No, Your Honor. Ms. Norcross is correct. There has been a mistake."

"I thought so." The judge jotted another note on his pad. "That's the last item on my list. Are we done here?"

Hope half rose. "Yes, Your Honor."

"Yes, Your Honor," Hez said as he shoved his notepad into his briefcase. "We're done."

***

The Baldwin County seat of Bay Minette was a bit of a drive, but Savannah couldn't bear to wait at home for news of Jess's bail hearing, and she'd been too nervous to sit in the courtroom. She waited on the wall around the park fountain where she could spot Hez the minute he started her way from the nearby courthouse.

Her watch seemed to tick each minute off slowly as she watched mothers with toddlers stopping to smell the flowers scattered in beds around the park. Ella had loved flowers and couldn't pass one without pausing. Savannah glanced at her watch again. Surely the hearing was over by now. Once she knew how much bail she had to raise, she could decide what to do. A call to her father wouldn't be fun, but surely he'd help her.

She spotted Hez before he saw her. His tight jaw and flushed cheeks didn't bode well, and she rose with her hand to her neck. He spotted her, and the glacial expression on his face eased into a tight smile that didn't reach his blue eyes.

She bit her lip when he stopped in front of her. "Bail is high?"

"Worse than that. Much worse. Two counts of capital murder plus embezzlement. But that's not the worst of it. She booked a charter flight to London for the day after tomorrow and didn't tell me about it. I waltzed into the courtroom confidently, expecting to convince the judge she wasn't a flight risk, and was blindsided by her complete and utter stupidity. And when I requested a short recess to find out what was going on, she refused to tell me what the trip was about. Of course the judge wouldn't release her. I couldn't even ask him to do something so foolish."

"Why was she going back to London? She was there three weeks ago." Savannah wrapped her fingers around his forearm. "She has to *stay* in jail? Until the trial? That's months, Hez!"

His warm hand came down over hers with a comforting pressure. "Probably a year." His jaw flexed, and he shook his head. "Savannah, she did this to herself. I can't represent her if she isn't honest with me. I looked like a fool to the judge."

"I'll talk to her. Please don't quit, Hez. She needs you." Savannah wanted to say she needed him too, but it wasn't fair to put that kind of pressure on him.

Her phone rang, and she glanced at the screen. "It's Jess." She swiped it on. "I'm here with Hez, Jess. I'm so sorry."

"I need to talk to you right away. I got permission for an emergency meeting. Can you come right now?"

"I'll be there in a couple of minutes." She ended the call. "Jess needs to talk to me."

"Try to convince her to be honest about what's going on."

"I'll try." She paused a moment. "Thank you, Hez. For everything."

"Of course. You know I'd do about anything for you."

It was wishful thinking to read more into his statement than he meant. She removed her hand and took off at a quick jog toward the jail. Her heart thudded with every step. Capital murder *and* embezzlement. Was there more to what was going on than Savannah wanted to admit to herself? She pushed away the thought—this was *Jess,* and she loved her sister with her whole heart. She had to have been framed.

She could barely think as she gave her name and was ushered into the room with her sister. Jess looked pale and subdued in an orange jumpsuit behind the window. Savannah slid into the seat and reached for the phone as Jess did the same on the other side.

"Thanks for coming," Jess said. "I need you to do something for me. You have to fly to London since I can't go."

"London? What's so important in London that you'd wreck your chances of getting out of jail until the trial?"

Jess pressed her lips together, and her gaze searched Savannah's for a long moment. She tucked a strand of lank blonde hair behind her ear and wet her lips. "My son."

The blood drained from Savannah's head, and she felt faint. "S-son?"

"He's ten, and his name is Simon. He's at boarding school in London, and he has a break right now. I promised to pick him up on Friday, so you'll need to fly there on Thursday. You'll have to explain who you are. Tell him I'm sorry I couldn't come." Her words flew faster and faster. "You can fly over and spend a few days with him, then take him back to school. Don't tell him I'm in jail."

"You have a son." Savannah could hardly believe the words coming out of her mouth. "Wow. Who's his father? And why did you keep him hidden all this time—hidden from *me*?"

Jess folded her arms. "We can talk about that later. I need your help now."

"Why didn't you tell Hez about this? It might have mattered in whether or not you got bail. Jess, you aren't thinking clearly." Savannah shook her head, trying to make sense of this surreal situation. "Your son—Simon—can't go back to school. You'll be in jail for months. What about his vacations, like at Christmas and next summer? I'll bring him here."

Jess scowled. "See, this is exactly why I never told you. Erik can never know he has a son. He'll use it to try to control me, and he'd be a terrible father. Promise me you won't ever tell Simon or Erik."

Everything about this felt wrong. Savannah leaned closer to the glass. "Every child has the right to know who his parents are. I mean, I agree with you about Erik, but your situation is a prime example of how the truth always comes out. You knew Dad wasn't your father, and you pressed for the truth until you knew. Simon will too."

Jess raked her hand through her hair. "It can't come out now. Erik will use my situation to try to gain custody of Simon. You can't let that happen, Savannah. You just can't." Her voice rose to a frantic note.

Savannah pressed her palm on the glass. "We don't have to say who he is. I have very little contact with Erik. I can make this work."

Her sister's strange behavior with her son emphasized to Savannah the trauma of her upbringing. Jess had wrapped her cold strength around her as a shield against their father's snide comments. Savannah had tried to help as much as possible, but she was a child herself and could do little to buffer either Dad's narcissism or Mom's passionate recklessness. And Jess letting anyone know about her pregnancy would have felt like she was no better than their ruined mother. It would have confirmed Dad's opinion of her. No wonder she'd hidden it all.

Jess covered her eyes with her free palm. "You have to help me."

How could she? She needed to leave in two days. Was there enough time to find someone to cover her classes? "You should have told Hez. He's livid about being blindsided."

Jess dropped her hand and sighed. "I know. Please don't let him drop me. I need him."

"I'm not going to manipulate him for you. Apologize and work it out with him on your own. Hez is a good listener. Tell him the truth about the trip. He'll understand."

But from Jess's expression, Savannah wasn't sure she'd tell Hez the truth. And without the truth, Hez was flying blind.

CHAPTER 27

KNOTS TWISTED IN HEZ'S STOMACH AS HE WALKED DOWN the jail corridor toward the interview room where Jess waited. He knew what he needed to say, and he knew the conversation could get ugly. Firing a client was never easy, even if it wasn't his sister-in-law.

The guard opened the door for him, and he went in to face Jess. He sat down as the door shut behind him. She watched him from the other side of the table. She had a good poker face, but he could see the tension in her rigid posture.

"Might as well cut to the chase." He took a sheet of paper out of his briefcase and slid it across the table to her. "I'm withdrawing. Here's a list of four good criminal defense attorneys. I can vouch for all of them."

She didn't take the paper. "I understand why you're upset, but I need you to stay on."

He groaned inwardly. *Here we go.* "Jess, this isn't your decision."

"Just until the real killer is caught. As my lawyer you'll have access to all the evidence, right?"

"Yes, and so will your new lawyer."

"Savannah will try to catch the murderer on her own, Hez. I tried to talk her out of it, but she wouldn't listen. She could be putting herself in a lot of danger. I need a lawyer I can trust to help her." She grimaced. "I need you."

Savannah going after a killer on her own? The thought rocked him. She could easily wind up dead. She didn't know the criminal world like he did. He had allowed Ella to go off alone and find death. Could he live with himself if he let the same thing happen to Savannah? But how could he represent Jess if she kept key information from him?

He leaned forward. "Why didn't you tell me about that London trip? You humiliated me in court."

Her face hardened, but she nodded. "I'm sorry that happened."

"It can't happen again."

"It won't. I was caught by surprise, and I couldn't make alternate arrangements at the last minute."

He sat back. "Alternate arrangements for what? You still haven't told me."

She stared at him in silence. "I had a good reason for what I did. You'll have to trust me."

He arched his eyebrows and said nothing.

She rolled her eyes. "Trust Savannah then. Ask her if I had a good reason."

"Jess, the police have your phone, your computer, your emails, your texts. They have everything. And you have to assume they know everything. If you keep information from your lawyer, you're just sabotaging yourself."

She scowled. "I said it won't happen again. Besides, if they have everything and they have to give it all to you, that means you'll have everything too, right? So you don't have to trust me if you don't want to."

He hated to admit it, but she had a point. "Well, your chances of winning are much higher if you don't keep important information on a need-to-know basis. You're not a lawyer, so you have no idea what an attorney needs to know. As you saw at the bail hearing."

"How many times do I have to say it won't happen again?" A hint of vulnerability softened her mouth and flashed in her eyes. "You either believe me or you don't. Your choice." She leaned back and crossed her arms over her chest in a gesture that came across as more resigned than angry.

He watched her closely as she spoke and decided she was being honest—at least to the best of her ability. Jessica Legare had never been an open person, and he doubted that would change. Oh well. She wouldn't be his first client who had a troubled relationship with the truth.

In any event, he had no choice. Not really. He couldn't withdraw if that meant Savannah going after a murderer on her own.

He sighed. "Okay, I'll stay in. But the real choice is actually yours. Either you can be straight with me from now on and have a shot at winning, or you can get ready to spend the rest of your life as a guest of the state. Remember that."

And there it was, right where Jess told Savannah to look on the shelf in the walk-in closet. The Chanel leather vanity case was vaguely familiar. Maybe it had been their mother's, but Savannah couldn't be sure. She carried it to the bed and unzipped the top.

A picture lay on top. Afternoon sunlight streamed through the windows on each side of the king-size poster bed and illuminated the contented grin on the boy's face.

Simon. His name was Simon. And he wasn't just any ten-year-old boy—he was Savannah's flesh and blood. Her own nephew.

She struggled with a sense of rising rage and betrayal. Jess had cheated her of watching Simon grow and change. She'd missed his first word and first steps. She'd missed his first faltering attempts at reading and the enthralling attention a child brought to every new thing. Savannah had included Jess in every aspect of Ella's life, but her sister hadn't returned the favor. And the last ten years could never be retrieved.

Moisture blurred her vision. Simon had the same blond hair as Jess and Ella. He fit in their family like a missing glove suddenly found after years of searching. He would have loved Ella. In her mind's eye Savannah could see him holding out his arms for Ella to run into with her first stumbling steps. She could see him swinging her and pushing her stroller. So much loss stole the strength from Savannah's knees, and she sank onto the edge of the bed with the picture in her trembling hand.

Why, Jess? How could you?

She finally gathered her composure and went back to the drawer where she found the address of the school in London along with his birth certificate. She gaped at the date on his birth certificate. He was born on their mother's birthday. A fresh wave of grief closed her eyes.

Did he even know he had an aunt? How would he feel when she showed up to get him when he was expecting his mother?

She would soon find out.

She stuffed the items in her oversize bag and headed for the front door. Through the window she spotted Hez getting out of his vehicle. Had Jess told him the truth? Savannah hated the thought of keeping such a huge secret from him, and he wouldn't say anything to anyone about this.

She wasn't sure she could hide her agitation from him, but she opened the door. "Did Jess need something?"

He shook his head. "I went by your place, and when I didn't see your car, I came by here on a hunch."

She glanced at Jess's beautiful yard full of flowers. Maybe the sunshine and the scent of roses would settle her some. "It's a beautiful afternoon. Let's sit on the porch. I could use some fresh air."

He held the door open for her, and she went ahead of him to the comfortable furniture on the wide front porch and sank into a lone chair instead of the sofa. She didn't want to sit too near him in case he sensed the turmoil inside her. Hez was good at reading people—especially her.

He settled on the sofa. "Jess wouldn't tell me anything about the London trip other than it was for a good reason. Did she tell you what was going on?"

Savannah watched a hummingbird flitter from rose to rose while she thought through her response. "She told me, Hez, but she swore me to secrecy. And while I wish she had told you, I understand her reasons for keeping it quiet." She finally met his gaze and flinched at the skepticism in his blue eyes. She couldn't fault him though—when had Jess ever made things easy for him? Or trusted him?

She searched his face for clues as to how things had gone. "Did you find her another attorney?"

This time he fell silent for several long beats. "She persuaded me to stay on to represent her."

"I'm shocked."

"She made a good case for it. The main reason I agreed is that Jess and I are both afraid the real killer will turn his attention to you. You're tenacious, and you love your sister enough to keep digging no matter how much the police and I tell you to stay out of it. I'll bet you're planning where to investigate next, aren't you?"

All thoughts of finding the killer had flown from her head the minute she heard about Simon, but he couldn't know that. When she got back from London, she'd focus again. The motivation to find the real killer had gotten even more urgent now that she knew about her nephew.

She gave a jerky nod. "The police aren't investigating any longer. They believe they have the killer in jail. If Jess is going to be freed, someone else has to get to the truth."

"As her attorney, I'll have access to everything the prosecution knows. There's no need for you to investigate on your own."

"But I'm going to, so you might as well clue me in on everything."

He heaved a sigh. "You can be the worst bulldog in the world. Does Jess's London trip affect the case?"

"No. It's a personal issue, Hez. Very personal with absolutely no connection to the case. Jess can't let this get out or it will adversely affect someone she loves very much. But I promise you it has nothing to do with the two murders. I'm going to London in her place to take care of wh-what needs to be done."

This time Hez's silence stretched out so long Savannah thought he wouldn't answer at all. He pressed his lips together and speared her with a hard stare. "Be careful, babe. While you're sure it's not related, the killer could follow you since you'll be alone. I could go with you."

Her lips curved in an involuntary smile at his worry. "I won't be gone that long, and it's not necessary. You concentrate on getting my sister out of jail. I'll be back next weekend."

The concern in his eyes only deepened. "I wish you'd tell me what this is all about."

If only she could. This was a heavy secret to bear on her own, but Jess was depending on her.

CHAPTER 28

SAVANNAH SQUARED HER SHOULDERS AND PEERED UP AT the looming English manor. She'd looked up the history of the place before she boarded the private charter plane. Fairhurst Boarding School had once been owned by the Fairhurst family, and Adam Fairhurst built his fortune by trading in the West Indies. He had built the imposing manor to impress his beloved with his wealth and power. The move had worked, and Elizabeth had moved in six months after completion. Their heirs sold it in 1970, and the school was formed a year later after renovations were complete.

The imposing mansion in the countryside was an hour from the airport. She stepped out of the rental car and glanced around the impressive estate before heading for the door. The rolling green hills and woods around the estate made her feel she should curtsy at the ten-foot carved entry doors.

One good thing had come from the trip—she'd finished her manuscript about the Willard Treasure, and it was ready to submit for publication. She rang the bell at the door.

"I'm here to pick up Simon Legare for his break," she told the woman who opened the door. The brunette was in her twenties and wore a harried expression.

The woman hesitated. "You're not Ms. Legare."

"I'm her sister, Savannah Webster."

"Mr. Lloyd needs to speak with you in his office. This way."

Savannah followed the woman wearing a neat white blouse and navy skirt through massive halls, their footsteps echoing from the high domed ceiling. The sound of children laughing came from somewhere off to the right, and through the window she spotted boys playing soccer in a wide green field.

The woman opened a tall door and motioned her inside. "I'll let Mr. Lloyd know you're here." Once Savannah stepped into the waiting room, the woman closed the door behind her.

Savannah glanced around and spotted a few books on ancient Welsh history she wished she could dive into, but that would mean sitting down. She was too much on edge to think about perching on one of the leather chairs scattered around the massive room. She paced the gorgeous area rug in front of the bookcases. What would Simon say when she showed up? How did she begin to explain why she was here instead of his mother? The story they'd concocted about Jess having an important meeting seemed inadequate now.

A man in a gray suit opened the far door and approached her with an extended hand. "Ms. Webster, please step into my office."

She immediately sensed some strain in his demeanor and followed him into a much smaller room than she'd expected. The decor was almost austere after the lavish woodwork and arched ceilings in the rest of the manor. It held only a utilitarian desk and chair with two other chairs on the other side.

She perched on the wooden seat of the closest chair and fumbled in her bag. "I have a letter from my sister. She also should have contacted you personally to explain the change in plans." Her fingers closed around the envelope, and she yanked out Jess's letter authorizing her to take Simon. "Here you go. If you fetch my nephew, we'll get out of your way."

He pulled out the sheet of paper and read it, then folded it back up. "Ms. Legare called, but unfortunately, it came through in the middle of the night and she left a message about your arrival. I recognized her voice, of course, so there won't be a problem releasing the boy to your care." He passed over a folder. "Here is his passport. Simon is packing his things and should be with us shortly. However, there's a problem, Ms. Webster, a serious problem. Since I was unable to speak directly to Ms. Legare, she does not yet know of this situation. I'm sorry to tell you that Fairhurst is expelling Simon, and he will not be allowed to return after the break."

The breath left her lungs, and she tensed with her hands fisted. "I don't understand. He's ten. What could he possibly do to deserve this punishment?"

"Please don't think of it as punishment." He steepled his fingers in front of him. "He's run away three times. He's quite determined to make his way to the U.S. His unhappiness is dangerous to his well-being, Ms. Webster. If he was injured whilst in our care, we would be liable. And beyond that, Simon is a sweet boy. I'd hate to see anything happen to him. It's best for him to be with his mother right now. If his emotional state improves, we could reconsider having him back at Fairhurst. Really, it's for the best."

What was she going to do? Before Savannah could gather her thoughts, the door opened behind them, and she twisted in the chair to see a boy standing in the doorway. She drank in the first sight of her nephew. He could have been Ella's older brother. He wore a Pikachu backpack, and his blond hair fell across his forehead just like Ella's used to.

Mr. Lloyd brushed past them. "I'll leave you to explain everything to Simon." He shut the door behind him.

She found herself on her feet and moving toward the little boy. No recognition registered in Simon's blue eyes, and he took a step back at her headlong rush. He eyed her open arms, and she dropped them to her sides.

She tried for a lighthearted, cheerful tone. "Hi, Simon. I'm your aunt Savannah. You're so much like y-your mom." She wanted to say like Ella, but that would be even more confusing to him.

"My code word is *Savannah*." He studied her face. "Mum said she had an older sister. Why haven't you ever come to see me before?"

How could she answer that when she questioned it as well? "We have a lot to catch up on." Did he know he was being expelled? "I—I have a nice inn nearby, and you can show me around."

"Is Mum in London? Why didn't she come?"

"There's a lot going on back home, and your mom sent me in her place." Lame. How would she explain all this to a ten-year-old?

The even bigger question was what was she going to do with Simon?

"You'll never find what you're not looking for," one of Hez's early mentors liked to say. The forensic techs who processed Jess's

house hadn't found any evidence that she had been framed, but they hadn't been looking for it. Hez wasn't a tech himself, of course, but he had seen enough of their work that he'd know what to look for. Or at least he hoped he would.

He didn't currently have any evidence that Jess had been framed, but that was his theory of the case. It had to be. The evidence the police found at her house was overwhelming. Either it had been planted or she was guilty beyond a reasonable doubt.

The most damning evidence came from Jess's laptop and the grove of trees behind her house. Ed was working on getting a copy of the laptop hard drive for Bruno to evaluate for evidence of hacking. Jess had agreed to hire both of them without hesitation, despite the fact that she was already paying Hez fifteen hundred dollars an hour. She apparently had made more money on Wall Street than he realized.

Meanwhile, Hez was trying to trace the steps of someone planting evidence in the trees behind Jess's home. He parked on the side of the road behind her house, where his car wouldn't be visible to anyone in the home. He picked a spot as far from other houses as possible, where he would probably be out of range of Ring doorbells or security cameras. The road shoulder was asphalt bordered by grass, which unsurprisingly held no tire tracks or footprints.

The trees started about five yards back from the roadside—mostly loblolly pines and silver maples decked in brilliant yellow autumn finery. Hez guessed that meant water was nearby, and the faint burble of a stream confirmed it as he approached the tree line. He picked a spot where the growth seemed thinnest and carefully pushed his way in.

Ten feet in, a little patch of white caught his eye. A twig had been snapped off at shoulder height. The break was recent, though he couldn't tell how recent. A deer or wind gust might have done it, but it was a hint that he was on the right track. He snapped a picture of it and moved on.

The sound of water grew, and he soon reached a little creek. It was only a couple of inches deep, but it was too wide to step across and the banks on both sides were soft and muddy. His gaze scoured the ground, searching for any unusual marks.

Jackpot! A partial footprint on one side and a full one on the other, with the heel particularly deep. Someone had taken a running jump from one side and landed heel-first on the other. The prints appeared to come from a man's boots, but Hez would need to consult with a forensic podiatrist to be sure. He would also need to hire his own forensic tech to come out and do an independent investigation now that he'd found something to investigate. He pulled out a pocket ruler and photographed it next to each print.

Hez's heart rose as he continued toward the house. He doubted he could establish reasonable doubt in jurors' minds based on a snapped twig and a couple of footprints, but it was a promising start.

He reached the spot where the techs had dug up the evidence. Yellow tape still fluttered from tree trunks marking a broad triangle around the hole that gaped at the foot of an ancient willow oak with a trunk like a cathedral pillar. He was only a few yards from Jess's rose garden, but the tree was so wide that it completely blocked his view of the house—and would have prevented anyone in the house from seeing someone burying evidence here.

He snapped a few more pictures, but he didn't bother with a more thorough investigation. This little piece of the crime scene had already been thoroughly documented by the police department's techs and investigators, and he had their reports.

He noticed two things in rapid succession when he stepped around the tree. The first was Jess's garden. Two rows of rose-bushes ran along each side of a flagstone path that paralleled the back of the lawn—and they were due for a trim. Anyone walking directly from the house to the big willow oak would have to squeeze between the bushes, tearing skin and clothing in the process. The only other option would be to enter the forest on the other side of the lawn and go through a hundred yards of underbrush, fallen tree limbs, and leaf mold. He raised his phone to take more pictures—and then he noticed the second thing and froze.

Someone was in Jess's house. He caught a glimpse of movement. A figure in black appeared for an instant in one of the windows.

Heart pounding, he ducked below the top of the bushes. He called 911 to report a burglary in progress. Then he found a gap in the bushes and crouched down to watch. He recorded the scene on his phone, though he couldn't get much detail even with the zoom maxed.

The burglar reappeared upstairs in what looked like Jess's bedroom. The intruder wore a black ski mask, but he was broad shouldered and around six feet tall—so almost certainly a man. He methodically went through the drawers of Jess's dresser, but he only shot a glance to the jewelry box sitting on top of it.

The burglar stopped. He pulled a phone from his pocket and held it to his ear for a moment. Then he jammed the phone back into his pocket and ran out of the room.

Hez pushed through the bushes, fighting past the clawing thorns. He raced across the grass and around the side of the house. The intruder was nowhere in sight. A silver SUV roared away from the curb two blocks away, tires squealing. It sped down the quiet street, then turned a corner and vanished.

A siren wailed in the distance. Hez stood in Jess's driveway, waiting for the police. He was now convinced that someone had set Jess up, though he might not be able to prove it in court yet. But why had they set her up? And what was that burglar searching for?

CHAPTER 29

THE LARGE DOUBLE ROOM ON THE FIRST FLOOR OF THE
Swan at Streatley had a terrace that overlooked the Thames.
It was comfortable and charming with a bucolic view of trees,
flowers, and water. The thought of exploring the old Victorian
homes and thatched cottages in town would have been appealing
under other circumstances, but the decisions left for her to
make about Simon's future swept away any anticipation.

Simon was in the bathroom changing out of his school
uniform, so she sat out on the patio away from little ears. It
was one o'clock here, so it would be seven in the morning back
home. Hez's number was at the top of her recent calls, and the
phone rang twice before his deep voice answered.

She clutched the phone as if it were his arm she had in her
grip. "Hez." Her voice wobbled.

"Savannah, what's wrong?"

"Everything." She squared her shoulders. "The reason for my
trip took a very unexpected turn."

"Can you tell me about it?"

His calm demeanor settled her agitation, and she leaned
back in the chair. "I tried to call Jess, but they wouldn't put the
call through. I really need to speak with her."

"She's used up her call privileges for the rest of the week. You can't speak to her until Monday."

"That's too late. I need to know what to do. The situation here is not what she thinks." The dull ache in her head went up another notch. "Is there anything you can do?"

"I can ask for an emergency call, but I'd have to explain what's going on."

"I—I can't tell you. Not yet." The news would be all over town if Hez had to explain.

She exhaled and rubbed her forehead. "I'll figure it out. Thanks, Hez." There was no choice—she had to bring Simon back to TGU. "Good luck with the preliminary hearing. I'll be praying it goes well."

"Thanks." He paused. "Be careful, Savannah. I spotted a burglar searching her home yesterday, and I'm pretty sure she was framed for those murders. Someone is out to get Jess, and I don't know why. I hope it's not related to whatever you're doing."

She glanced toward the bathroom where Simon was changing. Could this have something to do with him? That made no sense—but then, neither did the fact that she was in England with a surprise nephew. She looked up and down the narrow cobblestone lane that paralleled the river. Nothing but a couple of elderly tourists taking pictures of swans.

"Everything seems safe, but I'll keep my eyes open."

Savannah ended the connection and stared at her phone. Without her sister's input, Savannah was on her own, and she'd never missed Hez's strong, thoughtful presence in her life as much as she did right now. Talking to him had helped, but this was still her problem to sort out. She called up her flight back to Alabama and changed it to Monday, then purchased another seat for Simon.

He came out of the bathroom in jeans and a tee. "I'm hungry."

His mood had elevated with every kilometer away from Fairhurst. He'd taken the news of his expulsion with an arm pump of exuberance accompanied by an excited, "Get in!" He'd spent the drive to the inn chattering to her about football—soccer to her—and science, and she'd chuckled several times at his English accent and slang. But questions about the future would be coming any minute.

She dropped an arm around his shoulder. "So am I. Do you want to eat here at the inn or at a nearby pub?"

He leaned into her embrace. "Our favorite chippy place. It's just down the way, and they have wicked fish and chips."

"Lead the way, kiddo."

He pulled on his sneakers—or trainers, as he called them—and they followed the enticing aromas emanating from the line of restaurants down the street to a modest pub with outside tables overlooking the Thames. Savannah asked for a seat outside, and they settled at a shady spot near the sound of rippling water. Birds sang overhead, and the tension in her shoulders began to ease.

Simon leaned forward with an intent expression. "Mum has to take me home now, doesn't she? I don't have anywhere else to go."

"Is that why you ran away?"

He nodded. "I want to be with Mum." His blue eyes pinned her in place. "Do you know who my dad is? Mum won't talk about him, but I have a right to know, Aunt Savannah."

His plea touched her, and she reached across the table to take his hand. "Simon, your mum is a private person. You probably already know that about her, don't you?" When he gave a jerky nod, she squeezed his fingers. "She's always been that way. Until two days ago, I didn't know about you. I think she loved you so much she wanted to hold you close to her heart without outside interference."

He frowned and shook his head. "But she only came to see me five or six times a year. I don't think she loves me at all. But if I'm living with her, it will be better."

"I know she loves you. She's been trying to protect you."

"That's mental. I'm ten now and big enough to take care of myself." He puffed out his chest. "I'm learning jujitsu."

She managed not to smile. "You're getting bigger every day, but a mother always worries about her kid. Your mum thought you'd be safe and happy at the school."

His chin jutted. "I'm never going back there. I want to be with my mum." His grip on her fingers tightened. "And with you."

"You will be. We're flying to the U.S. on Monday."

He cheered and she smiled. Warmth and love unfurled through her being. This boy felt like he'd always been part of her life, and her heart ached at the forlorn expression on his sweet face. How had Jess been with him? Warm and affectionate in ways she couldn't be with other people? She'd been that way with Ella, and this boy was her own flesh and blood. So what accounted for Simon's lonely eyes? Was it because his father was Erik, and Jess found it hard to forget that detail?

Savannah released his hand as the server approached to take their order for fish and chips. Her decision had been made for her. There was no choice but to take him back to Tupelo Grove.

Her phone vibrated, and Beckett's face popped onto the screen.

You flew to England without telling me??!

The outrage in that terse message stiffened her spine. What made him think she had to answer to him in her personal life? Maybe it was time to extricate herself from their friendship. Because that was all it was ever going to be, and she couldn't deal with his unmet expectations.

Hez wasn't happy when Augusta Richards walked into the courtroom and sat in the front bench, immediately behind Hope Norcross. He also wasn't surprised—she was the obvious choice to walk through the prosecution's case. But he hoped to persuade her to take a fresh look at the case when he had enough evidence, so he had to be careful not to antagonize her on cross-examination.

The side door opened and Jess appeared, flanked by her entourage of guards. The guards sat in the front row a few feet from Ed. Jess took her place at the counsel table with Hez. She gave him a curt nod. "Any news on the burglar?" she whispered in his ear.

"No," he whispered back. "The police don't have any leads yet. The only evidence from the scene was a forced side door. No fingerprints, DNA, or anything like that. He also managed to avoid every security camera in the neighborhood. This guy was careful. He also left behind a lot of valuables. Any idea what he was after?"

"Have you heard from Savannah?"

Her evasion irritated him. If they'd had more time and hadn't been in the middle of a courtroom, he would have pressed her to answer his question. "Nothing since we last spoke. She's coming back tomorrow morning, so I—"

"All rise," the bailiff said. They got to their feet as Judge Hopkins took the bench. Once the case had been called and the lawyers had made their appearances, the judge turned to Hope. "Is the state ready to call its first witness?"

Hope stepped up to the lectern and put a neat stack of notes on it. "Yes, Your Honor. The state calls Detective Augusta Richards."

Richards took the stand and the clerk swore her in. The detective seemed unruffled. Her long legs didn't jiggle or twitch, and her brown eyes held steady on Hope, waiting for her first question.

"Detective Richards, how long have you been a police officer?"

"Fourteen years."

"How many murder cases have you investigated?"

"About two dozen."

"Were you the lead investigator each time?"

Richards shook her head. "No, but I was the lead most of the time. Maybe twenty of those cases."

"How did you become involved in investigating the murders of Ellison Abernathy and Peter Cardin?"

"Tupelo Grove University doesn't have its own police force. They and the town of Nova Cambridge contract with Pelican Harbor for police services. I live in Nova Cambridge, so I generally handle calls from TGU. That's what happened when Ms. Legare's sister found Ellison Abernathy's body."

"And when she also found Peter Cardin's body?"

A cold tendril of unease crept into Hez's heart at the mention of Savannah's discovery of both bodies. He'd thought she was in the clear. Had he been wrong?

Richards nodded. "Yes, but I probably would have handled that case in any event because of the strong similarities between the crimes."

Hope turned to the next page of her notes. "Please elaborate on those similarities."

"There are a number. Both victims were killed by deep stab wounds to the back, which appear to have come from the same knife. Neither was robbed. Neither crime scene showed signs of a struggle, which may indicate that the victims knew their killers and were caught by surprise. And both knew Jessica Legare."

"Thank you." Hope glanced at her notes. "Was there anything else that caused you to suspect Ms. Legare?"

"Yes. On October seventh, the day after the Cardin murder, the police department received an anonymous tip through our website. It stated that Jessica Legare had been embezzling funds from the university and making blackmail payments to both Abernathy and Cardin. The tip was accompanied by a picture of Ms. Legare passing what appeared to be a large amount of cash to Cardin."

"What did you do next?"

"I obtained permission from the Abernathy and Cardin families to check the victims' financial records. These showed a series of unexplained payments ranging from one thousand to ten thousand dollars."

"When you say the payments were 'unexplained,' what do you mean?"

"They didn't correspond to salary payments, investment income, gifts, or any other known source. And when we asked the victims' families about the money, they had no idea where it came from."

"Did you also obtain financial records from Ms. Legare and the university?"

Hope's question was leading, but Hez didn't object. The rules of evidence didn't apply in preliminary hearings. She could lead, put on hearsay testimony, and basically do whatever she wanted—and the judge would let her do it at this stage. Things would be different during trial.

"Yes. TGU's records showed a number of transfers that were not accompanied by invoices or other documentation. University administrators confirmed that those transfers were not authorized. The transfers went into accounts controlled by Ms. Legare, who made large cash withdrawals from them. Those withdrawals usually occurred a day or two before the payments to Abernathy and Cardin."

"What happened next?"

"We received another anonymous tip. The tipster stated that Ms. Legare kept records regarding the embezzlement and bribery at her home. Also, the tipster claimed to have observed Ms. Legare burying something at night in the woods behind her house. We obtained a warrant and searched Ms. Legare's home."

"What did you find behind the house?"

"We located an area of disturbed earth among the trees at the back of her yard. We excavated and found a women's fleece jacket confirmed to have belonged to Ms. Legare. It had a large bloodstain. A double-edged knife with a six-inch blade was buried with the fleece."

"Did you send those items out for forensic testing?"

Detective Richards nodded. "Yes. We sent both items to the Department of Forensic Sciences lab in Mobile. DNA testing showed that the blood on the fleece came from Ellison Abernathy. The knife held traces of blood from both victims."

"Did you also find relevant financial records?"

"Yes. We located a laptop that contained an encrypted Excel spreadsheet, which we were eventually able to decrypt. The spreadsheet recorded payments made to Rat 1 and Rat 2. The dates and amounts of the payments matched the payments to Abernathy and Cardin. We also located books in her library with titles matching notes found on the bodies."

"What were those titles?"

"*Something Wicked This Way Comes* and *Death Is a Lonely Business*, both by Ray Bradbury."

Hope turned to the judge. "One moment, Your Honor. I think I'm almost done." She flipped through her notes, then looked up. "One final question, Detective Richards: Do you believe there is probable cause to support each and every element of each offense alleged in this complaint?"

"Yes."

"Pass the witness."

Hez stepped up to the lectern as Hope sat down. Richards didn't move, but her brown eyes became more alert. "Good morning, Detective Richards. I'd like to start with the search of the woods behind Ms. Legare's home. Did your team search the entire area?"

"We searched until we located the buried items. I believe the search ended at that point."

"So no one from your team could have left footprints along the stream that runs near the side of the wooded area farthest from the house?"

Detective Richards leaned forward a few inches. "I believe that's correct."

"And no one from your team would know whether any footprints were there at the time of your search?"

"Also correct."

"Turning to the laptop found in Ms. Legare's home, did you evaluate it for evidence that it was hacked and the spreadsheet planted on it?"

"No, we had no reason to."

"Ms. Legare's home was burglarized after her arrest, correct?"

"Yes."

"Did you consider the possibility that the burglary was related to the crimes Ms. Legare is accused of?"

"Yes, though it's not uncommon for burglars to target empty homes."

"Is it possible that the tipster and the burglar are the same person?"

"Possible? Certainly, but I'm not aware of any evidence indicating that."

"Well, the tipster had pretty specific knowledge of what you would find in Ms. Legare's home and financial records, right?"

"Yes."

"The type of knowledge that could only come from having access to her home and records?"

The detective thought for a few seconds. "I'm not sure that's the only possibility."

"But it's the most natural one, correct?"

She shrugged one shoulder. "I suppose so."

"And someone with that kind of access could plant evidence, right?"

"Possibly."

"Are you aware that before coming to TGU, Ms. Legare was a managing director at a Wall Street investment bank, where her average annual income was roughly one million dollars?"

"I knew she had been on Wall Street. I wasn't aware of the specifics."

"Were you aware that her salary at TGU is less than one-tenth of what she made on Wall Street?"

"No, I wasn't aware of her current salary either."

"Okay, let's assume those numbers are accurate. Why would someone like that bother embezzling from TGU? If she wanted more money, wouldn't she just go back to Wall Street?"

"I can't testify about her motives, just what the evidence shows she did. Criminals often do things that aren't very rational."

"That's true," Hez conceded. "But would you agree that, unlike the criminals you mentioned, Ms. Legare is a very rational individual?"

"I don't know her personally."

Hez took a quick look at his notes. He'd gotten everything he could reasonably expect. Hope would have a hard time later arguing that investigators made the footprints in the woods or that the prints weren't there when they executed the warrant. And Hez was pretty sure he had raised a few questions in her mind without antagonizing Detective Richards in the process. "Pass the witness."

Hope half rose. "No further questions, Your Honor."

Judge Hopkins cleared his throat. "All right. Any additional witnesses, Ms. Norcross?"

"No, Your Honor."

The judge looked at Hez. "Do you have any witnesses, Mr. Webster?"

"No, Your Honor." There was no point in putting on his case now. Hope clearly had enough evidence to meet the low probable cause standard, so he had no chance of winning today. Laying out his evidence now would only tip his hand.

The judge turned back to Hope. "Does the state rest its case?"

"Yes, Your Honor."

"The defense also rests," Hez added.

Judge Hopkins swiveled back to Hope. "Any argument, Ms. Norcross?"

"Yes, Your Honor." She rose and stepped up to the lectern. "May it please the court. The evidence establishing probable cause is overwhelming and uncontested. The defense does not dispute that the murder weapon was found on the defendant's property, that a spreadsheet detailing payments to the victims was found on her computer, or any of the other evidence put on by the prosecution. Rather, the defense apparently thinks there may be another explanation for this evidence, that the defendant was framed by some unknown person or persons. But that is irrelevant. The only question before the court is whether there is a substantial chance that Ms. Legare committed the crimes charged in the complaint. The answer is yes. Thank you."

The judge looked at Hez as Hope returned to her seat. "Argument from the defense?"

Hez stood and moved to the lectern. "Thank you, Your Honor. With great respect to Ms. Norcross, the question of whether Ms. Legare was framed is actually very relevant. If she was, then the true killer is still at large and my client is wrongly imprisoned. Otherwise, I leave it to the court to decide whether the probable cause standard is met here. Thank you."

"I'll give you the last word if you want it," the judge said to Hope as Hez sat.

She glanced at Hez as she stood. "Thank you, Your Honor. If Mr. Webster has evidence that the defendant was framed, he should present it as soon as possible. He did not do so today. He merely presented a hypothetical alternative to the prosecution's theory of the case. That is not enough to defeat a finding of probable cause."

The judge nodded. "All right. I find that there is probable cause to believe that the defendant committed the crimes alleged in the complaint. In light of the severity of those crimes and the fact that the defendant is a flight risk, she will be detained until trial. Is there anything else either side would like to discuss today?"

"No, Your Honor," Hez and Hope said in unison.

"All right, this hearing is adjourned."

Hez had seen this coming and had warned both sisters, but he still didn't relish telling Savannah that Jess would have to rot in jail for months. Now the real work of getting her acquitted began.

CHAPTER 30

THE SUNSET GLIMMERED OVER THE TOPS OF THE TUPELO trees when Savannah arrived with Simon at her cottage. Her nephew yawned hugely, and his blue eyes were glassy from jet lag as he glanced around the living room. Marley pushed his nose into the boy's hand, and Simon rubbed the dog's ears.

The weekend with Simon had filled a hole in Savannah's heart, and she loved seeing him in her private space. "Here's my little abode."

"I've never been in a house before—only apartments and the dorm at school."

Though he said the words in a matter-of-fact tone, the reality of his ten years of life struck her hard in the gut. He had no idea what normal family life looked like. How could Jess have done this to her own son? Did reputation and money mean so much to her?

Savannah let him wander around a few minutes, then got him settled in the guest room and told him to try to stay awake another hour or two.

"I'll try. I'm knackered." He dutifully got out his iPad, but his drowsy eyes told her it was unlikely he'd manage to keep away the sandman. Especially with the dog curled beside him.

When she returned to the living room, she spotted Beckett getting out of his car.

"Great, just great," she muttered. She was too tired for this tonight, but she met him out on the porch and somehow managed a cordial smile. "What a surprise. I barely walked in the door."

"I saw you drive past my office window." His face was red as he mounted the steps. "You never answered my text. What was so important that you went gadding off without talking to me? I've been helping you, Savannah. We're partners."

His gall left her speechless for a long moment. He had power over her tenure. She at least needed to be polite. "It was personal, Beckett."

"Too personal to tell me?"

He wasn't going to let this go, and she was too tired to rein in her rising anger. "I think we need to clarify things between us. I enjoy your friendship, but I think you're overreacting. Our relationship isn't the kind that demands I tell you everything I do."

"Friends? We've gone way beyond friendship, Savannah." He pointed his finger at her. "You led me on and made me think you found me attractive—that you wanted to be with me. I was thinking of a future with you."

The building rage on his face alarmed her, and she softened her tone. "Beckett, we've never talked about anything like that. I think you misunderstood. You've never even kissed me."

"I can rectify that." He grabbed her by the shoulders and yanked her toward him.

The pain from his grip made her gasp. "Let go of me!" Savannah's pulse raced, and she shoved against his chest.

He immediately released her and held up his hands as he took a step back. "Sorry, but you made me so mad." His hand shook as he swiped it through his hair.

"What's going on here?" Hez's deep voice came from her left side, and he bounded up the porch steps to reach them.

Hez's presence calmed her, and she finally found her voice as she realized this encounter with Beckett might have ruined her future. "Your friendship is important to me, Beckett, and I'd like us to get past what just happened. We can talk tomorrow when we've both calmed down."

He gritted his teeth and whipped around to stalk to his car. The engine roared to life, and he peeled rubber pulling away from the house. Savannah exhaled a shaky breath as Hez stepped closer. He enfolded her in his arms without a word, and she sank against his chest. The steady beat of his heart under her ear calmed her enough that her trembling finally stopped. Why had she signed those papers? She should have talked with him and told him how she was feeling, but something stopped her every time she tried.

She lifted her head. "I'm glad you came when you did."

His eyes narrowed and his jaw flexed. "It looked like he was manhandling you. Are you all right?"

She took a step back and nodded. "I had to clarify our relationship, and he didn't like it." She rubbed her upper arms, which throbbed where Beckett's fingers had pressed. She glanced down at the marks that would soon be bruises.

Hez frowned when he saw her arms. "Beckett did that?"

"Yes." Beckett's strength had surprised her. "He got so angry so fast. It was a little scary."

He looked over her right shoulder, and his mouth dropped open as he stared through the window into the living room. "Who's the kid?"

She checked to make sure the door was closed firmly. The house was tight, and it was unlikely Simon could overhear, but she took Hez's hand and led him down the steps to the yard and farther away from little ears.

"You're scaring me, Savannah. What's this all about?"

"The boy is Simon Legare—Jess's son. I had to go see him in England at his boarding school. I wasn't supposed to bring him home, but he'd been expelled for running away. Jess doesn't know yet. I'm going to see her tomorrow and tell her. Would you be able to stay with Simon while I tell her what I've done? You might want to brace for the explosion."

"I can stay with him, but I'm confused. Why would she hide him?"

"She doesn't want his father to know of his existence."

"Erik?"

"Yes. He's ten and a great kid." She tugged at Hez's hand. "Come meet him."

She led him into the house to the living room where Simon sat punching buttons on the remote. He glanced up with a smile that so reminded her of Ella's. At the sight of Hez's widened eyes, she knew he saw the resemblance too.

How did she introduce Hez? He was still her husband, though he'd be her ex the moment the judge signed the divorce decree. She shied away from the thought.

Hez didn't give her the opportunity to decide. He smiled down at the boy. "I'm your uncle Hez. It's good to meet you. I guess you and I are going to hang out tomorrow." He settled on the sofa beside Simon. "You a gamer? I can bring over my Sony PlayStation."

Simon sat up and didn't look sleepy any longer. "Brilliant!"

Hez launched into a list of the games he had, and Savannah watched with a bemused smile. Hez always had a natural way with children, and Simon would grow to love him like Ella did.

———

Savannah's gut knotted, and her hands trembled as she slid into the chair on the other side of the window, two spots down from the other occupants. Jet lag burned in her eyes, and it was all she could do to return her sister's tired smile. Jess might have an alternative to keeping Simon in Tupelo Grove, but if there was a solution, Savannah hadn't found it.

Jess's hair was in need of a wash, and the skin under her hazel eyes was so dark, she looked like she sported two black eyes. And no wonder. According to Hez, the evidence against her was overwhelming, and the prospect of spending months in jail had to be devastating.

Jess reached for the phone, and Savannah did the same. Jess's gaze darted around to make sure no one was paying them any attention. "How's Simon?"

Savannah leaned closer to the glass. "I didn't know what to do, Jess. When I got there, the headmaster told me he'd been expelled for running away three times."

Jess gasped. "What? Is he all right? Where did he go? Someone could have snatched him."

"He's fine. They found him right away, but the headmaster didn't mention how far he'd gotten. He's very unhappy at the school and wants to be with you."

"That's not possible." Jess swept her hand around the tiny cubicle. "Obviously."

"Mr. Lloyd tried to call you several times, but he didn't reach you." She'd rehearsed this a thousand times in her head on the flight home, but the second Jess learned what she'd done, Savannah would be dealing with nuclear fallout.

"Thank goodness you agreed to go. Did it take much convincing for him to let Simon stay on?"

"He didn't agree, Jess. I couldn't reach you—Hez said you'd used up all your phone privileges and he couldn't get an emergency call arranged without knowing why it was needed."

Jess half stood. "You told Hez?"

"No. I took Simon to the hotel for the weekend like you'd arranged, but I had no choice but to bring him home with me."

The color washed out of Jess's face, and she shrank into her seat. "Y-you didn't." She leaned forward, and anger flared in her eyes. "That's not possible. Tell me you couldn't possibly be that stupid."

Savannah held her sister's angry gaze. "I didn't know what else to do. I don't know anyone in London, and I had no authority to enroll him in another school. Jess, he's an amazing kid. I love him already. He wants so badly to be with you. This kind of thing can't go on. He's miserable."

"Other kids grow up in boarding schools. It's a common enough thing. You have to get him out of town before anyone sees him." Realization dawned on her face. "Who has him now?"

"Hez is with him at my cottage. He seemed the safest person to tell since he's your attorney."

"Take him to New York," Jess said. "His old nanny lives there. He loves her, and she'll be happy to take him. Her name is Sarita Barnes. Her contact information is at my house. Don't let anyone know Simon is here, Savannah. Erik can't know about him! He just can't."

Savannah frowned. "Then when you get out of here, you need to move back to New York yourself and live with him. No child should have to be raised by other people. He doesn't think you love him! You have to fix that."

Jess was shaking her head before Savannah finished talking. "That's not possible. I have to save Tupelo Grove."

"And a pile of bricks is more important than your own child?" Savannah shot to her feet and wished there was no glass separating them. She'd shake some sense into Jess. "I'd give everything I own to have Ella back in my arms. Nothing is more important than your son. He's your legacy, not that soulless conglomerate of buildings. Do you think anyone else here would sacrifice their child for the university? It's not worth it."

Jess pressed her lips together. "Just do what I say. We can talk about what happens next when I'm out of jail."

"That's going to be months away—if Hez can get you acquitted. Simon doesn't want his nanny. He wants his family, his mother. Let me keep him, Jess." Her voice trembled, and she cleared her throat. "He reminds me of Ella in so many ways. He's got her coloring and eyes. Until I saw him, I hadn't realized how much she resembled you. He's a wonderful boy and deserves to be with people who love him. We could say I'm his foster mother."

"Sarita loves him. He'll be fine with her."

A guard opened the door. "Time's up."

Not now! Savannah wanted to beg for more time to convince Jess, but the stony expression on her sister's face destroyed any hope of Savannah keeping Simon with her. The thought of sending him away broke her. She didn't want to be the one to tell him his mother didn't want him even now. He'd think Savannah had rejected him, too, and it wasn't true. They'd bonded so well the past few days. She could see a future with Simon—years of laughter and fun with a child in the house again.

The guard led her sister back into the bowels of the jail. Savannah exited into the bright Alabama sunshine, but even the sun on her arms failed to chase away the chill in her heart. Maybe she wouldn't tell Simon just yet. There was always a chance the nanny wouldn't want him to come to her. Maybe Hez could get Jess to see reason. Wouldn't the jury look at a single mom with a little more sympathy?

CHAPTER 31

———

"SO NOW YOU KNOW," JESS SAID AS HEZ SETTLED INTO HIS chair.

He dropped his notepad on the interview room table. "He's a great kid, Jess. I wish you'd told me about him. If you had, you might be with him right now."

She glared at him and folded her arms. "We already talked about that."

"Yeah, and then you ducked my question about the burglar when we were waiting for the prelim to start. I'll try again: Any idea what he was after?"

He saw a momentary hint of indecision in her eyes. She nodded. "I'm not sure, but it might have something to do with that ridiculous embezzlement charge."

Good—that was the main thing he wanted to ask her about. "Tell me why it's ridiculous. What's really going on with those weird financial transactions? Did someone actually hack into TGU and your bank and plant fake financial data, or is there something I need to know?"

"This will take some explaining." Little stress lines appeared around her eyes and mouth. "The basic problem is that TGU's books are a mess. I knew there were problems when I took the

CFO job, but the accounting system was much worse than I expected." She sighed and rubbed her eyes. "Actually, there was no system. The CFO's office had one software program and the student aid office had another, and of course they weren't compatible. The president's office kept its own records. So did the law school and the business school. The history department actually kept its records in old-fashioned ledger books—when they kept records at all. I'm not even going to tell you what the English department did."

Hez took notes as she talked. So far, her story rang true. He'd heard grumbling from law school staff about being forced to convert to a new accounting system and run everything through Jess's office. "That's all interesting—but I don't see how that relates to the embezzlement charge."

"I'm getting to that. When I finally got overall numbers that were more or less reliable, I got two unpleasant surprises. First, TGU's finances are very . . . delicate. There's no margin for error. If one bank decided to call even one loan, we'd be in trouble. I'm the only one who knows how bad things are. If word got out, all the banks could call their loans. We could lose our accreditation. It would be a disaster—we'd go into bankruptcy and probably never come out. You can see why I got a little defensive when you wanted to poke around in our books."

Hez nodded. He'd been uneasy about TGU's finances from the moment he set foot on campus in July. "Okay, but I still don't understand how that relates to you getting charged with embezzlement."

"That was the second surprise. I found a lot of stuff that wasn't on the books. For example, Ellison Abernathy's official salary was supplemented by money coming in from a private foundation in Birmingham. Funds would appear in an obscure account controlled by the CFO's office, then be withdrawn in cash and handed to Abernathy."

"That sounds fishy, to use a technical legal term."

"It is fishy. I'm pretty sure it was set up that way to evade taxes—and possibly to hide a bribe. Anyway, I've been gradually moving this stuff onto the books. I'm going as fast as I can without doing something that will get noticed by the IRS or our lenders, but cleaning up this mess will take years. In the meantime . . ." She shrugged. "Well, I'm stuck continuing some accounting practices I don't like."

Now Hez got it. "And that could appear to be embezzlement and blackmail payments if taken out of context."

"Exactly. Was I moving money out of university accounts and then handing envelopes of cash to Abernathy and Cardin? Yes. Was I embezzling or paying them hush money? No."

"I think I understand." Hez chewed on his lower lip as he went over Jess's convoluted story. "What about the spreadsheet on your laptop—the one showing payments to Rat 1 and Rat 2?"

"That's fake. Maybe the burglar planted it on an earlier visit."

"Maybe. He forced a side door last time. Did you notice any damage to your doors or windows?"

"No," she admitted. "Maybe it was planted remotely."

He jotted down a note to check with his computer expert, Bruno. "And why would the burglar have come back?"

"Probably because there's a lot of cash in the house, thanks to TGU's irregular finances."

"It sounds like whoever framed you knows a lot about this stuff."

"Well, they know about the payments to Abernathy and Cardin. Most of the department heads and administration veterans know at least something about the off-the-book payment streams—but I'm not sure who knows what."

Hez reviewed his notes. "Okay, that's all the questions I have right now—I'm sure I'll have more as I dig deeper. Is there anything else I should know?"

"Nothing I can think of." She held her hands palms up. "You know all my secrets now."

He doubted that was true, but maybe he knew enough to get her acquitted.

Ten minutes later, he was in his car and driving back to Pelican Harbor. He didn't love Jess's story, but at least he now had a defense for the embezzlement charge and an explanation for her payments to Abernathy and Cardin. It would be complicated to put on in front of jurors, and they probably wouldn't like the fact that Jess played along with shady accounting practices. They might be willing to acquit her, though.

But what would the cost be? Jess's comments about bankruptcy haunted him. Would he have to upend Savannah's life and destroy her family's legacy in order to exonerate Jess?

***

She didn't want to do this. Savannah gritted her teeth and punched in the old nanny's number Jess had given her. The call to Sarita Barnes began to ring through, and Savannah settled on the swing on her front porch. Marley lay beside her, and he growled when Boo Radley roared over at the pond. A breeze touched her face with the scents of moss and pine.

The longer she was with Simon, the more she wanted to keep him close and see him grow up. He was loving it here, too, and she'd even taken him out to the Gum Swamp late yesterday and shown him the platforms she and his mom had built in their swamping days. He was already thriving, and she was about to upend his life again.

The call got dumped to voice mail, and she left a message explaining who she was and that she was calling to see if Sarita would be available to take Simon. She clicked off her phone and heard something behind her, but when she turned, it was only a fox squirrel hopping off the porch.

Her phone sounded, and she answered it. "Good morning, Sarita. Thanks for returning my call so quickly."

"Good morning, Ms. Webster. Simon is back in the States?"

"He is. Jess would love you to take charge of him again."

"I wish I could. That young man is very dear to me, but I took another position a year ago, and I can't. I have a couple of friends who might be looking for a nanny position if you'd like me to inquire for you."

Savannah pressed her fingers to her forehead. A stranger? She would have to hand her nephew over to someone none of them knew? Surely Jess wouldn't want her to do that.

"Ms. Webster, are you there?"

"Sorry, yes, I'm here. I was trying to decide what to do."

"It may take a few weeks for me to find someone, but I will be very careful with any recommendations. I want Simon only with someone I could trust completely."

"Okay, see what you can find, and I'll tell my sister. I appreciate your help." After a few more pleasantries, she ended the call. Marley rose and stretched before nosing her. She wrapped her arms around his neck and buried her face in his soft fur. Even the best dog in the world wasn't going to make her feel better about this.

A car stopped at the curb, and she gasped. "Dad?" She jumped up and hurried down the steps to hug him. His familiar scent of pipe tobacco and lemon gumdrops enveloped her, and he looked as assured and handsome as ever, though his auburn hair had softened to brown with the years. He'd help—wouldn't he?

"How's my girl? We have the big game this weekend, so I thought I'd surprise you. That quarterback, Will Dixon, is setting new school records."

"I'm sure his mom is proud." She had to keep him out on the porch so he didn't see Simon. Jess would die if he found out she'd had a child out of wedlock. "I'm so glad to see you. Let's sit on the porch. It's a beautiful fall morning."

He inhaled as he followed her to the porch. "Ah, the scent of gardenias and roses. There's no place like Tupelo Grove." He stopped to pet Marley, who came to greet him. "Good boy."

An idea began to form as they settled on the porch chairs. She could stay at his condo in Pensacola with Simon. It shouldn't be hard to find a sitter while she worked, and she'd be out of the neighborhood without running the risk of someone spotting Simon.

"I've missed you. Hey, Dad, you still have your condo, don't you?"

"Of course. It's my sanctuary."

"I have an emergency and really need your help. Could I borrow it for a few weeks?"

His brown eyes narrowed, and he frowned. "Aren't you up for tenure here? You're not quitting, are you?"

"No, no, nothing like that. It's not something I can talk about. It would only be for a couple of weeks."

He shook his head, and a thick lock of hair fell over his forehead. "No can do, Savannah. I like my own space, and besides, it wouldn't be that convenient for you. I'm sure you can find something closer."

She hadn't meant she wanted to live with him, but she could hardly say that. Her initial bubble of hope deflated. "I understand." Dad's life revolved around golf, the occasional TGU board meeting, and his money.

He studied her face. "What's going on?"

While she frantically tried to come up with a way to deflect his question, his phone sounded. "It's Beckett. I need to take this. Let's do dinner one night this week." He swiped on his phone and ambled back toward his car.

Beckett. She still had to deal with his behavior too. What a mess she had on her plate. She watched her dad get in his blue sedan and drive away. No matter how much she wished she could forget how he'd treated Jess, reminders of his selfishness always surfaced. She needed to realize he was never going to change.

The door stood ajar when she went to the front door, and she frowned. Had Simon been listening at some point? She hoped he hadn't caught the gist of the conversation with Sarita. She called for her nephew and he didn't answer. His room was empty, and she picked up the iPad on his bed. The screen lit, and she saw a newspaper article about Jess's arrest. "Oh no," she said under her breath. She'd put off his questions, so he'd gone looking for answers.

She went back through the house again, calling for him. The refrigerator stood open, and the back door was unlocked. She hurried outside and called for him again. Her agitation mounted with every step. Had he overheard her plans to ship him off? If so, he might have run away again.

CHAPTER 32

HEZ LOVED DIRT. HE STARTED PLAYING BACK IN LAW SCHOOL during study breaks, and he quickly got addicted. So when Simon said he enjoyed racing games, Hez couldn't wait to go home and dig up all the Dirt he had. He'd managed to locate almost the entire series, which he now carried in a box with his PlayStation. Regrettably, Savannah had banned all of his war games.

He walked up the path to her cottage, humming a catchy theme from *Dirt 5*. He bounced up the steps to her porch and knocked on her door. It creaked open.

"Savannah?"

No response.

He set the box of games on a chair and pushed the door open. "Savannah?" he called more loudly. "Simon?"

Silence.

His heart hammered as he walked through the empty house, calling their names. It felt like the awful moments he always relived in nightmares, searching the empty house for Ella and finding the sliding door open.

The cottage's back door stood ajar. The familiar horror threatened to strangle him as he pushed it open. She'd been attacked once. He should have made sure she was using her security. Horrific images of finding her and Simon lying in a pool of blood ran through his head.

Please, God. Don't let it happen again.

"Savannah!" He stepped out onto the back deck. She was his whole world, and she had to be safe. He stopped and called her name again.

"Over here!" she called from a brushy area at the back of her property.

The tightness in his chest eased, and he jogged to her. He didn't even try to check his impulse to embrace her. She trembled against him and he buried his face in her hair. Holding her in his arms felt so right.

Let her go. He forced himself to drop his arms and take a step back. "Where's Simon?"

"I—I don't know." She hugged herself and he instinctively put a comforting hand on her arm. "I've searched everywhere. He's not here, and he's not answering his phone. I'm afraid he overheard me talking about sending him to New York and ran away."

"Where would he go?"

"I'm not sure. He doesn't know anyone here except Jess."

"Have you told him where she is?"

She shook her head. "No, but he figured it out on his own. I kept ducking his questions, so he got on his iPad and found an article about her arrest."

Hez winced. "Poor kid. Do you think he might be headed for the jail? I can ask them to give me a call if he shows up and hold him until we can get there."

Her shoulders sagged with relief. "That would be great. I'm so glad you came."

Her gratitude stirred a warm glow in his heart, despite the stress of the situation. He made the call. No blond ten-year-olds had shown up and asked to see Jess, but they promised to let him know if one appeared.

Savannah's brows drew together in a quizzical frown. "Hmm. How would he get there? He'd have to take a bus, wouldn't he?"

"Good thinking! Yes, two buses, I believe. I'll figure out the route and start checking stops along it. Maybe you should stay here in case he comes back." He hesitated for a moment. "Do you think we should call the police?"

Before she could answer, her phone rang. Her eyes widened as she looked at the screen. "It's him!" She answered and put the phone to her ear. "Simon, where are—?" She gasped and her face turned pale. "Stay where you are. I'm on my way." She ended the call and gripped Hez's arm. "He's in the swamp—a gator has him trapped in a tree!"

Pines crowded against the path Savannah and Hez had taken, and downy woodpeckers chattered angrily at them from the boughs. She paused to catch her breath enough to shout for Simon. Beside her, Hez waved away a horde of flies and added his voice to hers.

"About now is when you need an old-time southern tracker," Hez said.

She slipped her hand into the crook of his arm. "There's no one I'd rather have with me right now. He's only ten and he doesn't know his way around. Poisonous snakes and gators are everywhere. And mosquitoes and ticks." Her voice wobbled at all the things that could have happened to him. Wildlife might be the least of the danger. "We have no idea what tree he's even in."

"Try calling him again."

"I've tried three times. I don't have a good signal."

He laid his other hand on top of hers. "He's a smart kid, Savannah. Maybe he's heading for the jail to see his mom."

"Not right through the swamp. It would make more sense to catch a bus." She took a few steps and studied the trees.

It had been a while since she'd been in this small offshoot of the Gum Swamp, but she used to know every inch of its turgid waters. "Jess and I built a camping platform over a small pond back here. Simon was very interested in it, but I don't think he could have found it by himself."

"Seems a dangerous place for kids."

"It was more of a hideaway for us. When Mom would start drinking or take a pill, Jess and I would run off here so we didn't have to watch things spiral down. Dad would yell, Mom would cry, and we didn't know what to do. Out in the swamp we didn't have to know what was happening."

Her phone sounded, and Simon's picture showed on the screen. "It's him!" She swiped it on. "Simon, where are you?"

"Aunt Savannah, you have to come! I'm afraid I'm going to fall, and the gator will eat me."

"Are you on a platform?"

"I couldn't make it to that one you and Mum built, but I can see it from here. I'm on a tree limb."

She heard a gator roar as he spoke. "We'll be there as fast as we can. Stay on the phone and tell me when you see us."

Hez followed her when she turned and plunged through murky water. The mud encased her ankles, and she caught a glimpse of leeches beside a cottonmouth that slithered away. She shuddered and yanked her feet free of the muck.

Hez made a sound of disgust behind her, and she turned to see him fall onto one knee in the swampy water before recovering. He muttered and swiped a muddy hand over his face, leaving a trail of brown over one cheek and down his neck. Once she was sure he was okay, she plunged on through the swamp. The water rose above her knees, and she kept an eye out for gators. This was not the best situation, and she would have to check for leeches when she got out of here.

The bank on the other side drew nearer, and the water level fell to her calves, then to her ankles until she stumbled up the slippery slope of mud. Her feet gained purchase on the weedy dry ground, and she paused to locate the platform she'd built with Jess. There it was, ten feet to her left.

"You there, Aunt Savannah?"

"I'm near the platform, but I don't see you."

Hez slogged out of the water to join her. "Any sign of him?"

She shook her head as she scanned the treetops. He'd been wearing a green shirt this morning, which would easily blend into the remaining leaves. A movement ten yards away caught her eye, and she saw a gator under a tree. Simon sat in a fork of the tree and was waving his hand. "I'm here!"

"I see you." She ended the call and started that way.

Hez picked up some sticks and threw them at the gator. He then found a heavier branch and wielded it like a baseball bat, whacking the undergrowth and water as he approached the gator, shouting at it the whole time. It hissed and lumbered away. While he had the gator distracted, Savannah ran to the tree and reached up toward the boy. "Lower yourself down, and I'll help you."

Simon's tearstained face peered down through the leaves, and he nodded. He shut his eyes and hugged the tree trunk as he lowered himself toward her waiting arms. She grabbed his calves and helped ease him down to the ground. With a rock in each hand, Hez moved closer with his attention on the fleeing gator.

Once he was on the ground, Savannah palmed the boy's face. "What were you thinking to come out here alone?"

His gaze dropped away from hers. "I—I wanted to explore."

He was lying. She took a step back and held out her hand. "Give me your phone."

His blue eyes darted back to her face, and he bit his lip. He reached slowly into the pocket of his shorts and pulled out his phone. It didn't have a lock on it, so she was able to see what was on his screen with one swipe. It was the page for the public library in town.

She turned the phone around to face him. "What's this about?"

His chin came up. "I want to find my dad, Aunt Savannah. I thought maybe I could find something at the library. I'm ten, so my dad was dating Mom eleven years ago, right? I thought there'd be pictures or articles mentioning the school or my mum." He balled up his hands. "You should have told me about her. I know she's in jail."

"I saw the article on your iPad when you went missing. And you're right, Simon. I wanted to tell you, but I knew it would be hard to hear."

Hez moved closer. "I'm defending your mom, and we'll get to the truth. I know this is all confusing, but you have to trust us. No more running off, okay?"

The boy hung his head and scuffed a muddy shoe on the weeds. "Okay." His eyes were full of tears when he raised his head. "I haven't even gotten to see Mum."

"I'll see what I can do," Hez said.

But Savannah saw the doubt in his eyes. They both knew Jess would never agree to let Simon see her in that place. And there was no way she'd reveal her son to the community like that.

I stare at the insides of my eyelids, willing myself to sleep. I've barely slept the past few nights, and I need rest. A storm is coming, and I will need every ounce of energy and focus to survive it.

I try every relaxation trick I've ever learned. I clear my mind, focus on a peaceful place, and relax every muscle in my body one at a time. I even count sheep. None of it works. My brain insists on staying on high alert, attuned to every little night noise—even though I know that the hooting of the owl outside and the hiss of the wind on the roof mean nothing.

The real danger is miles away at TGU. I put it there, iron-ically enough. I planted the bomb that will bring down the whole rotten edifice. But somehow the fuse was lit too early, and now I'm trapped here, waiting for the explosion.

When will the bomb go off? That's out of my control—but it will happen soon. Savannah and Hez now have all the pieces to the puzzle. Once they manage to put them together, it will all be over.

Can they be stopped from solving the puzzle? That question has tortured me through many sleepless hours. Brute force won't work. That would simply draw attention from the cops who caught Hernando Morales and nearly got me. The last thing I need is an entire state-federal task force scrutinizing the same puzzle pieces.

I may be able to misdirect Savannah and Hez. If I can just point them in the wrong direction for long enough, it may be possible to salvage the situation. But I will need to know exactly what they've already figured out so I know what truths need to go into the lie I will tell. And I will need to tell the lie in exactly the right way at exactly the right time.

I can't just ask them what they know, of course. I'll need to be subtle. Just raising the subject with Hez could tip him off. If I play my cards right, I may be able to get the information I need from Savannah. She used to trust me. Maybe she still does.

All I can do now is wait for the right moment. And try to get some sleep.

CHAPTER 33

SAVANNAH SNEAKED A PEEK AT HER WATCH. TEN MORE
minutes. She turned the item on the table around to face her
class of fourteen students. "What can you tell me about this
artifact?" Her class had been engaged all year so far, and she
was determined not to lose the momentum in spite of the
problems facing her. Only a few more weeks and Thanksgiving
break would give her a chance to think.

The students gathered around the item and studied it for
several moments. Her brightest student, Dominga Steerforth,
swiped a lock of black hair behind her ear and shot up her
hand. "It's Mezcala stonework. I think it's andesite?"

Savannah nodded. "Time period?"

"Between 300 and 100 BC." Dominga's voice gained confidence. "Its provenance locates it in Mexico."

"Very good." Savannah shifted and glanced at her watch
again. If she ended class now, she'd have time to run to the
library before going to Hez's office to relieve him of his
babysitting duties. "Good job, and since you identified it
so quickly, I'm dismissing class a little early. Have a good
evening."

The students chattered excitedly on the way out, and Savannah grabbed her purse and hurried to her car in the falling dusk. She paused to check Simon's whereabouts. The app she'd put on his phone showed him still in the building where Hez worked. Was this a day he met with Will, Jane's son, for tutoring? If so, she had a little time. She could zip to the library, then gather Simon. Maybe Hez would agree to join them for dinner. She had chicken out for alfredo, and it was one of Hez's favorite recipes she made. She told herself she only wanted him to join them so they could discuss what to do about Simon, but she wasn't so delusional that she didn't recognize the rationalization for what it was.

She kept a close eye on the time as she parked in the Nova Cambridge Library lot and hurried inside. As she approached the desk, she pulled out her phone and found a picture she'd snapped of her nephew.

The librarian, a woman in her thirties, greeted her when she reached the desk. "Can I help you find something?"

Savannah extended her phone. "I know this will seem like a strange request, but have you seen this boy?"

The woman adjusted her round glasses and glanced at the photo. "That's Simon. He was in yesterday. He was working on some genealogy and asked to see newspapers. I showed him how to find the Alabama digital library resources. We have all those old newspapers and journals available digitally. He doesn't even need to come in here to access them."

Savannah tensed. "Was there a particular time period he asked about?"

The woman's brown eyes held curiosity. "He was particularly interested in 2012 to 2014. He printed off a page of engagement announcements."

Oh no. It had to be Jess's engagement to Erik. He was a smart kid, and he'd figured it out. Savannah thanked her and turned to leave.

Her phone dinged and she glanced at the screen, which announced a new charge on her credit card. An Uber? Hez wouldn't use her card to order an Uber, and besides, he had a car. She checked her app and watched a few seconds. Simon must have stolen her card, then called an Uber and gotten away from Hez somehow. No wonder the school had expelled him. The kid was a juggernaut of determination.

The icon on the app moved along Tupelo Street and turned on Pecan Street. The breath left her lungs. He was heading for Erik's house. This couldn't get any worse. Jess was going to explode when she heard about it.

Savannah shot a text to Hez. *On Simon's tail. Stand by. I might need help.*

Jess would absolutely kill her if Simon announced himself to Erik. As she drove toward Pecan Street, she prayed Erik was still teaching and she'd have a chance to retrieve the boy before any harm was done. She parked on the street and hopped out of the car. Mossy oak trees shaded the single-story house from the fading light, and she didn't spot her nephew until she rounded the south side of the house.

He stood at a partially open window, and when she called his name, he glanced her way before he shoved the pane up the rest of the way. He threw himself inside before she reached him, and she grabbed at his ankle but missed. She dove inside the house after him, and the fall to the hardwood floor knocked the breath out of her for a minute.

She struggled to her feet beside a queen-size bed. "Simon?" The room was empty, and she went through the open door into the quiet living room. She followed noises down the hall to the office, where she found Simon crouching in front of an open desk drawer. His back was to the door, and he thumbed frantically through a sheaf of papers.

"Simon Legare, what do you think you're doing? We are leaving now." She grabbed his arm, and he jerked it away.

He stood and turned to face her with his hands fisted at his sides. "I'm off my trolley at all the secrets! I have a right to meet my dad, Aunt Savannah. He doesn't know about me, does he? I don't even know who I am or where I came from. How would you like to live your life wondering if something is wrong with you that makes your own parents not want you?"

When his voice quivered, she saw through his anger to the pain driving him. "Oh honey, your mom loves you. You don't understand everything going on here." She took his hand. "Let's go. I'll see about getting you in to see your mom. Let her explain it."

Savannah had no idea how she'd get Jess to open up to her son, but her heart broke at the torment in Simon's blue eyes. He let her embrace him, and as she held him, she spotted a jade statue on top of Erik's desk. Her mind cataloged it as an Olmec figure. When Simon stepped back, she moved past him to pick up the piece. Jade was always a pleasure to hold, but even as her fingers registered the patina on the surface, she spotted a provenance letter on TGU letterhead. It identified the piece as part of the TGU collection and was signed by Professor Wilson

Fremont on behalf of the Tupelo Grove University History Department. There was no Professor Wilson Fremont.

Erik was behind this scheme? It was the only explanation for why the figurine was in his possession. He was a European history professor with no legitimate interest in the item. She pulled up the camera on her phone, snapped pictures of the jade piece and the provenance letter, then sent both pictures to Hez.

"Aunt Savannah?"

At the sound of Simon's voice, she realized they had to get out of here. Now. "Simon, we're in grave danger. Come with me." She took his hand and turned back toward the door.

But wide shoulders moved into view, and Erik's blue eyes pinned her in place. His gaze moved from her to the boy and back again.

Bruno Rubinelli said the words Hez had been hoping to hear: "Your girl was hacked. No doubt about it. And the rat spreadsheet is fake."

Hez and Ed exchanged a victorious glance across Hez's battered desk. Hez turned back to his computer monitor, where Bruno's face watched from a Zoom window. Sunlight played on his hairless head, and the sound of distant waves came through the speakers, so Hez guessed Bruno was enjoying the secluded California beach he was rumored to own. It was only a guess, though—the background behind Bruno was the logo of his company, Whacktastic: a deranged child holding an enormous sledgehammer.

Hez's phone buzzed with a text from Savannah—something about being on Simon's tail. What was she on his tail about this time? Simon had been behaving himself all day, as far as Hez could tell. The kid had been sitting in Hez's office, quietly playing on his phone for the past few hours, and he didn't complain when Hez parked him in a dingy empty room so they could meet with Bruno. Hez made a mental note to check with her later, but he had more important things to think about right now. If Bruno was right, this could give him the evidence he needed to exonerate Jess. "Great news! Tell me about it."

Bruno grabbed a can of Red Bull from off camera and took a swig. "Someone put a keystroke logger on her laptop about two months ago. I haven't figured out how they did it yet. She had pretty good security, but there are ways around that. Maybe a spear-phishing email from someone she trusted." He talked fast, and Ed scribbled furiously to get everything down. Hez was glad he had his intern taking notes. There was no way he'd be able to simultaneously talk to his computer expert and transcribe everything he said.

"Keystroke logger—that would have recorded her passwords, right?"

Bruno's head bobbed. "Yup. They got her passwords, and then someone got in and manually uploaded the rat spreadsheet sometime after 2:00 a.m. on October 16. They also removed the logger at the same time."

Hez's phone buzzed again, but he ignored it. "Are you absolutely positive it happened after that?"

"Yup. She backed up her laptop to the cloud every night. The last backup happened at 2:00 a.m. on October 16. That backup had the logger but no spreadsheet. The copy of her hard drive you gave me had the spreadsheet but no logger. Ergo, someone removed the logger and added the spreadsheet after the backup. QED," Bruno added with a flourish of his Red Bull can.

Hez sat back, his mind whirling. The police raided Jess's house on October 15, and they'd had her laptop ever since. Whoever planted the rat spreadsheet and removed the telltale logger almost certainly got to the laptop while it was in police custody. "Could the hacker have done that remotely?"

Bruno shrugged his thin shoulders. "Hypothetically possible but unlikely. They would've needed to install a VPN to do that, and I didn't see one in any of the backups. Plus, if the laptop was turned off, someone would need to physically turn it on first."

Someone in law enforcement had set Jess up. Savannah socialized with the chief of the Pelican Harbor Police Department, and her best friend worked there. Could his wife be putting herself in danger? Or maybe inadvertently tipping off the killers about the investigation?

He needed to warn her when she came to get Simon.

Erik crossed his tanned, muscular arms. "Savannah Webster." His gaze darted to Simon. "What are you doing in my house?" He still wore khakis and the red shirt Savannah had spotted him in this morning when he entered the history building.

Her tongue didn't want to unravel the circumstances of how she came to be standing in his home office, and she had to get out of here and call the police. Erik was the person behind everything that had happened, and she struggled to tamp down the fear souring her tongue. "I—I can explain."

Simon, blue eyes alert and eager, took a step toward him. "You have to be Erik Andersen, right? You were engaged to my mum."

Erik stiffened. "I'm Professor Andersen, but I don't know your mother." His blue eyes clouded with confusion. "Who's the kid? I've never even been to England. Who's he talking about?"

The suspicion on his face deepened, and Savannah took a step toward the door. She had to keep his attention away from the desk where she'd spotted the artifact. "There's been a misunderstanding, Erik. I'll take him and get out of your way. I'm so sorry for the inconvenience."

Simon jerked his arm out of her grasp. "Bollocks! I knew Mum didn't tell you about me." He took another step and reached toward Erik. "I'm Jessica Legare's son. *Your* son."

Erik's face went red, then white. His mouth sagged, and his square jaw tightened as he stared at Simon for several beats. "That's impossible, kid. Savannah, what's going on here?"

"My mum is Jessica Legare." Simon fumbled in his pocket and withdrew a folded paper from the pocket of his shorts. He unfolded it and shoved it in Erik's face. "You were engaged to her eleven years ago. I'm ten."

Erik's gaze roamed over Simon's face, and Savannah saw the instant it clicked for him. His eyes flickered, and he took a step back. "You're Jessica's son? She said . . ."

"She never told you she was having a baby, did she? She locked me away in a boarding school and never told me about my dad either."

Savannah winced at the pathos vibrating in Simon's voice, and she wanted to scream at her sister for what she'd done to this little boy. All of Jess's secrets had knotted into a tangled mess that just might destroy all of them. This man had orchestrated everything and had framed Jess for murders she didn't commit. He wouldn't allow his hard work to unravel now.

She licked her lips and seized Simon's hand again. "I'm going to take him home now, Erik. I don't think we should discuss this in front of Simon."

Erik's face flushed. "Jess *lied* to me. I always knew she was secretive, but this is over the top. Why would she have kept something this important from me?"

Savannah could have listed the reasons, but they would only inflame the situation and put her and Simon in more danger. She edged toward the door with Simon, who kept trying to tug out of her grip. "You need to talk to Jess about this, Erik. Simon is too young to take in all the layers of what happens in a relationship."

"So you're saying you agree with him, and he's really my son? Jessica has hidden him away for *ten years* and you let her?"

"I only found out about Simon myself last week."

Erik reached out and grabbed the doorjamb to steady himself. "Her own sister. She kept this secret even from you." He swiped a big hand through his hair. "I can't take it all in."

His gaze lingered on the boy, and a crafty smile lifted the corners of his mouth. Savannah could see the wheels turning as he realized what kind of leverage this might give him over Jess. She had to get Simon out of here right now. She took another step toward the door, and Erik's gaze went over her shoulder to the artifact on the desk.

His shoulders tensed, and his lips flattened. He reached out and closed the door before she could reach it. "I think there are some things we need to discuss."

Savannah's gut clenched, and she pulled Simon against her. *Please come, Hez.*

CHAPTER 34

WHERE WAS SIMON?

The kid wasn't in the room where Hez left him. Maybe he was in the bathroom. Hez had told him to stay put and not let anyone see him, but the meeting with Bruno lasted an hour and Simon had drunk both cups of root beer Hez got with a takeout meal of "Mac's and cheese" from Mac's. Simon had never tasted Mac's root beer before, and it was love at first sip.

Hez walked down the hall to the men's room. No one there. His stomach muscles tightened.

Maybe Savannah had picked up Simon early. He pulled out his phone and looked at her texts. Cold horror washed over him as he finally focused on what she'd said. She wasn't "on his tail" in the sense that she was mad at him—she was chasing him. And the pictures with the text *At Erik's house* made it only too clear where the chase led.

He dialed her number. "Please pick up, please pick up, please pick up!"

The call went to voice mail.

He jerked open the bathroom door and raced for the staircase leading to the exit nearest the parking lot. He took the stairs two at a time, almost falling on the narrow, worn steps. Then he was out in the pale November sun, sprinting for his car.

Nausea rose in him as he ran. He'd done it again. He was supposed to be watching a child, but he let work distract him as the child wandered into deadly danger. He had learned nothing from Ella's death.

He prayed he wouldn't be too late this time.

Savannah suppressed a shudder at the coldness in Erik's eyes. There was no other way out of the house but through the door he barred with his body. If only she had a weapon of some kind. She clutched Simon's hand, and this time, he didn't try to pull away. Even he realized the confrontation had segued into something more dangerous than telling his father about his existence.

Erik's jaw flexed, and he jerked his head toward the desk. "You searched my desk, didn't you? What have you and your nosy husband dug up?"

"Nothing. Like I said, I just came to retrieve Simon and prevent him from confronting you."

"I don't buy it, Savannah. That's a cover, and we both know it. You think if you can pin something on me, you can get your sister out of jail, but I won't be the fall guy for this. Spill it— what else have you dug up?"

"Nothing, Erik. I don't have any real idea of what's going on at TGU."

Her phone sounded with an incoming call, and she started to answer it, but Erik stepped forward and snatched it out of her hand. He held it aloft, and she caught a glimpse of Hez's face on the screen before he clicked the side button and sent the call to voice mail. When the screen went black, he tried to turn it on again, but it was set for face recognition. Erik gritted his teeth and swore.

Simon squeezed her hand, and he signaled something with his eyes she couldn't decipher. She gave a slight shake of her head. The last thing she wanted was for him to be in the direct line of fire for Erik's rage.

Erik's mouth twisted, and he stared at her. "You don't really know your sister and what she's capable of. Look what she's done to her own kid. Why do you think we broke up? She's got more secrets than the CIA." He clicked on the phone and put the screen in front of her face until it came on, then scrolled through her apps. "Let's see what you've been up to."

She watched him open her photos, and her fingers tightened on Simon's. Erik would see the photos she took of the artifact and provenance letter. When he swore again, she knew the situation was about to get worse.

Erik's scowl darkened, and he deleted the photos. "I think I'll have to call in the boss to find out what else you know. You have no one to blame but yourself. You shouldn't have poked your nose into things that don't concern you." He stared at Simon. "I'm sorry you're here right now, kid. It makes me seem like a bad guy, and I'm not."

Simon jerked his hand out of Savannah's grip. "Aunt Savannah is the nicest person in the world! You'd better not hurt her." He pointed at the phone in Erik's hand. "You deleted the pictures, so just let us go. She doesn't have any proof of anything."

Erik pulled out his phone. "Sorry, it doesn't work that way. She's nosed around too much. You can stay here with me, though, and we can get acquainted. Jess will have to cooperate now."

Savannah glanced around for a weapon again, but there wasn't even a lamp or a paperweight to use. As Erik called up a number, the door burst open behind him, and Hez rushed into the room brandishing a tire iron above his head.

———

Hez took in the scene in an instant. Faces pale, Savannah and Simon stood behind an expensive-looking walnut desk. They appeared to be unharmed. Thank God. Erik Andersen stood on the other side of the desk, half turned toward the door, his eyes wide with shock.

Andersen reacted first. He held up his hands, each of which gripped a cell phone. "Whoa, whoa. No need for violence."

Hez stepped into the room, keeping the tire iron cocked and ready to swing. "What's going on here?"

Andersen took a step back. "Breaking and entering, I think. But you tell me—you're the former prosecutor." He nodded at Savannah and Simon. "I caught them a minute before you barged in. I'm going to call the police on all of you." He started to dial on the phone in his right hand.

"He's not calling the cops," Savannah said, her voice tight with fear. "He's calling his boss!"

Hez tensed to bring the tire iron smashing down on Andersen's phone, but a better idea hit him. He nodded and pulled out his own phone. "Good, the state police can arrest both of you when they get here."

Andersen looked up from his phone. His finger hovered over the surface. "The state police?"

Hez nodded. "I have friends there. Former prosecutor, you know."

"I . . ." Andersen breathed a shaky sigh. "Look, we all need to talk."

"Why?" Hez pulled up the pictures of the letter and statue, then held up his phone. "We have all the evidence we need. You've been stealing artifacts from the Willard Treasure and forging the provenance documents. Cardin lost one of those, so you killed him." Andersen opened his mouth, but Hez ignored him. "We have video of you arguing with him, so don't bother denying it. You also murdered Abernathy to cover up your crimes. And you framed Jess for all of it."

Simon gasped. "My dad framed my mum?"

So Simon and Erik both knew the truth. That was unfortunate. "I'm afraid so, Simon."

Tiny beads of sweat glistened along Andersen's hairline. "You've got it all wrong. I didn't kill anyone, and I didn't frame Jess. I didn't steal anything either."

Hez flicked a glance toward the statuette on Andersen's desk. "Then where did that come from?"

"It . . . was brought to me. I don't know where it came from. I just get the artifact and write the letter—that's it."

"And you get paid, right?"

Andersen bristled. "I'm done answering your questions. And you really should stop asking them. If you don't, you'll wind up in a world of hurt."

"Where I'll join you, I guess." Hez smiled and held up his phone. "You just confessed to aiding the trafficking of stolen goods, and I recorded the whole thing."

Andersen's face went gray under his tan. "Turn that off!"

"Sure thing." Hez tapped the Stop button and saved the recording. "Just uploaded it to my cloud, which is password protected. I put Savannah's pictures there, too, by the way."

"What . . . what do you want?" Andersen's voice was barely more than a whisper.

"Answers. Let's start with who you were about to call when I came in. Who's this boss of yours?"

"I—I can't say."

"Sure you can."

Andersen licked pale lips. "No, you don't understand. He'll kill me. He already killed Cardin and Abernathy. He'll kill you, too, if you don't stop poking around." He turned to Savannah and Simon. "All of you."

CHAPTER 35

SAVANNAH FINGERED HER BRACELET AND TRIED TO CALM her racing pulse now that Hez had taken charge of the situation. A placating tone had replaced Erik's rage, but his warning about what his boss would do to them rang with authenticity. She stared at his frightened face a long moment before she moved to the desk and picked up the statue. The jade warmed in her hand, and she ran her thumb over the smooth texture.

Something about the artifacts had troubled her from the very first, and staring at the statue, she still struggled to decipher her unease. She picked up the provenance letter identifying the item as part of the Willard Treasure. This Olmec piece was exquisite and should fetch a high price. She should have recognized it and didn't. Why had she never seen it? She set it and the letter back on the desk and tried to figure out the questions swirling in her head.

Wait a minute. Olmec. Willard looted an Aztec city that had been abandoned soon after the Spanish conquest of Mexico. The Olmecs were the first known Mesoamerican civilization. They occupied the Veracruz area starting in 1600 BC until about 400 BC. And though the university had acquired a few Olmec pieces through the decades, there had been none in the Willard Treasure since it was a completely different time period. The Aztec civilization hadn't arrived in central Mexico until AD 1300, well over a millennium and a half later.

She stepped to Erik and held out her hand. "My phone."

He hesitated and glanced at Hez, who still held the tire iron ready. Erik shrugged and placed the phone in her hand, and she scrolled through the pictures she'd taken in the warehouse nearly three months earlier. She enlarged the pictures of the boxes and crates and studied them.

Then it hit her and she gasped. "Hez, this isn't part of the Willard Treasure. It's too old." She turned the phone around to show him. "It's not that someone is selling off the Willard Treasure. There aren't boxes and crates missing—there are too many! We had it all wrong. No one is stealing from the Willard Treasure—they're parking smuggled artifacts in the warehouse and writing fake provenance letters claiming they came from the Willard Treasure. They're using the Treasure's reputation to smuggle newly looted treasures."

Hez's blue eyes narrowed as he assessed her sudden insight. "An ongoing laundering operation, not just theft and embezzlement."

"Exactly." She turned her attention back to a wide-eyed Erik, who had begun to shuffle his feet. His panicked gaze shot to the door, but Hez and the tire iron still blocked the path of escape. "Who is your boss, Erik? You might as well tell us. Once Hez calls the state police, it will all come out anyway. They'll go through your bank records, your computers, everything. You can't hide it."

"I don't know anything. I just provide the letters—I don't know what he does with things after that. My role is too small for you to bother with."

Hez advanced toward Erik with the tire iron. "Tell us what you know."

His gaze zipping between Hez and Savannah, Erik shook his head. "You don't know what he'll do to me! You don't want to get involved either. He'll kill anyone who stands in his way." He broke for the door and tried to barrel past Hez, but Hez swung the tire iron in an arc that caught Erik under the chin.

Blood streaming from a small cut, he lurched back with his hand to his face before he stumbled and fell onto his backside. The force knocked his phone from his hand, and it flew across the floor to rest by Savannah's feet.

He pulled his hand back and stared at the blood smeared on his fingers. "I can't tell you more. He's a sociopath." His voice wobbled.

Who would paralyze Erik with so much fear? Savannah leaned over and grabbed his phone. She stepped to Erik's prone form and leaned over to hold the phone in front of his face to unlock it, then pulled up his call history. The number he was about to call before Hez arrived was at the top, and as soon as she saw the name, it all clicked into place.

Beckett Harrison. The provost was in a perfect position to handle all this. And after the way he'd reacted when she clarified their relationship, the title of sociopath made perfect sense. She turned the phone around to show Hez.

He stared at the name, and his eyes turned steely as he seemed to make the same connections she did. And they both knew they had no proof of anything. She hoped Hez had some kind of legal wrangling up his sleeve, because it would be hard to sleep tonight knowing Beckett was out there plotting his next move. And she believed Erik—Beckett might target Simon.

Andersen made his move while Hez was distracted by the phone. He bull-rushed Hez, sending him sprawling. Savannah and Simon screamed. The tire iron flew from Hez's hand and rang dully as it hit the hardwood floor. Hez scrambled away and grabbed for the iron.

Andersen lunged toward Savannah, snatching the phone from her hand. Hez lurched to his feet and raised the iron to defend his wife, but Andersen was running for the half-open door.

Simon started to run after Andersen, but Hez caught his arm. "Let him go. You'll just get hurt if you try to stop him."

Simon tried to jerk free. "But he's my dad! He'll listen to me."

Hez kept his grip as Andersen vanished. "That doesn't mean much. Not to a guy like him." Simon glared up at him, his face full of anger and pain. "I'm sorry, Simon. You deserve better."

A chilly breeze blew in through the open door and Savannah rubbed her arms. "Should we stay here until the police arrive?"

Hez shook his head. "It'll take a while for the state police to get someone here, and they probably won't do anything without a request from the DA's office. I'll give Hope a call as soon as I'm back in my office."

A little furrow appeared between her brows. "What about the local police?"

"They've been compromised." He told her about Bruno's findings. "I'm reluctant to involve them until I know who we can trust."

Savannah shivered. "Let's get out of here."

Hez nodded. "I'll walk you to your car."

She blinked in the autumn sun as they stepped outside. "Do you think they'll have enough to arrest Beckett?"

"I'm afraid not. The only evidence we have is our testimony that we saw Beckett's number on Erik's phone and a convoluted story about smuggled artifacts. That's not even enough to get a search warrant. It's not exactly probable cause to believe Beckett committed a crime." Hez sighed. "We'd need Erik's cooperation, and that's obviously not going to happen."

Simon snorted. "I can't believe my dad is such a git."

Savannah patted him on the back. "At least you've got a great mom."

"And she's the one in jail." Simon shook his head. "If we get some evidence on this Beckett, they'll let her out—right, Uncle Hez?"

"Maybe, but there's no 'we' in this, Simon. I'll handle it." Hez glanced at Savannah and added, "With your aunt's help, of course."

Simon frowned. "I can help too!"

Hez could hardly believe his ears. "Like you did today? You could have gotten yourself and your aunt killed—do you understand that?"

Savannah put an arm around Simon's skinny shoulders. "Hez is right, honey. What you did was very dangerous. You need to leave this to the adults."

Simon jerked free of her arm as they reached her car. "She's my mum!" He opened the passenger door without another word, got in, and slammed it.

The moonlight came through the slits in the blinds, and Savannah stared at the pattern of light and dark across her legs. That was like life—it alternated between joy and pain. Today could have gone in a very bad direction, and she was grateful Hez had gotten there in time.

Simon's deep breathing from the bedroom next door was a sweet reminder that God had taken care of them. Her nephew was safe, and she and Hez had weathered the storm together. More and more she felt the divorce paperwork she'd signed was the wrong direction to take. What would Hez say if she asked him to cancel it?

She rolled over and stared at the lit numbers on the clock. Just before midnight. Hez was a night owl, and she suspected he was awake thinking about the events too. She grabbed her phone from the nightstand and shot a quick message to him.

You awake?

Instead of an answering text, the phone sounded. She swiped it on. "That was fast."

"You okay? You're up late."

His deep voice soothed her agitation, and she sat on the edge of the bed. "I keep thinking about what might have happened if you hadn't shown up. I don't know where Simon and I would be right now if you hadn't busted in. You brandished that tire iron like a sword." Her chuckle ended in a hiccup she barely managed to keep from morphing to a sob. "I didn't know you had it in you."

"I didn't either. I usually do battle with words. This was a new experience for me, but I was so afraid, Savannah." He fell silent for a long moment. "I was scared I'd lost another child on my watch. It was like watching Ella's death unfold all over again. I should have had Simon stay in the room with me, but I was absorbed in work like usual."

When his voice wobbled, she rushed to reassure him. "Simon is old enough to play a game in another room. No one could have suspected he'd run off."

"The school would beg to differ." He chuckled, then exhaled. "I called Hope. She's going to have the Major Crimes Unit take a look at the evidence. I could tell she was very interested in Erik and Beckett. This might be our break. I've been up working on a package for her. I want to get it to her tomorrow while it's all fresh. I'm cautiously optimistic. She's a good DA and can utilize the excellent investigators on the MCU team."

"Does that mean we might get Jess out of jail?"

"Maybe. With the right breaks, we might have the real culprits in jail and Jess home by Christmas."

"Oh, Hez, that would be wonderful!"

"Don't get overly optimistic yet. There's a lot of road to travel before then." He cleared his throat. "I got your paperwork and filed it. You were gone to England when it came. I can leave as soon as Jess is free, and you'll be able to resume your life as soon as the judge signs the divorce decree. Paperwork is pretty backed up in that courtroom, but the judge should get to this soon."

Her tongue dried, and she clamped her lips shut. All she wanted to do was tell him she wanted to put the divorce papers in the shredder and have him move back in with her. She was beginning to think maybe he really wanted a divorce, and the thought made her heart shrivel.

"Savannah, you there?"

"I-I'm here. Listen, I'd better go." She ended the call and held her head in her hands. She wasn't ready for things to end.

She tried to lie back down, but her heart wouldn't calm in her chest. All the what-ifs echoed in her head. Tears leaked from the corners of her eyes, and she thrashed in the bed for another thirty minutes before sitting up again.

What should I do, God? She stared at the ceiling while she prayed, and a whisper of an answer came. *Truth.* What was that verse in 1 John? *"Dear children, let us not love with words or speech but with actions and in truth."* She still loved Hez, but she hadn't told him or been truthful with him about so much. So what if she was afraid? That didn't dictate how she should behave now.

A cool breeze touched her face, and she realized she didn't hear Simon's deep breathing. She went out of her bedroom to Simon's door. The breeze grew stronger, and the curtains moved at the window by his bed. She moved farther into the darkened bedroom and touched the mound on his bed. It was all sheet, pillow and comforter. No boy. She pushed the curtains aside and found the window raised all the way to the top. A box from the closet had been pushed in front of the window.

Simon had escaped again. No wonder the school expelled him.

Her hands shaking, she called up the tracking app. Her eyes widened and she gasped. He was at Beckett's house. How did Simon even know where that was? Had he somehow hacked into her contacts?

She shot him a text. *Simon, get out of there now!*

The message showed delivered, but he didn't appear to have read it. Had Beckett already found him? She checked the app again, but Simon's location no longer showed. She needed Hez. Before she could call him, she received an incoming call. The blood thundered through her veins, and she swallowed hard.

"Beckett?"

"Savannah, I have terrible news for you. I was about to call you and let you know that there was a boy in my yard, but before I could get to him, some very bad people in a black van grabbed him. I found his phone in the yard when you texted him just now. His name is Simon? I think I know where they're taking him, but you need to come here as quickly as you can. Don't call the police. That will just make things worse. Trust me and get here right away."

Trust him? She'd rather trust Boo Radley with a raw steak. "I-I'm on my way." She ended the call and rushed to her room to pull on clothes.

CHAPTER 36

HEZ'S PHONE RANG AS HE WAS NEARLY ASLEEP. HE LOOKED over and saw Savannah's face smiling at him from the screen. Why was she calling?

He hesitated for a moment before answering. She'd seemed upset when he mentioned the divorce earlier in the evening. Was she having second thoughts about ending their marriage? Or was she just avoiding thinking about something painful even though she knew it was necessary? What would he do if she hinted that reconciliation might be possible?

He sighed and shook his head. No, she'd made her wishes clear ever since he set foot on campus. He shouldn't overthink the situation. She was probably just calling about Jess's case or something.

"Hi, Savannah. What's up?"

"They kidnapped Simon!"

He bolted upright in his bed. "What? Who kidnapped him?"

She described her conversation with Beckett. "Should we call the police?"

He tried to force his brain to function. His mind went back to the time he called 911 to report a burglar in Jess's house—and the man got a warning call a few seconds later. "The last time I called them, someone tipped off Beckett immediately. If that happens now, he might kill Simon."

"Wh-what should we do? He's expecting me any minute."

"You can't go over there alone."

"I don't have any choice! If I don't go, he'll kill Simon."

The desperation and fear in her voice tore at him. He stared into the darkness outside, thinking furiously. He couldn't mess this up. He needed to make exactly the right move here. "Okay, but you're not going alone. Stay on the phone with me. If you have it on speaker, I'll be able to hear everything—and I'll record it. If you can get him to admit something incriminating—even just that he knows where Simon is—that will be enough to get the MCU or the FBI involved tonight. And once you have that admission, get away from him as soon as you can. You can say you need to use the bathroom and then go through a window— whatever it takes to get out of his house. I'll be parked around the corner as backup if anything goes wrong."

"Thank you! Are you ready to go?"

"Almost. There's one thing I need to do first." He went over to the closet and opened a small safe he kept there. He took out his Glock 22 and bullets. He prayed he wouldn't need them.

Though it was nearly one, lights blazed from the windows of Beckett's house. Savannah parked in his driveway and glanced into the shadows before she slid out and shut her car door. Her heart thudded against her ribs. She switched her call with Hez to FaceTime and kept the phone in her hand. The hooting of an owl drowned out the faint sound of her sneakers on the walk to the porch, but Beckett must have seen her headlights because he opened the door and stood waiting for her.

She went up the steps and stopped a few feet from him. "Where's my nephew?" The dark yard left her uneasy, and she edged slightly closer to the porch light's illumination.

Dressed in joggers, he reached toward her, then dropped his hand when she crossed her arms over her chest. "I know Hez has trash-talked me and you've believed him, Savannah. That's clear by the way you've both cut me out of the investigation. But the university is my life, and I've been investigating on my own. You won't believe the information I found. I was about to call you when my security camera alerted me to an intruder in the yard. I spotted the kid right off. He was skulking around in the shrubs at the front of the house."

That sounded like Simon. She gave a slight nod for him to continue.

"I think he was followed here. I noticed a panel van parked at the curb, and at first I thought maybe he stole it and drove it himself until I realized how small he was. I opened the door to call to him, and two guys charged out of the van and grabbed him. One of them pulled a gun and marched him inside my house."

So plausible. So truthful sounding. If she didn't know Beckett better, she might have been taken in by his story. "Did you recognize either of them?"

He shook his head. "They wore ski masks. The evidence I'd gathered was spread out on the kitchen table, and one of them gathered it all up. They took everything I had and took it to the van along with Simon." He stepped out of the way. "They tossed my house. See for yourself."

She went past him into the entry and spotted the disarray in the living room. Someone had pulled everything out of the storage spaces under the end tables and left it on the floor.

Beckett followed her. "They'll exchange him in return for any evidence you and Hez have collected. If you don't, they'll kill Simon. You also have to hand over your phone so they can search it. And they want you both to quit the investigation."

She moved farther into the living room and gave a furtive glance around. Maybe Simon was in here somewhere. "You think Jess is guilty, don't you, Beckett?"

He shrugged. "You have never seen your sister clearly, Savannah. She's got an ego the size of the Gulf. All she cares about is herself."

"That's not true!" She breathed in and out to calm herself. "Jess is no murderer."

"These guys mean business. Let's start by taking your phone to them." He reached toward the hand clutching her iPhone.

She took a step back and jerked her hand away. "Where did they take him? How are you supposed to contact them to give them any evidence?"

"They gave me a number to call. I'm sure it's a burner phone. Are you trying to get Simon killed? They've already had him an hour. If he annoys them, they may shoot him."

He was trying to scare her, and he was doing a good job of it. Every minute away from her nephew terrified her, and it was hard to think through the fear. "Could I see the video your camera took? Maybe I'll recognize them."

"I told you—they wore ski masks."

"I might recognize their clothing or their builds. Something might be familiar."

"You're wasting time, Savannah. The clock is ticking on Simon's life."

"I think you know more than you're saying, Beckett. Why won't you let me watch the video? Unless there's something you don't want me to see."

His eyes glittered, and his mouth flattened. He took a step toward her, and his phone rang. His scowl deepened as he answered it. He walked a few feet away and said, "Go."

He was too far away for her to hear what the caller was saying, but Beckett gripped the phone tightly enough that his fingers went white. He gritted his teeth and swiped off the phone before starting toward her.

She backed away and glanced around for a weapon. Nothing was handy in the living room.

He clenched his fists and turned to glare at her. "I told you these guys were dangerous, but you didn't listen. I told you to come alone, and again, you didn't listen. Now you'll have to pay the consequences."

Her mouth went dry. Did they see Hez parked nearby? "What do you mean? I'm here alone."

"You are now. They grabbed Hez too. And you're next."

Feet pounded toward her from behind, and she whirled to spot two men rushing her from the doorway into the kitchen. Her gaze went to the guns in their hands, and she began to back away. Beckett grabbed her by the shoulders, and one of the men yanked a black hood down over her head before marching her into the night.

CHAPTER 37

HEZ OPENED HIS EYES. HE WAS LYING ON HIS BACK STARING up. The moon peered down on him through a gap in scudding clouds. A cold wind blew drizzle into his face, and he shivered.

He started to sit up, but his vision swam and he felt like someone just drove a spike into the left side of his skull. He groaned and sank back to the ground.

Then it all came back to him: following Savannah over to Beckett's house, parking around the corner, straining to hear their conversation. He'd been so focused on his phone that he hadn't noticed anything wrong until someone jerked open his car door and yanked him out. Before he could reach for his gun, something slammed into the side of his head and everything went black.

Where was he—and where was Savannah? Fear sent his heart racing. He sat up again, moving more carefully. He was in an overgrown graveyard, sitting on a grave. The tombstone identified the occupant as Andre Legare (1905–1983). So he was in the Legare family cemetery. Why?

Hez got to his feet and tested his limbs. He was stiff and chilled to the bone from the rain, but he found no injuries other than an enormous lump on the left side of his head. He wasn't bound and no one else was in sight. His captors had apparently just dumped him on Andre Legare's grave. Again, why?

Someone moaned in the grass to his right. He staggered over and saw a woman struggling to get up with a cord binding her wrists. An ornate marble tombstone loomed over her, and a black hood concealed her face.

He pulled off the hood and damp auburn hair spilled out. "Savannah! Are you all right?" He saw no sign of Simon as he knelt to untie her. His head pounded so hard he fought nausea.

"I—I think so." She looked up at him with unfocused eyes. Then she seemed to come fully awake. Her eyes went wide. "Hez! What happened? And where's Simon?" Her voice shook and she glanced around wildly.

"I don't see him, but when you can stand, we'll search for him." He hugged her tight. "Thank God you're okay!"

She hugged him back, burying her face in his chest. They said nothing for a moment, drawing comfort from each other's embrace. How long had it been since she'd clung to him like that?

"I thought they were going to kill both of us," she whispered. She lifted her head. "Why did they leave us here?"

He hated to let go of her, but he helped her to her feet. "I was about to ask you the same thing. The last thing I remember is someone knocking me out on the street near Beckett's house."

"I think they got me right after you." She started to shiver. "D-did you get the evidence you need?"

To his surprise his phone was still in his pocket. He pulled it out and checked it. A welcome screen came up, and he stared at it, trying to think past the pain in his head. "It's been completely wiped and returned to factory settings."

She took out her phone—and it also had been wiped. Her hands shook, so he took off his jacket and wrapped it around her shoulders. The smile she gave him warmed him to the tips of his toes, despite the wet November chill. "Thank you."

He put an arm around her and she leaned her head against his chest. "Let's get out of here and find Simon. We need to figure out our next move, which we can't really do standing in the middle of a cemetery."

She nodded and cupped her hands around her mouth. "Simon!" The only answer was the startled flutter of birds' wings. "I can't bear to think what could be happening to him. He must be terrified." Her voice wobbled.

He'd tried not to think about the boy's fate. If Beckett had harmed him . . .

Hez started walking toward the cemetery entrance as fast as his unsteady legs permitted, and she fell into step beside him. "I'll call Hope as soon as I can get to a functioning phone. She might know who to trust in the Pelican Harbor Police Department, and if she doesn't—"

Savannah gasped and grabbed his arm. "Simon!"

Hez followed her gaze. Simon lay on Ella's grave. There was a package of candy on his chest.

They rushed to the grave, calling Simon's name over and over. Relief flooded through Hez when the boy opened his eyes and sat up. The candy slid off his chest as he got to his feet.

Savannah gathered their nephew into her arms and held him tight. Hez squatted down to get a closer view of the candy. Justin's peanut butter cups. The same candy that lured Ella to her death.

Moonlight bounced off the white gravestones and illuminated the bizarre scene they'd found. Savannah couldn't let go of Simon. He clutched her and sobbed with his face pressed against her. She wept, too, as she patted his back to try to comfort him until his shakes stopped and the sobs turned to hiccups. His hair smelled of mud and rain, and he shivered with the cold wind penetrating his wet clothes.

When his grip loosened, she pulled back with her hands on his shoulders and gave him a gentle shake. "What were you thinking going to Beckett's? You have to stop running off, Simon. You'll be the death of me. These guys aren't playing around!" She took off Hez's jacket and wrapped its warmth around the boy.

Simon pulled away and wiped his dirty, tear-streaked face on the arm of Hez's jacket. "I have to help my mum, Aunt Savannah. I thought he might tell a kid something he wouldn't say to someone who could get him in trouble."

Hez stepped closer and put his hand on the boy's shoulder. "What do you remember, Simon? Did he answer any of your questions?"

Savannah's first instinct was to protect Simon from being interrogated right now, but she pressed her lips together and let Hez handle it.

Simon crossed his arms over his chest. "I pounded on his door. When he opened it, I asked why he had framed my mum. He just stared at me and had this creepy grin. He said, 'You don't know anything, do you?' Then he waved at someone behind me. A guy in a ski mask picked me up and carried me to a van. He poked a needle in my arm, and I woke up here."

Simon shuffled his feet and looked down at a crunching sound. The bag of peanut butter cups was half under his left shoe, and pieces had spilled out of the crushed packaging.

Savannah bent down and grabbed it. "Where did you get this?" The sweet scent of the candy made her want to gag, and she dragged her thoughts away from the horrible memories.

Simon stared at the bag in her hands. "It's not mine. I'm allergic to peanuts."

"It was on your chest when we found you," Hez said.

Savannah's mouth went dry as she stared at the candy before she raised her gaze to lock with Hez's. "Who have you told about the candy?"

He shook his head. "No one knew. I mean, when the police showed up, I mentioned Ella had probably been headed for the candy when she fell in the pool, and they jotted it down. Did they ask you about it?"

"They never really said anything about it when they followed up with questions. So who else knew?"

Hez took a step back. "You're saying someone left the candy here as a warning?"

A glance at Simon's curious face made Savannah check her initial response. "I don't know what it means."

But she knew. They both did. Beckett was warning them that if they poked around, Simon might die. But how did Beckett know Ella had likely gone after the bag of candy? It wasn't something she'd talked about with anyone other than Hez. Not ever—even to Nora. Even she and Hez hadn't discussed it much after a couple of early fights about who left the bag where it would tempt Ella. Neither of them remembered leaving the bag out there by the pool.

So how had Beckett found out?

Hez exhaled. "Maybe a snitch in the police force gave him the file."

It would make sense, but it was a cruel thing for Beckett to reference. It showed her the true depth of his depravity. They were up against a monster.

CHAPTER 38

HEZ NEEDED TO BE MENTALLY SHARP, NEEDED IT MORE THAN he'd ever needed it in his life. Savannah, Simon, and Jess all depended on him outsmarting Beckett and his cronies. But Hez's postconcussion brain fog was so bad, he couldn't outsmart the lock screen on his office computer. He struggled with it for twenty minutes, until Simon looked over his shoulder and told him he had caps lock on. Hez had promised to keep the boy continuously in sight today, and he was glad he had.

When Hez finally got into his computer, he couldn't find his investigative file. He initially thought the problem was his inability to focus, but after a dozen fruitless searches, he realized the truth: His files had been erased. Everything related to the murders, the artifact smuggling, and the university's finances was gone. The online backup was missing as well. All the pictures Savannah had sent him had vanished, too, so he had no proof that there had ever been extra boxes in the warehouse or that Erik Andersen was in possession of a looted artifact. They were back to square one. Maybe even further back than that.

Hez groaned and leaned back in his chair.

Simon looked up from his phone. "Is something wrong, Uncle Hez?"

Hez gestured at the monitor on his desk. "They somehow got into my computer and deleted everything I had on your mom's case, plus a bunch of other stuff."

"Does your phone unlock with facial recognition?"

"Yes."

"Do you have remote access for your computer?"

"Yes."

"And you let your phone remember your passwords?"

"Yes."

"Then all they had to do was hold your phone up to your face to unlock it and they could get into everything, right? From there they could wipe everything, including your iCloud backup."

"Yep." Hez nodded slowly as he thought it through. "You're a smart kid, Simon."

The boy smiled at the compliment. "One of my mates used that trick to get into his mum's Amazon account. He nicked her phone while she was taking a nap, put it in front of her face, and ordered a VR headset for himself at school. We all had great fun with it until she got the bill."

Hez chuckled. "She must've been furious."

Simon nodded. "She took away his phone, his Switch, and his tablet. She even made the poor bloke wear one of those GPS trackers—the kind people put on dogs—for the rest of the term so she knew where he was every second, even when he went to the loo."

"Here in the States, we might call that 'cruel and unusual punishment'—though after last night, I can think of someone who could use one of those trackers."

Simon looked at his shoes. "I just . . . I want to help."

"Which is the exact opposite of what you did yesterday. Aunt Savannah said you'd be the death of her, and that was almost literally true last night. I'm surprised any of us woke up this morning."

Simon's reply was barely audible. "I know."

"We'll involve you whenever it's safe, but you have to trust us." Hez stood, drawing a warning tweak from his head. "Speaking of which, let's take a little walk. There's something I want to check."

The crisp air cleared Hez's head a little, and he enjoyed Simon's inquisitive chatter as they walked across campus. The one positive result of his nephew's penchant for running away was that there was no longer much point in keeping him hidden. He had already introduced himself to everyone who might want to harm him or use him for leverage. So there was no longer any reason not to show the boy the buildings named after his ancestors or spend a few minutes watching football practice, which Simon found fascinating, especially since Will Dixon was on the field.

Half an hour later, they arrived at their destination: the history department warehouse. Hez opened the door, using his university key card, and took Simon back to the room housing the Willard Treasure. As he'd expected, the extra boxes from Savannah's pictures were gone. He checked the security log and found that someone had entered the warehouse overnight using her key card.

The pieces finally fell into place. He sighed and turned to Simon. "I know why we're alive, kid."

Simon frowned up at him. "What do you mean?"

"Beckett and his friends didn't have to kill us to keep us quiet. All they needed to do was get rid of the evidence we'd discovered. Once they did that, killing us would have been counterproductive because it would have gotten the police involved, and honest officers might have been assigned to the case. As things stand now, all we have is a wild and completely unprovable story. After last night, we don't have a single shred of evidence that Beckett, your dad, or any of their friends broke a single law. It was the perfect crime."

And Beckett had the perfect patsy for his murders. If Hez didn't come up with some new evidence soon, Jess would spend the rest of her life behind bars—if she was lucky. If she wasn't, Hez would be defending his first death penalty appeal.

Savannah stood and examined the ground around her family grave plot. Last night had been terrifying, and she was still trying to wrap her head around what happened. They'd awakened in the old part of the Legare cemetery. There had to be a reason they'd been dropped here. She hadn't been able to sleep after they'd walked back, and coming to the cemetery again only ratcheted up her tension. Even the trees rustling overhead and the soothing sound of a wind chime a few graves over grated on her raw nerves.

She'd left Simon with Hez. If anything had happened to him yesterday, it would have been her fault. He was her responsibility, and she knew he had a habit of running into danger, but she had somehow let him escape. Again. She shuddered at the thought of living with that kind of guilt. Hez had carried that weight, and she hadn't lifted a finger to help him.

The more she saw of the new Hez, the more she regretted signing those divorce papers. He seemed settled and content about it, but something inside her soul shriveled at the thought of going through with it. She'd rationalized what *she* thought was best instead of asking God what she should do. And he was impressing the need for truth on her heart.

What would Hez say if she told him she'd changed her mind? And how did she even bring it up?

The crunch of feet on the oyster-shell pathway alerted her, and she turned to see Beckett approaching. She refused to show fear and stood to face him. What was he doing here, of all places? She said nothing as he walked toward her.

The smile on Beckett's face didn't reach his brown eyes. "Glad you seem fine this morning. Scary night, wasn't it? I was terrified for you, but fortunately I managed to keep you all alive."

"How did you know where I was?" When his lips tilted in a smirk, she fisted her hands. "What? You were watching me?"

"The campus has cameras all over, Savannah. It wasn't hard to figure out your location. It never is."

An unnamed threat was just under the surface of his expression and words. Bile rose in her throat at how he'd put Simon in danger. "What do you want?"

"Nothing much. Just ensuring you understand how important it is to leave the investigation to me, or future events might turn out worse for you. And Simon. I understand what's going on and how to handle it. You don't. Stay out of it."

"You don't need to threaten me."

"Is that what I was doing? I'm sorry—I intended merely to assure you I can handle things without any help from you or Hez. It was a close call last night. It took a lot of persuasion for me to avert an unfortunate incident."

Cold fear shuddered down her back. "Simon has nothing to do with what is going on at the university."

He shrugged. "You and I know that, but certain other people might not look kindly on him barging in where he isn't wanted. I hesitate to say this, but that put a target on his back. I have convinced those involved it was an aberration and it won't happen again. Will it?"

On that, at least, she could wholeheartedly agree. "Absolutely not!"

"Good. And you and Hez will leave things to me."

"I understand." But she refused to say they would stop. She couldn't—not while Jess was in jail.

"Does Hez?"

"I'll make sure he knows your demands."

"Demands?" He let out a theatrical sigh. "I'm just trying to explain the situation and keep you safe." He glanced at his watch. "I have class in half an hour, so I'd better get back to campus. Don't you have a class late morning yourself?"

Beckett's smarmy fake concern made her skin crawl. "I'm leaving shortly too."

He gave a satisfied nod, and she watched him move back down the path toward the picturesque view of the campus with its beautiful old buildings and green spaces. From up here the decay and urgent need for upkeep couldn't be seen. Beckett's true nature had been that way—handsome on the outside and rotten under the facade. He'd been very good at masking his true wicked nature. It sickened her that she'd ever considered him a friend.

When he disappeared down the steeper slope, she exhaled and started that direction too. There had to be some way to find the truth without putting her nephew in danger. Jess was facing a conviction for two charges of capital murder, and Savannah's greatest fear was that her sister would be sentenced to death. Maybe Hez would have an idea how to get Jess released. Once that happened, Savannah could whisk her and Simon out of Beckett's reach and get to the bottom of what was going on here.

So many things were riding on the truth. She'd read Ephesians 6:14 this morning in her devotions, and it had told her to stand with the belt of truth. More truth. Beckett couldn't silence her or frighten her. There had to be a way to bring the evil being done here to light.

Hez was sure hell had fluorescent lights—the kind that buzzed and flickered constantly. Like the one in his office. It had annoyed him for months, and the maintenance staff had ignored several requests for a replacement. Hez's concussion-induced headaches made the situation intolerable, so he decided to take matters into his own hands. He went to Home Depot, picked up a replacement bulb, and took it to his office. And that's how he discovered the bug.

He got up on his chair and took the cover off the light fixture—and a tiny microphone fell out. He stared at it for a long moment. His first instinct was to smash it and then search his office for more. Then he'd search Savannah's office, her cottage, and his condo.

He lifted his foot to crush the little spy, then stopped. Even if he was able to find and destroy every single bug, Beckett and his minions would just install new ones and hide them better. Or they might conclude that Hez and Savannah were continuing to investigate despite Beckett's warning and simply kill them.

He lowered his foot and gently replaced the bug. With a twinge of regret he decided not to replace the satanic light bulb. If he fixed it, Beckett might notice and realize that the bug had been found. Hez sighed and put the cover back on the fixture.

His office phone rang as he got down from the chair. The number looked vaguely familiar, but he couldn't quite place it. He picked up the receiver. "Hello, Hezekiah Webster."

"Hi, Hez. It's Hope Norcross. I'm calling to give you a heads-up that Erik Andersen has disappeared. The forensic techs found drops of blood on his living room floor, and his home was ransacked. Also, someone emptied his bank accounts around the time he vanished."

The phone was probably bugged, so Hez chose his words carefully. "Is the blood his?"

"I'm waiting on DNA results. I'll send you a copy as soon as I have them."

"Thanks. Do you agree that everything related to Andersen's disappearance is subject to disclosure because it indicates that whoever is targeting university employees is still at large, which undermines the state's case against my client?"

"Well, I'm sure you'll argue that. So I'm making this disclosure out of an abundance of caution to avoid any claim that the state is withholding exculpatory evidence." Hope paused. "And I was hoping you might be able to give us a hand. You said you would give me a package on Andersen and a Beckett Harrison. When do you think you'll have that ready?"

Hez winced at the mention of the package. That was the last thing he wanted Beckett to hear. He had to do some fast damage control and get her off the phone. "There won't be a package. Sorry. I, uh, misplaced the materials I was going to send you."

Surprise and disappointment mixed in her voice. "You did?"

"Yeah, I did. Hey, I'd love to chat, but it's been a rough couple of days and I was just about to head out for a run."

She was silent for several seconds. "You know, we used to go running together after work. Want to knock out a five-miler? Slowpoke buys coffee and beignets at Petit Charms."

She'd picked up on his hint. "That would be great. I'll meet you in half an hour outside your office."

CHAPTER 39

SAVANNAH STUFFED THE STACK OF PAPERS INTO HER BRIEF-case and motioned for Simon to follow her from the classroom.

"Are you chuffed? You're smiling."

She nodded. "I texted Hez to meet us at the beach."

She didn't dare say more. Hez had warned her he'd found a bug in his light, and she didn't want Beckett to realize they might have some evidence after all. No one would overhear them at the waterfront.

Simon chattered all the way to the beach. When they walked toward the water, she spotted Hez. He lifted a hand in greeting when they neared. His eyes were red rimmed and shadowed.

"Headache?" she asked.

He nodded. "Comes and goes in intensity."

She checked her impulse to embrace him, and her longing for him only increased her awareness of how much she didn't want the divorce. Once this was over, she would tell him how she felt.

He glanced around. "I checked on the security footage you asked about. My computer expert still had a copy, and I brought it."

Simon was listening with rapt attention, but she didn't dare let him out of their sight. He was as vested in getting his mother out of jail as they were. "Jess's fleece is the key."

His frown was an obvious attempt to follow her through the pain of his headache. "The one with blood on it?"

She stepped close enough to catch a whiff of his familiar cologne. "It was always in her office. The HVAC worked overtime right over her desk. She wouldn't have worn it outside into the heat and humidity. It had to have been stolen from her office."

"And the security footage might show it."

"Exactly." She gestured to a nearby bench on an empty beachside bike path. "Let's take a look."

The three of them moved to the bench overlooking the waves, and Hez sat between Simon and her. She leaned against him, relishing his warmth and closeness on the lonely winter beach. "It will take some time to review all of the footage." He pulled out his laptop and launched the file.

She leaned against him. "I'd guess someone stole it the night before we found Abernathy. Events unrolled quickly, and I think Beckett was boxed in and had to act fast to throw suspicion onto Jess."

Hez nodded and fast-forwarded through the video to 7:00 p.m. the night before Abernathy was murdered. "I'll run it at double speed, and we can pause it if there's any movement. This footage comes from a camera on the backside of the office building."

They watched in silence for half an hour as the camera picked up a rabbit and then a dog nosing through the shrubbery. The camera's time showed 12:02 a.m. when Savannah saw another movement, this one a figure. "Stop."

Hez paused the video and zoomed in to get a better view. "I can't make out his face with that hood over it."

"Me neither. Go forward slowly." The footage went frame by frame, and they watched the man enter the door with a key. He exited six minutes later, and this time the camera caught a good picture of his legs. He was wearing shorts.

"He's got something in his hand!" Hez froze the screen again and enlarged the picture. "Do you recognize it?"

Savannah clutched his arm. "It's her fleece. You can see the Goldman Sachs emblem. And look at the man's leg. Beckett has a scar like that on his knee. It has to be him."

Hez exhaled. "We've got him."

"I don't think so." A figure stepped from the shadows. Beckett's grim stare was punctuated by the gun in his hand. The barrel pointed at Simon's chest. "All of you get up. Slowly. No sudden moves or Simon is dead."

Savannah would have risked her own life, but she couldn't risk Simon's. Still clutching Hez's arm, she rose along with him. Simon glanced uncertainly at Hez before he stood and slipped his hand into Hez's. "Let the boy go, Beckett. We'll come with you."

"I'm afraid I can't do that. Remember, you brought this on yourself. If you'd just left it alone like I told you, this wouldn't have had to happen."

Hez needed to buy time. If he didn't, they were all dead. And he needed to get that gun pointed away from Simon. "Hey, Beckett!"

Beckett glanced toward him and the gun muzzle moved just enough. Hez stepped to the side and hurled his laptop at Beckett's head like a Frisbee.

Beckett ducked and the laptop sailed over his head and dug itself into the sand ten yards behind him. He smiled, but it wasn't the nice kind. "Nice try." He turned to his masked henchman. "Go get that. It's got evidence against us."

Beckett aimed his gun toward Hez as the henchman dutifully loped after the laptop. Savannah launched herself at Beckett, slamming into him before he could point the gun at her. A split second later, Simon and Hez were both on Beckett too. He gave a hoarse shout and fell backward under their combined assault. The gun went off.

Hez put all his weight on Beckett's right arm, forcing it to the ground. He put a knee on Beckett's right wrist and punched him hard in the jaw. Beckett went limp and the gun clattered onto the path.

Hez reached for the weapon. Just as his hand touched it, Beckett's henchman crashed into him. They both went sprawling. The henchman got to his feet before Hez—but Hez had the gun. Still on his knees, he pointed it at the henchman and gasped, "Freeze!"

The man froze, every muscle tensed.

Hez struggled to his feet. "Down! Lie on your stomach, hands behind your head." The man reluctantly complied, cursing under his breath. Hez turned to Savannah and Simon. They were both on their feet and seemed uninjured. "Are you okay?"

Savannah examined her limbs and took a tentative step. "I—I think so."

"Me too," Simon added.

Hez breathed a sigh of relief. Beckett's wild shot had missed all of them. Thank God. "Good. Call 911 and get someplace safe. I'll keep an eye on these two until the police arrive."

Savannah pulled out her phone. "I always have terrible reception here. I'll be right back. Come on, Simon."

The two of them headed toward the parking lot while Hez kept his gaze locked on the men on the ground. Beckett groaned and sat up. His eyes came into focus and went wide.

Hez trained the gun on Beckett's midsection. "Stay where you are."

Beckett spat blood and glared up at Hez. "You think this is over, don't you? It's not. This is much bigger than you could possibly realize."

"Oh, really? Well, maybe you can get some cooperation credit by explaining it all to the DA's office. If you're lucky, they might even agree not to ask for the death penalty."

Beckett looked past Hez, and his swollen mouth stretched into a lopsided sneer. "Oh, I'm lucky all right. And you're not."

Footsteps sounded on the path behind Hez. He started to turn—and caught a glimpse of a large, masked man carrying Savannah's and Simon's limp bodies over his shoulders. Before Hez could react, someone clamped a wet rag over his face. A sweet chemical scent filled his nose and lungs, and blackness took him.

Savannah's head pounded, and she licked dry lips as she blinked and tried to clear her vision. Why couldn't she move?

The drone of an engine penetrated her fuzzy brain, and she smelled seawater as she rolled over. The vibration of an inboard motor alarmed her, and she struggled up with her hands bound behind her.

The sun was low in the sky, but there was enough light to spot Hez and Simon prone on the boat's deck beside her. "Hez! Simon!" She pitched her voice in a hoarse whisper. She spotted the rise and fall of Simon's chest and his color was good so she knew he was alive, but Hez's pale face frightened her. Was he dead? She couldn't lose him too. He was positioned where she couldn't detect if he was breathing. She scooted toward him with her ankles zip-tied. Hez and Simon were also bound.

She leaned down to Hez's face and felt a puff of air from his lips. "Thank God, thank God." Her voice trembled, and she blinked back the moisture in her burning eyes. "Hez, wake up."

He muttered something, and his eyes opened. She stared down into the beautiful blue color that had anchored her for so many years. She brushed her lips across his. "I thought you were dead."

A crooked smile chased away the pain in his face. "You can't get rid of me that easy."

"I don't want to get rid of you. I love you. I tried to tell myself I didn't, but it was a lie."

His gaze widened, and he struggled to sit up. "I wish you'd told me that when I could move my hands."

Her chuckle ended on a sob. Being tied up aboard a boat meant only one thing. "Me too. I'd rather go overboard with your arms around me."

"You could kiss me again."

She started to lean down again, but a noise behind her brought panic surging in her chest, and she turned to see Beckett coming toward them with a pistol in his hand.

Simon stirred and woke crying. Savannah scooted toward him. "I'm here, honey."

"Ah, you're awake." Beckett motioned to cut the engine to the man piloting the boat. "You have no idea how much pleasure it brings me to see you both helpless." His cold expression changed to a grimace when his gaze went to Simon. "I wish the boy didn't have to pay for your mistakes."

"This is crazy!" Hez struggled to sit. "You can't just dump us overboard and let the sharks take care of the evidence. We'll be missed. They'll trace the gun and the boat back to you."

Before Savannah could shout out a warning or scream, Beckett drove his foot into Hez's abdomen. Hez's pale face went even whiter. His eyes closed briefly, and his jaw clamped shut. His throat worked and she saw his effort to contain a groan.

Beckett was breathing hard. "I've wanted to do that for a long time. But the best part of my plan is that *you* will be blamed, Hez. Your credit card is on record for the boat rental and the gun purchase. Poor, unstable Hez. He couldn't handle the thought of the looming divorce, and he went off the rails again. I'm not going to feed you to the sharks. I'm going to leave clear evidence of murder and suicide. No legacy, Hez. Just the sad epitaph of your instability."

"No!" Savannah struggled against the ties on her wrists. "No one who knows Hez would believe he'd hurt anyone."

Why wasn't Hez objecting or struggling? A smile pushed its way past the pain on his face. "You forgot one thing, Beckett."

Beckett barked out a derisive laugh. "And what's that?"

The noise of a loud engine pushed into Savannah's awareness, and a horn blared. Someone shouted, "U.S. Coast Guard. Stand by for boarding."

Hez's grin widened. "You forgot to search me. Raise my shirt in the back." Beckett stepped over and yanked up Hez's shirt to reveal a small rectangular box at his waist. "Jane, Augusta, and Hope heard every word you said."

Beckett took a step back as the Coast Guard swarmed up the side of the boat.

The bailiff cleared his throat. "All rise. The district court for Baldwin County is now in session, the Honorable Achilles Hopkins presiding."

Hez, Jess, and Hope got to their feet as Judge Hopkins limped up to the bench. He sat with a grunt and picked up his trademark yellow pad. "All right. We're here on the defendant's motion to dismiss in *People v. Legare*, is that correct?"

Hez nodded. "Yes, Your Honor."

The judge flipped through an accordion folder of papers. "I don't see an opposition on file from the DA. Was one filed?"

Hope shook her head. "No, Your Honor. We have determined not to oppose the motion. I apologize that we weren't able to make a decision before the filing deadline."

Hez resisted the urge to let out a victory whoop. Hope had hinted that there was an internal debate at the DA's office over whether to dismiss all of the charges against Jess or just the charges related to Abernathy's murder. Hez had filed a motion to dismiss to force a decision out of them. It had been a gamble, but it just paid off.

The judge put down the folder. "Okay, well, at least that makes today's hearing easy. Does either side have anything they'd like to put on the record before I enter an order?"

"The People do, Your Honor." Hope glanced at Hez. "We would like to thank defense counsel for assisting law enforcement in gathering critical evidence that led to the arrest of two very dangerous men and is about to result in the dismissal of charges against Ms. Legare. Mr. Webster wore a wire and deliberately put himself in grave danger to achieve justice. The People appreciate that."

Hez's face warmed as Hope spoke. He hadn't expected that little speech, and it left him uncharacteristically tongue-tied. "I, uh, well, thank you, Counsel. For my part I appreciate the DA's willingness to listen to my then-unproven story and devote significant law enforcement resources to investigating it. And I'm grateful to Ms. Norcross personally for realizing something was off during a routine phone call and inviting me to go for a run so we could talk in person. If she hadn't done that, things might have turned out much differently."

Judge Hopkins gave a broad smile. "And the court appreciates the professionalism and character shown by both of you. This is how the system is supposed to work. Case dismissed."

Hez turned to Jess. Tears pooled in her eyes and her voice was rough. "Thank you!" To his utter amazement, she hugged him.

Five minutes later, he was in the corridor outside the courtroom, phone in hand. He couldn't wait to tell Savannah the good news. But before he could dial, someone called his name.

He looked up and the clerk from the domestic relations court-room hurried toward him, carrying a sheaf of papers.

She held out the papers as she walked up. "Oh, good! I'm glad I caught you. I saw you had a hearing on today's calendar, and I wanted to get these to you before you left. I'm sorry it took so long to get them signed."

He took the papers, and his joy and excitement vanished like a candle being snuffed out. Judge Jefferson had finally signed the divorce decree. A black abyss swallowed his heart.

Savannah was no longer his wife.

He walked out of the courthouse and over to the coffee shop where Savannah and Simon waited. A brisk December breeze chilled him as he crossed the courthouse square. Christmas carols blared from storefront speakers.

Savannah stood up from a booth as he walked into the coffee shop, hope and anxiety battling in her eyes. Simon's face appeared around the edge of the booth.

Hez swallowed hard. "The hearing went as well as it could. The DA dismissed all charges. The jail should be processing Jess's release right now. She should be home in time for dinner."

Simon punched the air. "Yes! That's ace!"

Savannah threw her arms around Hez's neck and kissed him hard. He kissed her back and wrapped her in his arms, savoring the taste of her lips, the tropical scent of her hair, and the warmth of her body after the cold outside.

She finally released him and stepped back, her face flushed and happy. He hated what would come next, but he had to tell her. He held out the divorce decree. "As I was walking out, the clerk handed me this."

She took the paper and read it. The color drained from her face.

Hez glanced around. They couldn't have a private conversation about their future in the middle of a busy coffee shop while their nephew listened. "I'll text these to you. We need to talk. Let me know when you're ready."

He motioned to Simon. "Let's go get your mom."

CHAPTER 40

DIVORCED.

Savannah drove to Jess's house on autopilot and parked in the driveway. Hez had said nothing about how to fix this. Could he be relieved this had happened now? But no, she was being emotional. He hadn't wanted to discuss it in front of Simon, that was all.

Wasn't it?

Her heart warred with her head. Simon would be happy to see them living together again. Maybe Hez had used his presence as an excuse to examine his own feelings. A lot had happened since he showed up in her classroom asking for a second chance.

She shoved open her car door and got out with her phone clutched in her hand. The documents had pinged into her messages a minute ago, but she couldn't read them. Not yet. She spotted Nora getting out of her car to walk up the drive.

The wind blew Nora's brown hair around her face, and she poked her glasses up on her nose. Her smile faded when she reached the porch and caught sight of Savannah's face. "What's happened?"

When Nora hurried up the steps toward her, Savannah's control crumpled. She sank into her friend's embrace, and the comforting press of Nora's arms around her released the floodgate holding back her tears. Savannah sobbed against her shoulder until she managed to get a grip on her emotions. The familiar scent of peppermints and Nora's vanilla shampoo strengthened her as much as Nora's patting her on the back.

Nora's brown eyes were soft with concern when she released Savannah and stepped back. "I'm so sorry. I thought for sure the charges would be dropped."

Savannah swiped the back of her hand over her wet cheeks. "It's not that. Jess is being processed for release right now. I realized on the boat I didn't want the divorce. I still love Hez, and I thought he felt the same. But look." She thrust her phone with the decree on the screen into Nora's hand. "The judge signed the decree. We're divorced."

Nora glanced at the decree. "Let's get inside out of the wind. We can talk while we decorate for the celebration."

Savannah unlocked the door, and they stepped into the house. The place had a still, expectant feel as if it knew Jess would be home soon. "I should be focusing on Jess's release, but I can't think past this news." She sank onto the sofa and stared at the document on her phone.

Nora sat beside her. "You can always get remarried. What's driving this fear you have?"

A few minutes ago Savannah would have said she didn't know, but the truth bubbled up. "Hez tossed it back in my court again. He said we needed to talk and to let him know when I was ready. He didn't try to reassure me it would be fine."

"What did he say when you told him you loved him?"

"He said I could kiss him again, but he didn't say he loved me too."

"Maybe he wanted to show it. It sounds like you have doubts yourself. You both suffered such trauma. Are you worried you can't get past all of it for a true fresh start?"

Savannah slumped against the back of the sofa. "Maybe." She choked back fresh tears. Everything in her wanted Hez back in her life.

Nora squeezed her hand. "I can't tell you what to do. You and Hez will have to figure it out together. You could part on good terms and be friends."

Savannah shook her head. "I don't think that would work, not when I still love him. And I *do* love him, Nora. I'm not sure it's what he wants now, though. Wouldn't he have said something about getting remarried if that's what he thought we should do? Maybe our marriage seems like too much work. Jess's release today rested on his shoulders. He worked tirelessly to bring Beckett to justice. Rebuilding things won't be easy. We've been apart so long, and we're different people than we used to be. Grief has changed and reshaped us."

Nora fished a tissue from her purse and handed it to Savannah. "Life usually does, but we grow and adapt together. I don't think Hez has forgiven himself for Ella's death, and that'll make everything harder. You both have to be ready to face the demons from your past."

The past four and a half months had been full of trauma and fear. She'd hoped being truly with Hez again would help them both get beyond the past, but what if Nora was right and rebuilding caused more stress?

She shook her head. "I have to know what he's thinking. He said to let him know when I was ready to talk. I'm going to tell him to meet me at Ella's grave tomorrow morning."

Hez stood at Ella's grave with Savannah beside him. But he also stood at a crossroads all alone. If he stayed on the path he'd followed for the last two months, he would leave for Birmingham in less than two weeks. His contract at TGU ended in three days when he handed in his final grades. His lease ended eight days after that. And his marriage had ended yesterday. Everything he had planned to do here would be finished soon.

When Savannah heard about the decree, her white face and stricken green eyes had been his only hint of her feelings. Was she waiting for him to make a move—or was she relieved this had happened? Maybe those moments on the boat had been pure fear of dying.

Winter had turned the grass gray-brown, relieved only by a splash of color from the flowers Savannah brought. The little stuffed puppy he had left seemed cold and forlorn.

The inscription on Ella's headstone caught his gaze: *"For where your treasure is, there your heart will be also."* After his last visit to the cemetery, he had read the passage in Luke that it came from, so he now understood that Jesus had been talking about storing up treasure in heaven. Blake had told him it had nothing to do with his money but his actions. And Hez had no idea how that worked. Not yet. Blake had promised to help explain it, and Hez realized he was finally ready to listen, to maybe accept that God might forgive him. It seemed impossible, but what if it was true?

Jess paid him almost half a million dollars for representing her, so he now had enough seed money to start the Justice Chamber basically anywhere he wanted. Jimmy had even offered to let Hez use a couple of empty offices at Little & Associates, provided Hez was willing to consult for the firm in his spare time. It seemed like the ideal setup, except . . .

There was that crossroad. Or there might be a crossroad anyway. He needed to find out.

He cleared his throat. "Everything went wrong that day, and it kept going wrong for a lot of days after that. And it was my fault." He looked from the grave to Savannah. "I-I'm sorry."

She took his hand in hers. "You don't need to keep apologizing. It could have happened to anyone."

"But it didn't just happen—I *let* it happen because I was focused on my work instead of our little girl."

"You've changed. I see it every day."

"Have I? I've tried, but just the other day, Simon ran off when I was watching him. You noticed, but I didn't. I even ignored your texts saying that you were going after him. What if he had died?" He shook his head. "I love you, Savannah, but is that enough?"

She squeezed his hand. "It's enough for me."

The tenderness in her eyes overwhelmed him. His vision blurred and he stared down at Ella's grave. "It wasn't last time—and that still lies between us, doesn't it? I hid behind bottles and briefs until you couldn't take it anymore and left. How do we know that won't happen again?"

"But look at us now! You're not hiding and I'm not leaving. I've forgiven you, Hez. God has forgiven you. You don't have to keep carrying around the guilt of the past. Just let it go. You can have a fresh start."

He wanted to believe that, wanted it with all his heart. But he knew himself too well. "What if I mess up that fresh start, Savannah? What if I hurt you again?"

"Then I'll forgive you again. As many times as I have to. And you'll forgive me. I'm not perfect, you know." She took his other hand and turned him to face her. "Hez, you have a second chance. Right here. Right now. Are you going to take it?"

Something in him broke. It felt like a dozen steel chains snapping at once, or a dam collapsing and flooding a desert with life-giving water. He pulled her into his arms and she nestled against his chest. "Yes," he whispered in her ear. "Yes."

Boo Radley roared from down by Tupelo Pond, and she smiled as she looked up at him. "I think that old gator just gave you your marching orders." She wrapped her arms around his neck. "It's time you kissed me properly."

CHAPTER 41

THIS WAS THE MOST ACTIVITY IN JESS'S MANSION SAVAN-
nah had ever seen. With Jess and Simon's help, she'd decorated two live Christmas trees in white twinkle lights and
blue ornaments, and they reflected back the joy she felt inside.
The scent of pine and cinnamon mingled with the aroma of
cranberry-brie appetizers that a waiter had just carried past.
The many gifts for Simon were nestled under the main tree,
and small gifts for everyone in attendance stood under the
other tree.

People thronged the massive living room and spilled into
the dining and kitchen areas. Through the large windows and
patio doors that opened onto the deck, the beautiful golds
and reds of sunset settled into her heart. Everything was as
it should be. She'd even finished her book, so she could enjoy
the holidays without edits and research hanging over her. She
spotted Hez by the fireplace talking to Hope, Jane, Nora, and
Augusta, and she headed that way.

When she reached them, Hez took her hand and pulled her
into the circle of his arm. His blue eyes crinkled in a loving
smile. "Jane says I can stay in the condo as long as I like."

"I thought she wouldn't mind." Savannah leaned her head against his chest as his hand settled around her waist. "Where's that little cutie pie of yours, Jane?"

She gestured toward the smaller tree with the gifts. "Will and Reid have their hands full keeping Dolly out of the presents. We made the mistake of letting her open one today, and she wants *a-l-l* the packages."

Savannah turned her head that way and saw Will scoop up the little girl, who was dressed in a pink princess dress. "She's so darling." She felt only a faint stab of pain at the sight of Dolly's delight. It was as it should be. Ella was somewhere in heaven enjoying herself too.

Will was a strapping, broad-shouldered young man now, and he easily lifted his little sister to his shoulders while Reid watched with a smile. Dolly squealed and tugged on her brother's dark hair.

Simon had been Will's shadow all evening, and it felt good to see her nephew settle into life here. Once she'd been released from jail, Jess had said nothing more about sending him back to boarding school, and the two were already building a better relationship.

Hez's hold at Savannah's waist tightened, and his gaze lingered on the women clustered around them. "I want to thank all of you for working to find the true killer. Once a person is caught in the system, not every police department keeps digging for the truth. None of you discounted what we brought to you. Thanks to your desire for the truth, Jess is free to live her life with her son."

"It's a miracle." Savannah's attention was caught by genuine laughter ringing out from her sister.

Jess clapped her hands together and gestured for everyone's attention. "I'd like to thank all of you for standing with me. It was a hard few months, but this will be the best Christmas I've ever had." She nodded toward her son, whose joyous grin was brighter than the Christmas tree.

Jess picked up an armful of packages. "I have a little gift for you." She moved through the crowd handing out presents. Professors Hinkle and Guzman accepted their gifts with a solemn thank-you, and she moved on to Oscar Pickwick, the elderly guard who put his *Pokémon Go* game away long enough to tear into the wrapping.

When Jess came toward Savannah and Hez with their little entourage, her eyes misted. "Thank you all for never giving up, for digging into the truth. I'll never forget what you did for me and for the school. I have a chance to save TGU now, and I'll make sure the university is around for a long time."

Savannah left Hez's side long enough to hug her sister. Jess returned the embrace. "Thank you," she whispered in Savannah's ear. "I love you, you know."

"I know. I love you too." Savannah blinked back tears and unwrapped her gift to reveal an antique framed map of TGU's streets. "It's beautiful." She held it to her chest.

When Jess went back to gather another armful of gifts, Savannah took Hez's hand, and they moved to a quiet spot on the other side of the big tree. "She seems so much better, Hez. She told me she loved me."

"Who could *not* love you?" He reached out and pulled her close enough she could feel his heart beating against her ear. "This is a new beginning for all of us, babe. I intend to grasp my second chance with both hands and never let go," he whispered against her hair.

She lifted her head to stare up at him. Promises, commitment, and love were a steady light in his eyes, and she sent the same wordless message back to him. It didn't matter if they settled here or moved wherever God took them. They had time to figure out all the nuances of when they'd remarry and where they'd go from here. The past five months had wrought a miracle in their lives, and she was grateful, so grateful.

He smiled down at her. "Let's take a walk on the beach when this is over. I want to kiss you without an audience."

And there was nothing she'd like better. She tucked her hand into his arm. "I think we can duck out in about an hour."

EPILOGUE

I OPEN THE DOOR SLOWLY, TAKING CARE THAT THE HINGES don't squeak. Simon lies on his side, facing me. He's fast asleep, exhausted by the excitement of the party. Shafts of moonlight from his windows bathe his face in silver-white light. He looks like an alabaster angel.

I close the door with a soft click and stand in the dark hallway, unsure what to do. It's past midnight and my body yearns for bed, but thoughts whir around my head like electric humming-birds, and I know I won't be able to sleep.

I go downstairs to the now-empty living room. A few lingering embers glow in the back of the fireplace. The scents of woodsmoke, pine needles, and cinnamon mingle in the air—the smell of Christmas. The room is silent, but I can almost hear the echoes of the laughter and conversation from a few hours ago. I stand alone in the middle of the shadow-filled room, and I smile.

It was the perfect party—and the perfect lie. Every moment of the evening was genuine, but the event was deeply fake. This was not the celebration of a fresh new beginning for TGU, but the last note of its swan song. I almost expected a hand to appear in the middle of the party and write *"Mene mene tekel upharsin*" on my living room wall. Yesterday's secrets have grown into today's lies, and tomorrow's verdict is coming fast.

It's bittersweet to know this was the last Christmas party I will hold in this house. A year from now, I'll be gone and so will the university. It's almost completely hollowed out now, a decayed facade ready to collapse when touched by a breath of wind. And the wind that's coming will be a hurricane. My family has been waiting for this for generations, and nothing can stop it now.

Will Savannah get caught in the storm? I hope not. I engineered Tony Guzman's hiring and did everything I could to maneuver Savannah out of tenure contention—and if she doesn't get tenure, she'll basically have to leave at the end of the school year. And I no longer need to worry about Beckett trying to keep her here.

The thought of our former provost makes me chuckle. He pictured himself as the dashing mastermind behind everything and had no idea of the real game I was playing. My partners will make sure he keeps his mouth shut. He planned to marry a Legare woman to smooth his path into the university president's office. From there, he wanted to run for senator or governor, his campaign paid for by our smuggling profits. When I turned him down flat, he set his sights on Savannah—but I knew my sister would eventually see what a malevolent buffoon he is.

Still, Beckett was more cunning than I realized. He almost got away with framing me for two murders. If it hadn't been for Hez, I'd still be behind bars and Beckett would be the one enjoying the afterglow of a grand holiday party.

I'm grateful to Hez, but I'm not thrilled that he'll be staying. My former and future brother-in-law is too clever for his own good or anyone else's. With Beckett and his puppet, Deke Willard, behind bars, everyone will assume our little operation has been wrapped up with a Christmas bow—and Beckett and Deke are smart enough not to say otherwise. But Hez is sharp enough to see the loose ends on that bow and start pulling on them. Hez needs to leave as soon as possible, and he needs to take Savannah with him.

I frown at the thought of Hez taking my sister away from me. He's always been an intruder in our relationship, and he hurt her badly the last time they were together. If he does it again . . .

No, I won't worry about that. Not tonight.

I take a deep breath and blow it out slowly, forcing my muscles to relax one by one. Today is a good day. I can't lose sight of that. I am in a good place now—much better than I had any right to expect a month ago. I am free. Beckett is in jail. Erik is gone, so I can finally have Simon with me. Even that old grifter Ellison Abernathy is gone. I can rebuild the TGU side of the operation entirely on my own terms. Our friend in the police department is a bit of a wild card but one that can be managed.

I yawn and discover that I am finally tired. I go back upstairs to read myself to sleep. I curl up in bed and pick up an old favorite I've read a dozen times: *Death Is a Lonely Business.*

A NOTE FROM THE AUTHORS

___

DEAR READER,

The book you hold in your hands is such a labor of love for both of us, and we wanted to tell you the story of how our partnership began.

In the summer of 2021 I (Colleen) got an email from Rick as follows. *Hi, Colleen. Oddball question for you: Do you play Pokémon Go? I do it with my kids, and the game just suggested that I send you a friend request, which implies that you play too. True?* ☺ *—Rick*

We've been friends for years and have served on the American Christian Fiction Writers board together for a long time, but I didn't know much about *Pokémon Go* other than my grandsons wanted me to play. Thus began getting to know my longtime friend in a new way. I saw his kindness and patience with me and my family as we learned this new game, and we exchanged many emails a week with our fun new pastime.

I had always wanted to write a legal suspense, but I knew I didn't have the knowledge to make it authentic. The idea of cowriting had been fermenting a while, but cowriting can be tricky—you can start off as friends and end up hating each other by the time it's all over. But I really felt God was nudging me and that I should listen. After praying about it for a while I sent Rick this message on May 25, 2022: *I know this might sound crazy but what would you think about the two of us cowriting a new series? I really love your writing and I just thought it might be fun. No pressure if cowriting isn't something you've ever thought of doing.*

Rick's response: *Wow!! I'm incredibly flattered! You're right—I hadn't thought of cowriting, but I can't think of anyone I'd rather do it with! I'd love to explore the idea! Did you have anything in particular in mind?* I was the one who was flattered he'd even consider it! Rick leads a team in the California Attorney General's Corporate Fraud Section. He's racked up over $1 billion in wins and has had cases on the front of every major newspaper. But more than that, he's a terrific writer, and I've always loved his books.

And so we embarked on the most fun we've ever had with writing. Our joint writing process is something we call Plantsing because it's a mixture of Rick's plotting and my seat-of-the-pants intuition about where the story should go. I would veer us off course and Rick would immediately embrace the added layer. Such fun to discover our story together! Our partnership works because we respect each other so much. Rick has fabulous ideas and complex plots, and I bring emotional layers to give depth to those plots in new ways.

We aren't going to tell you who wrote which part—that's the fun of discovery as you immerse yourself in the story. And even when I wrote a scene, Rick edited it and tweaked it. And when Rick wrote a scene, I did the same so every scene had both of our touches on it.

Our hope is that you enjoy reading our books as much as we have loved writing them together! Drop us a note and let us know what you think!

COLLEEN COBLE
https://colleencoble.com
colleen@colleencoble.com

RICK ACKER
https://www.rickacker.com
contactrickacker@gmail.com

ACKNOWLEDGMENTS

Our huge thanks go to our HarperCollins Christian Publishing family for trusting us to do this new thing of writing together! Embarking on something different is always a little scary, but the team saw our excitement and caught our vision for how great this new partnership could be. We are so very grateful, especially to publisher Amanda Bostic who has always been able to steer us all through the murky waters of publishing. Thank you so much!

A special thanks to our freelance editor Julee Schwartzburg who went above and beyond the call of duty in reading the first half before we were done to make sure we were hitting all the right notes and that the cowriting felt cohesive. Her praise for the way it flowed bolstered our confidence and helped us so much. Thank you, Julee!

Thank you to agents Karen Solem and Julie Gwinn for your help in figuring out the new direction as well. We both appreciate you so much.

A heartfelt thanks to Anette Acker, Rick's sweet wife! She read every word and offered great suggestions and was a much-needed sounding board for direction and brainstorming.

ACKNOWLEDGMENTS

We had good author friends read the manuscript before it went off to the publishing house, too, and their unanimous delight in our first book together was such an encouragement! Thank you, Denise Hunter, Lynette Eason, and Robin Miller!

A heartfelt thanks to our beta readers as well. These readers are longtime fans who unanimously loved the book and thought it felt very cohesive. Thank you, Nikki Bee, Deb Blower, Cat Brown, Chandler Carlson, Kay Chance, Jodi Edwards, Kathy Engel, Marcie Farano, Gay Lynn Hobbs, Emily Kalanithi, Per Kjeldaas, Janith Marker, Beverly Moore, Bubba Pettit, Gail Pettit, Dawn Schupp, Barbara Stone, Joni Truex, Jody Wallem, Ruth Ann White, and Leah Willis!

Honestly, it has felt like God himself dreamed up this partnership and handed the idea to us, and we're so thankful for His guidance and provision for this new venture!

DISCUSSION QUESTIONS

(Includes spoilers)

1. The book begins and ends with the same line, in Jess's point of view each time: "Death is a lonely business." How does this statement apply to Jess? What death(s) does it refer to? Is Jess's determination to destroy (or kill) TGU the only thing that keeps her alone?

2. Were you surprised by the epilogue, or did you suspect Jess all along? What do you think is motivating her?

3. Does the book's first and final line apply to any other character? How might things have turned out differently if Hez hadn't tried to cope with Ella's death alone?

4. Why does Hez have so much difficulty accepting God's forgiveness? Is it related to his desire to undo the past?

5. Do you ever struggle with trying to earn God's forgiveness?

6. What mistakes did Savannah make? Why did she make them?

7. How did Savannah's childhood affect how she responds to difficult situations in close relationships?

8. In chapter 10, Professor Guzman argues that the Willard Treasure should be sent back to Mexico. Do you agree with him? Or do you think the Treasure should stay

where it is? His comments echo a longstanding debate between historians. Some think important artifacts should go back to their country of origin, even if they were excavated legally. Others think those artifacts should stay in American and European museums, where they can be better preserved and more people can see them. What do you think?

9. Where do you think the story will go in the next books of the Tupelo Grove series?

LOOKING FOR MORE GREAT READS? LOOK NO FURTHER!

THOMAS NELSON

Since 1798

Visit us online to learn more:
tnzfiction.com

Or scan the below code and sign up to receive email updates
on new releases, giveaways, book deals, and more:

@tnzfiction

THE PELICAN HARBOR SERIES

Available in print, e-book, and audio

DON'T MISS THE GRIPPING NEW STAND-ALONE NOVEL FROM COLLEEN COBLE AND RICKER ACKER

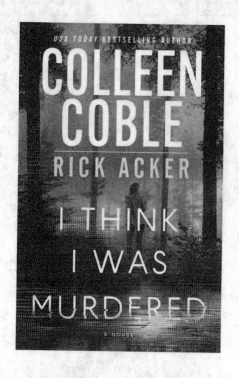

COMING NOVEMBER 2024

Available in print, e-book, and audio

Thomas Nelson
Since 1798

ABOUT THE AUTHORS

Emilie Haney

COLLEEN COBLE IS THE *USA TODAY* BESTSELLING AUTHOR of more than seventy-five books and is best known for her coastal romantic suspense novels.

Connect with her online at colleencoble.com
Instagram: @colleencoble
Facebook: colleencoblebooks
Twitter: @colleencoble

ABOUT THE AUTHORS

RICK ACKER WRITES DURING HIS COMMUTE TO AND FROM his "real job" as a supervising deputy attorney general in the California Department of Justice. He is the author of eight acclaimed suspense novels, including the number one Kindle bestseller *When the Devil Whistles*. He is also a contributing author on two legal treatises published by the American Bar Association.

You can visit him on the web at rickacker.com.